WALKING WOUNDED

for Marian Zeifel,

    friend of the family and
Linda's eighth grade teacher,
with my thanks and best
wishes,

Steve Thompson

19 July 81

WALKING WOUNDED

STEPHEN J. THORPE

DOUBLEDAY & COMPANY, INC.

GARDEN CITY, NEW YORK

1980

All characters in this book are fictitious, and any resemblance to persons living or dead is entirely coincidental.

Library of Congress Cataloging in Publication Data

Thorpe, Stephen J., 1944–
Walking Wounded
I. Title
PS3570.H684W3   813'.54
ISBN: 0-385-15900-5
Library of Congress Catalog Card Number 79-6892
Copyright © 1980 by Stephen J. Thorpe

For Linda and Richard

Lines from the "Sesame Street" theme are used by permission of Children's Television Workshop.

PART

ONE

1

Inside the cabin Sherwood dries breakfast dishes and stacks them in the cupboard, wipes crumbs off the counter into a pie plate to put out for the sparrows and juncos. "Are the guitars packed?" he calls. No answer from the other room. He leaves the plate by the wash pan, pulls on worn combat boots and then his army overcoat. In an effort to stall leaving a minute longer, he rubs his hands together over the pot-bellied stove, and finally goes to lean in the doorway to the workroom. "How cold is it?"

"Cold." Seated on the floor at his low bench, Art brushes back his bowl-cut hair and rearranges a red bandanna worn as a headband. "It was two below last time I looked. You could go tomorrow."

"And then tomorrow I could go tomorrow and if I put it off long enough the post office would send our disability checks back."

"Sorry, Woody."

Sherwood pushes himself off the doorframe and tramps into the workroom. The finished guitars are wrapped in wool blankets and strapped together on an army surplus pack frame that leans against Art's workbench. "See you this afternoon," he says and he thinks, maybe. Town and people planning futures in ways we can't imagine anymore. Don't want to see them and don't want them to have to look at you, do you, O'Neal? He shakes his head, trying to put the thought out of it, but can't. Nothing to do except shoul-

der the pack, pass through the kitchen, carry the pie pan out to
the feeder platform and try not to make the trip worse by antici-
pating it.

At the first pine trees he stops and looks back at the clearing,
the thin smoke rising from the chimney, and wishes winter were
over. All summer they have kept Art's second-hand jeep near the
cabin, but they drive it infrequently and the hills they used then
to coast-start it are covered with snow. The trek to town now begins with a half-mile walk through deep drifts to the edge of the
trees, then another plodding mile over wind-scoured ridge to the
small shed above the one downhill stretch of road that is usually
blown clear.

Breathing hard from the hike, Sherwood beats open the frozen
latch on the side door of the shed, loads guitars into the jeep,
then fills and lights the squat kerosene heater and slides it under
the engine. Cold air in his windpipe creates the deep tickle that
he expects to grow into a last, heart-stopping pain. He tries to
slow his breathing, though he would rather it came here than on
some crowded street. Better alone than with terrified strangers
who could only watch; better with strangers than with friends.
There is no chance the starter will work. He hasn't been out in a
month. At least the antifreeze is still liquid in the radiator. After
an hour of slow heat he tries the starter and gets one sluggish
turn. "Someday you aren't going to start," he says. "Someday
you're going to cough all the way to the bottom of the hill and
I'm going to drop you in that wide ditch and leave you there."
Laughing, he pulls out the heater, takes off his gloves and warms
his hands. They wouldn't take you in the psych ward, he thinks,
so here you are, O'Neal, in the sticks talking to a half-frozen jeep.

"Hear that, Dr. Brodie? I'm talking to a jeep." Sherwood rolls
down the heater wick, pushes wide the doors of the shed. A bunt-
ing chirrups at him from the stand of young pines near the road.
"Yeah, I'll talk to you too. I'll talk to anything as long as it
doesn't talk back and doesn't know how to care." Gear shift in
neutral, he strains against the weight of the jeep for three short
steps, then climbs into the seat. Wind bites through the cab before he can pull the door shut. Feels like a fifteen-miles-an-hour-
second-gear day. He coasts off the steep bank to the road, turns on
the ignition as the wheels cut through crusty snow and dig into

gravel. The transmission whines. Halfway downslope he rams the shift into second and pops the clutch.

The jeep slips to one side, sputters and coughs and lurches down the ruts. "Come on." A frozen rock bounces the frame against the springs. The engine pops to bounce it again and again. Swearing, working the choke and pumping at the gas, Sherwood wedges himself between seat and wheel and hangs on until he is on his way, revving down the hill to scare up three cottontails before he roars past the wide ditch. "Done it one more time, O'Neal." The heater begins to kick dusty-smelling warmth into the compartment. The tickle goes out of his throat. His death won't be official this morning.

By the time he reaches Custer the sun has begun to soak into the asphalt streets and melt the edges of dirty snow piles that fill the gutters. The floor of the post office is already smeared with watery mud, but the room with its thick tables and combination boxes is deserted. "General delivery for O'Neal and Johnson," he tells the balding man behind the stamp counter.

"Haven't seen you in a month. Been snowed in?"

"No."

"Figured you'd be down. Your checks are here."

"That's good."

"Package too." The man sorts through a pile of letters, drops six in front of him, then leans over the counter. "You boys still comfortable up there?"

"Sure."

"You're the ones got the place by Bear Mountain?"

"That's us."

"Doing what I felt like doing after I got back in '45. Friend of mine did it, you know."

"Oh." You don't want to know me, mister. A day or week or month from now you'll hear I died and you'll feel bad for nothing.

"He fixed up an old homesteader's cabin near Moon. Lived up there most of a year, I guess. It's good there's two of you."

"When we get along."

"Get along or not. Jim should have had somebody out there with him. Didn't come in a couple of months that spring and I finally had the sheriff run out and see how he was doing. You know, that damned fool'd shot himself. In the gut." He shrugs. "The sheriff figured he lived a couple of days."

Dull pain flits back and forth below Sherwood's rib cage. "Rough."

"We never did find out how it happened." The man slides letters across the counter, lifts a package up and pushes it beside the letters. "He didn't leave any note. I sure as hell know how he felt, though."

"Yeah." Sherwood goes through the pile, puts the checks in his overcoat pocket and considers the others one at a time: two from Art's mother and one for Art from A. K. Schumwalter on Willow in Berkeley. He puts that in with the checks. The last is for him from a lawyer in Woodgrove, California. "These'll have to be returned." He gives the letters from Art's mother a little shove back. "I don't know about this one from the lawyer." He stuffs it into his pocket. "Maybe my sister has decided to sue me."

"I sure feel bad about this lady's letters."

"It'll be worse if she finds out he's really here. Believe me."

"I guess I sort of know how he feels." The man stamps both letters, "Addressee Unknown" and scoops them into a mail sack. "What's in the box?"

"Neck blanks. For guitars," Sherwood says. "See you in a couple of weeks." Fingering the lawyer's letter in his pocket he hurries away from the postal clerk's sad stare. Bank, music store, grocery store, and then out of here. Next time, O'Neal, you're going to horse the jeep back to the cabin and make Art come too.

At the bank he cashes his January disability check, deposits Art's endorsed December check and cashes a personal check from Art that converts his November check to cash. The process is cumbersome, but it *is* better than trying to drive in with Art, who hates coming to town more than Sherwood does.

His third stop is Jorgensen's Music, a narrow shop in the middle of the next block. Two of the six guitars Sherwood has already left on consignment are missing from the front rack, but the woman who reads *Tiger Beat* at the counter doesn't know what happened to them. "Mr. Jorgensen will be back in half an hour," she says.

"I'll wait." Sherwood unpacks the new instruments and settles into an old cane chair hidden between a bank of amplifiers and a drum display. Jorgensen has mentioned sending some of the guitars to a store in Rapid City—but if the missing ones have been sold, that will be five hundred dollars more for Art this month. A couple of sales wouldn't hurt morale at the cabin.

"Want a magazine?" the woman asks.

"No thanks." He slides the overcoat off his shoulders and takes out what he assumes will be a summons from the lawyer, one more of Marion's attempts to bring him out of isolation. The envelope contains a letter and a short, handwritten note:

Dear Sherwood,

This will introduce Don Holmes, a friend and executor of my estate. I am leaving you all I have; the house, enough insurance to take care of payments and taxes for three or four years. Of course, you'll have to take Jamie.

Don tells me that your mental record might make it hard for you to get custody, but you'll do it. If things ever come to this, you'll have to get off your supposedly dead ass. It will be up to you to tell Jamie who his family was.

What's this? he wonders. Signed, "Love, Marion," dated January 1974, just before that last visit with them. Shock tactics? Some spur-of-the-moment gesture she's never bothered to set straight? Steady the hand, O'Neal. Turn to the letter.

Dear Mr. O'Neal,

With deepest regret I inform you that your sister, Marion O'Neal Howard, was killed in an automobile accident near her home in Dawville on the eighteenth of December. Notification has been delayed because I have had a great deal of trouble locating you.

Pursuant to your sister's last wishes, I have been in contact with Dr. Kevin Brodie of Martinez, who assures me that when you left his care a year ago you were physically and mentally capable of caring for your nephew. He believes that the records of your treatment demonstrate this and he recommends that I ask your permission to release those records to the court.

At this point I am assuming that you will comply with your sister's wishes in regard to your nephew and I wish to warn you that Child Protective Services is already involved because your

medical history does indicate some doubt about your ability to
care for a child. When Marion talked to me about this last
year, I anticipated having to notify CPS, but I do not know
how they became involved so early.

Your nephew, James Patrick Howard, is currently lodged in a
foster home with George and Doris Ransler, 212 I Street in
Dawville, at county expense. A jurisdiction hearing has been set
for February 3, 1975, at 10:00 A.M. in the Valley County Courthouse. Would you please make your wishes known to me well
before that date.

Erica Riggs, a neighbor and a close friend of your sister, has
asked me to ask you to get in touch with her by mail at
Marion's address.

A few typing errors and he has been clumsy with the white-out
fluid. No secretary's initials, no copies? Signs off, "With deepest
regrets, Donald Holmes." Who is this guy, Marion? What gives?
Past tense, O'Neal: What gave?

Past tense? Oh no. With one dangling hand he taps arhyth-
mically on the bottom of the chair. Only a year since his last visit
with them?

Though the time seems longer, he has no trouble recalling Jamie. Three years old then, he was a slight child with dark, excita-
ble eyes and a head of fine, startlingly black hair. He had already
developed an attachment to his "Uncle Sher." Marion said Sherwood was the only man Jamie let wear his security blanket: a
great, shaggy coat of goat fur discarded by his long-absent father
and later adopted as the symbol of male presence in the child's
life.

He remembers the thin voice chanting, "Sher, Sher, coat, Sher,"
inviting him to put on the coat and take Jamie into his lap; and
the memory drags up the rest of it:

They have been in South Dakota a year. Before that they were
two years in Martinez, before that, San Jose; and before that Sherwood was alone in military and veterans' hospitals where doctors
dug junk out of his heart, tried to convince him his flipping out
was just a bad dream and that it was normal not to remember the
accident. He laughs. It has been five years. Five years he wasn't
even supposed to have; only one year since that day with Jamie.

A year? Sherwood and Art were living in Martinez where they were both on-again-off-again outpatients at the psychiatric clinic. The care they were getting wasn't doing either of them much good, but Sherwood helped Art whenever he could. With Art's coaching, and a joint now and then to help him relax, Sherwood had reduced his blackouts from half an hour a day to no more than ten minutes every fourth or fifth day. Sherwood's trip to Dawville and the baby-sitting stint while Marion went out of town was to be a trial run, Art said. If Sherwood succeeded, Art would reveal what he called phase two of the master plan.

Sherwood hadn't been worried about watching Jamie. Marion's house was on a quiet street. Even in downtown Dawville there would rarely be enough excitement to flip him out, and Jamie would give him reason to remain conscious.

Saturday, that weekend, Jamie kept him on the go all day. By the time he put the child in bed for the night he was too tired to pick up the litter of toys on the floor and too restless to sit and stare at the mess. He waited until Jamie was asleep, then walked a block to the park to get some air and to smoke his bedtime joint.

A light rain fell and the park was deserted. From the swing he could see the porchlight and watch the front door of Marion's house. He was still trying to calm down—so the joint would put him to sleep, not keep him stirred up—when he noticed someone running toward him. The man had to be setting some kind of speed record for field boots on wet grass from the far end of the park to the restroom building near the playground. Behind the runner came a swarm of bearded men and long-haired women, some carrying night sticks or baseball bats and shouting slogans about "enemies" and "The People's Revolutionary Commune." Their quarry climbed the back of the building and flattened undetected on the top of the overhanging roof.

The kids searched the park, pounded on garbage cans and poked under bushes, and finally turned their attention to Sherwood. He offered to share his joint with them, found they were paranoid that he might get them busted, and drove away the lot of them by lighting up and yelling "pot" as loud as he could.

Probably he should have left the fugitive to fend for himself, but the weather was nasty. He took the man to Marion's. Another drifter, one more displaced ex-soldier who had put in a few years trying to get back to normal and then had given up to tramp the country in an attempt to figure out what had changed. He wouldn't say how he'd gotten involved with the commune group, only that they were in the old apartment complex across the park and that he intended to get as far away from it as he could. Eventually, Sherwood invited him to stay, then went to bed—and a long restless night of dreams about student revolutionaries breaking into the house, killing the drifter and kidnaping Jamie.

The guest left without breakfast in the morning. Sherwood settled Jamie onto the kitchen floor with blocks and a stuffed kitten while he fried eggs and pancakes. Things were fine, then everything went wrong. One minute he was at the stove and the next he was flipped out, working his way through the dreamlike sequences in Okinawan bars toward the rifle range. Fear and darkness. Spongy wet grass that pulled at running feet. Humid air tasting like gun metal in the throat. Flapping red cloth. Terror. And then the hospital.

He woke to the odor of burning eggs and an empty silence in the house. Jamie wasn't there. From the front door he could hear the child's screams for help and finally he found him on the opposite side of the block, shrieking his lungs out at traffic through the busiest intersection in town. Soaking-wet training pants hung off his buttocks, and rain dribbled down his face. All Sherwood could do was nod apologetically to shocked faces behind the windows of churchbound cars, snatch Jamie into the goatskin coat and run.

Jamie was inconsolable the rest of the day. He had thought Sherwood dead and once Sherwood understood the reaction, he knew he had to get away from anyone who might care about him so no one—especially Jamie—would have to bear the full impact of his death when it did come. The place he would have felt most comfortable, a vets' hospital, wasn't a possibility. According to his records nothing was wrong with him: a little metal in the heart, all removed during the course of five operations. The records didn't explain the conversation that Sherwood had overheard after his final operation. "Cross our fingers," one of his doctors had said. "To live a year, that boy's going to need more than the usual allotment of luck." Nor was there any documentation of the sympathetic pains, like lightning down his rib cage, that made it feel dangerous for him even to read about death. Admission, however, was by the record. No way into a terminal ward. Nor could he commit himself to the quiet security of a psych ward. He had tried. Rules for admission there were complicated, but they amounted to this: As long as he wasn't dangerous to himself or to others, as long as he could survive, could eat out of a garbage can and find shelter under a bush somewhere, he was legally competent. Functionally sane. Sanity he didn't care about, but he didn't feel competent and he was definitely dangerous to others. He felt dead, should have been dead for some time and the fact that he still had one short step to take into death made him a source of inevitable pain for anyone who cared about him.

When he went back to Martinez, Sherwood had no choice but to go along with Art's master plan, phase two: the escape from California. For most of their two years out of the hospital they had been changing apartments regularly to keep away from Art's parents, who had been pressuring Art to come home. Hitching a rented one-way trailer to Art's jeep, packing, and moving cross-country was hardly more trouble than hauling everything across town; and it was the best thing he could do for Art, best for Jamie, best for Marion, though she wouldn't agree. . . .

The woman behind the counter ruffles pages of her magazine. "Are you feeling okay?"

"Some bad news." He stares at the lawyer's letter. Who was this guy? he wonders. Not just some lawyer, Marion? Fleeting stitches of pain dance through his arms and legs as he tries to avoid any image of how it happened to her; which muscles tore, which bones snapped before the impact snuffed out her caring. Should have stayed, O'Neal. It should have been you.

"You're sure?"

"Yes." Thumb and forefinger move automatically to the corners of his eyes and he smudges tears on the bridge of his nose.

"Can I get you a cup of something? You look kind of pale."

"I'd appreciate a cup of coffee." Folding the letter and the note together he slips them into the coat pocket. He can't think what to do, but he can't imagine letting Jamie go to an institution, a succession of foster homes. Adoption, maybe? How is that done? Permission from some agency; an advertisement in a local paper: "Wanted, good home for bright, four-year-old boy"?

The front door of the shop opens. Mr. Jorgensen, a tall, weathered man with a mane of hair that has gone gray in streaks,

stamps snow off his shoes onto the doormat. "Sherwood." His
voice carries down the narrow room. "Good news. I sold two.
Local boys. They been singing in bars around the hills for three,
maybe four years, and they came in and took that pair with the
matched grain in the tops."

"I was afraid you'd sent them to that other store."

"No. Sold. Happy New Year!"

New Year? "Happy New Year."

"Here's the coffee." The woman comes out of the back and
hands Sherwood a cup that is still wet from washing. "I'm on
break now, Mr. J."

"Fine, Trudy. I'll write you a check," he says to Sherwood.
"Two new ones, I see. Those go to Rapid City. Aren't you feeling
well?"

"Do I look that bad?"

"Around the eyes." He points to the area of his own eyes with
four fingers of one hand. His bushy eyebrows slide toward wrinkles at the bridge of his nose.

"My sister was killed. I just found out."

Mr. Jorgensen shakes his head. "Too many young people die.
First the war, now . . ." He throws a hand past his face.

"She left a kid."

"The poor grandparents. But they'll enjoy—"

"They're gone, same thing . . . car wreck."

He shakes his head again. "Bad. Fathers can't care for children."

"His father left them a long time ago. He's in South America
somewhere."

"That's no good. Who will care for the child?"

"I'm the only one left."

"Get married." The thick eyebrows rise into peaks, pull together again. "Will you bring him to Custer?"

"I'll have to go to California and figure it out from there. Art
couldn't stand a kid at the cabin."

"What about Arthur?"

"He'll have to come with me," Sherwood says. A worse problem
than it sounds. "He can't get supplies or go in or out by himself."

"But is he in some kind of trouble?"

"What do you mean, 'trouble'?"

"There was a man here asking about Arthur Johnson, Jr. A detective, he said." Mr. Jorgensen strides to the front of the shop and looks through a clear spot in the fogged window. "He has been here about two weeks. Come look. The green car across the street."

By the time Sherwood reaches the front, the car is moving, but he catches a glimpse of the heavy face that seems to protrude between a narrow-brimmed hat and a coat collar. "What does he want?"

"He knew all except where you live. I said Bear Mountain, but that's a lot of country."

"Not enough, I bet." Probably the man comes from Art's family and if they want him that much, Bear Mountain won't be big enough. "We aren't in trouble with the law, if that worries you."

"You will be leaving Custer?"

"Not right away."

"I was thinking, if you didn't want to take the guitars, I could give you one hundred fifty apiece for them." He picks up one of the new ones and examines the finish. "The work is good. And the tone, but the design is bulky. Not everyone would want such an instrument."

"Two-fifty. If you have local musicians using them, you can probably up your price."

"I cannot tie up so much money. But Arthur is a veteran." Mr. Jorgensen smiles. "Two hundred?"

The check he gives Sherwood is for seventeen hundred dollars. Sherwood cashes it at the bank and withdraws the five hundred he had stashed to save Marion the expense of a coffin. Another six hundred dollars in Art's account is untouchable. They will have to transfer that later. For now, Sherwood has over three thousand dollars, most of it in hundred-dollar bills, and Art's January check.

Sherwood makes his usual stop at the downtown supermarket, but he buys sparingly; no cases of canned goods or twenty-five-pound bags of potatoes this time, no roasts or steaks. Whether they like it or not, they will both be on a plane for California in the next few days. From the market parking lot he can see two green cars. One is a Ford parked beside the corner service station, but the Buick idling at the curb up the street is more suspicious. The driver wears a hat, and the car follows the jeep out of town.

After he takes the turnoff, Sherwood still catches occasional sight of the Buick in the rear-view mirror. Whoever the man is, he doesn't care who knows he's there, and that cocky presence wipes out the usual calm of the trip back to the cabin. Sherwood feels a growing pressure, as if the world he has managed to leave has caught up with him again. He is tempted to turn the jeep around, go back and run the man off the road, but he can't do that now. He taps the wheel and laughs. "Dangerous to myself or others." Until he does something about Jamie, he can't afford to wind up in a psych ward.

He reaches the shed and then watches until the green car pulls around the bottom of the hill and stops. With hammer and tire iron he knocks the frozen front hubs of the jeep into lock position. If the man wants Art, he's going to have to walk. Hubs locked, Sherwood climbs back behind the wheel, shifts into four-wheel drive and churns up the ridge.

"Why now?" With a rattle of casters Art pushes off with the short sticks like ski poles, and sends his plywood platform rolling across the room. "No one has bothered us before."

"I don't know. Maybe it took him this long to find South Dakota or maybe your folks only hired him two weeks ago."

At the window Art grabs a rope hung from one of the rafters and climbs. The muscles in his chest and shoulders ripple under his T-shirt, and the stumps of his legs, amputated at midthigh, beat the air. Anchoring himself to the sill, he peers through the frosted glass. "You're making it up so I'll go with you to get your sister's kid."

"I wish I were."

"What's he going to do? Come up here and drag me home? Draft me?"

"I don't know, Art."

Art lets himself down the rope hand over hand. Once on the platform he lifts his sticks as if to move, but only sits there. "You're not making it up."

"No."

"Sure as hell my father told this guy to haul me home so he can stash me out of sight for good this time. You'll help me? Won't you? Help me stop him?"

"The best I can."

"Okay. We get out of here. To your sister's place if we have to."

"I'll have to go there."

"I can make crates for my tools and forms." He stares around the room, mutters half to himself, "All this quarter-sawed spruce. Lose some of it if it gets dinged. Lose it all if I leave it. Pack the rosewood inside. Never be able to replace that. Cost us to send it."

"The money is to use when we need it."

"We're really clearing out, aren't we? Can we wait until tomorrow?"

"I don't know, man."

"You're pushing me, Woody."

"I'm not, damn it. He is."

"You'd go anyway."

"I could take more time. With this guy around, I'm not sure. Maybe we should. . . ." He throws out his hands and lets them drop.

"What about the kid?"

"Art, I don't know that either. You think I want to go back to California?"

Pushing his platform so his back is to Sherwood, Art shakes his head.

"I think I'll hike down to the edge of the trees and see what he's doing."

"What good will that do?"

"Who knows? You want me to drive you down for a look? Maybe if you saw the guy, you'd be as scared as I am. I'll just feel better if I know he isn't sneaking up on us."

"I'll pack," Art says.

Sherwood takes the binoculars and walks back along the jeep tracks to the ridge until he can see the curve of the road at the bottom of the hill. The car is still parked next to the wide ditch. Peering through the glasses, he sweeps the next ridge from the car to a line of trees that is half a mile away. There are deer trails cut through the snow, but no sign that a man has been that way. He focuses on the car again, then on the isolated stand of pines between the shed and the road. While he watches, a figure comes out the side door of the shed. The man wears a tweedy-looking overcoat and a narrow-brimmed hat with a little red feather stuck in the band. Apparently he catches sight of Sherwood about the same time Sherwood notices him because he stops and raises the binoculars that hang around his neck.

His trousers are gray and tucked into insulated boots of yellow rubber. A black, boxlike purse that is probably a tape recorder hangs from a strap over one shoulder. His breath comes in puffs and it drifts away from his mouth as small white clouds. "Who are you?" Sherwood says to himself. He is aware of his condensed breath rising around the edges of his own binoculars. "I suppose you know who I am." On impulse he raises one hand and waves. No response. "What's with you? You think I don't see you?" Sherwood wants to go down and ask what the man wants, but before he can start, the figure lowers his glasses, turns and disappears over the bank toward the road.

Stamping his feet and walking in circles to keep warm, Sherwood watches until the figure appears again at the bottom of the hill to stop and look up through his glasses. Another wave is ignored. "We might as well be rabbits." The man gets into his car. Exhaust billows as he starts the engine, but he doesn't leave. "You're not stupid enough to stand out here and freeze, are you?" Sherwood turns and tramps back through the trees to the cabin.

According to the clock beside the stove, he has been gone forty-five minutes. Art has already packed the workboards and forms and the supply of rosewood into one long home-made crate; now he's arranging tools among folded clothes in a shorter one.

"He's still there and he knows we know. I imagine he expects us to run or he wouldn't be waiting."

"And we're going to do what he expects?"

"You remember your training about what to do if you're a POW? Best chance to escape is in the first few hours after you're captured."

"Yeah. That's right." Art places the last of his rasps and files and arranges a layer of books on top of them. "But I don't like going back."

"If you can figure out any other place you want to go, I'll take you there and get you set up."

"There isn't anyplace else, Woody."

Quiver in the voice. This is hitting him hard, O'Neal. "I'm sorry," he says. He pulls his suitcase from under the bed and dumps his one drawer of clothes into it. "Maybe we should plan to get Jamie and come back. Maybe he wouldn't look for us here again right away, or is that too obvious?"

Art's answer is the sound of his hammer against the lid of his second crate.

There is no reason to take the bedding or any of the food and, Sherwood decides, there is no real reason for him to take any clothes. His old clothes that Marion stored in her basement are probably in better shape than those he has with him. He kicks the suitcase into a corner and packs a paper bag with his toothbrush and the crusty razor, shaving brush and soap cup he has used since basic training.

The crates, when Art finishes them, weigh nearly a hundred pounds apiece, but Sherwood manages to wrestle them into the back of the jeep. He carries Art piggyback and helps him get settled in the passenger seat. Mercifully, the engine starts.

"Why don't you check on our friend, Woody. We might be able to leave the easy way."

Sherwood nods, climbs out, stuffs his hands in his pockets and only then remembers the letter from Berkeley. He leaves it for Art to read while he slips through the trees far enough to catch sight of the green-painted metal at the bottom of the hill. Exhaust still rises from the back of the car. He watches until he sees the detective move behind the windshield.

"Still down there," he tells Art as he climbs into the driver's seat and throws the jeep into gear.

They creep away from the cabin in four-wheel drive, up a fire road around the base of the mountain to an unpaved secondary that runs north and then east to the highway. Muttering to himself, Art fingers the letter and torn envelope; finally tears off the return address and stuffs it into his pocket, throws the letter and the rest of the envelope out into the snow.

2

By late afternoon they have shipped Art's crates via Greyhound from Rapid City, abandoned the jeep at the airport and flown Frontier Airlines to Denver. Everywhere is confusion; knots and crowds and streams of people, solicitous airline employees who offer assistance and fold-away wheelchairs for Art, noise, arrows that point the way, signs that flash instructions. Flight schedules flicker on television screens. Sherwood imagines that his eyes have taken on a crazy cast with the strain of moving Art from one place to another and having to explain again and again that Art is fine, that their baggage is taken care of, that he can manage. Finally he gets them both aboard a 727 for San Francisco, lets the stewardess take the wheelchair and collapses into a seat.

He is barely aware that the plane has taken off, then he lapses into a long sleep broken by short periods of half-waking consideration of the more sensible escapes they might have made. At least they could have driven the jeep.

"We should have had a gun," Art mumbles.

For a moment Sherwood isn't sure whether he has heard or whether the thought was his. He comes fully awake. "What time is it?"

"About five-thirty."

Light reflected from a bottle on the stewardess' cart seems to grow into a silver disc that swims in his field of vision. Something red flutters at the edge of sight. He rubs his eyes to wipe these things away, but knows they won't go. "Art, I'm flipping out. What time is it?"

Art holds up one arm and looks at his watch. "Five twenty-one and six seconds," he says.

The fluttering stops. Sherwood is aware of Art's hands loosening his belt and shirt collar, aware of Art pushing the seat tray out of the way and forcing the seat back. "Relax, Woody. I got you."

Another circle of light joins the first and another and then Sherwood is in the Club Texas, the narrow-fronted bar just off Gate Two Street in Koza. Twisted streamers of red ribbon hung with round mirrors still decorate the bar from a New Year celebration a number of days or maybe weeks ago. A tall Eurasian girl dances on a dais to the left of the stage. Half a dozen of the mirrors catch the footlights to sparkle around her face and black ponytail. He would like to meet her, but he isn't on the make and he doubts his limited Japanese is up to explaining that all he wants is a friend. He has 116 days left in the Army, and his mind is already on his new life—off The Rock and free. A civilian.

One of the bargirls brings Sherwood another scotch. The front door opens and a distracted, pale-looking kid comes in with his head lowered as if he's looking for a fifty-cent piece on the floor. Kenny Marr. His hair is mussed and his red shirt rides askew on his shoulders. As island jargon has it Kenny is drifty from being stoned most of the time. Usually Sherwood enjoys his company, but recently Kenny has had trouble with the new company commander, and his response to the trouble makes Sherwood uneasy. Tonight all he wants to do is sip this last drink and listen to the band a while before he goes back to the barracks. He would rather not hear about someone else's troubles.

Kenny pairs up with a bargirl who calls herself Lisa and leads her to Sherwood's table. "How you doing, Woody?"

"Fine. How about you?"

"Crummy. Lang gave me two weeks' extra duty. I have to clean every damned weapon in the company."

"The guy is a bastard," Sherwood says.

"I'm going to have to kill him."

Sherwood tries to pass off the remark, but Kenny has told him drunken firsthand tales of spilled brains, severed limbs, terror and more nastiness than any twenty-year-old kid should hear let alone live through. No doubt the threat is not to be taken lightly. "Think civilian, Kenny."

The grass is thick and wet and it pulls at his boots. "Not yet," Sherwood calls. "I'm not ready yet." The dream turns over and rolls on.

The band wraps up its set. Drummer and lead guitar player climb off the stage and push through the bar to smoke a joint in the alley. Sherwood now has ninety days. The Eurasian dancer's name is Tsuko. She works the bars for money to go to business school and, like Sherwood, she is not on the make. She steps off her dais, wriggles feet into zoris and comes to sit beside him. "We go to Moon Beach tomorrow, *ne*, Sherwood?"

"Not tomorrow. We have to go to the rifle range for record firing. It's silly for a bunch of clerks, but what can you say? Let's go Sunday."

"Sunday," she says. "You come too, Ken-knee." She touches Sherwood's knee and laughs. "Bring Lisa, *ne?*"

Kenny shakes his head and answers in pidgin, "No can do. Have to work arms room. Extra duty. *Wakarimas-ka?*" He sounds like he's about to cry. "It's the shits," he says to Sherwood and then, for Tsuko's benefit adds, "*ne?*"

She nods and winks at Sherwood. "I can speak English, Kenny," she says.

It is morning.

Lead gray, the East China Sea tosses under solid overcast. Record firing. Eighty-nine more sunrises. Almost home free with no chance now of being sent to Vietnam. Feelings of relief; undercurrent of nagging guilt. Sherwood rides to Bolo Point with a carload of other men who are "short," who have little time to serve. The shortest man in the groaning Ford has only seventeen days. Desk soldiers and short-timers to a man, they all find it funny that they have to fire their M-14s and they wear the uniform of the day —fatigues, baseball caps, ammo belt with clip pouches and canteen, field jackets and empty field packs—with amused resignation.

That evening the seventeen-day man is having his getting-out party. "I'm glad to get away from this turkey outfit," he says. "But I leave The Rock with some regrets." He has promised his Okinawan girlfriend he will come back and marry her. The girl knows he won't come back. Tsuko has told Sherwood that already six GIs have promised to come back for this girl. "I have friends here," the seventeen-day man says. "They'll take care of her for me."

Red flags fly along the edges of the rifle range. MPs patrol the perimeter and the road, ready to turn away off-duty soldiers and Okinawan families who have come to eat picnic lunches on the spectacular sea cliffs beyond the range. Sherwood moves up the line.

A line of shuffling men.

He is moving toward a truck where Kenny pulls rifles from the racks and hands them to the men who file past, then . . .

Nothing.

His time has a hole in it. In place of events, Sherwood finds terror; slippery grass like quicksand and air that burns in his chest. The terror is familiar and not so bad this time. Kenny seems to be near him, but leaving. Sherwood wants to follow. Instead he feels hands that hold and lift, needles in his arms, tubes that dangle beside his face. Bright lights shine in his eyes. Men in smocks and masks pass back and forth and he asks them to leave him alone. The dream drags on like a snake down hospital corridors that shift and echo and change. Always the same green walls, the same red blood; alcohol and vitamin scents in antiseptic air. Everywhere he asks what has happened to Kenny and finally a voice answers with the question, "Where did you see him last?"

"Koza."

"Was that in Saigon?"

Another person, a woman, is present. Sherwood can't turn his head to see her. "He was brought in from Okinawa, Doctor."

"How the hell did he get a heart full of shrapnel on Okinawa?"

"An accident. The one he keeps talking about, Kenny, was killed."

"Killed," Sherwood repeats. The word doesn't seem to have meaning.

"He's scheduled for more surgery in the morning."

Coughing, the doctor flips through pages on a clipboard. "I see."

The nurse comes near the bed. "Are you awake? Do you know what happened to you?"

He opens his mouth to tell her. Nothing comes. He can't move and pains shoot from his shoulders to his groin when he tries; but he has no images. Heart full of shrapnel? He has no recollection of it. None at all. "I was killed," he says.

Leaning near his face, the nurse shakes his shoulder. "Are you all right, mister?"

The pain is unbearable. A babble of voices washes around him, then Art says, "Leave him alone. He's having a blackout. Five twenty-four and eight seconds, Woody. Nine seconds, ten seconds . . ."

"How much time?"

"Three minutes."

"I'm coming out," Sherwood says. Three minutes? He can feel the faint vibration of the airplane through his seat back and that helps him place himself before he opens his eyes. Are they going to get worse again? he wonders.

"Pulse got up to one-thirty. Longer this time, but not a hard one."

Sherwood feels Art lower his wrist onto the armrest. A worried-looking stewardess kneels in the aisle. Faces poke over the seats ahead. "I'm okay." He stretches his arms, then laughs at himself for hoping the gesture might make it appear he is simply waking up. "If I can just sit a minute and get my bearings," he tells her.

"Would you like to come back where you can be alone?"

"No."

"I can have the pilot radio ahead for a doctor to be waiting."

"Art can take care of me."

"You're sure?" Her eyes fix on Art's tucked, empty pants legs.

"He's sure," Art says. "We'll need the wheelchair when we land. That's all."

She hesitates a moment more, then rises and moves down the aisle. One by one the curious faces withdraw. "I'm having my doubts about this," Sherwood whispers. "If it makes you feel any better."

"It doesn't, Woody. You know it doesn't; but if they get worse again, we can handle it. Just promise you won't let my family get me."

"Right."

"San Francisco Airport is too close. If they do get me, you'll come get me out?"

"I'll do it, Art. You know I'll do it."

Art nods, but he doesn't look sure. Finally he turns away and stares through the window, eyes withdrawn until they are almost blank.

Sitting rigid in his seat for fear any movement might drop his resistance and let the dream come flooding back, Sherwood watches Art out of the corner of his eye. You're not in such good shape yourself, old friend. Haven't seen you like this since we left the hospital for good.

Announcement of their arrival brings them both alert. San Francisco time is four-thirty. The temperature is fifty-two degrees and it is raining. "I'm going to miss the snow," Sherwood says. Art doesn't answer.

The stewardess brings the wheelchair as soon as the plane has stopped and she keeps a way clear so they are among the first off. Sherwood's paper sack and both their military overcoats are piled on Art's lap as he hurries the pace with strong thrusts of his hands. "Come on, Woody. Rent us a car and get us out of here. I feel eyes, man. I have a bad feeling about this. It's like an ambush."

"Bus or taxi?" Sherwood says. "Those car agencies only rent to licensed drivers."

"I forgot." Art twists around. "How's it look behind us?"

"Relax. We're surrounded by people. What can happen?"

"If that guy figured out we split, if he figured out about the plane? One phone call is all it would take."

"I'm moving as fast as I can."

"Watch out ahead. Damn. The guy with the coffee."

"I see him." The man is in his fifties, tall and dressed in a gray wool suit with a dark tie. He leaves a styrofoam cup on the counter of a closed concession stall with a careless gesture that suggests familiarity with styrofoam cups and airports. A pretty woman in nurse's whites responds to an impatient wave of the hand that has just discarded the cup, and follows him into the concourse. Automatically, Sherwood angles the chair to pass around the man and the nurse, but Art brakes with his hands and brings them to a stop.

"What's the matter?"

"It's no use, Woody."

The man steps up to Sherwood, hand extended. "You would be
Sherwood O'Neal," he says. His shake is firm. "I'm Arthur Johnson, Sr. If you want to bring the chair, I have a car waiting."

Sherwood tightens his grip, ready to run, but Art has locked the
wheels. He sits forward, braced on his arms, his mouth an awkward gap in his face. The nurse has come up a little behind
Arthur, Sr. She is small, a little taller than five feet with a tiny
waist and skinny legs. Dark, short hair surrounds her face like a
fringe that seems to tumble down her neck in small, loose curls.
Her eyes are brown and damp and they are locked onto Art's face.

"Karen," he says.

Her feet scuff the dirty floor. "When I answered the ad, I
didn't know it would be you. I wrote, but you didn't answer."

"He got you? *You?*"

She shakes her head, but can't continue to meet his gaze.

"Thank you for bringing my son home, Sherwood. Come
along." Arthur, Sr., claps a hand on his shoulder and watches,
wary now and ready for a chase. "Mrs. Johnson would like to meet
you, to thank you in person."

"Remember your promise, Woody?"

"I won't forget."

"Either bring him or back off, young man. I'm losing patience
and you're blocking the way here."

"Please come, Art," the nurse says. "I'll help you. I really can."

"You, of all people."

Face flushed as if she might cry, she looks at him again. "How
else could I even have found you?"

"Take the chair," Arthur, Sr., orders her. "Enough fooling
around." He turns on Sherwood. "What's the matter with you?
Do you want money? Is that it? Do I have to bribe you to have
my own son?" His hand comes out of his pocket to point at Sherwood with a tight roll of bills.

"No. No." Spreading his arms in a gesture of surrender, Sherwood backs away from the money. "You'll write, Art?"

"I'll have to."

"You don't need money, huh?" A corner of Arthur, Sr.'s, mouth
lifts in a hint of contempt. He waits until he is sure the nurse has
replaced Sherwood behind the chair, then without a word having

passed between him and his son he does a smooth about-face and strides down the concourse. The nurse follows, guiding the chair with professional ease.

Should do something, O'Neal, but what? Alone, Sherwood can't act. He can hardly make sense of the fact that he is more than a thousand miles from the bed he woke in this morning. Out of circulation for too long; off in other countries, in hospitals or tiny apartments within walking distance of the psychiatric clinic, in the isolated cabin. His own country feels foreign to him. The thought that he might come back and do something for Jamie seems crazy. He couldn't do anything for Art. He hasn't even managed to keep his few possessions—the overcoat and the bag of shaving gear are now gone out of sight with Art in his chair. Slowly, the movement of the other deplaning passengers sweeps him into the main lobby, there to be jostled out of lines for several shuttles into the city until he gives up and pays a cab to take him to the Greyhound depot.

People in the rain, loitering on the dirty sidewalk in front of the bus terminal, make Sherwood uneasy. Inside is worse than out. Scrubbed tile floors, molded plastic chairs with TV sets bolted to their reinforced arms; thick odors of whiskey, wet wool and warm skin. Alone now, he has to look at this place and these people in a way he doesn't quite understand and he feels threatened. He can't reconcile all this with the postal clerk or Mr. Jorgensen, with memories of bargaining in the Okinawan open-air markets; tiny people with lively eyes full of good humor and the ubiquitous courtesy of the oriental bow. Here in the depot everyone who crowds around him stares with dull, indifferent eyes that bulge or sink into pasty-looking skin. They don't respond to one another. Tired mothers try to shush boisterous children who disobey until they are caught and held immobile to scream themselves into mimicry of the pervasive stupor. "My God." His voice is absorbed by background noise. A gust of foul-smelling air hits his damp clothing and he shivers. Ceiling speakers blare unintelligible instructions, and Sherwood approaches an open ticket window. A pock-faced man stares at him.

"Ticket to Dawville," Sherwood says, finally. He gropes in his pocket and comes out with a hundred-dollar bill. It is too big and he knows it. He tries again and again until he finds a twenty that he pushes across the counter.

The man takes the bill, makes change and slides it back with a ticket on top of the money. "Gate six," he says.

Cramming paper and coins into his shirt pocket, Sherwood follows a sluggish flow of bodies through wide doors and into a long shed broken into sections by banks of coin-operated lockers. Cigarette butts and pieces of broken glass litter the asphalt; and a section of newspaper stuck to the floor in a puddle of soda pop catches his eye with the headline: FORD TELLS CONGRESS: THE STATE OF THE UNION IS NOT GOOD.

Feel better when you get out of this city, O'Neal, he tells himself, but the Bay Bridge and then countless strung-together suburbs pass relentlessly. Sherwood had hoped for vague humps of distant mountains and the occasional twinkle from an isolated farmhouse. Instead he is assaulted by light: approaching headlights and a slowly shifting pattern of taillights; lighted houses, sheds, factories, chain restaurants, shopping centers along the freeway, the lights of vehicles on roads to right and left, porchlights, streetlights, neon and mercury vapor in Fairfield, Travis Air Force Base, Vacaville; navigation lights and landing lights that spin and flash and whirl through the sky overhead and beyond it all, halo after halo of reflected light from distant cities that glow against the night clouds and a haze of rain. Another flipout, O'Neal? Could you handle one without Art? He tries to ignore the questions, but can't do it any more than he can keep his eyes closed. When the driver announces, "Dawville," Sherwood stumbles off the bus with hardly any idea where he is.

At least he has been in Dawville before and as soon as he gets his directions straight the seven-block walk under the dripping trees of half-familiar, sparsely lighted streets calms him. Marion's house is as he remembers it, white paint and gray trim that has gone chalky with time. The rain gutters haven't been cleaned again this year and water runs in streams off leaves caught at the edge of the roof. Rank grass soaks his shoes as he crosses the lawn.

Somewhere he has a key that Marion gave him, but finding it doesn't seem worth the effort. He passes around the side to the basement stairway window where he knows there are no locks on screen or sash. The only thing he can find to pry open the screen is the key to the front door, but he is too tired to bother going back. The window opens without trouble and he hoists himself inside.

The odor of Marion's cigarettes seems to ooze from the walls, to rise out of the worn carpeting on the stairs, but through it he can smell bleached cleanser and fresh floor wax. The kitchen counters are scrubbed clean. Not a dish, jar or sack stands where Marion would have left it. He finds an open box of crackers in the cupboard, fills the tea kettle and puts it on the gas stove. "Something warm." The oddly polished house deadens the sound of his voice. "Check it out, O'Neal," he says. Keep a steady heart.

Dining-room table and piano lack their usual thin coat of dust. Mail and rolled papers are piled neatly in the front hall. There is a stack of wood by the living-room fireplace and, absently, Sherwood puts kindling and logs on the grate, crushes newspaper and starts a fire. He kicks out of his shoes, then strips off wet shirt and socks, and drapes them over the firescreen to dry.

"What, exactly, do you think you're supposed to do here?" He pads barefoot into the little cubicle hall that connects the living room with Marion's room, the bathroom and Jamie's bedroom where a dim night-light shows books and toys arranged with adult precision on the shelves. Pieces of wood smeared with tempera paint stand or hang as decorations. The crib is gone, replaced by a single bed that would dwarf the child Sherwood remembers. He counts the shapes of at least a dozen stuffed animals around the pillow and turned-down covers.

This last touch, the turned-down covers, starts a dull pressure in his chest. Too much hope. The door into the little hall between kitchen and basement stairs is already closed. He backs out of the room and pulls the inner hall door shut, as if that will close off the image. Marion's room is too dark to see, but he can imagine her clothes hung neatly in the closet, the spread pulled tight across her bed. Turned down. Waiting. Can't look at it. Eyes closed, he reaches for her doorknob and pulls it until the mechanism latches.

In the living room his fire casts light enough for Sherwood to notice that the sofa, the rocking chair and a pair of floor lamps are gone. The only furniture remaining is the old green chair Marion bought from Goodwill so she would have a place to nurse the baby. For a moment he is angry that anything is missing, but then he throws up a shoulder in an uneven shrug. No amount of furniture could bring back the lived-in clutter that marked her life. "Sorry, Marion," he says. Feeling guilty as hell, aren't you, O'Neal? Guilty it couldn't have been you instead. Leave Jamie with a mother at least. Grandparents dead in a car wreck a couple of months before Jamie was born. Father wasted by the war and crawled off to be someone's mercenary.

Sputtering from the tea kettle that has boiled over draws Sherwood back to the kitchen. He turns off the gas, pulls open the refrigerator for light enough to see, rummages through cupboards until he finds a cup and a box of bouillon cubes. Two cubes in the cup, hot water. He fishes a spoon out of the silverware drawer and carries his drink and the box of crackers to the hearth.

"So empty there might as well not be anyone here at all. Nobody but us ghosts." He had thought he would squat, Okinawan fashion, with his back to the fire for warmth, but the damp has made his knees stiff. As long as the body is animate, it might as well be comfortable. The chairs he drags from the dining room leave long scuffmarks on the freshly polished floor. He pulls the green chair in front of the firescreen, places one of the wooden chairs as table and the other as footstool. The crackers taste stale, but the bouillon warms his throat.

Shifting light from the fire teases with a suggestion of the silver discs that can drag him back to the Club Texas. He is more tired than he has been in a long time. Another flipout? The thought of losing that time without Art to watch the clock and take his pulse and be there as anchor at the end of the dream frightens Sherwood enough to put him near the threshold. A blackout now would be one of the old kind that used to last for hours and leave his heart pounding and his skin clammy. He imagines the band, can almost hear the beat of the drum. Instead he hears a light rapping against wood. "Marion?" he calls. "Are you there?"

Taps come again, a series of three, a pause, a series of four.

"Is someone there? Marion?" Could she be there? A spirit, finally to take you to your death, O'Neal?

A woman's voice calls, "Is anyone there?" and it sounds far away, as if coming through water or loosely packed earth.

Sherwood can feel his hair stand up at the back of his neck, but he answers, "Yes. I'm here."

The front door rattles against the lock, then a key slides into its slot. He twists around in the chair, coming fully awake. A small wave of bouillon slops over the lip of his cup and drops into a fragrant puddle on the floor. Slowly the door opens and a voice resonant with fear asks, "Who is it, please?"

"Sherwood."

A long, relieved, "Ooh," echoes in the nearly empty room. "I'm Erica Riggs. We met once." She steps into the firelight, blond and tall, a large woman who seems oversized but avoids any impression of being overweight. Her smile pulls soft skin tight over rounded cheekbones and bunches faint laugh lines around her eyes. A curlyhead child snuggled against her shoulder gives Sherwood a sleepy, round-eyed grin. "This is Josie. I thought I'd put her on the couch for a minute, if you don't mind?"

"The couch seems to be gone."

She grimaces. "I forgot. That damned bitch," she says. Then, without explanation, "May I put her in with Jamie?"

"Jamie isn't here. She can use his bed."

For several minutes he sits quietly and listens to her talking to the child in Jamie's room. He has met her before, but all he can remember about her is that she married young and left her husband shortly after the child was born. When she comes back she stops in the hall doorway and leans against the frame. Her coat hangs open on loose jeans and a blue workshirt; her eyes search his face as if to avoid looking at his scarred chest. "I'm sorry I forgot. It's just, Marion used to do this. Be here with the lights all off and just the fire. It was a kind of signal that we should come over." She brushes hair out of her face with the back of her hand. "Aren't you cold?"

"A little."

"There's a robe in Marion's closet."

"I couldn't go in there."

Pulling her coat together, Erica nods. "I know. By the time I got to her room, I was all cried out."

"You cleaned up?" Of course. Who else? "Thank you."

She disappears into the hall again and returns with a thick terrycloth robe. "You'll catch cold."

That might solve the whole problem, he thinks. The robe is warm and dry. He lifts his cup and offers her the chair. "Would you like some bouillon? I didn't find any coffee."

"No thanks." She drags another of the dining-room chairs to the fire and sits with her legs propped across the one Sherwood has given her. "Josie saw the light from her window. We thought Jamie might be home. She hasn't seen him since right after the accident. They're good friends." She laughs, almost as if to apologize for her fast, nervous statements, but then adds, "They can't help it. They're the only kids in the neighborhood. You haven't seen him yet?"

"No."

"Doris Ransler took the sofa and the rocking chair, I imagine. The lamps too."

"She's the one who has Jamie?"

"Yes. I'm sorry. I didn't know if you'd come and, with working . . . I couldn't have given him the attention he needed. If I'd known they were going to put him with her, I would have taken my vacation. Something. But Marion said you . . ."

Her lips make a tense line, then relax. "I don't like Doris Ransler. Can't stand her. I had to take Josie to the hospital for a cut chin. Doris works there as a nurse. Nights in the emergency room. And she accused me of hitting Josie."

"Oh."

"I'm sorry. I just don't like her."

"Who would? Maybe I should see about Jamie tonight."

Erica checks her watch. "No, it's late. If you did anything unusual, she'd make trouble. She . . . Someone from Child Protective Services has already been to see me about you. Doris knows. . . ." Her voice trails off and she stares at the fire.

"That I've been a mental patient? That I tried to commit myself?"

"Other people have told me she's a troublemaker. I'm glad you're here now."

As if you might be able to do something permanent, O'Neal. He nods and is aware of his breath escaping in a long sigh.

"Marion told me," Erica says. "About you."

"But she didn't believe it."

"You aren't going to stay?"

"I'll make sure he has a good place, but it wouldn't be fair." He thumps his chest with a fist. "I'm not really crazy, damn it. I just can't take on responsibilities as if I were going to be around to-morrow. Something as simple as a cold could start an infection in there around any bit of junk they couldn't get out. A piece of metal or scar tissue can break loose any time, block an artery. One minute I'm here and the next, just a body that would have to be moved. The last thing Jamie needs is to have me say I'll stick with him and then die."

For a moment Erica watches Sherwood, then she turns her head away to stare out the window. Almost immediately she looks at him again and with a shock that registers as a shudder up his back Sherwood recognizes that the gesture, the entire double take is something this woman has picked up from Marion. For a mo-ment he recalls his sister, eleven years old and wanting him to take her swimming in a deep hole about half a mile down the creek, eyes large and pleading, looking at him, looking away and back again, afraid he'll say no, but determined to do everything in her power to persuade him; then Erica lets her eyes close and the illusion is gone. He can see from the resigned slump of her body against the hard-angled chair that he has come on too strong about his death. He is sorry and at the same time is aware of her there, hardly an arm's length away.

Finally she stretches up from the slouched position. Her nipples raise faint areas of shadow on the fabric of her shirt. "Don't you think it will be just as hard on him if you're here a while, then leave again?"

"Not if I'm careful."

Erica shakes her head. "You don't know much about children."

"I may need some help."

"Any help you want, Sherwood." Her eyes have turned on him, but the reflected firelight makes them hard to read. Her tone of voice is measured, as if she isn't sure of her words. "Don't look so frightened." She hesitates. "I'm not looking for anything perma-nent," hesitates again. "Marion and I were good friends. I trusted her. I know a lot about you and maybe I trust you just because you're her brother. Okay?"

Too much all at once. Is she making a pass or is this your imagination, O'Neal? He shakes his head, as much to clear it as to say no.

At first she looks hurt, then she turns away and laughs to herself. "Maybe I *am* getting old." Seconds later she shakes her head. "Is there any chance Jamie will be here tomorrow? We'd like to see him."

"Come for supper. I'll try to have him here."

"I'll bring a casserole."

"No. You work and I know how to cook. What time is best?"

"Five-thirty." She is on her feet and close to his chair. "Will you be okay here tonight?"

"Yes."

She bends over and kisses his forehead. Her breasts hang loose inside the shirt, and the warm scents of her skin and a sweet perfume envelop his buzzing head. "Sorry," she says. "You look like you need that and I wanted to do it. Welcome home, Sherwood."

He nods and watches her wrap up in her coat. His head feels heavier as she moves away and her perfume thins in the air around him. Her murmuring to the child comes like ghost whispers from the bedroom, then Josie moans and grumbles and finds her shrill little voice, "But Mommy, I want to stay and see Jamie."

"Tomorrow, honey. We'll see him tomorrow after your school." She returns to the living room with the child perched on one hip and tucked inside the coat. "Good night, Sherwood." With a whirl of bright hair and a last protest from Josie, they are gone.

Sherwood works his bare feet closer to the fire. His chest feels hot and Erica's odor lingers where her hair touched his face and shoulder. For several seconds he wonders what it would be like to be alive, to pull himself out of the chair and call her back. He can feel the weight of his tired legs, the rush of air into his lungs. His eyes blink in mild irritation from the fire's heat. Remembering her mouth on his forehead arouses him, as if this body that holds him refuses even now to accept its own end.

No, he thinks. Jamie first, then Art, and if you're still here after they're on their own, O'Neal, it's back to the cabin. Alone this time, like the postal clerk's friend, the way it should have been in the beginning.

3

Come morning Sherwood's neck and shoulders are stiff from sleeping in the chair, and his feet, drawn under the cushion, are as cold as the dead ashes in the fireplace. He stretches, tries to work the kinks out of his knees, then goes into the front hall and opens the door. A south wind has come up. It brings a gentle warmth and carries the scent of more rain. Down the street, sidewalks and diveways divide patches of trim lawn into squares and trapezoids and triangles that look like small oriental garden plots or fields from some fairytale landscape laid out below the bare branches of cork oak and Chinese hackberry and smooth, white English walnut trees grafted onto rough black walnut stumps. The yard in front of Marion's house is tufted with crabgrass, and the sidewalk is littered with sticks and late sycamore leaves. "Bet it wouldn't hurt to muster a little civic pride," he says.

His first impulse is to find Jamie, but he doesn't want to start wrong by showing up too early. Just an uncle dropping by to visit his nephew and nothing more. He closes the door and prowls the house in search of a working timepiece. The clock above the sink reads nine thirty-six. By the stove timer-clock it is eight twenty-four and an old wind-up clock in the basement is stuck at four thirty-two. As a last resort he goes to the telephone, where a penetrating female voice announces, "The time . . . is seven-forty . . . and fifty seconds."

"Too early," he tells her. Ten-thirty ought to be about right. In the meantime, he can think about what to do for Art.

Sooner or later, Sherwood will have to spring Art from his parents, and Sherwood assumes that when he does, the detectives will be out again. There are no good hiding places on the ground floor of the house, though he notices that the bathroom door opens against the curtained entrance of a large, low-ceilinged shower cubicle. In an emergency someone could sit quietly in the shower and not be discovered by a cursory search. The basement, too, offers minimum cover. The area is divided into two large rooms with closets, a central hall, a bathroom with tub and toilet on a platform two feet higher than the concrete floor, and an unfinished utility room. From the utility room a crawlspace about three feet wide extends under the bathroom platform. With a door to hide the opening this could serve as a temporary hiding place. "Not perfect, but reasonable."

As he stands up from examining the hole, he feels faint. Sparks dance in front of his eyes and, expecting to flip out, he steps into the hall, lies down to wait and worry about how he'll get through without Art. You need him, O'Neal. Have to wait for a letter saying where to pick him up, but you'll be there. No question. He can imagine Art, exercising daily to keep his incredible arms and shoulders in shape, working out and waiting, impatient to be free. Have to be ready for him. He'd be miserable if they caught him again, flat on his back under Marion's downstairs toilet.

Silver discs and the Club Texas don't materialize. Sherwood stares at the ceiling. His stomach growls. "Hungry," he says. That sensation of being in a foreign country hits him again. He feels lost and without clear direction. A decent place to sleep, meals, things that fell out naturally when he was with Art, are going to take a little thought and preparation. "So hungry you're about to faint, O'Neal."

Slowly he gets up and climbs the stairs to the kitchen, where the cupboards are stocked with prepared foods that he doesn't know how to use. "I hope California markets still stock meat and potatoes and flour." Forty-nine dehydrated ways to jazz up hamburger are not going to cut it. Wishing he had thought to grab his army overcoat from Art's lap, he leaves the house and walks through the park, past the place on the corner where the kid-revolutionaries were hiding out last year, and down two more blocks to the local Sambo's.

The noise and the people in the pancake house make him nervous, but a round-faced girl in white shows him into a quiet back dining room and seats him beneath a picture of a round-headed caricature in turban and red shorts. "Coffee?" she asks. Sherwood nods and stares at the tabletop. When she returns with the pot he asks for ham and eggs and toast.

"How would you like your eggs?"

He hesitates. "It doesn't matter," he says, then looks up to see her standing, weight on one leg with a fist jammed into her hip and a cocked smile at the corner of her mouth.

"Come on, man. Don't give me a hard time. Scrambled, over easy, sunny side . . . ?"

"Scrambled, I guess." He wonders if he looks as clumsy as he feels.

The smile twitches and her mouth turns down to look concerned. "Are you okay?"

"Yes."

She moves away with a long look back. Didn't handle that at all well. "Thanks," he says, then pulls his neck into his collar and peers around the room. The only other diner is four tables away and she doesn't seem to have noticed his fumbling. Like Sherwood she sits a little hunched in her chair, but her back is to the window, the vista of parking lot and garbage cans. The occasional nervous movement of one leg crossed over the other, the tense line her mouth makes as she prepares to light a cigarette, the shy tilt of her head; all suggest that she feels as self-conscious as he does. Even when the waitress brings her food, the woman keeps her eyes on the newspaper folded beside her plate. She is tall and slender, a red scarf is knotted jauntily at her throat. Once when she turns her head he notices that there are several streaks of blond or gray in the dark hair that brushes her face; then his breakfast arrives and he loses track of her in his attempt to eat without spilling anything.

By the time he has choked down the last forkful of dry egg, she is gone. A group of collegiate-looking types has moved in across the room. The waitress pours him another cup of coffee. "Are you feeling better?"

"Much," he says. Wonder if the shy woman felt any better when she left? "Thanks." He tilts his head toward her empty table.

"You noticed her, huh? Know exactly what you mean. Sometimes she'll have a second cup of coffee and a cigarette, but if someone else comes in," the waitress hits one palm a glancing blow across the coffee pot, "out the door. I know how she feels."

Sherwood nods.

"Yeah. I figured, you too. Are you an artist or something?"

"No."

"I am. It's so sterile in here, like to drive me batty. If you don't mind, I could tell her you noticed her. In a nice way. Just to spice up her day the next time she looks so down."

Caught by the girl's sincerity, Sherwood nods again, realizes his mistake but can't change it now. He hands her the check and a twenty-dollar bill, and runs. With two hours to kill and nothing to do, he goes back to Marion's, where he builds a fire and stares at the flames.

Precisely at ten-thirty Sherwood knocks on the door of 212 I Street, a freshly painted but ramshackle frame house near the railroad tracks. Through one of the windows he hears a child crying. A girl about six years old opens the door and asks him, "What do you want?"

"I'm Jamie's uncle."

She looks at him, eyes wide and maybe a little frightened, "Oh," and with a gesture more coy than her age would seem to allow, she brushes down the hem of her dress. "I'll get Mommy." She wipes her nose with the palm of her hand and slams the door in his face.

Inside the house a voice scolds—too far away for him to catch the words. An interior door bangs and he hears the voice again, nearer this time. "What the hell do you want now?" Silence follows. The floor creaks on the other side of the front door. "Who are you?"

"Sherwood O'Neal. I've come to see Jamie."

A short, dumpy woman opens the door wide enough to step outside. "You'll have to come back. He's asleep."

In spite of plump cheeks and chin, her face has a pinched look. She brushes back a string of black hair and lets her hand slide down one sagging breast that looks obscenely like meat inside a sack of sweater, marked with a smear of lipstick or catsup or, maybe, blood on one sleeve.

"I'll wake him." He takes a step toward the door, but she doesn't budge. "He's been too long without family."

"Where were you when he needed you?"

"I beg your pardon."

"I'll get it out in the open right now. I don't like the idea of some mental case barging in here any time he feels like it. I don't know what they're thinking of, wanting to let this poor, disturbed child go to a psychotic."

Disturbed?

She places both hands on the backs of her fleshy hips and throws out her chest. "It isn't right at all and I'm going to raise hell, let me tell you."

"I think you'd better let me see Jamie."

"Are you threatening me?"

"Not yet."

"You get out of here or I'll call the cops. I have two of my own and I take these other urchins out of my own feelings for children and the county doesn't pay me hardly enough to feed them, let alone buy clothes and I've just bought him a whole new outfit; and I don't have to put up with some maniac. . . ."

"Are you asking for money?" He reaches into his pocket and drags out the wad of bills.

The greed in her eyes is unmistakable.

Sherwood peels off a hundred-dollar bill and waves it in front of her. "I want to see Jamie."

"You're trying to bribe me."

"Lady"—he adds a second bill and stuffs them into her waiting hand—"I bribed you and now I'm threatening you. Get out of my way."

"You're crazy."

"Bet your fat ass."

She glances at the money as if to make sure it is as much as she thought, and Sherwood seizes the lapse to brush past her. He knocks the door back on its hinges and steps inside.

The living room is filthy, knee deep in toys and broken furniture and piles of books and magazines and newspapers and dirty dishes there so long that dust has gathered on the dried food. A white, starched nurse's cap seems to accentuate the squalor from a solid perch on the back of Marion's rocking chair. The place stinks of rot and human excrement and death.

"I haven't had a chance to clean up the . . ."

"Where's Jamie?" Uneasy feeling about this, O'Neal.

"Upstairs," she says.

For a moment, he is relieved. The crying child seems to be behind the nearest downstairs door. "Which room?" He strides to the stairs, knocking over a bowl of moldy spaghetti, and climbs two at a time.

The woman is right behind him, her voice whining now, "I've done all I could for him, but he's been impossible all the time I've had him. He's being punished. You're asking for trouble if you impose a different authority. . . ."

"If you've hurt him, I'm going to hurt you." He hopes he sounds crazy enough to make her shut up.

"Are you saying I've abused him?" she shrieks.

"Hope I don't have to, lady. Just hope."

In the upstairs hall he passes a bathroom, then has to decide among four closed doors. He throws open the first on the left and stops in shocked silence. The woman pants audibly at the top of the stairs.

This room is unfurnished except for two of Marion's sofa cushions thrown askew into the corner. A stench of human feces issues from piles and slimy puddles on the floor, and there, across the filth, sits Jamie. His hair is matted like black seaweed against his pale scalp. One thumb is crammed into his mouth, and his other hand strokes the thick furry coat that he has tried to push onto a cold radiator as if to keep it out of the dirt. The diaper pinned around his hips is stained a yellowish brown. Awed by the scene, Sherwood calls softly, "Jamie?" Dark, vacant eyes turn on him. "Hang tight a second. I'll get you out of this."

He turns on Doris. "You bitch." His voice is a growl, low and full of menace and it sends her scrambling into the stairwell. "If I see you again, I'm going to kill you." The second she disappears, he turns back to the room. "Jamie. My God, little dude. If I'd known, I would have come sooner." He fights back a bitter laugh. "They didn't even treat me this bad when they thought I was a nut case. Come on. Let me slip into the coat." He crouches and gathers up the child and the stinking fur. A mucus-filled, yellow fluid oozes out of the diapers. Tugging them off, he uses the outside to wipe away as much of the mess as he can. "There's a bathroom right outside. Let me clean you up." He picks his way out and down to the bathroom, where he runs a tub of warm water.

The tile floor is coated with gray scum, but the room isn't littered. Sherwood finds soap and towel. "Aren't you going to say anything? It's me, Sher. Uncle Sher. Remember?" He thinks he sees a flash in the child's eyes, but Jamie's only real response is to drag one sleeve of the coat into the water after him.

With a washcloth Sherwood scrubs at caked-on filth until Jamie whimpers. The small buttocks and upper legs are covered with a rash, and there is one open sore. "Nothing we can do for it here." He dries Jamie, wraps him in a dry towel, pulls on the coat and gathers the damp body inside the fur.

Downstairs the crying has stopped. From a far corner of the living room the six-year-old girl watches Sherwood with large, animal eyes. "Mommy put him in the shitty room," she says.

"How long was he in there?"

She shrugs.

"Since this morning? Yesterday?"

"He had to go in there a lot. He wouldn't talk at all."

"Where's your mother?"

The girl casts a glance over her shoulder. "Are you going to kill me too?"

"No." The word is too angry to give her any reassurance, but he can't bear to stay under her sad, frightened gaze. He runs out of the house and down the block, keeps running until his breath comes in gasps. "I won't kill anyone," he whispers.

Jamie, he discovers, has fallen asleep.

The sky is broken into bargelike clouds that move slowly north. With Jamie a dead weight on his left arm Sherwood walks through the Tuesday-morning car-and-bike traffic of downtown Dawville. He feels conspicuous wearing the smelly coat and carrying the child, but no one pays any attention. Before the Army he would have hated it: people too busy to notice each other. That he is glad of it now surprises him. "Before the Army," he mutters. "How long since you thought about anything before the Army?" He can't remember. By the time he arrives at Marion's he has become preoccupied with a numbness in his left arm. He would have assumed that the work he did at the cabin kept him in reasonable shape. Not enough strength and staying power to handle a child?

He puts Jamie in bed without waking him, tapes a Band-Aid over the sore, and tugs pajamas over the unresisting limbs. The sleeping child looks normal, almost happy, but Sherwood wonders. The little he knows about children doesn't allow for that vacant stare. He remembers a child who wouldn't walk anywhere if he could run and who couldn't go more than a few seconds without making some word or sound.

"Sleep, little guy." You haven't spoken. Didn't even cry when I washed the sore. "Things will look better when you wake up." He pulls up a chair and drapes the coat over it so the cleanest sleeve rests on the bed near Jamie's hand, then he tiptoes out of the room and collapses into the chair by the fireplace.

Unsure of yourself, O'Neal, he thinks. Hanging here like a loose end, and you're going to be doing it longer than you thought. Jamie's situation disastrous. Have to figure a way to convince Art he should stay too. Sherwood's thoughts wander to finding or building a decent hiding place for Art. "All right. Let's put this scene together." He is amazed at how tired he is already, but he has things to do so he finds a pencil and an old envelope and installs himself at the kitchen table to consider them. He writes Art's name in the top right corner, draws a box around it, then doodles an ornate No. 1 on the paper. "You'd better find a decent place to sleep." He writes it as:

1. Sleeping place—sofa for living room?

2. Make this place look more like a home—lawn, outside of windows. Cleanliness. There's going to be flack about your mental health.

Is a clean mind a healthy mind?

3. Clean rain gutters.

4. Food. Check the market downtown to see what you can buy that might be real food. After Jamie wakes up.

Sherwood looks around, trying to gauge how long the outside work will take. The clock above the sink is at one-fifteen.

5. Set clocks.

Jamie doesn't stir for the rest of the morning and most of the afternoon. By four o'clock Sherwood has dragged a single bed out of the basement and covered it with throw pillows to make a couch. He has washed the windows on the front and south sides of the house, hacked through the wet grass of the lawn with Marion's dull mower, cleaned all the boxed food from the cupboards and stashed it in the utility room, and has studied at least twenty-five recipes for the hamburger he has taken out of the freezer to thaw. For the past year, he and Art haven't considered hamburger to be fit for human consumption, but Sherwood manages to pack together a meatloaf that doesn't look like it will fall apart in the oven. A package of pinto beans presents him with more familiar fare and he sets a pan of them on the counter to soak. The only vegetable he can find is a box of frozen peas. He puts that on the drainboard, dumps frozen orange juice into a pitcher of water and mixes up a batch of cornbread. He worries about the child in the other room, but he waits. He has no way of knowing if Jamie sat awake all night in that room and needs sleep, or if he sleeps to escape just as he, Sherwood, slept away almost two years before Art found him.

Finished with supper preparations, he props his feet on the kitchen table and watches the clock move around to a quarter till five. "Time enough," he says, finally. Erica and Josie will be here soon. He gets up and crosses the kitchen to listen at the door to Jamie's room, opens it carefully.

Jamie is awake. He sits in the middle of the rug, the shaggy coat pulled around him, and he stares at his carefully ordered toy shelves with what looks like mild interest. The dark eyes flicker and shift toward the movement of the opening door, but then they move away again and the interest goes out of them.

"Little dude?" His voice brings no response. Sherwood squats on his heels and waits. Nothing happens. Except for a twitch now and then, Jamie doesn't move. His shoulders slump. The muscles in his thin arms are tense. Words bubble through Sherwood's head, words of comfort, words of commitment that he can't say. Can't tell that lie, O'Neal. All you need to do to destroy Marion's kid is promise to be here, to make sure he's with you when your heart does give out.

Minutes run together. The stove timer signals that the meatloaf has been in forty-five minutes. The time is five-fifteen. Sherwood gets up to shut off the buzzer, comes back. Jamie doesn't appear to have noticed the movement or heard the racket. The scent of browning meat works its way into the room. "We're going to have to talk to each other, Jamie. I'll be staying here awhile."

It occurs to Sherwood that he might have to squat in the doorway all night, but then the front door thumps open and Josie's excited voice echoes through the darkening house. "Jamie, Jamie. Are you home, Jamie?" She darts into the room, all warmth and excitement, cheeks flushed and bright orange coat askew over one shoulder. "Jamie." Throwing out her arms, she drops to the floor beside him and engulfs him with hugs and noisy kisses.

Erica appears in the opposite doorway, her coat pushed back on her shoulders in a more sedate reflection of Josie's enthusiasm. "Don't you two believe in light?" Her hand brushes the switch.

Sherwood blinks in the sudden brightness.

"What *are* you doing in the dark?"

"He's had a rough time. I think we're trying to decide how we're going to communicate."

"Mommy," Josie says. She scoots around to study Jamie's face. Erica kneels between them and puts an arm around Jamie's shoulder. "My God." She tries to pick him up, but as she does he loses his grip on the coat and lets out a cry.

"The coat," Sherwood says.

She grabs it, feels the grime and at the same time gets a whiff of the fur and lets it drop again. Jamie's shriek fills the room, then chokes off from lack of breath.

At least he responds to something. Sherwood takes him from Erica and retrieves the coat. One more cry drags through a long sob into silence and Jamie goes limp.

"That bitch. That goddamned stinking bitch."

Erica's anger makes Jamie stiffen against Sherwood, and Jamie's face turns red in preparation for another scream. "Easy. Keep things low-key. Let's not flip him out all the way."

She covers her eyes with both hands and sinks to the floor. Beside her Josie offers comfort with her arms and nuzzling curly head. "What's wrong with Jamie, Mommy?"

"This is too much. What did she do to him?"

"She might not have had to do much."

"I should have taken him. I could have. . . ."

"Maybe she tried."

"I damn well doubt it and you aren't any better sitting here in the dark staring at him." Her voice rises and Sherwood feels tension come into Jamie's arms. "Christ. Your own sister's child."

"I know what he's going through," Sherwood says softly. "What he needs most right now is calm. Okay? I'll put in the corn bread. We can all eat in about twenty minutes."

A long silence, then Erica shakes her head.

"Come on. I think Josie was getting to him before you turned on the light. It's going to take a little time."

"Okay," she says, finally. "Give me a minute and I'll come help."

Leaving her with Josie draped around her neck, Sherwood takes Jamie into the kitchen where he installs him, coat and all, in the high chair. Josie's voice seems to follow them from the bedroom. "Will Jamie get better?"

"Of course he'll get better, baby, but we'll have to love him a lot."

"He's sad because his mommy died, isn't he?"

"Yes, but for a while we shouldn't talk about that."

"Can I go see him?" She comes out of the bedroom and with a side glance at Sherwood, perches on a kitchen chair.

"Do you think he knows who you are, Josie?" He puts the corn bread into the oven and drops the half-frozen block of peas into a pan of water.

"Yes, but he looks afraid."

"I'll bet he is." Adults haven't done well by him. "Maybe Marion told him I died and he thinks I'm a ghost."

Josie giggles.

"Marion told him you'd taken a job in that place, wherever you were, in South Dakota." Erica is dry-eyed and her voice has steadied. "He was hurt that you left without coming to see him and didn't at least send a card once in a while."

"I didn't see any other way."

"She told me you were stubborn."

"She wasn't exactly a diplomat herself. If everything else had been normal, things would have worked out." He waves a tired hand in the direction of the high chair. "Who could anticipate this?"

For a moment she bristles, then shakes her head. "I'm sorry. . . . take my own guilt out on you. What did Doris Ransler do to him?"

"I don't know for sure."

"You should report her"—she hesitates—"to the foster home people, at least, maybe to the police. He's been abused. What else could you call it?"

Doris Ransler can make more trouble for you, O'Neal, than you can make for her, and you know it as well as you know your own scar.

"I mean it. You should tell someone."

"Let me think about it. Things are coming too fast."

"Yes," she says, "I suppose they are."

The peas boil and become tender. Sherwood pulls the meatloaf out of the oven to keep it from burning. The cornbread is still half liquid in its pan. Supper turns out to be meatloaf and peas with hot cornbread and honey for dessert. "This cooking with gas is going to take practice," he says. "I'm used to a wood stove."

"You did fine. Jamie ate like he was starved."

"That's what counts."

Jamie looks better after the meal. His eyes track Josie around the kitchen as she darts between Erica at the table and Sherwood at the sink. Dishes done, Sherwood carries him into the living room and props him in the green chair so he can watch the evening fire. Josie puts on a show of jumping and dancing and clumsy four-year-old somersaults in the center of the floor. Oblivious to the stench of the coat, she sits with Jamie between acts and chatters about her nursery school. Sherwood spreads out on the end of the bed, and Erica settles cross-legged near the fire.

"You're going to have to do something about the coat," she says.

"I thought if I could get it away from him, I'd have it cleaned."

"You could try wool cleaner."

"There's still the problem of getting him to part with it."

"A piece might be as good as the whole thing. Security blankets work that way sometimes."

"I'll try."

She turns and looks at him, takes a long breath and lets her eyes drift back to the fire.

And what was that she was going to say? Something about security blankets, O'Neal. You knew that look once; another gesture she's picked up from your sister. This business of the mimicked expressions troubles Sherwood a little, but at the same time he is aware that he's inclined to trust Erica simply because she was close enough to Marion to imitate her. He stifles a yawn.

"You're tired."

"A little jet lag, maybe."

"We'd better go." She stretches her legs in front of her as if to get up. "Are you as sure about what you're doing as you seem?"

Shrugging, Sherwood watches Josie stroke Jamie's hand. "I'm not very sure about anything."

"May we come tomorrow?"

"Please do."

"Say good-bye, Josie. Sherwood and Jamie need their sleep and so do we." Erica is on her feet and she bustles around the house to find her dark coat and bundle Josie into her orange one. Before Sherwood can say his thanks, they are outside and on their way up the street in a light drizzle.

"Time for a showdown, little dude." He finds a pair of scissors in Marion's sewing closet and approaches the chair. "If we don't get the stink out of the coat, someone is going to come in here to check on us and decide I'm not fit to see about your welfare." Jamie stares straight ahead. His eyes look red in the firelight. "We're going to wash the coat, Jamie. I'm going to snip off a piece you can take to bed tonight." He looks for a clean corner, doesn't find one and finally cuts off a band of sleeve that has been turned up inside. Jamie lets him slide the loop over his shoulder. "Now we'll get one for the other side." The second loop separates along a seam. He slips it onto Jamie's other arm and gently tugs the bulk of the coat out of the chair. Slowly, the dark eyes move to Sherwood's face. "Want to watch?" Lifting the child, he drags the coat into the bathroom.

"I wish you could get it together to talk, small friend. These one-sided conversations are going to get to me after a while. I'm supposed to be about half nuts and it's not acceptable for me to be doing something that looks so much like talking to myself."

The wool cleaner turns out to be in a bottle under the sink. Sherwood runs a tub of cold water, adds twice as much of the liquid as the instructions advise and drops the coat into the brew. "That should cure it." He looks down at Jamie, who sits on the floor, a pained grimace on his face. "It's okay, man. As soon as it dries you can have it again," he says, then he notices that both hands dig like clawed paws into the pajama crotch. "Use the toilet, Jamie."

Jamie stares at him.

"It's easy." Sherwood lifts him to the bowl. The small legs don't offer any resistance against the floor so Sherwood holds him to let him relieve himself of a stream of urine and a long sigh. "What's the matter here? Your legs don't work, or you don't want to work them? We're going to have to concentrate on finding you some will to live. The world isn't all rooms full of shit and people who disappear without a word. There's more to it. A lot more." Isn't there? He carries Jamie to bed and tucks him under the covers. "Time to sleep again. Are you thirsty?"

The child doesn't respond.

Sherwood gets a glass of water, holds it for him to drink and then puts it on the bookcase beside the bed. "Call me if you need anything." As if on signal, Jamie closes his eyes. "Pancakes for breakfast, okay? You used to like that."

First the coat, then sleep. The water is shot through with gray-brown fluid tendrils that extend from a haze around the coat. He sloshes fur back and forth until it becomes a blur in the liquid, then drains the tub, and fills it a second time. The water turns milky almost immediately. A third tub brings out as much dirt as the second, but the fourth remains more or less clear. Sherwood pulls the plug and leaves the coat to drain.

In the living room the fire has burned to a low flicker. Easing off his shoes, he stretches out on the bed and closes his eyes. He needs sleep, but the telephone rings before he can get deep enough not to hear it. The instrument is hidden in the hall closet.

He drags it back to the bed, flops down and lifts the receiver. "Marion Howard's residence."

"Are you the man who took Jamie this morning?" Though it has a conciliatory tone, the voice is strident. Unmistakably Doris Ransler.

"Yes."

"I think we should come to some kind of understanding."

A shudder tugs at the skin between his shoulder blades. "I don't have anything to say to you, lady."

"You threatened to kill me. If you don't listen, I'll have you locked up." She pauses. "Do you understand? I can do that to you."

"It should be the other way around."

"I want you to understand that what you saw here today was because I've been sick. I haven't been able to take care of things and my husband ran . . ." She lets out a short, barking cough. "That little monster was crapping all over the house. I had to do something. I was responsible for him, for his discipline."

"I hear you," Sherwood says.

"If they inspect me right now, it won't be fair. It wouldn't be right. Do you understand."

"You want to trade my silence for yours?" He hears a gasp at the other end of the line. "Either it's that or I'm going to have to listen to your nasty voice another five minutes to figure out what you're trying to say because it's obvious you won't say it yourself."

"You understand well enough."

"Consider it done." He slams down the phone, peels back the bedclothes and rolls under them fully dressed.

Sleep doesn't come. The weariness that almost carried him under dissolves in anger at Doris Ransler and at himself. She can clean up her house, he thinks, fumigate the shitty room to erase any evidence against her, but you can't wipe out your fear, can you? Can't wipe out the mental record that is sure to damn you for the threat that both she and her daughter heard. "If you're shot for stupidity," he grumbles, "you'll deserve your fate."

The fire collapses into a layer of coals that dulls over with cold ash. A streetlamp outside sends a pale shaft of light across the bed. Around him the house groans and cracks, and a wind beats branches of the Chinese hackberry against the shingles. Jamie seems unnaturally quiet, then Sherwood hears a swish and a thump. Fingers scrabble against wood. The door opens. For a moment the house is silent, then knees and hands bump the floor. Jamie crawls across the hall, and Sherwood hears him rise to open the door of Marion's room. A little animal sniffing the lair for a trace of its mother. He doesn't cry out or whimper. Sherwood waits. Marion's bed creaks. The crawling sounds resume as Jamie moves out of her room and into the hall again.

"Jamie?"

No response.

Sherwood listens for sounds of him getting back into bed, but they don't come. Fell asleep on the floor? He is about to go check when he hears the scrape and slap of hands and knees. Jamie crawls into the living room, stops, pushes himself into a sitting position and stares for a long time at the bed and Sherwood, who watches through slitted eyes. The pieces of coat dangle from each small hand.

Spotlighted by the streetlamp, afraid the slightest movement might break the child's concentration, Sherwood holds his breath. At length Jamie lets out a hiss that might be breathing or the beginning of a word, drops onto hands and knees and crawls to the side of the bed. He pulls himself up, tugs down the covers and wriggles under them to lie, back to Sherwood, curled and still.

"Jamie?" Sherwood pushes up on one elbow. He can see the face in a beam of streetlight, its round, dark eyes wide open and staring straight across the room with an intensity that can only be expectation. "Little dude," Sherwood says. He lets his hand fall on the shoulder so small it seems that one reassuring squeeze could crush it. "We'll make it, man. Try to get some sleep."

Jamie's eyes close slowly and by the time the upper lashes touch the lower, his breathing has deepened.

Crazy, O'Neal. There're only a couple of ways this can end: Jamie somewhere else and you in the mountains or dead. He can't count on you. One day and you've made a total mess of things. Lying there, watching rain through the light fall like sparks or silver discs to take him back to the Club Texas, he waits for the flipout and wonders for the first time if it would make any difference if he remembered what happened to him.

4

Hazy dreams about his parents: driving the pickup into town, the three of them talking about the condition of the range on either side of the road where the land unfolds with grass all winter brown and snow patches under the north faces of each ridge; saying good-bye at the depot for what he now realizes will be the last time—the pain of their death and that vague unsettling guilt, both absent this time—and then the bus and the plane and Okinawa, lush and green under the monsoon rains, neon signs of Koza blurred by downpour. With image after image, the dream drags up anticipation from wherever he has packed it away.

The feeling is so strong that it wakes him and he lies still, letting his eyes wander the textured ceiling. Feet slap the sidewalk outside. Someone laughing, probably a student and probably drunk, cuts across the lawn, slips on the wet grass, gets up again and runs down the street toward the park.

"You felt like that once. Not mortal at all and full of infinite possibility." He shrugs to himself. His hand touches Jamie's leg.

The child is rigid and trembling.

"Jamie, man." Sherwood puts his hand on the small chest. The pajamas are soaked with sweat, and Jamie's heart beats wildly. His face is contorted as if to pull cheeks and eyes and knotted forehead into his open mouth. "Hey. Wake up. You've having a bad dream."

The open mouth contracts a little, as if he wants to scream but can't.

"Come on, man. Wake up." He lifts Jamie by the shoulders. The child's eyes pop open, crazed eyes like Dracula in his coffin with the hero already in the crypt and the sun only five minutes from setting. "It's okay. I'm here. Sher. Remember?" Eyes soften and close again. Arms and legs relax. "You do your own flipping out, don't you, little dude?" And don't you know that immobilizing terror, O'Neal? "You're too young to get like that. You still haven't had your chance to be twenty and immortal."

Jamie is limp and quiet. Sherwood gets up, rummages dry pajamas out of his dresser, changes them for the sweaty ones and tugs the fur loops on over them. The time is one-thirty. He stokes up the fire, but falls asleep almost immediately. When he wakes again, Jamie is out of bed. Sherwood finds him in the bathroom, sitting beside the tub, his pajama bottoms heaped in a puddle of urine and his eyes fixed in a blank stare at the floor.

"It's okay, Jamie." He runs his hand over the dark hair, watches the head half turn until Jamie can look at him out of the corner of one eye. "No harm done. Look." Wiping the puddle with a bath towel, he throws the towel and pajamas into the tub. "Got the coat clean. It's still wet. We'll have to use saddle soap on it to keep the leather from cracking, but it won't stink anymore." Some of the fur is already dry. Sherwood drags the coat up and pulls the sleeves through the towel racks. "Pretty steady drip. It may take three or four days to dry. Let's get you dressed and see about breakfast, okay?" He finds underwear and pants, a sweatshirt and a pair of slippers with bulbous duck heads sewn over the toes. Being careful not to separate Jamie from the rings of coat, Sherwood dresses him and pushes on the slipppers. "Ducks, huh? Ducks on your toes. Quack, quack. Come on, duck toes. Let's make some pancakes."

With a lot of hair ruffling and a patter of quacks to fill the silence, he hauls Jamie to the kitchen and puts him in the high chair, dumps water and baking mix into a bowl, adds a little cornmeal, Roman Meal cereal, honey, oil, powdered egg, powdered milk. Jamie sits askew at the table with his head rigid, but his eyes move to follow the activity from counter to refrigerator to stove. The griddle smokes around the edges. Sherwood turns down the flame and spoons out three small cakes, cooks and flips and lets them cook again.

"Okay, my friend. What are you going to have on these?" He stacks the pancakes on a plate, butters them, then bends low so his face is level with Jamie's. "Jelly or syrup?" He crosses to the high chair with slow, heavy steps.

The eyes live. They sparkle at his stalking advance and in one corner of the neutral mouth, a hint of smile. "I know you're hiding in there, Jamie. Jelly or syrup?" The smile spreads. "Or mud?"

A short bark erupts from Jamie's throat.

"Great, man. Jelly?"

Jamie shakes his head.

"Syrup."

He doesn't nod, but his eyes flicker toward the bottle on the counter.

"Okay." Sherwood claps him gently on the shoulder, slides the plate in front of him and grabs the bottle. "Syrup. Say it, okay? We're going to have to talk. There's a lot that has to be said if we're going to get this act together in time. The way I see it, I'm here to turn you into the healthy kid you were, teach you a few manners and get you set up for the rest of your life.

"That doesn't mean I'm *not* going to be part of the rest of your life. . . ." Whoa back, O'Neal. Eyes going wary. Don't let them get blank again. "Naw. Go ahead and eat. We can take time to hash that out." He laughs. "For now we have to figure out what we're going to do with this particular morning."

Going to have to figure out what to do with a lot of mornings and hope the heart holds in the meantime. "We can start by getting some kind of real food. None of this powder-and-water junk."

Exactly what he will have to do with a lot of his time becomes apparent after breakfast. He mops syrup and pancake off the table, off the floor and the high chair, off Jamie's hands and face, then puts him on the floor so he can stay or go while Sherwood does the dishes. Dishes take about fifteen minutes. Half an hour of rummaging through closets yields an umbrella, the Gerry pack Marion used when Jamie was a baby and the fatigue jacket he had thought lost at Bolo Point. Shoes for Jamie finally turn up, placed neatly under the bed. The shoes fit, but for no obvious reason it takes ten minutes to get them on the wiggling feet.

Jacket comes next with coat-sleeve loops crossed over it like ban-
doliers, then a better wash job for the hands and face.

How did Marion manage? Handled a kid and held down a job?
Started to go to the store at eight o'clock and here it is a quarter
past nine and we're not out the door yet. "There has to be something about this I don't know, man. Maybe a lot of things. Might
help if you'd talk a little, tell me what's going wrong."

Jamie's legs are still like rubber. Sherwood wrestles him into
the pack, then as an afterthought, puts the pack on the bathroom
scale. Total weight is twenty-nine pounds. "That can't be enough
—not even ten pounds a year. Exercise is what you need. And
food. Let's go to the store."

On his back twenty-nine pounds is plenty. He pops open the
umbrella at the door and they set out for town.

The grocery where Marion shopped is a small family store on
the edge of downtown, one of the last essential services among all
the novelty shops, real estate offices and banks. Sherwood jockeys
a cart and the Gerry pack through the narrow aisles, loads up with
potatoes and carrots and cabbage, chops and a roast and a
chicken; bok choy, rice vinegar, dried mushrooms, noodles, even a
small packet of dried squid. Peanut butter, milk, honey, yoghurt;
his confidence is on the rise. Food hasn't gone all to boxed din-
ners in a year. The produce is both better and cheaper than in
South Dakota. He can live the way he knows and get by. A little
Midwest, a little Far East. At the checkout stand a cheerful white-
haired woman rings up his supplies without comment, then, as he
offers one of his hundred-dollar bills, she notices the Gerry pack.

"Is that you, Jamie? You need some candy?" She reaches into
her apron pocket and comes up with a thin candy cane left over
from Christmas. To Sherwood's surprise a hand shoots by his neck
and takes the candy. The woman smiles. "You forget how to say
'thank you,' Jamie?"

"Thank you." The voice is hoarse, but the words are clear. Sherwood cranes his neck, tries to catch a glimpse of the child behind
him.

"Jamie's a favorite. He's always so bright and cheerful. You're
Marion's brother."

"Sherwood."

"I heard. I'm terribly sorry. Did you come to take care of Jamie?"

"Yes."

"You aren't married, are you?"

"No."

One eyebrow goes up. "It takes time to raise a child."

"So it seems." Money too. Fifty-eight dollars' worth of food? Didn't buy a case of anything. Cost more to live here in spite of the cheap produce.

The sacked groceries fill five bags. "Could I leave some of these here and come back?" he asks.

"No car?"

"No."

"That's right. Marion said you didn't drive. Something about a wound. In Vietnam?" She leans toward him and whispers, "Take the cart. Bring it back as soon as you get the chance."

"Thank you." The woman seems willing to carry the conversation farther, but Sherwood waves and pushes the cart out into the rain. "Jamie, small friend. Are you feeling better all of a sudden, or have you been holding out on me?"

Jamie munches candy, almost in time with the slap of Sherwood's feet on the wet sidewalk.

The umbrella is cumbersome. He finally wedges the handle between his shoulders and the pack. It keeps them both dry that way, but it is uncomfortable and the groceries get soaked. Back at Marion's he peels sodden paper bags away from his supplies and loads the shelves of cupboards and refrigerator. Jamie plays on the kitchen floor, picks up pieces of the brown paper and plasters them on the wall or smears water across the floor with his hand. When Sherwood finishes stashing the food, Jamie follows him into the living room and watches until a fire crackles in the fireplace. "All right. You have a room full of toys in there, and I know you know how to play with them. Why don't you get us a couple of trucks or cars and we'll see if we can't carry on some normal activity?"

"Truck?" Jamie cocks his head to one side.

"Right. Two trucks. You know about the number 2?"

"Two trucks." He drops from a sitting position onto all fours and disappears into the bedroom, where he bangs around for several minutes. Shortly he appears again, pushing his hands ahead of him on a chipped red fire truck and a white ambulance van.

"Good. You have a way to go to catch up with Josie, but it looks like the basic material is still there. Suppose I find us some blocks to go with the trucks?" On one of the higher toy shelves he finds a net bag of alphabet blocks, takes it into the living room and builds a house on the floor. "Okay. You're the fireman. Got that? Help, fireman. My house is on fire. Get that truck up here and put out this fire. Help."

With a short laugh Jamie pushes the truck up to the block building and rams it through the wall.

"No, that's not . . ." Several of the blocks have fallen on top of Jamie's hand and he stares at them. Can't blow it, O'Neal. He doesn't need you getting after him. "Oh-oh. The fireman had an accident. Here comes the ambulance." He runs the ambulance up to the house, plucks blocks away from Jamie's hand. "Looks like you're hurt, fireman. Have to take you to the hospital." Imitating a siren, Sherwood puts the small hand on top of the ambulance, drives it toward the bed, then lifts a grinning Jamie onto the rumpled spread. "All right. This fireman has hurt his hand. Legs too, I see. Just look at those legs. Can't walk on those. We'll fix the hand. Like this. Then the legs, the left one, pull it, work it a little bit. Hip seems to be okay. Knee. Foot."

Jamie giggles.

"Tickling helps, huh? Other leg. Foot. Okay, now the knee and the hip. Good, good. Now the *tummy*."

Doubling with laughter, Jamie kicks the tickling hand away.

"Those legs are fixed. Try 'em, little fireman. See how they work."

With cocked head he studies Sherwood's face.

"You guessed it. I'm trying to psych you out. Come on. Let's build another house."

Jamie slides off the bed to his knees and crawls to the fire truck, watches Sherwood rebuild the house and they go through the wreck-and-doctor routine again—again and again. "You could do this all day, couldn't you?" Finally the game degenerates into running the truck around the floor, ramming it into houses and walls and scattering blocks from fireplace to kitchen door.

At noon Sherwood makes peanut-butter sandwiches. Jamie's

eyes start to droop while they eat, and when Sherwood puts him down for a nap he falls asleep within minutes.

A couple of words and a few giggles the first morning, Sherwood thinks. He'll be all right, but he's short on stamina. Have to ask Erica if that little ride and playing with a toy truck should tire him that much. "And what about you, O'Neal?" he mutters. The morning has worn him out. He wants to sleep, decides he better not and then wakes up to the sound of someone knocking on the front door.

She is a distinguished-looking woman, his caller; about fifty years old in dark-colored pantsuit and raincoat, large purse over one shoulder and a zip-lock plastic case of papers in her hand. Curled brown hair with a little gray showing here and there; her nose is small and her teeth straight, but Sherwood's attention is drawn to eyes the same age-brown color as her hair. The eyes are sharply observant—wary, but neutral. "I'm Patricia Chapman," she says. "Valley County Child Protective Services."

Oh Lord. Erica turned Doris in and Doris called the cops. He can see by the half-official, half-hostile set of thin brows over those wary eyes that his fear shows on his face.

"Are you Sherwood O'Neal?"

"Yes. I was asleep. Come in."

The stiff, self-assured way she walks into the room gives him the same pressured feeling that made him want to run the detective off the road outside Custer. She seems to pass judgment on the chair pulled in front of the smoldering fire, the unmade bed, blocks and trucks on the floor. "Is the child here? You're not supposed to take charge of the child until the court decides you are . . ."

"Josie," he blurts. Control, O'Neal. Think control. "She couldn't go to school today and her mother couldn't stay home."

"Is she sick?"

"Yes. It's just a cold, I mean. But I needed the practice. With a kid. You know? Erica left her with me." He puts his finger to his lips in a gesture that feels wide-eyed and jerky. "She's asleep. Josie." Oh brother.

"I see." The woman takes a red clipboard out of the plastic case.

"Sit down, please. The chair. I haven't made the bed yet."

She sits and writes something on a form clipped to the board. "Try to relax, Mr. O'Neal. I'm not against you. I'm here to see if I can determine what is best for the child. Our goals are . . . should be, the same. I'm not certain that you can practice taking responsibility for another human being, but your motives are obviously sincere. I'll be sure to take that into account along with everything else. Please try not to think of me as the enemy."

"That won't be easy." Sherwood sits on the edge of the bed, watches her nod and smile faintly to herself.

"I take it you want custody of your sister's child."

"He should have some kind of chance, and right now I'm the best he has."

"Have you visited him?"

"Yes."

"And what do you think of the foster home?"

Sherwood feels his mouth turn down in a sneer. "It's okay."

"That's good. Our caseload is heavy right now and there wasn't any other place for the child. . . ."

"Jamie," Sherwood says.

"For Jamie. Now, would you mind telling me a little about the foster home? Did you meet the Ranslers?"

"Just the woman. Doris."

"You didn't meet Mr. Ransler? When did you visit?"

"This morning." Whoops. "Before Josie came."

"And the house was clean? Jamie seemed happy there?"

Lady, if you're out to get Doris Ransler for something, you'll end up having Sherwood O'Neal in the process. "I'd be better for him. I'm family. The last. It's just him and me."

"You're Irish, aren't you? Close family ties?"

"I don't know about my Irish. When we were a family, we were all close."

The woman nods and writes. "When was the last time you visited your sister?"

"A year ago."

"If you were close, why haven't you seen them for so long?"

"Haven't you seen my record? You aren't here because you know?"

"I want to hear your version." She takes a deep breath and studies him with an unembarrassed stare. "You are a single man with a mental record, which makes you totally unsuitable except that, if we are to place Jamie with a willing family member, you're our only choice. We would rather have a child with some member of his family. The fact that you want custody also counts in your favor."

Sherwood nods.

"Do you want to tell me why you stayed away so long?"

"I was afraid I'd die and leave Jamie hanging." Lame, O'Neal. She can't understand that. Why would she want to? He shrugs. "A lot like he is now. It doesn't make good sense the way things are, but it seemed the most reasonable course at the time."

"Why change your mind, then?"

"Because except for a father who ran out on him to see the world, I'm the only family he has. Who else would care about him as much as I do? Who else can tell him about his mother, about his grandparents?"

"You have a point about the family history, but about the care? Our foster homes are very good."

"Not what . . ." Blew it, you dope. Shut up.

"Then you don't approve of the Ransler home?"

"Lady, as you've pointed out, I'm a known psych case and to most people that means psycho. I don't want to make trouble that can only come back at me. The only thing I'm interested in is making sure Jamie has a chance for a more or less normal life. Okay?"

"I understand your feelings." Her eyes seem to probe his face. She starts to say something, then shakes her head. "You know that the jurisdiction hearing is February 3?"

"I have it in a letter."

"That's probably as far as we can get for today, then. You may make arrangements with the Ranslers for the child to visit you. As often as is convenient. Expect me to come again. I'll want to make at least one other impromptu visit. We'll have to get fairly well acquainted. If you are granted custody, I'll be making at least weekly visits."

"What?"

"We don't just give him to you. It isn't that simple. Ever. And with your record . . ."

"Damned Army." Too nasty. Get a grip.

"Bitterness won't help you get the child."

"He's not 'the child,' lady. His name is Jamie. Got that? Jamie, and damned right I'm bitter. I get myself blown open in some freak accident I can't even remember—probably would have been court-martialed for it if they hadn't decided I was a lifetime basket case.

"It wasn't so bad when it was just me telling myself I was already dead, but having to beg someone to let me make sure Jamie doesn't live the rest of his life in shit. . . ." Too much, O'Neal. Careful. "And you come in here, lady, calling him 'the child' like he's just a number on that piece of paper you keep scribbling on and you don't even know his name. Yeah. I'm bitter." And dumb. He realizes he has gotten to his feet and he sits back on the bed. "You're probably right, but I can't help feeling bitter." How do you ask her not to write this on her forms, O'Neal?

"You don't know what happened to you?"

"No. I think a kid I knew did something flaky with some explosives. He was killed, I was hurt, but I don't know how it happened. There was an official report . . . my shrink told me about it, trying to jog my memory. No luck, though. It's just a blank. Nothing."

She watches him closely and he can't shake the feeling that he is being studied. Finally, she nods. "My nephew was killed in Vietnam. I don't suppose any of us really know what it was like."

"I was never there. The guy who was killed had been."

For the first time her gaze falters and her eyes glisten with a slight film of tears. "I'm sorry. I was close to my sister's boy." Head lowered, she slips her clipboard into the plastic case. "In the future, I'd appreciate it if you call me Pat or Patricia or even Mrs. Chapman. Anything would be better than 'lady.' I'm glad to meet you, Mr. O'Neal."

"Sherwood." He shakes the hand she offers. "I guess I'll see you before the hearing, Mrs. Chapman."

"Don't worry."

Easy enough for you to say, lady. He holds the door for her, watches her cross the street to a weathered-looking red Volkswagen, get in and drive away. "Damned if I can see what's going on," he says. Hang on until the hearing and hope there's a clear course after that. You're barely making it so far, O'Neal. All you need now is for her to find out you have Jamie and why. Child Protective Services and Doris Ransler right down your neck.

Jamie is still asleep. Sherwood calls Marion's lawyer friend, Donald Holmes, but he can only get a secretary who tells him that if he wants to release his medical records to the court, he will have to submit permission in writing, which would best be done at his earliest convenience. Also, if he would meet Mr. Holmes in the office at nine o'clock on Monday, the third of February, other details could be gone over then. He says fine and writes the note giving permission to the judge or whoever to dig into his medical and psychological history, then prowls the house, thinking about a place for Art. The hole under the basement bathroom still looks best; some sort of rope-swing arrangement so he can get up and down the stairs. The problem will be how to get the rope down and hide it and still make it so Art can get it up again when he wants.

Ready to start working, Sherwood has his field jacket in hand and is halfway to the front door before he realizes he can't go out while Jamie is asleep. Since he is stopped anyway, he sits down to try to figure out how to get to the ceiling of the stairwell so he can screw eyebolts into the stringers, and finally notices the hatch to the attic in the ceiling of the back hall. Grabbing a flashlight from the top of the refrigerator, he drags the high chair under the opening and scrambles up.

Seen from inside the attic, the house looks well crafted. The two-by-fours and two-by-sixes are actually two inches thick and the fancy curves of the dining-room and living-room ceilings are formed by curved joists that were probably hand-cut. Someone has taken a lot of care putting the house together and that care has produced the oddity that will provide the ideal hiding place. Above the bathroom, Sherwood finds a hole left over after the low shower ceiling, a sunken room about five feet square and four and a half feet deep; torturous size for a man with legs, but perfect for Art. Rough measurements are enough for a start. The project will require a bundle of lath, a thin sheet of plywood and some plaster for the top cover, thicker plywood for a floor, hinges, nails.

In the garage he finds a dust-covered workbench equipped with hammer and rusty saw, paintbrushes, a few odd putty knives, clamps, several crescent wrenches and three or four sacks of mixed nails. He takes twenty minutes to sweep off everything, sort some of the nails and hang the tools on the wall where they belong, then he goes back to the house to check on Jamie.

Still asleep. Have to give him iron pills or something. Can't go for supplies until he gets up. Sherwood makes a pot of coffee and carries a cup to the fireplace chair. The rain has stopped. Clouds scatter in the light south wind and the afternoon sun casts large, geometrical patterns on the dining-room floor, creates a shadow city around the spilled blocks and throws shifting reflections off the fire truck, the piano keys. Points of light seem to grow and pulse. Steam from the coffee smells like a night heavy with warm human odors and stinging scents of cheap liquor. . . . Here it comes. Where are you, Art? Need him, O'Neal. Sherwood presses his eyes closed with thumb and fingers. "Not now." A thumping noise distracts him, then comes a rasp and a squeak. A voice.

"Legs not better yet, Sher."

"Jamie?"

"I rested."

"Good." Sherwood opens his eyes. Jamie sits in the hall doorway. "Your voice is working, though, isn't it?"

The child nods.

"Legs'll come. You'll have to try. Legs get flabby on you if you don't use them. Are you ready for another ride in that pack? I want to get some things at the hardware store and we should take the grocery cart back."

"Candy?"

"Maybe a small piece. Do you need to use the toilet?"

Jamie thinks, then nods and crawls into the bathroom. Sherwood follows and holds him up. "You may sleep a lot, little guy, but you're resilient."

They bundle into jackets and the pack and are off again, Jamie in his bandolier coat loops and Sherwood with the umbrella stuck like a saber in his belt. A couple of pirates with a grocery cart for a ship. At the hardware store he buys the plywood, lath, plaster, forty yards of thick rope and a dozen eyebolts.

"Going to build the kid a swing?" the clerk asks.

"Sure." Or aren't you? He pays and arranges to have the material delivered. "Okay, Jamie. Let's see if we can find that piece of candy."

The streets and sidewalks of downtown are rain-washed clean
between buildings all squat and squared off. Brick and concrete
and window glass that casts reflections and shadows in the afternoon sun like blocks arranged on a floor. Over the flat rooftops,
bare trees branch helter-skelter in such profusion that twigs and
limbs seen down distant streets combine to create an illusion of
gray haze in the clear air. Pushing the cart ahead of him, Sherwood crisscrosses the business district, peers into windows at sta-
tionery supplies and used jeans and potted plants. He is mildly curious about the life he has been ignoring in his own country and
he searches the displays for something he might want or need.
Nothing attracts him. Flyers stuck to the glass have changed from
what he remembers the last time he noticed such things—before
the Army. Politics has been replaced by a wide range of religious
and philosophical movements that don't mean anything to Sherwood.

The white-haired woman is not working at the grocery, but she
has filled an ice-cream carton with candy canes. He buys half a
dozen, gives one to Jamie and continues up the street past a few
rundown houses, a gas station, a motel, Sambo's.

"Sambo, Sambo," Jamie says.

"We can eat there sometime, if you want. Sound good?"

No response.

"You okay back there?" Sherwood cranes his neck to catch a
glimpse of sticky smile and Jamie's nodding head. "Good. Let's
head home." He walks down the block, cuts through a large parking lot, crosses the next street and they are in the park: picnic
tables, concrete trash containers, jungle gym, slide, swings.

"Swing, Sher."

"Too wet, man. Too . . . Aw why not?" Slinging the pack off
one shoulder, he lifts Jamie out of the canvas seat, wipes off a
swing with his sleeve. "In you go. Can you hold on?"

"Push me." The face is alive, almost like that of the three-year-
old who started that disastrous weekend a year ago by offering the
coat. Sherwood pulls back the swing and lets go, watches the
small legs flail enthusiastically in what looks like an effort to
pump.

"Push faster."

He should talk better than that. Josie speaks in sentences. "A little faster, maybe," he says.

"More. Faster."

"Go easy, okay? You can't even walk and here you are trying to fly."

"Faster. Faster-raster."

"Hang on and pay attention to what you're doing. You're scaring me." Sherwood sits in the next seat and kicks himself to swing side by side with Jamie. He has visions of the hands weakening, letting go the chain, Jamie falling face first into the wet bark of the playground; but Jamie holds on. Water beads his forehead and cheeks, runs down his chin and neck to soak the collar of his jacket. His fine, black hair flies out from his head, first as wild fuzz and then as wet strands that cling together and flop in time with the still uncoordinated kicks. A lot of improvement over yesterday; a whole lot. At length, Sherwood drags him protesting out of the swing, shoulders the pack and carries him home zipped half inside the fatigue jacket.

Erica and Josie are already at Marion's, building a tower of blocks in front of the fire. Their faces are serious as they turn to watch Sherwood put Jamie on the floor.

"How's he doing, Sherwood?"

"Not walking, but he can swing with the best of them and he's saying a word or two, aren't you, Jamie? Coming along."

"I can too walk," Jamie says. He stands for a moment as if concentrating on what he wants to do, then he takes a step toward Josie. His feet tangle almost immediately and he falls, lands shoulder first and his head snaps against the floor.

Sherwood expects him to cry, but Jamie doesn't move or make a sound. Oh-oh; back to square one. "Hey, small friend?" Before he can move, Erica is beside Jamie, trying to lift him. Jamie pushes her away, turns to Sherwood and finally lets out a whimper. "It's okay, man." Picking him up, feeling ribs and shoulder and the side of his head to make sure nothing is smashed or snapped, Sherwood carries him to the green chair. "No blood. No bones broken." But how much time in that room? Not moving or seeing anyone. Have to watch out he doesn't hurt himself trying too much too fast. "Just a bump, but I'll bet it hurt. Sit with me here until you feel better."

Josie follows them, tries to comfort Jamie with a hand on his arm, but he turns away from her.

"She's trying to help you feel better, Jamie. It's okay."

"He is a lot better than yesterday," Erica says. Her voice sounds flat.

"We had a good day. Brought home some supplies, had some candy, took a look around town. Decided we'd have breakfast at Sambo's soon."

"Me too." Josie brightens. "I like Sambo's."

"Josie too," Jamie says. He twists around in Sherwood's lap and gives her a shy smile.

"Sure she can come too." He lets Jamie wiggle off the chair onto the floor. "We had a social worker here this afternoon. She sounded like they'll probably let me take Jamie. She wasn't excited about the idea, though." No response. "Erica?"

Erica sits on the bed, shoulders slumped forward and back bowed. "He didn't want me to touch him."

"I told her it was Josie in the other room asleep," he says. "Erica? With a cold, so if anyone asks you, I was taking care of her today. For practice, okay?"

"You seem to be picking up the fine points." She shakes her head as if throwing off an unpleasant thought, "Supper's on. We should eat it soon."

Sherwood is aware he has missed something, is about to ask what's the matter, but Josie breaks in, "Mommy made pigs in blankets," and his chance is gone.

Dinner is hot dogs baked in biscuit dough—an established favorite with both children—spinach, carrot strips and corn on the cob. Josie monopolizes the conversation trying to get Jamie to talk to her, but he is withdrawn again. All he'll eat is half a hot dog and several bites of corn.

"Too much candy this afternoon, man. We'll have to watch it."

"Candy, Sher?"

"If you eat the rest of that hot dog."

"You sound like a mother, Sherwood."

"Practicing for the judge."

Her head cocks to one side and an eyebrow shoots up in question, but he shakes his head. Not a word about my going back, not in front of Jamie.

"You're going to try to get custody?"

"It's the only way to start." He picks up plates and moves to the sink. "If you three want to go in by the fire, I'll do the dishes. Jamie, you could show Josie the game with the fire truck."

Jamie seems willing, but he clings when Sherwood lifts him out of the high chair. In the end, Sherwood goes in with Jamie and Josie to knock down blocks with the fire truck and ambulance while Erica does the dishes. At eight he reads both children a story, puts them to bed in Jamie's room, gets glasses of water and carries them in to find that Jamie is already asleep. Sherwood is also exhausted. He stretches out on the living-room bed to watch shadows the fire throws across the ceiling.

"Are you warm enough over there?" Erica pushes the chair closer to the fire.

"Yes."

"Are you tired? I could take Josie home."

"No. I need to talk to someone."

"I'm listening."

No doubt. Could get a lot of troubles off your chest, O'Neal; open up a little and find out how much things have really changed all the time you've been gone. "I just can't figure out what's been going on."

"Who can?"

"That isn't what I mean." Or is it? Were you making a pass night before last, or was that just overactive imagination? "Maybe it is. Just this vague uneasiness. Nothing is quite the way I think it should be. I've been out of touch a long time." He rubs his temples. "I have a lot of things to do and I don't seem to be going about any of them right."

"As far as I can see, you're doing fine, Sherwood. Do you want to get down to specifics?"

"I thought I would." Don't know how to, though, do you, O'Neal? Not without getting too involved. "Do you have a car?"

"Yes."

"Any chance I could borrow it in a couple of weeks? I have to pick up a friend of mine in San Francisco."

"If it's running then. It doesn't always start."

"Maybe I could fix it. Or have it fixed."

She shakes her head. "It needs a new starter. I'll get one the first of the month."

"Let me do it for you. I know a little about engines. I kept Art's jeep running."

"He was the man who lost his legs?"

"Yes. Marion didn't like him."

"She told me, Sherwood. Is he who you're going to pick up?"

"He's the one."

From the set of her chin he half expects her to deliver Marion's lecture on Art's shortcomings, but she stares into the fire. "What was it like?" she asks, finally. "Living alone in the hills?"

"Not as romantic as it sounds. Wood to chop, water to carry, meals to fix and clean up after, but it was quiet. Deer and rabbits and wild turkeys in the yard most mornings and evenings. I suppose anyone could get used to it, except that being alone isn't easy even if you have good reason."

"You had your friend. Didn't you?"

"We left each other alone most of the time."

"Then why . . . ?"

"Bring him here? Because he's my friend. Because when I was flipping out for hours at a time, spending most of my life in a nightmare and saving sleeping pills so I could stop it all, he stole the pills and then coached me and woke me up and helped me get the nightmare under control. Now he's stuck where he doesn't want to be. Even if he weren't my friend, I'd owe him. Did Marion tell you about that?"

Erica nods. "Where is he?"

"His parents have him. Either I get him out or he'll do something crazy to one of them or to himself and they'll put him away in a hospital." Art's father striding down that concourse, shoulders back and back straight. Art like a ramrod in the chair. Nurse to push the chair and act as interpreter, as buffer. "I don't know how things came to that. Both his parents insisted Art go in the Army. Serve his country. That's the grudge I've heard most from him, but no doubt there's more. His father is some kind of middleman between the military and various arms manufacturers. He used to be based somewhere in the Midwest, but he moved out here when Art was wounded. Can't seem to let Art go."

With a shudder Erica gets up and throws another log on the

fire. "That's too bad." She wraps arms around herself and watches the flames. "I go on the assumption that if I give Josie lots of love now, she'll have some for me when she's older, but sometimes I wonder if she'll be any better than I am."

"You're okay."

"Am I, Sherwood? A twenty-eight-year-old woman alone with a four-year-old kid? I couldn't stand to live with her father. . . ."

Sherwood waits for her to continue, but instead of sitting down again she paces into the dining room, where she picks up her coat, slips it on and grabs Josie's coat by the collar.

"I'd better go home," she says. "Have to work in the morning."

Whenever Jamie sleeps Sherwood works on the hiding place in the attic. First he puts down the floor, then adds Sheetrock walls, a fold-down shelf with a thin, foam-rubber pad that will make the hard bed Art likes, a ceiling nailed to the underside of the rafters, tight-fitting trap door. On top of the plywood ceiling he spreads plaster, puts down lath that he has finally had to pilfer from a demolition site near the center of town in order to match color and texture of lath already in the attic. He splices around the hole and trap door with great care, using pocket knife and razor saw to avoid any straight line that might betray the camouflage. The project takes all the craft he had learned in his father's carpentry shops as a child, from the various workrooms where he has helped Art build guitars. In the end Sherwood is pleased with what he has built.

His time with Jamie dissolves in a repetition of meals cooked and eaten, dishes done and floors swept. He picks up after Jamie, washes his hands and face, picks him up after falls that become more and more frequent as he regains confidence in his ability to walk. Everything takes time: washing clothes in Marion's basement machine that only works on the wash-and-wear cycle, hanging clothes to dry on ropes strung in the back bedroom, making constant trips to the store for milk or juice or eggs, none of which he can seem to remember all at one time. Always moving, no sense of progress; always feeling you could drop your guard and

wake up one day to realize you'd been here a full year, but you
don't have a year, O'Neal. So watch out.

That first weekend he buys a calendar, picks the thirteenth of
July as the day he will go back to the cabin, calls it zero and numbers backward to 185 days on the nineteenth of January. In the
Army they called it a short sheet. It is antimilitary yet also vaguely
military; he feels better as soon as he hangs it on the kitchen wall.

Once the coat dries Jamie discards the sleeve loops and lives in
the thing, drags it around the house with him, plays with cars and
trucks in the hills and valleys of its fur, eats with it draped over
the back of the high chair and rides on Sherwood's back with
sleeves and tails crammed under, around and over him in the
pack. After one or two accidents Sherwood learns that the pile of
goat hair on the floor always has a child inside—two whenever
Josie and Erica come for supper—no matter how flat it looks.

Wet weather keeps them away from the park, but as part of his
preparation for Art, Sherwood screws two eyebolts into the frame
of the attic hatch and hangs a swing that cuts its arc through the
stairway door and over the stairs. A pair of old web belts laced to
the ropes with heavy string makes a safety strap and Sherwood begins to give Jamie pumping lessons: "Just backward from what
you'd think, small friend. When you're all the way back, throw
your legs in front of you. All the way front, then you tuck them
under. Back, throw 'em out. Then tuck. Throw, tuck. You have to
remember, man, it's just backward from what you'd think."

Additional elements of Art's route to and from the attic build
from the swing. A rope hangs from the rafters to halfway down
the swing ropes, pulled through an eyebolt to catch on a large
knot. Access from the top of the rope to the trap door is provided
by an innocent-looking twenty-foot ladder that rests flat across five
brackets. With a string tied to the knot, Art will be able to pull
the rope up through the eyebolt, across the ladder and into his
hole. Sherwood covers all his carpentry and plasterwork with dust
from Marion's vacuum cleaner. The attic looks untouched. Natural. Never tampered with. Not even a footprint remains on the
rafters.

Art's crates arrive by bus on the Tuesday of the second week.
Sherwood borrows Erica's car, fixes the loose wire in the starter
and hauls the boxes to Marion's, where he wrestles them into the

bedroom at the foot of the stairs. That Friday, Art's letter comes
in the mail:

Dear Woody,
    Wed, 29th. 10 pm–3 am. Park on the street and watch the
third story front. Man without legs can't climb. Ha. Some problem with this nurse they hired, but it's a long story. She'll get
this out for me. May join us later.

A piece of city map pasted to the bottom of the page shows
him the freeway off-ramp and several routes through the maze of
streets to a small "x" in a yellow area in the city that looks
wedged between large areas of green and red.

Sherwood isn't sure how he'll manage to be both legs for Art
and Uncle Sher to Jamie, but Sherwood has had enough close
calls to realize how much he needs Art to help him through his
flipouts.

29 *January:* one hundred seventy-five days until he is to return
to the hills. Erica and Josie arrive for an early dinner and marshmallows toasted over the fire. Jamie and Josie eat little of the
meal, stuff themselves with as many of the sweets as Erica will
allow, then move into the dining room to play secret games under
the coat. Sherwood sits in the green chair, and Erica lies on a
blanket in front of the fire, dangles a marshmallow over coals in
an effort to toast one perfectly brown all around.

"When do you have to go?"

"Eight to be safe. Don't wait up. I'll probably be back after
midnight, maybe as late as four or five."

"Right. I'm a working woman. Need my rest." She pulls a hot
marshmallow off her stick and hands it to Sherwood. "You won't
reconsider this?"

"I can't."

"What if you're caught?"

He shrugs. "It isn't illegal." Except for the driver's license that
you can't get without lying about the blackouts.

"But it isn't knocking on the door and saying, 'Hi, I'm here, let's go,' is it? Have you thought about what could happen? What it could mean to your custody case?"

"I can't worry about everything that might go wrong." He looks around for the coat and finds that it is in the living room, close to the chair and moving closer. Erica is about to say something more, but he touches her leg with his toe. "There's a fuzzy creature with ears sneaking up on us."

Josie's face pokes out of the fur and then comes the top of Jamie's head as far as his eyes. "Jamie wants to know if you are going away tonight," Josie says.

"Yes. For a while. I'll be back before morning."

"He worries you might go away and die."

You might act slow, small friend, but you don't miss much. "No, I'm not."

Face serious, Josie nods.

"Jamie?" the child's face rises the rest of the way out of the coat. His mouth quivers. "Come up here." Sherwood grabs him by the arms and pulls him into his lap. "I'm not going very far. Don't worry. You play with Josie a while more and I'll tuck you in before I go."

The children drag the coat back into the dining room, but Sherwood is too aware of their huddled presence to try to say what's on his mind. By seven-thirty Erica still hasn't roasted her perfect marshmallow. Sherwood refuses to eat any more.

"Time," he says. He rubs his palms on the chair arms and gets up. "Come on, Jamie. Let's put you in the sack. If we wait any longer, Erica will have to do it."

"I wanna play, Sher."

"That's okay with me, but you'll have to let Erica put you to bed."

Erica looks doubtful, but Jamie nods.

"No guff? You'll go right down when she says?"

"You come back, Sher?"

"Sure, I'll come back."

"Okay." Dragging coat, Jamie gets up and trots into his room. He returns with the sleeve cuttings looped over one shoulder and he hands the coat to Sherwood. "Cold out," he says.

"Oh man. Are you sure?" He scoops up Jamie and the coat and holds them in a cumbersome ball against his chest. Too much trust. Erica's eyes look shiny. "Okay, small friend. I'll need it. It's probably the coldest night of the year out there. Thanks." He sees the self-important set of the small head, sees pleasure curl the edges of Jamie's mouth. No messing up now, O'Neal. With a quick kiss on the forehead, Sherwood lets him down. "See you-all later."

From the house to the car he shrugs constantly, trying to find a comfortable position under the bulky, vaguely familiar weight of the coat. The sleeves are too long in spite of what he has cut off and he has to tuck under a new length of cuff. Once he is on his way, he is glad for the extra warmth. The heater in Erica's battered Ford station wagon doesn't work.

On the freeway the car almost drives itself. The steering feels a little sloppy in tight turns, but is snug on the straightaway. Erica, cautious Erica, has already worn a groove in the accelerator at fifty-five miles an hour. Fitful spates of rain blur the windshield beyond the capacity of the groaning wipers. Again the lights stun him, but he is kept alert by the tickle of goat hair against his neck and wrists.

He misses the off-ramp in San Francisco and has to cast back and forth for twenty minutes before he finds his way back onto Art's piece of map. Eventually he finds the place, located across from a hospital—an illuminated sign for the emergency entrance points down the street. The house is a well-kept Victorian with a high wrought-iron fence in front. The narrow yard has been bricked over. Empty planter boxes flank the door and to one side there is a bench of gray concrete. Sherwood passes the house the first time and pulls over the lip of hill above it. He can walk back and watch from the shadows at the end of the hospital or drive around and park there, but either way he will be uncomfortably exposed. There are no trees along the street, and the dark, staring windows of the hospital are like half-closed eyes. No more than a dozen cars are parked on the street at this time of night and among them Erica's Ford will be conspicuously old.

Finally, Sherwood drives around the block and parks up the hill from the house; far enough from the hospital, he hopes, so that he won't draw the attention of bored patients sitting up late. He shudders. You wouldn't have missed it, would you, O'Neal? Not for a second. Now that he is on the spot, the escape seems too hastily arranged. He opens the window for a little air and a better view, and waits.

Nothing happens. The dashboard clock doesn't work and he hasn't thought to bring a watch. To make matters worse, the clouds that covered the opening phase of the operation begin to separate and flood the ground with light from a moon only two days past full. He has yet to see a cop or night watchman, but with the hospital, he knows they will be around.

His nervous attempt to keep watch—on the patchwork of dark and lighted windows, the front of Art's parents' house, the street behind and ahead of him—exhausts him in short order. The city seems alive with the sound of distant sirens and each one raises the hair on the back of his neck.

What to look for? Some signal. A note dropped by paper glider? Third floor. Window on the right. Was closed. Now open. The window is open and while Sherwood watches, a thick climbing rope drops and comes snaking down the front of the house. Without hesitation, Art heaves himself over the sill and surveys the street. Not more than a minute now. The moon has even gone behind a cloud.

Far off a siren breaks away from the background noise. "Can't be for us," Sherwood says. Art dangles from the rope. He has started his descent, not rappeling, but climbing down three stories hand over hand. Sherwood can't be sure, but he thinks he glimpses a second figure leaning briefly out the window as if to speak down the rope. Art moves faster. The siren veers off a little, then shifts tone again and approaches. Sherwood touches the key in the starter. "Come on, man. Get it down here."

Level with the second-floor windows now, Art hangs up and looks around. At the same time a flashing red light appears over the hill above and comes speeding down. Sherwood wants to start the car, but his hand is frozen on the ignition. The siren sets the air vibrating with its scream. In seconds the noise and the flash are almost on top of him. Blood whistles in his ears. His terror crosses the breaking point and becomes an adrenalin-edged calm. He will save Art if he can, but he can't let himself be caught. Rolling over the back seat, he crawls to the cargo bed, lifts the hatch and feels underneath for the jack handle. Street, walls, blank windows all pulse with red light. The siren lets out an earsplitting shriek, drops a tortured half tone and then cuts off mid-wail. Tires hiss on the pavement as the vehicle shoots on down the hill.

Smashing heart seems to catch thick air in Sherwood's throat. He peers out the back window in time to see an ambulance career into the emergency entrance. The houses across the street remain closed; not even a light comes on. Art is no longer in view and the last of the rope disappears into the third-floor window. Jamming the jack handle into his hip pocket he crawls over the seats and out the door, sprints across the street. Art is already at the fence, hiding in the shadow of a scraggly bush that hangs over from the adjacent yard. He pushes a length of four-by-four with a groove cut in one face through the fence. "Put this over the spikes," he says, "and let's get the hell out of here." Sherwood fits the wood onto the spearlike tips of the uprights and Art swarms over. "Catch me on your back. Gonna need your legs."

"Right." He takes the weight, grabs the stumps, "hang on," looks both ways and runs. Panic still rides high in his throat and Art feels weightless, like an empty field pack that is only a flapping annoyance. His feet slap the damp pavement. He heaves Art through the open window of the car and dives in after him.

"Easy, Woody. Slow down, man, we're in the clear. Look."

The windows are still empty except for the one on the third floor, where a lone figure in white waves an "all clear," then disappears.

"The nurse?" Sherwood asks.

"Karen." Art lets out a laugh giddy with excitement. "Now start this heap and let's move out."

Erica's jack handle makes an annoying hard spot against the back of the seat. Sherwood grinds the starter until the engine catches, then he pulls into the deserted street. "I thought we'd had it."

"Yeah. It gave me a scare too. I knew what it was, but I was afraid you'd be jumpy enough to think it was a cop and run and there I'd be."

"You came close."

"You wouldn't have run?"

"Maybe." He pulls the jack handle out of his pocket and passes it across the seat. "I wasn't going to be caught."

Art runs his hands over the metal bar, holds it in a shaft of streetlight to see. "Man," he says. His head shakes back and forth and he laughs. "Man, oh man." One stump beats on the seat, lightly at first, then harder and faster, and his head shakes harder and faster and his laughter rises to a gleeful, half-crazy giggle. "Christ, oh Woody. You're great, man. Know that?"

All Sherwood can do is nod. By the time he reaches the freeway the steering wheel is the only thing that holds his hands steady and he has to concentrate hard to keep an even pressure on the gas pedal with his trembling foot. He feels raw and spent and he drives twenty miles at sixty-five before he remembers that he can't afford to get tagged for speeding. Beside him Art has quieted and he looks at all the lights as if half afraid they'll disappear before he can get enough of them.

"Damn them anyway," he says, finally. "I let them drive me away from here once, but now . . . You weren't thinking we'd go back to South Dakota right away, were you?"

"Not right away. I have to go through a custody hearing for Jamie."

Art hesitates. "Maybe we shouldn't go back at all. Maybe we could figure some way to go underground. Maybe pick up new ID. Disappear on paper and we'd be gone. We could live anywhere."

"Maybe," Sherwood says.

Nodding, Art stares out the window. "Maybe," he whispers. He falls silent, watches the light for several miles. "Custody?"

"It's the only way. The bitch who was supposed to take care of him had him stuck away like an animal in a filthy room."

"Mmmm."

"What's the matter, Art?"

"Nothing."

"Did you see Brodie?"

"Sure. Threw everything I could grab at the first three guys they brought in. All phonies. Draft dodgers. After the third one gave up, they finally took me to see Brodie."

"How is he?"

"The same. No bullshit. He won't sign any commitment papers on me that I don't want."

"That's Brodie, all right."

"Not a chance he'd sign papers."

Sherwood taps the wheel.

"No way he'd sign."

"Was it bad with your folks, Art? You sound like it was bad."

"Don't crowd me." He takes a deep breath and lets it out slowly.

A few cars work their way past in the fast lane, but Sherwood has the freeway mostly to himself. Clouds begin to spread out across the sky; show bright edges in the moonlight and scattered stars through dark places between. "It's only me, man."

"Hell, Woody. You know I'll tell you what happened. Just don't push, okay? I have to figure some things out. What about the kid?"

"He's going to need me for a while."

"That's bad. My father'll be after us. I don't know if he'll call the cops or hire someone, or both, but he'll be looking this time for sure. I ripped him off." Slipping out of a small backpack that Sherwood didn't notice in the excitement, Art digs around in it and comes up with several small paper packets. "It's his grease money, man. Political contributions or bribes or whatever he does with petty cash he keeps in the wall safe. I think I got about five thousand. We're going to have to travel light."

"I hear you."

"So? Can you find a place to dump the kid when we have to run?"

"We're fine for a while."

"Not a chance are we fine. He won't sit on his hands a year, hoping I'll give up and come dragging home. Not now."

"I figured I'd have to hide you. Built a place. No one is going to find you if we're just a little careful."

"How fast can you get the kid taken care of?"

"Not that fast, Art."

"How fast?"

"There's a hearing next week, then another one a couple of weeks after that, I think. Once I have custody, I'll try to find a place, but that will take time too. I've allowed six months and I suspect it'll take most of that."

"Six months." Art drops the money into the pack. "I'm on the run and you're trying to hang us up with a kid and court hearings and lawyers and I don't know what. What's wrong with a foster home?"

"Plenty."

"Damn. Social workers?"

"One of those."

"I don't believe it, man. A couple of weeks ago it was the two of us. To the death. No sweat. What's going on? We go back a long way. What was it, about three years ago I came cruising into your room? They had you stuck off in that dead-end hall and you were so flaky you didn't know your name. The bastards. We have to stick together, Woody. They'll screw us if we break the front."

"I know, Art, but he's my sister's kid. I'm the only one there is to take care of him and until I find a better place, there's no way out. What about this nurse? Karen?"

Art shakes his head. "I don't know. She's . . ." He hits his stump with a clenched fist. "I knew her before the Army."

"I figured that out at the airport."

"Well, it's complicated. Complicated. Sooner or later, I'll have to do something about her, but right now she's probably the first person my father will have watched."

"Yeah. Right after yours truly."

"That's what I've been trying to tell you. We'll have to move."

"Don't decide that for sure until you've seen the place, Art. I don't think we'll have to let him rush us this time."

Unconvinced, Art rests his head against the back of the seat and closes his eyes. The road drops and twists through the coast range and then lines out on the floor of the Sacramento Valley past Vacaville and The Nut Tree, the transformer station with its lines of pylons that stand like eerie giants, each one alone but linked to its neighbors by sagging cables. Sherwood steers with his palms, finally relaxing, but worried. Get it together, Art. You're the strong one. Dragged me out of those flipouts. Got me up and moving around. I'm just a pair or legs, man. Only difference is there will be two of you using them for a while.

The Dawville off-ramp swings them over the freeway, under the railroad tracks and into the center of town, where the Wells Fargo time-temperature sign flashes 2:38; 45 degrees. "We're here, Art."

Art stirs and grumbles and finally wipes the sleep out of his eyes as Sherwood stops in front of the house. "It isn't very big."

"It's big enough." He gets out, loads Art onto his back and crosses the wet lawn. Inside, the living room is warm and a little smokey from the fire. Erica hasn't left any lights on, but the streetlamp through the window shows him the blocks and stuffed animals on the floor. Sherwood doesn't realize where she is until Art whispers, "Who's that on the bed?"

"Must be Erica." And aren't things complicated enough without her there? "She loaned me the car and stayed with Jamie."

"Can we trust her?"

"Yes."

"Moving out a little, yourself," Art says, then when Sherwood doesn't respond, "Where do I sleep, man? I'm beat."

"Hope you saved a little strength." He carries Art into the back hall, hits the light and points to the attic hatch. "Up there. There's water and I left some rolls and apples in case you're hungry."

"No." Art looks put upon. "An attic isn't going to cut it. If someone gets in here looking, they won't miss it."

"Go on up and look."

Shaking his head, Art leans off Sherwood's back to grab the swing and climbs. At the top he wraps the rope around one stump for support and pushes the hatch cover into the attic. The second rope drops out. "Thought that out well enough," he says. He disappears through the opening. Sherwood can hear heavy breathing, then the ladder creaks. For several seconds Art is silent and Sherwood tries to imagine his reaction to the tiny room; floor and walls painted white, sheets and blankets pulled tight over the mattress with hospital corners, a new book on North American hardwoods he found in the local bookstore, current *Esquire* and *Playboy*, chinning bar and chamber pot. Finally, a low chuckle issues from the hatch. The ladder pops as if something were scampering across it, and Art's face appears above Jamie's swing. "Damn, Woody. It's incredible. It's not in the attic, not in the house. Like it's suspended between. A no-man's-land."

"I put a couple extra blankets up there. It'll probably get cold, but the space is so small, I was afraid a heater would suffocate you."

"It's beautiful, man. You were right. Maybe we can hang in here . . . at least for a while." Art pulls his face out of sight. The rope snakes up and the hatch cover drops into place.

Sherwood is alone, left to face Erica all warm and smelling of sweet powder in his bed. Quietly he opens the door to Jamie's room. In the dim light he can see the children, covers pushed around their waists. They lie face to face, each with one arm draped over the other, one head of curly brown and the other of fine black hair that breaks the outline of Jamie's head in little knots and tufts. Jamie sighs and his hand wags a series of soft pats against Josie's back.

"Keeps the night terrors away, small friend?" Sherwood asks softly. Have to remember to comb his hair once in a while. He slips out of the coat, covers them with the fur and then, oddly unsettled, he backs into the hall and closes the door. For two weeks now he has felt that Jamie needed him every minute, waking and sleeping, and he is puzzled that Josie can fill the place he thought was his own. He flips on the basement light and climbs down in search of a place to sleep. The bedroom at the foot of the stairs is empty except for Art's crates of wood and books and tools. There is a stack of three old mattresses and half a dozen large pillows in the other bedroom, but when he looks for blankets he discovers that the only extras are in the attic hiding hole. It is Marion's empty bed, then. Or Erica.

He can't face Marion's room. His own death is already established and will finish itself soon enough. No sense tempting Fate on sheets meant for someone who won't ever use them. Erica, it seems, is inevitable. He climbs up, turning off the basement and back-hall lights as he passes, then makes his way to the living room.

"Sherwood?"

"Yes."

"Did it go okay? I thought I heard someone."

"Everything is fine."

"I didn't know if you wanted anyone to use Marion's room." She hesitates. "Should I move in there?"

Feel the same way about it, don't you? "It's okay." He strips off shoes, socks and shirt; unbuckles his belt. What now, O'Neal? Uncomfortable or immodest? You've been gone too long.

As if sensing his uncertainty, she throws back the covers to let him in. She sleeps without clothes. Natural. No self-consciousness. Her body looks pale and smooth in the streetlight. Pushing off pants and shorts, he can feel her warmth even before he slides against her. Arms and legs wrap around him. The heat of her belly is startling against his back. "You're cold," she says.

Cold and crazy, O'Neal. She's a good woman and you already owe her. But dead or not, you're going to stick to this vow of chastity for others' sake through only so much of this. He nods. "Good night, Erica."

"Good night."

Too soon, gray light pours through the windows. Jamie is beside him, the small upper body pushed under the covers as far as the scant space will allow. The coat trails behind him on the floor. His face is bright; pleased and surprised at once as if he half expected that Sherwood wouldn't return. Josie stands beside Jamie, shivering in heavy flannel pajamas and plucking at Sherwood's arm. "Do you and Mommy love each other?" she whispers.

"In a way, I guess," he says. "What are you two doing out here in the cold? What time is it?"

Josie props hands on her hips. "I can't tell time."

"Oh."

"Jamie and I were thinking this is a good morning to go to Sambo's."

Erica groans, opens one eye to look at her wrist watch. "Go back to bed, Josie. It's six o'clock, for crying out loud."

No possibility of going back to sleep now, so Sherwood winks at the children and holds a finger to his lips. "Can you guys dress yourselves?"

"I can," Josie says, "but not my shirt or tie shoes. Jamie used to."

"You help me, Sher."

"Okay. Get back into bed until I can get dressed."

They scamper into Jamie's room. Sherwood rolls out, pulls on his clothes and follows to find Josie already dressed in pants and socks and Jamie struggling into his underwear. "Great, man. Snuggle under the coat and keep trying while I get Josie fixed up.

Shirt. Shoes, tie 'em and now. Jamie." Underpants on backward, but they're on. A first is a first and time for corrections later. He dumps Jamie into a pair of elastic-top britches, tugs on a warm sweatshirt. "Okay now. Shoes and socks. Josie, if you'll find your coats, we'll be on our way."

She tears out of the bedroom, wheeling like a small bird through the hall and into the front room and comes back with Jamie's jacket. A second pass brings her back with the orange coat already on. Two kids dressed this fast? Can't have been more than ten minutes, a record for sure. He is proud of himself. "That's it. Quiet now. Don't wake Erica."

"Coat, Sher."

"Fine." He takes one of the sleeve loops and tries to hang it over Jamie's shoulder, but Jamie takes it off. Tag, you're it, O'Neal. He pulls on the goat coat. "Okay. Let's go."

At least this time in Sambo's he is too busy to feel self-conscious. From the minute they walk into the starchy-smelling warmth of the restaurant, the children are restive, wanting first the stuffed tigers on the shelves behind the counter, then the balloons, then gum from the gumball machine. Apparently used to such things, the waitress with the round face helps him herd them toward the back room. "She said to say hello," she says.

She? Sherwood glances at her name tag—"Bonnie Dawson"— then at the face. Finally he remembers the woman at the other table. "Thanks," he says.

The waitress, Bonnie, shows him to the same table, sets up both children with picture menus and balloons, takes orders for pancakes and eggs and bacon and juice. The woman is at her table again, same red scarf, same slightly embarrassed slump of her shoulders. Sherwood sees the startling blond streaks in her hair as she turns to look at him. He nods.

She smiles back, a faint smile that acknowledges the children without understanding why they are there, then she returns to her coffee and newspaper as if she hadn't noticed him.

"Who is that lady?" Josie asks. "She smiled."

"Shh. I don't think she wants our attention."

"But she smiled."

"We shared separate breakfasts once before. It's more comfortable that way."

"But, Sherwood."

"We're going to make her nervous if we sit here talking about her." The damage is already done. Adjusting her scarf, the woman folds her paper, picks up her purse and leaves an almost full cup of coffee to send up steam like smoke signals from her empty table.

Bonnie returns with orange juice and coffee, distributes the glasses and fills Sherwood's cup. "She left already?"

"I think we made her nervous."

"No. She thought it was great that someone was friendly, you know, not just staring or making a pass."

"Something wasn't right. Maybe it was the kids."

"Cute kids. They yours?"

"Jamie," Sherwood makes a ceremonious bow and waves his hand, "is my nephew. Josie is a friend of ours. We thought this a perfect morning for dining out." His exaggeration drags a laugh from Jamie, but Josie's face is serious. "You look a little down, Josie." He reaches across the table and gives her shoulder a light squeeze. "Not even a smile for the lady who's going to bring our breakfast?"

"That's all right," the waitress says. "Sometimes I feel serious too."

Josie gives her a faint smile.

"I'll have your pancakes in a minute."

Whatever has bothered Josie seems to evaporate when the pancakes and bacon appear. She is cheerful again, Jamie's mouthpiece. "He wants syrup on his pancakes."

Sherwood spreads butter, pours syrup and cuts pancakes for both children, then hands a fork to Jamie. "See if you can eat with this instead of your hands, small friend." Jamie's effort with the fork is more for show than utility, and he finally gives up. Sherwood lets him, cleans him up afterward with a napkin dipped in his water glass.

"Sure are good kids," the waitress says when she brings the check.

Having no idea they can be any other way, Sherwood accepts the compliment as a statement of fact. He leaves a tip, small this time since the money that seemed inexhaustible at first is going at an alarming rate. The bill takes even more, then he makes a fast exit past the gum machine with a child dragging on each hand. "That was fun, kids. We'll have to do it again." They dash to Erica's car, Josie's feet smacking the sidewalk, Jamie dangling along on his arm.

By the time they tumble all logy with sweets into Marion's living room it is past seven o'clock. Sherwood sheds the coat, gives it to Jamie and Josie, who pull it into the chair by the fire, then Sherwood shuffles into the kitchen, where Erica sips coffee and reads the morning paper. "Anything in there about Art Johnson?"

"No." She is dressed and made up for work, and Sherwood is surprised by the air of polish, or maybe chic, that has supplanted the evening earthiness he's used to. "It's all last night's news." She laughs. "I'm the only person I know who's given up the TV news because it ruins my morning paper. Then, I rarely get to read more than a couple of pages. I haven't seen your friend yet."

"The less said about him for a while, the better."

"What happened?"

Five thousand dollars? Sherwood shakes his head. "Come to dinner tonight and I'll introduce you."

"I'd like to, but . . . Do you think you could take care of Josie tonight? My baby-sitter can't make it and I have to go out."

"Sure."

"I may be late, so you don't need to wait up. Then we're going to the coast for the weekend. Will you need me to watch Jamie while you're in court Monday?"

"That would help."

She nods and gets up from the table. Both the gesture and the movement seem languid and self-satisfied in a way that Sherwood doesn't understand. "Monday morning, then. I do appreciate you taking Josie to breakfast. I can't remember how long it's been since I got to read the whole paper. What a luxury."

"I owe you."

"Not really, but thanks. Come on, Josie. We have to get your clothes changed for school." The ease with which she gets Josie into her coat and out the door surprises Sherwood.

Moved pretty fast this morning, O'Neal, but that was to get them somewhere they wanted to go, not off to school.

Jamie follows them onto the porch and waves, finally comes

back inside and retrieves the coat from the chair. "Is there a person in the attic?" he asks.

"Yes."

He nods as if to say, 'I thought so.' "Josie said there wasn't."

"That's good. Don't talk to anyone about the man in the attic, Jamie. If the wrong people found out we had him up there, they would probably take you away from here."

For a moment Jamie's eyes search Sherwood's face, then he turns away, stares at the fire and finally turns back. "To some bad place," he says. "Was I someplace bad? Then you came?"

"You don't remember?"

"Some bad place." He sits down and pulls the coat around his shoulders. "I don't want him in the attic."

Oh-oh. Where to now? "Having him there isn't a problem as long as the wrong people don't find out. Can you put up with that? If the wrong people catch him, they'll put him in a bad place like the place you were when I got you. Then I'd have to get him out again because he's my friend the same way you are. I have to help both of you. If we don't tell anyone he's there, I may be able to set you both up so you won't have to worry about bad places again. Okay? Got that?"

Jamie's eyes go distant; not blank, but not all there either. His mouth twitches. He shakes his head, finally nods a consciously serious nod.

"I know it will be hard. Just don't say anything about him to anyone."

"Got that, Sher."

"Great. Now, if you'll find something to play with, I'll clean up here."

Blocks, ambulance, fire truck; Jamie plays while Sherwood does Erica's breakfast dishes and makes the bed and worries about how to keep Art hidden. Pull the shade in the stairwell. Maybe hang a blanket between the hall and the kitchen so no one on the street could see him come down the swing. Too contrived? Is the swing good camouflage, or just obvious? Puttering, waiting, he tries to read Erica's paper, but the front page is taken up by accounts of a Weather Underground bomb that wrecked a building in Washington, D.C., and another that failed to go off in Oakland. Thoughts about explosions make his scar itch. But you understand how the bombers feel this morning, don't you, O'Neal? Fugitive mentality. He stuffs the newspaper in the trash and goes into the living room to play blocks and draw pictures with Jamie.

About nine o'clock Pat Chapman calls. "I had hoped to meet with you again before the hearing," she says. "But I'm afraid I won't be able to come to Dawville at all this week. The hearing will be in Courtroom No. 2."

"Okay," Sherwood says.

"Monday at ten."

"Right."

"If you need a ride . . ."

"I can come by bus." Self-sufficient, see: Won't that get a point or two, lady?

"Fine. I'll see you Monday, then. Good-bye."

"Yeah. Bye." He listens until she hangs up, then shakes his head. Not in best form, O'Neal. Not even close.

No more than five minutes later the phone rings again, gives Sherwood a flash of that pressured uneasiness. "Two weeks without a ring and now this thing goes off twice in a row," he says under his breath. "Can't be good. Hello?"

"Sherwood," a voice says. "This is Brodie. I'm calling about Art."

"You what?" A trick?

"This is Brodie. Doc Brodie, remember? Martinez. I'm coming up for your hearing Monday."

Finally he recognizes the voice. "That makes me feel better about a lot of things. How you doing, Doc?"

"I'm fine. How about you? Got any of that memory back?"

"Nope."

"Still thinking of yourself as a dead man, then?"

"Yeah, but I'm with my nephew and it's not something he should have on him, so let's not talk about it, okay? Basically I'm in good shape. What's this about Art?"

"He split from his folks' house in San Francisco last night, got away with a pile of money and I don't know what else. His father's furious. Knows Art escaped, but he's saying Art was kidnaped and the cops are checking everyone who knew him."

"Whoops."

"I thought you might want to know. You're doing okay with your nephew?"

"I'm doing fine, Doc."

"You don't sound fine."

"That's for other reasons." He drags the phone by its twenty-five-foot cord to the window, and looks up and down the street. No flashing red lights yet. "I'm sorry to be short with you, Doc, but I'm as busy as I am fine. See you at the hearing, okay?"

"Sure. Is there anything I can do?"

"Don't think so, but thanks, Doc. Many thanks." He drops the receiver into its cradle. Cops? Art's here and not supposed to be and Jamie's here and not supposed to be and we're going to have real cops? Hands shaking, Sherwood hauls the high chair to the head of the stairs and hoists himself through the attic hatch. The trap door to Art's hole is open and the light from inside makes a bright patch on the rafters.

"Art?"

"I hear you, man. Is it all clear?"

"The story is you were kidnaped and the cops are checking. They saw Brodie and they'll probably come here. I'll bang on the wall when I see them; drop the hatch, kill the light and keep quiet."

"Check."

"You hungry?"

"No."

He climbs down, drags the high chair back into place. Jamie looks up from his crayon scribbling in the dining room. "Matter, Sher?"

Gotta sound calm. If he's scared it'll blow the show. "Some police might come and look around. You just stick close to me and pretend you can't talk, okay?"

Jamie's eyes grow large, but he nods. "Got that."

All that trust that if he does what he's told, things'll be fine. Sherwood paces into the living room, stands in front of the fireplace, stalks through the dining room to the kitchen, back through the dining room. He has already hung the blanket in the back-hall doorway and now, afraid it will look too contrived, he takes it down, folds it and places it across the foot of Jamie's bed. Must have forgotten something: Art's stuff downstairs. Have to leave it and tell the story the way it happened. If Marion had any dope stashed, we've had it.

By the time lunch is over and Jamie has settled down for a nap, Sherwood is so soaked with sweat that he has to take a bath, change clothes and roll on a heavy dose of Marion's deodorant. Still the house seems to reek with the odor of his fear. He cracks open a south window to let rain-scented wind circulate through the rooms.

The police finally arrive at about one o'clock: a white car with a black-and-gold shield on the door, red and blue and yellow lights on the roof. At least the lights are off. A man with curly red hair knocks on the door and identifies himself as Officer Clayton. Sherwood guesses the man is in his late twenties. Clayton's partner is about forty and has close-cropped black hair. Campbell is his name and as Clayton introduces him Sherwood realizes he has been too rattled to bang on Art's wall.

"Are you Sherwood O'Neal?" Clayton asks.

"Yes."

"Do you know Arthur Johnson?"

Sherwood nods. "We shared a cabin in South Dakota until a couple of weeks ago."

"Have you heard from him the past few days?"

What happened to that damned letter? "Not since his father kidnaped him at the San Francisco airport."

"Kidnaped, you say?"

"I imagine it was legal enough. Art and I flew out here together. His father showed up at the airport and took him when we landed. Art didn't want to go with him, but he didn't have much choice so what else would you call it?"

"He was kidnaped last night. From his father's house."

"Don't bet on that."

Officer Clayton takes off his hat. "You don't think so?"

"All the time I've known him, that's three years now, Art has hated his parents. They sent him off to war. He lost both legs in Vietnam and he's still bitter. My bet is he found a way to leave and took it."

"The kidnapers also stole a large amount of money."

"Art was bitter enough."

Campbell starts to say something, but Clayton silences him

with a wave of his hand. "His service record doesn't square with that. He was in Nam for a second tour when he got it."

"That's news to me." What gives, Art?

"Were you here last night?" Clayton asks, and when Sherwood nods, "You may be asked to prove it."

"I can, if I have to. Would it help if I just let you check the house so you'll know he isn't here?"

"We're willing to wait for a search warrant," Campbell says. "Two men are watching the back."

Sherwood can't help himself. The tension that has been building all morning breaks loose as laughter—thirty seconds of irrepressible chuckles and guffaws that leave his eyes full of tears.

"Listen, fella."

"I'm sorry, but sending four armed cops to catch one man without legs is funny."

The redhead laughs. He keeps it short, but he seems sincere.

"Come in," Sherwood says. "Be quiet if you can. My nephew is asleep in the other room."

"Anyone else in the house?" They are both wary, careful not to turn their backs on Sherwood, and their hands hover near their guns.

"Just the two of us," Sherwood says. "The living room and dining room are here. Bathroom and bedrooms through the hall. Jamie is in the room on the right. The only hiding places I can think of in there are under the bed and in the closet." They're looking for someone who's been kidnaped and you're going on like you know he's hiding, O'Neal. Careful. "I don't think you'll ever find him if you're looking for kidnapers. Art split. Bet on it." Too lame. His hands begin to tremble. *Don't cough, Art.*

Campbell steps into the bathroom and pounds on the shower stall. "Solid house."

"Please don't wake Jamie," he says and hopes they can't see his relief that Art doesn't pound back.

The two check hall closets, the bathroom cupboards. Clayton goes quietly into Jamie's room and looks under the bed, pokes in the closet. Campbell takes Marion's room. "Who stays here?"

"That was my sister's room. She was killed in December. Accident. I haven't been able to go in there yet."

"December. Oh yeah. Howard her name? Volkswagen bug and a tank truck. I was on that one. Nasty."

Sherwood winces. A sharp pain runs the length of his scar and spreads across his chest. He turns away and almost runs into Clayton in the doorway. "It's tough," Clayton says. "I still haven't gotten over buddies I lost in Vietnam."

Campbell shrugs. The two men follow Sherwood through the house to the back hall.

"Basement down the stairs. The boxes in the first bedroom are full of Art's things. His name is on them. We both expected to come here and we shipped them from Rapid City. The attic is through that hatch. As far as I know it's the only way up there."

"Do you have a ladder?"

"I haven't found one yet."

They search the basement first, commenting that Art will probably either come or send for his boxes if, in fact, he has not been kidnaped. Both seem to accept Sherwood's statement that he would be inclined to let Art have his things without notifying them.

In due course they drag the high chair under the attic hatch and, to Sherwood's relief, Clayton climbs up. "Your ladder is up here," he calls. "It looks like about a twenty-footer. Want me to see if I can pass it down to you?"

"No. There isn't a smaller stepladder?"

"Sorry." Clayton moves away from the hole, sweeping the attic space with his flashlight. He is back in less than a minute, sits and lets his feet dangle into the hall. "Clean, Bill," he says. "How old is this place?"

"Beats me," Sherwood says.

"They don't make 'em this well anymore." He hangs, lets himself down until his feet touch the chair, then dusts off his pants and steps to the floor. "Okay, Mr. O'Neal. We appreciate your cooperation. We'd appreciate it more if you give us a call in case you hear from him."

"If I hear from any kidnapers, you can count on it."

Clayton nods. "If he does show up here and he has run away, would you ask him to get in touch with me?"

"I'd tell him you said so."

"Seriously. We have an active veterans' group here. I was 173rd

Airborne, myself. As long as he isn't wanted for anything, we have a drop-in center on campus, peer counseling, that kind of thing. We might be able to help him and the other way around. How about you?"

"Okinawa was as close as I got to the war."

"Air Force?"

"Army."

"A veteran is a veteran," Clayton says.

"Thanks." Half elated, half terrified that he might still blow it with the worst already over, Sherwood sees them out and stands in the doorway until the backup men come around the house, huddle with Clayton and Campbell and, finally, all four of them leave.

6

Light rain so fine it is almost mist envelops the house at sunset. Sherwood feeds Jamie and Josie, then stokes up the fire. Sherwood expects to have to entertain them with games or stories, but they disappear under the coat at his first inattentive moment.

"You guys interested in a bath?"

No response.

"Want some more marshmallows?" brings them out long enough to eat as many as he will allow, but no longer. They move from the living room to Jamie's room and back through the central hall to the dining room as a single fuzzy creature. Only when he insists they get ready for bed do they emerge from the coat. Josie puts on her pajamas. Sherwood helps Jamie into his, reads them an abbreviated version of "The Ugly Duckling" that Josie has brought along, then tucks them in and says good night.

Jamie's eyes are already drooping, but Josie plucks at Sherwood's hand. "Are you really an ugly duckling, Sherwood?"

"Not that I know of. Why?"

"Mommy said you were like one."

Oh-oh. Dangerous ground here. "She was probably talking about you or Jamie."

"Oh." She nods, as if that makes some sense, then purses her lips. "But we aren't ugly."

"That's true, but neither am I." With my shirt on, at least. "Maybe she meant someone else."

"Yes. Joe. He's ugly."

"That's it, then. She must have been talking about Joe."

"Maybe." Doubt shows on her face. She reaches up and takes his hand, drops it. "Sherwood?"

The gesture and the look on her face recall her that morning; standing beside the bed, shivering in flannel pajamas. About to bring up the sticky question of what Sherwood O'Neal was doing in bed with your mother, aren't you? That and what she's doing now, out with this ugly guy who is undoubtedly named Joe. "Good night, Josie," he says. "You need your sleep and I have a lot of things to do before I can get any sleep of my own."

Nodding solemnly, she rolls over and puts her arm across Jamie's shoulder.

Sherwood waits until he's sure both children are asleep, then he rehangs the blanket between the back hall and kitchen, bangs on the hatch, listens to the muffled thump of trap door, the creak of rafters, and finally the thud of rope that hits the hatch cover in a gob. Art's voice sounds distant through the panel. "There isn't any handle on the inside of this door."

"There are probably still a lot of little things I missed," Sherwood says. He pushes the hatch up with a broom handle, and Art catches the edge, pulls it out of the way. He comes down the rope hand over hand and balances on the swing seat.

"Damn, am I hungry. Did my boxes come?"

"They're in the basement. I fixed the shades so no one can see in. In case you wanted to work. I left a hammer so you can get the crates open. You want help getting down the stairs?"

Art shakes his head. "How did it go with the cops?"

"They may keep an eye on me, but they don't know you're here."

"Anyone watching the house?"

"Not that I've been able to spot so far."

With a quick nod, Art lets himself off the swing, raises his body on his hands and walks on them around the edge of the blanket into the kitchen. "What about food?"

"How about some eggs and toast?"

"Got any bacon?"

"No. With Jamie to think about, it's too expensive."

"Eggs and toast, then. Half a dozen of each. And coffee. Nice house." He surveys the kitchen with Marion's ruffled curtains on the windows, a stuffed frog on its side under the table and Sherwood's short-sheet calendar tacked beside the stove. "Bring the food downstairs, would you, Woody? I want to take a look."

"Sure." He makes toast in the oven, fries all six eggs together in a small pan, pours two mugs of coffee and takes everything down on a tray. Already Art has pulled the top off one of the boxes, assembled his rolling platform and is organizing tools and guitar parts in one corner of the room. "One rope right in the center of the stairwell, Woody. I can get up and down on something like that fine. If we leave the lights off, I won't make a silhouette on the shade. See if you can get those doors off the closet, would you?" He attacks the food, and even as he eats with one hand, fishes tools and clothes and books out of his box with the other and hurls the things into separate piles on the floor. Sherwood drags the closet doors off their runners and unscrews the hardware from the tops. In less than an hour they have a workshop with the doors up on short legs made from damaged pieces of the crates, tools spread within easy reach and one already assembled guitar hung on the north wall to await purfling and binding.

"Now to work," Art says. He coughs, turns his back to Sherwood and fiddles with something on the bench.

"You want some help?"

"That depends, Woody. What's the short sheet for?"

"I don't know. I've been pushed and it felt better to think there'd be an end."

"Hoping you'll get that long, likely. A couple of weeks in the world haven't changed you. How much money do we have left?"

"Two thousand, three hundred forty-six dollars and seventy-nine cents. Give or take a nickel. I figure two thousand even is yours, but I'm going to need to use it for a while. To pay off bills and feed us. Marion had insurance and I'll pay you back as soon as that comes through. Before I set up anything for Jamie. Okay? Otherwise, we'll probably lose utilities and we won't have anything to live on until the disability checks start coming."

"You had my check sent here?"

"Yeah. You didn't tell me there'd be cops hunting you as a kidnaping victim or a safecracker."

"Damn it."

"Relax. I can send it back. Say you never showed. Things will be a little tight."

Art slaps the bench, turns his platform to face Sherwood. "How much insurance?"

"I don't know. There'll probably be some kind of inheritance tax out of it and property taxes to pay. I'm supposed to see Marion's lawyer Monday. He should be able to tell me what I have to do to keep this place from being auctioned out from under us."

"I'm going to need money, Woody. I did a lot of thinking up there today. Your short sheet goes to July, right? Well, I figure I should be out of here and on my own by, say, the first of June. What I'm going to need help with is getting a new identity."

"Whatever I can do."

"You remember telling me about how you flipped out on the kid? And you picked up some guy running from a gang that was supposed to be some kind of revolutionary group?"

"He's long gone. I don't even remember his name."

"Not him. That gang. If those dudes are any good, they'll know all about fake identification."

"That's trouble, Art." And crazy too. What do you want to get away from so much?

"Come on, Woody. Don't make me bargain for your help."

"Bargain?" The two thousand for my help? Oh no. "It's that important? A new identity?"

"What other choice do I have?"

What other choice, Art? Not the two of us anymore. That's clear enough. Sherwood shrugs, shakes his head.

"All you have to do is set up a meeting for me. I'll take care of the rest."

"How are you going to do that?"

"I'll do it. You'll see."

"Can you wait until I get Jamie set up?"

"Sure. A couple of months. I'll need that to get ready anyway."

"I don't mean just custody hearings. I want to get him settled wherever he's going to be with all Marion's money in a trust fund and the house secure in his name or sold or whatever. If I don't manage that before July, then I'll stay and finish it and help with this ID thing no matter how long it takes. Okay?"

"Yeah," Art says. He raises a questioning eyebrow, "Unless something happens so I need it sooner," holds out his hand and watches Sherwood until he takes the hand and shakes. "We'd better wait until morning to hang that rope in the stairwell."

"Right." Brushed off. "Don't work too hard." Sherwood stands awkwardly near the door for another minute, watching Art open and sort through the box of guitar neck blanks from that last morning in Custer. Sherwood remembers the post office, the girl in Jorgensen's and Jorgensen himself saying, "Fathers can't care for children." Things looked simple then. Finally Sherwood turns away, climbs the stairs, wanders into the living room where he stokes up the fire and drops into Marion's green chair.

"No end in sight now, is there?" He half wishes he could flip out and spend a few minutes in a world both simple and predictable, but the noise of Art's hammering holds him back. Finally he gives up wishing and stares at the fire, at small blue flames that pop between the logs to flare orange for a few seconds, then flash out in gouts of smoke. Coals spill down the heap of ashes onto the hearth as if to push into the room and for a moment he sees the fireplace as a throwback, a smoke-blackened hole in one wall of the house, essentially the same here as on ancient fogbound moors. Glowing pits of warmth and comfort. Fire tamed and carried from shelter cave to farmhouse to suburbia. There was a fireplace in the house on the ranch south of Laramie. Family all sitting around the fire. Lights out. Watching the coals in the dark. And here you sit now, O'Neal, hoping you'll have time to find as good a place for Marion's kid.

The memory of his family surprises him. He hasn't really thought about them since the accident. Brodie used to try to get him to talk about them during some of their sessions, but he refused. He still doesn't want to think about their wreck. Just like Marion. Now he isn't even sure how he found out that his parents were dead. Probably Art found out and told him. No. They were killed the month after his accident. It must have been before he met Art. As he tries to remember, he comes up against a series of images of his father: carving a wooden horse-head to glue onto a broomstick, showing Sherwood how to cut a toy rifle out of a piece of board, walking with him and Marion into the meadows and the hills around the various ranches he worked when they were children. "Have to set it up so Jamie doesn't miss any of that."

He puts more wood on the fire and stirs up the coals. A little later he gets up to do it again. He never exactly falls asleep, but he isn't fully awake either. Memories drift in and out of focus until, finally, he hears Erica laugh and slip her key into the lock and tell someone to be quiet.

She is halfway across the living room before she notices that the bed is empty. "Sherwood?"

"Over here." He pushes the chair around. The man with her is in shadow. He is broad and tall, and Sherwood makes out mustache and long sideburns.

"You didn't have to wait up. It's after three."

"I fell asleep."

"How was Josie?"

"Fine."

"This is Joe Soames. Sherwood."

The man steps into the room. "Glad to meet you," he says. His face is pleasant and his eyes gleam with intelligence. The sideburns are muttonchops.

"How do you do." What to say?

Erica goes in for Josie. The man stands in the middle of the room, hands relaxed at his sides. Sherwood envies his ease, slaps the arms of the chair a couple of times and shifts his feet. "Would you a like a cup of coffee?"

A gruff, "No thanks," seems to fill the room.

"Have a good time?" Sounds like her father or something.

Joe Soames stares, then nods. Erica comes back with Josie. "Thanks, Sherwood. Do you need me on Monday?"

"I'm afraid so. Is that all right?"

"Of course." She carries Josie into the hall where Joe holds the door, nods to Sherwood and then closes the door behind them. The tap of Art's hammer comes up from the basement. Sherwood waits until Joe's silver Porsche pulls away from the front of the house before he undresses and rolls into the bed.

First thing he hears in the morning is the hammer, still going. He has slept only four hours, but he feels fine. Up and washed, he starts coffee and mixes up a batch of pancakes. By the time Jamie

wanders into the kitchen, Sherwood has most of breakfast cooked
and warming in the oven.

"I hear pounding, Sher."

"That's Art. You want to call him for breakfast?"

Jamie shakes his head. "I thought he was a ghost."

"Hey, Woody." The voice echoes a little in the stairwell and
Jamie presses against Sherwood's leg. "I smell food."

"Want me to bring it down?"

"I'll come up. See anyone on the street?"

Sherwood checks out the window. The day is clear, no clouds
for the first time since he has come to California. Cars up and
down the block are coated with heavy dew, but halfway down
Sixth, he glimpses someone ducking behind the dash of a Lincoln
with its windshield wiped clean. He moves out of sight of the car.
"Could be," he calls.

Bumping softly as he lifts himself and drops onto each step for
a higher grip, Art comes up. "Why don't you slip mine under the
blanket."

"Sure." Sherwood loads a plate, fills a coffee mug and passes
them into the hall. He fills plates for Jamie and himself and sits at
the kitchen table so he can keep watch on the Lincoln. "Fancy
car. Doubt if it's cops. Probably a private detective again."

"I'm too tired to care. I think I'll rack out. Pound on the wall if
he tries to get in."

"Okay." He pours syrup on Jamie's pancakes and cuts them.
"Eat, small friend. It's going to be a beautiful day. We'll have to
check out the park."

Jamie's eyes are large and they fix on Sherwood.

"Are you scared, man?"

"Why doesn't he come out?"

"He doesn't want anyone but us to know he's here. You want
to meet him?"

"I don't know."

"Come on." He picks Jamie up, carries him to the blanket and
ducks under it. The child's eyes grow larger and Sherwood realizes
that in spite of all the talk and preparation, Jamie has expected
some kind of game or imaginary friend. This vision of Art, sitting
legless on the floor with his mouth full of pancake, isn't something to be passed off with a shrug.

Art nods and holds out his hand to shake. Jamie's arms turn to steely wires around Sherwood's chest.

"This is my friend Art, Jamie. Go ahead and shake hands."

"But, Sher . . ."

"It's okay. He isn't a ghost."

"His legs are broke."

Art's laugh is short and bitter. "Art Johnson, terrifier of little children."

"I know, man. Jamie, shake hands with Art. He lost his legs in the war and he's going to feel bad if you're scared of him. He's just people. Like us."

Slowly, Jamie unwraps his arms and legs and lets Sherwood lower him to the floor. He flinches when Art envelops his small hand in a large, calloused palm, but he doesn't pull away.

"Okay, Jamie?"

Jamie nods and clings.

"We better get back to our breakfast before it gets cold. See you tonight, Art."

"Be sure to hit the wall if anyone comes."

Back in the high chair Jamie picks at his food and keeps his head tilted slightly toward the hall. Finally, after Art has pushed his plate and cup under the blanket and climbed up to dangle and swear and knock the hatch cover back into place, Jamie eats.

"Why are his legs broke off, Sher?"

"It happens a lot in war," but that's no explanation is it, O'Neal?

Jamie shakes his head and looks out the window. "Did his legs die?"

"Yes. After they were—off."

"But Art didn't die?"

"No." Is it that logical; such a violation of the body should bring death? "In practice you can ruin a lot of your body and still not die."

"Does it hurt? If your legs break off?"

"When they're first off, yes. Art's legs don't hurt him now." At least not that way.

With a nod, Jamie puts his attention on his pancakes, but he still seems uneasy. Sherwood leaves the breakfast dishes in the sink and fills the morning with a trip to the grocery store, yard

cleanup and finally an hour and a half in the park. Not until
Jamie is fed and put down for his afternoon nap does Sherwood
get to the basement to check out the order Art has created in his
new shop; tools rearranged within easy reach, the charcoal-heated
bending pipe set up and a set of sides bent and clamped into the
form, the purfling and binding already strapped to one assembled
guitar and, on the second bench, all alone and obviously the
prime project, the painstakingly sanded framework and tight fric-
tion joints for what will become a pair of artificial legs.

"Hard into it, aren't you?" Sherwood whispers. "Shoulder chip
and drive and all. I wish you best luck, old friend."

Monday morning Sherwood leaves Jamie with Erica and
catches a bus past the green and brown lawns and bare trees, the
neat houses buffeted by a hard north wind; onto the highway past
farmhouses that seem caught between the open fields and the asphalt, a weathered drive-in that doubles as Sunday-afternoon flea
market, almond orchards and finally up a long stretch between
black walnut trees to the county fairgrounds, service stations, liquor stores, rice driers and grain elevators of Woodgrove. Belatedly
he has realized that the court is a civilian branch of the same government that gave him the U. S. Army, the same government that
gave Kenny and Art to Vietnam, and his palms are damp with
nervous sweat. He feels tall and skinny and alone, half lost in the
great pile of Jamie's coat and at the same time glad he has the fur
to hide in. The bus drops him half a dozen blocks from the lawyer's office, and the cold wind whistles down the streets as if to
drive him deep into the protective warmth.

The personal tone of the letter about Marion's death has led
Sherwood to expect an overweight, teary-eyed man; pudgy and
soft. In fact, Donald Holmes is about thirty-five and in good physical shape. His face is squared at the jaw with a large, hawklike
beak of nose, but all potential fierceness of the face is damped by
a tangle of curly blond hair gone thin at the top and grown thick
around the ears. A desktop picture shows him looking somewhat
more formidable beside a small, light-haired woman and two
little blond girls.

"Sherwood O'Neal." He stands and leans across the desk to shake hands. "Sit down, please."

Sherwood likes him immediately, for the hair if for no other reason. Trying to hide ears big as yours, O'Neal. Sherwood shakes hands, hangs the coat over the back of the chair and sits.

"Judge Gavin isn't going to like that coat. Too nonconformist."

"I can leave it here. I just don't dare lose it."

"It is distinguished-looking." He tips his head, picks up a pair of glasses and puts them on. "That isn't Jamie's coat?"

You know Jamie well enough to know his coat? "He gives it to me when I go off without him. It's to make sure I'll come back."

"Yes. He did the same thing with Marion sometimes. I think, perhaps, you should wear it. Gavin being Gavin will have to make some remark. We'll gain a few points."

"You knew Marion."

Donald Holmes nods. "She came in well over a year ago to make out a will. Wanted to be sure Jamie would be taken care of in case something happened to her." He picks up a sheaf of papers and taps to straighten it, top and sides. His eyes avoid Sherwood's. "I'd like to cover a number of things before the hearing."

"Okay."

"The estate consists of the house, a twenty thousand dollar life insurance policy, six hundred dollars in a savings account, three hundred twelve dollars and seventeen cents in her checking account. The house is yours. She put your name on a joint-tenancy deed, so in essence the property is not changing hands. You are the named beneficiary on her life insurance policy, so that money is yours less nine hundred fifty dollars and thirty-two cents to cover the cost of burial. There will be inheritance tax on money in the bank accounts, but it won't amount to much. I can probably clear that up in a couple of months.

"Market value of the house is about forty thousand dollars if you think best to sell it. Eighteen thousand four hundred thirty-four dollars and thirty-four cents is outstanding on the mortgage, which puts the total value of the estate at approximately forty-one thousand dollars, contingent upon the selling price of the house. Of course, I'm donating my services. . . ." His head is lowered and his attention fixed on a sheet of figures in neat columns. "It

all looks so tidy this way," he muses, then coughs. "I assume you
do want custody of Jamie."

Okay, O'Neal, how much do you tell this guy?

"Or don't you?"

"Yes. Of course."

"I think at this point we can get custody without too much
trouble. Child Protective Services is ready to give you tentative approval and that's a major hurdle. You apparently impressed Pat
Chapman. We also have a good judge. Judge Gavin raised two of
his brother's children after the Korean War and he's a strong
believer in family. Your mental history is the only real problem
and I don't think it will finally weigh against you. I released your
medical file to Judge Gavin and I know he has read the report of
the inquiry into your accident. You're aware of its contents?"

Sherwood shakes his head. "I haven't read it. I was in bad
shape the first two years. Later I was a psychiatric outpatient for a
couple of years, then I was living in a cabin in the mountains. All
I know is what Brodie told me, trying to jog my memory. There
was what they called 'an explosive device of undetermined type
and origin,' probably a mine or shell left over from World War
II. There were still a few of those around.

"Whatever it was, Kenny and I were ordered to stay away from
it, but we didn't. I don't know why. Kenny had been in Vietnam.
Maybe he thought he could handle it, or maybe he didn't give a
damn. He was killed. I was almost killed. At one point they were
going to court-martial me for disobeying a direct order and as-
saulting a noncommissioned officer. The charges were written up,
then dropped without explanation and in the end they gave me
an honorable discharge with total mental disability.

"None of the official version takes into account these flipouts I
still have about things that happened before. We were on the rifle
range, and Kenny had talked about killing one of the officers, but
an explosion? I don't know what blew up. Maybe if I could remember that I'd remember the rest."

Holmes nods. "The conclusion of the board of inquiry was that
you suffered a nervous breakdown and were mentally incompetent
when you disobeyed the order to stay away from whatever ex-
ploded. No mention is made of the alleged assault. The whole report looks like a snow job to me."

"But the breakdown would explain why I can't remember."

"That was the official line until Dr. Brodie got involved in your case." He opens a folder and reads, ". . . retrograde posttraumatic amnesia complicated by guilt feelings that stem from an unrelated incident, probably the death of the subject's parents, during the amnestic period."

"Yeah. That sounds like Brodie."

"Any other time in the history of this country, a mark like this on your record would damn you for life, but in light of later events and disclosures about military policies and practices . . ." He laughs. "The language of the report is obviously designed to cover up the facts. There are so many inconsistencies and gaps that I'm afraid there's little doubt the Army lied about whatever happened. This is even more obvious when one considers the dreams as Dr. Brodie has transcribed them."

Dreams? Just wrote those flipouts off the record, didn't you, Doc? Wonder if I could get a driver's license.

"Of course, depending on your court and judge, reaction to the report might still go against you. In this case, Judge Gavin was an enlisted man in the Pacific during the Second World War. He had quite a reputation for hating officers. Refused three field commissions.

"I think I can get him to disregard the inquiry report for all purposes related to any custody hearing involving Jamie. That leaves your mental record and we can handle that. Essentially, it shows your steady improvement to a point from which you were able to discontinue outpatient treatment and move halfway across the country as companion to a double amputee. No small responsibility."

And *that* is Art, summed up to make you look good, O'Neal. A double amputee.

"Do you understand what I'm saying, Mr. O'Neal?"

"Sherwood, please." It all adds up to saying that just because something happened doesn't mean anyone will be able to sit down later and figure out what it was, even the person it happened to.

"All right. Sherwood, then. Do you understand?"

"Yes. Is there anything I can or should do about it?"

"No. The only thing you can do anything about, really, is to establish how you intend to support yourself and Jamie."

"I have a disability pension."

"That will be a liability with Judge Gavin. He isn't at all sympathetic toward anyone on the public dole, whatever their reason.
Also, since your mental disability stems directly from something
we are going to ask him to disregard, we should anticipate that
Judge Gavin will want you to become self-supporting. Do you
have any skills?"

"I've been out of circulation too long, I'm afraid."

"College degree?"

"In English."

"Would you consider going back to school for another degree
or a teaching certificate?"

"Is it necessary?"

"It may be, unless you're ready to settle for short-order cook or
something else along that line."

"I see. How soon would I have to start doing that?"

"Soon. I can probably get you six months to a year of grace for
education, apprenticeship or whatever."

"Okay." No problem at all!

"Think about it. Maybe you have skills you could use that you
haven't thought about in terms of occupation. One last thing,
then we should go. Are you ready to take Jamie if I can get him
placed with you today?"

"Absolutely." As long as no one goes along as county delegate
when I pick him up.

Sherwood follows Donald Holmes out of the office across the
street and up a long sidewalk through a little courtyard in the center of the courthouse grounds. The area is hardly more than a
wide spot in the walk with benches and thick railings of sculp-
tured concrete inside a low screen of hedge that adds an air of ordered intimacy made tenuous by the fierce north wind. Fallow
earth in planters and urn-shaped pots seem ready to throw up
mats of flowers at the first hint of spring. Drawn to the place,
Sherwood almost asks the lawyer to stop a minute, but there isn't
time.

The hearing room is closed and cluttered, its aura of venerable
age marred by an arbitrary arrangement of preformed plastic

chairs among the pewlike benches for spectators and prospective jurors. Odors of polished wood and sweeping compound remind Sherwood of schoolrooms and janitors pushing brooms over worn flooring of deserted hallways. Donald Holmes motions him to an oak table on one side of the judge's bench and then crosses to greet Pat Chapman and a man with soft eyes where they sit at an identical table across the room. Pat gives Sherwood a pleasant nod. He hears mention of Dr. Brodie.

Come on, Doc. These people seem nice, but I could use a familiar face to jack up my courage. Be good to see you come in the door, tugging your sideburns and feeling as out of place as I do. Sherwood pinches his earlobe. In spite of the tic, pulling at his sideburns, Dr. Brodie is not just another neurotic psychiatrist. He was in Vietnam, under fire twice and wounded in July 1973, just a month before the American withdrawal. Sherwood came to respect him in the hospital because he knew what he was talking about and managed to remain slow with both advice and leading questions. He was also the only one in the hospital who cared anything about Art.

Not until Brodie slouches into the courtroom with only two minutes to spare does Sherwood remember that the tic is not nervous, but is rather Brodie's inability to get used to the sideburns he has grown to spare patients and friends the sight of an ugly scar that runs from his right ear to his jawbone. He has added a mustache since Sherwood last saw him. Taking in the room with wary eyes, he crosses to sit beside Sherwood and ask, "How are things?" He has lost a little weight and his hair is thinner, but he is still Brodie.

"Not bad, Doc. The mustache looks good."

Brodie grins. "It gives me something else to grab. I decided I'd break myself of pulling the sideburns, too distracting to patients, by stroking the mustache. Then I can shave and just pet my lip. How's Art?"

"Later, Doc. He's okay."

Across the room Pat Chapman laughs at something one of the lawyers says. Donald Holmes comes back, shakes hands with Brodie and sits beside Sherwood. "This won't take long," Holmes says.

"Who's the guy with Mrs. Chapman?"

"Ron Jarvis. He's Jamie's lawyer."

"I thought Jamie and I were on the same side."

"It's the adversary system. Clumsy at times and seldom perfect, but it's what we have and we can work with it."

The bailiff comes in and stations himself at a small desk near the door. Another door, behind the bench, opens a crack. Bailiff announces, "Juvenile court of Valley County, state of California is now in session, Judge Harold Gavin presiding. All rise."

Judge Gavin is white-haired and wrinkled, but his step is quick. He takes his place behind the bench and greets the lawyers as they sit. "We are here to decide who shall have jurisdiction over James Patrick Howard." His eyes sweep the room, stop at the coat draped over the back of Sherwood's chair. "Age four years, presently residing in a foster home at 212 I Street in Dawville, California. Is that information correct, Mr. Jarvis?"

"It is, Your Honor."

"Seeking custody of the child is Sherwood Patrick O'Neal, uncle on the mother's side, currently residing at 558 C Street in Dawville. Is that correct?"

"Yes . . ." Sherwood's voice comes out a growl around a frog in his throat. Can't come down to a simple question of correct addresses, can it? He coughs. "Yes, Your Honor."

"What is your age, Mr. O'Neal?"

"Thirty-one."

Judge Gavin writes on a three-by-five card. "No need to be nervous, Mr. O'Neal. You aren't on trial. We're trying to decide what is best for your nephew. All of us here are trying to decide together. It is serious business, often difficult, and we have to try to take into account every side presented. CPS would prefer to put a child with a willing relative and I accommodate them whenever possible. In this case, the court is required to proceed with caution. You are a single male and the care of a child is one area in which a single male is traditionally considered less than qualified.

"In addition there is certain doubt about your qualification in general. You have been under psychiatric care and also have tried to gain admittance to several mental wards in veterans' hospitals. You receive government compensation for total mental disability. This would appear to stem from a military accident that took place on Okinawa on the twenty-seventh of February 1970, but

I'm afraid that, having considered the official inquiry into the accident, I am at a loss to say whether your purported disability was the cause of the accident or resulted from it. A number of things suggest that even the inquiry board was concerned you were not being treated fairly." Judge Gavin coughs. "Though how they could make the humane recommendation that you be honorably discharged and at the same time approve that obviously fabricated report is beyond my imagination.

"Fortunately, it is not the task of this court to make any ruling about whether your treatment by the United States Army was just or unjust. We are concerned solely with your present ability to act as legal guardian for a minor child.

"At this early point in the proceedings I see no alternative to placing James Patrick Howard under jurisdiction of this court."

Sherwood starts up, but Donald Holmes catches his arm. Brodie is already on his feet. "Your Honor, Sherwood O'Neal is sane and competent. I don't think it is at all just . . ."

"You would be Dr. Kevin Brodie?" Judge Gavin shuffles through his three-by-five cards, finally turns up the one he wants and writes something on it.

"Yes, Your Honor."

"Please sit down, Doctor. This is only a jurisdiction hearing. Placing the child under jurisdiction of the court does not mean that Mr. O'Neal will not be granted custody. Mr. Jarvis?"

"We concur, Your Honor."

"Mr. Holmes?"

"Several small matters, Your Honor. We would like to discredit the official report on Mr. O'Neal's accident for the purposes of these hearings."

"I quite understand. Will counsel please approach the bench."

The two lawyers huddle in front of Judge Gavin, who speaks rapidly in a low voice. ". . . official report didn't establish . . . disobeyed order . . . possible humanitarian motives . . . probable whitewash . . . most likely a case of misjudgment, but it is not clear . . ."

"Misjudgment, hell," Brodie mutters.

First Holmes nods, then Jarvis. The judge says something Sherwood can't make out and the three men laugh.

"We are agreed that the official report has no direct bearing on

Mr. O'Neal's present competence to care for his nephew. You had something more, Mr. Holmes?" Judge Gavin glances at the clock.

"Yes, Your Honor. First, Mr. O'Neal has anticipated that caring for a child is not consistent with mental disability and at the disposition hearing he will present a plan to become self-supporting and thereby effect an official change of status regarding his competence. Second, I would like to draw your attention to the coat Mr. O'Neal has worn into the courtroom this morning." Donald Holmes lifts the coat from the back of the chair and seems momentarily surprised by its weight.

Gavin's response is a dry, "I noticed."

"This coat belonged to Jamie's father and it has passed to Jamie as a sort of security blanket. He knows what is happening here today and has sent the coat with Sherwood as a symbol of his trust."

The judge's forehead wrinkles in a half scowl.

"It's true, Your Honor." Brodie is on his feet again. "I knew Sherwood's sister and Jamie, and when they used to come to Martinez, Jamie would bring the coat and whenever he was with Sherwood, Sherwood was wearing it."

"I see."

Thanks, Doc.

Across the room, Pat Chapman stands. "Your Honor, Jamie had that coat or one very like it when he was first brought to the shelter home and I remember he wouldn't part with it. I also took it with him to the foster home."

Judge Gavin nods and coughs. "You seem to have made a favorable impression on quite a number of people, Mr. O'Neal. I surmise, Mr. Holmes, that your last item would be to request temporary custody until the disposition hearing?"

"Yes, Your Honor."

"Mr. Jarvis? Any objections?"

"None, Your Honor."

"Mrs. Chapman? This would be agreeable with CPS, is that correct?"

"Yes, Your Honor."

"Then it is the decision of this court that James Patrick Howard be made a ward of the court and further that he be placed in the temporary custody of Sherwood O'Neal under close supervi-

sion of Child Protective Services. Final disposition will be decided
at ten o'clock, Monday, the seventeenth of February in this courtroom. Dr. Brodie, may I see you in my chambers for a moment?
Hearing is adjourned."

Almost too easy, but what happened here, O'Neal? A lot of
things follow directly from this and it all slipped by like a ghost.
Would the defendant please give a summary of the substance of
the proceedings? Can't do it, can you? A general impression, you
have, but what happened? It's almost worse than not remembering anything.

The bailiff calls, "All rise," and Judge Gavin exits through the
rear door. Brodie strokes his mustache, tugs at a sideburn and follows the judge into the back room.

"It just occurred to me," Sherwood says to Donald Holmes.
"Why hasn't anyone mentioned Jamie's father?"

"We covered him at the detention hearing, the one that placed
Jamie in the foster home. For one thing, Marion has had a war-
rant out on him for three years. Nonpayment of child support.
Last she heard of him, he was wanted on a drug-related charge in
Mexico more than a year ago."

Pat Chapman leans across the table to shake Sherwood's
hand. "Congratulations. I want to come along when you pick up
Jamie. When would be best for you?"

"Tomorrow morning?"

"Fine. I can bring the papers with me, if you don't want to wait
for them today."

"Thank you." Logistics problem. Don't want to leave him at
Doris's so long she flips him out again. No more than thirty seconds alone with her.

"What time would be convenient?" She studies Sherwood's
face. "Is anything the matter?"

"No. Would nine to be too early?"

"Not at all." She shakes hands with Holmes and with Sherwood again, then returns to the other table and her zippered plastic case.

Donald shakes Sherwood's hand. "That came off well. If you
can manage with Jamie for the next two weeks, there shouldn't
be any question. Think about what you can do to get off disability. Any plan will serve for a start, but try for some kind of supple-

mentary income as soon as possible. I'll see you get a check for the
insurance in a couple of days."

"Thanks. Thanks for everything."

"Call me if you need any help. Please."

"I will. Thanks."

"I only hope . . ." He hesitates, then shakes his head. "Good
luck." Paying careful attention to the movement of his hands, he
gathers up his papers.

You aren't going to charge for your help and you "only
hope . . ."? *What were you to Marion?* Sherwood watches him go,
watches Pat Chapman and the other lawyer leave. In a few
more minutes Dr. Brodie comes out the door behind the bench
and saunters up to Sherwood.

"Thanks for coming, Doc."

"You need a ride?"

They walk together out of the courtroom, down the hall into a
wide gallery with plaster curlicues along the edge of the ceiling
and half columns embedded in the walls. Outside they cross the
lawn past the little courtyard with its shrubbery and concrete
benches. Brodie pulls at his sideburns all the way to the parking
lot posted "FOR JURORS ONLY." "Didn't catch me," he says.
"Let's get out of here before they do."

"I'm hiding Art at the house," Sherwood says. "The cops have
already searched the place and couldn't find him."

"Figured that's what was going on, but I've had some bad moments over it, worrying that he might have gotten into some trouble and I wasn't doing anything because I assumed you'd sprung
him. Is he okay?"

"I've seen him better. He's making a pair of legs, getting ready
to go out on his own."

Brodie nods, half absently, "That's a battle I thought we'd lost.
The legs. What changed his mind? Hmm . . ." He concentrates
on making the turn from Main Street onto the highway. "How
about you?"

"Are you supposed to ask me a lot of questions and then give
that judge a call?"

"I'm going to let him know how I find you, Sherwood, but this
is me. Brodie. Remember? I'm not taping conversations, so if you
want to talk off the record, just say so."

"Sorry, Doc." Have to level with someone. "I'm going to do this custody thing, and if I get Jamie I'll find a good place for him. A home, Doc. As good as the one I had. Then I'm going back to the hills."

"I thought you said Art was going on his own."

"Without Art, Doc."

"Your nephew won't change that? You're still finished with yourself except for a few details you have to tidy up?"

"What would you do?"

"Tough question." Brodie shrugs. "Put it this way. What will you do if you go back to the hills and end up having to live there alone for fifty years?"

"It does sound bleak, Doc, but I can't count on that. Jamie needs someone who will be there for sure."

Nodding, Brodie hums tunelessly to himself. "Can you get away with it? Take legal custody and then give him away? Won't there be some legal conventions involved? Like these hearings?"

"First thing first, Doc. I don't want my long-range plan to hurt the custody part of it. I'm a lot better than where they had him."

"You aren't looking for an argument?"

"No."

"Or someone to point out once again that your medical record says they got all the shrapnel out?"

"Doc, I heard those guys talking about me when they thought I was asleep. Five operations and each time they told me they got it all. Nurses'd cluck their tongues and look damp-eyed and say, 'Oh you're doing fine'—but doctors, nurses, not a one of 'em had a shrapnel scar anywhere. Would you believe them?"

"Of course I would. Aw. Hell, Sherwood. I don't know."

"Are you feeling okay, Doc? You looked a little tired back in the courtroom."

Arms straight from the steering wheel, Doc Brodie pushes himself against the seat, then laughs. "See that? Trying to get a little distance from the windshield as if it were the problem. People crack up thinking like that." He laughs again, then shakes his head. "My father died the first of the year," he says. "I've been fighting Viet Cong in my sleep ever since. Better the last couple of weeks, but I don't know. I thought I'd gotten the whole experience under control, then his death triggered these memories, some of them things I had completely repressed, and now I wonder if I'll have to go through the war again every time something in my life gets shaken up or someone close to me dies."

"That's rough," Sherwood says.

"Part of what bothers me is that these things that are coming back aren't . . . pure. If you know what I mean. My own feelings about this are still confused, but I'm beginning to suspect that part of wanting to forget was the assumption that the things I was forgetting had some sort of independent reality. That they existed —in some sense, at any rate. Now, seeing my past boil up because of things happening to me in the present, I realize that the past, my past, isn't there anymore except as I see it now and even in regard to that goddamned war, that leaves me with a tremendous sense of loss. Ironic, but I've forgotten it as effectively as you have. And I can't get it back. Ever." He taps the wheel. "You don't mind hearing this?"

"Not at all. That's how I felt right after the hearing. Like I missed something important."

"Yeah. Missed something. I was on good terms with my father, and we saw a lot of each other so there's no problem with that kind of guilt." He leans back against the seat. "I know what you mean about the doctors who didn't have shrapnel scars. I haven't seen you in a year and here I am telling you things I feel uncomfortable telling colleagues.

"The worst of it is I just feel lost, like I've lost rudder and anchor; taproot. Part of me is missing and I have to reorient myself without that part and it's harder than I thought it would be. And then, last, with him gone, I've lost a kind of immunity or protective barrier. In the normal course of events fathers die before sons and now he has died and I have to face the fact that I'm next.

"If it makes you feel any better, Sherwood, I understand you one hell of a lot better than I did before."

"Wouldn't wish that on anyone, Doc, but at least you see why I can't hang around long enough to do the same thing to Jamie."

"You didn't hear me say I'd have been better off without a father."

"Not the same thing," Sherwood says. He directs Dr. Brodie into Dawville, onto B Street and then down Sixth past the Lincoln that has been parked there all weekend. The man behind the wheel glances up from the newspaper as they drive by. "I'm pretty sure that's a detective. Art's father, probably."

"He doesn't care if you know he's there, does he?"

"No. He's just waiting. Marion's is the house on the corner."

Sherwood lets Brodie in at the front door and motions him into the living room. "Jamie," he calls.

Feet slap the floor of the bedroom and a squeal turns to cries of, "Sher, Sher." Jamie appears in the central hall, arms out and hair flying. He misses the turn, smacks into the doorframe and tumbles onto the living-room floor.

Damn, he can't stay on his feet. Going to take a bad fall if we aren't careful. "Oh-oh," Sherwood grabs him before he can cry and pulls him into the folds of the coat. "Are you okay, small friend?"

The dark eyes look a little dazed. A white lump on Jamie's forehead turns red while Sherwood watches. No doubt it hurts, but Jamie is too excited to cry. "Come see. I made something."

"That's a good-sized bump."

Jamie feels his forehead. "Hurts. Come on." He wriggles down and starts across the floor.

"Don't run, man." Sherwood follows him into the bedroom, where Erica sits beside a board covered with gobs of white glue and various-sized pieces and chips of wood.

"It's a boat, Sher. Can I take it in the bath?"

"Good boat. Maybe when it's dry."

"I found the scraps in the basement," Erica says. "How did it go?"

"Temporary custody starting tomorrow. You don't suppose you could take him to Doris's and duck into a back room when I come with the caseworker?"

Erica purses her lips. "Okay. You couldn't take Josie again to-night?"

"Sure." He watches her stand awkwardly, her joints apparently stiff from sitting on the floor. "Did you know this lawyer of Marion's?"

"Don? I met him a couple of times."

"What was it between him and my sister?"

"What was it between Don and Marion?" she says. For a moment she studies his face, then shakes her head. "A lot more than I could tell you in five minutes—and I'm going to have to work late as it is."

They find Brodie in the center of the living room, chin on his hand with one finger idly stroking his mustache. Sherwood makes introductions, then watches the two of them eye each other warily. Erica finally breaks off looking at Brodie to track a car passing in front of the window, then turns back to face him. "Are you another one who can't get out of the Army, Doctor?" she asks.

Before Sherwood can protest, Brodie laughs and claps his hands together. "That's very astute. The answer is a qualified yes. Civilian employee at a veterans' hospital, but it isn't all looking for security in familiar surroundings. I do understand some of the problems better than a lot of people."

"I bet you do."

"Erica, what are you . . . ?"

Brodie cuts Sherwood off with a wave of his hand. "Know exactly what you mean," he says. "Sherwood and Art have been holding together as a castoff remnant of the Army for quite a while, but don't let that mislead you. No one dies the day he's inducted, and getting out isn't like being born either."

Erica's eyes widen a little, then she smiles. "Sorry. Just feeling bitchy, I guess. I'll bring Josie about six o'clock, Sherwood." With a quick nod and a nice-to-meet-you-Doctor, she is out the door.

"Sorry, Doc."

"I don't know why you should be. We both know there's a lot of truth in with all her resentment." He raises a questiong eyebrow, watches Sherwood's face, then shrugs. "Is there a chance that I could see Art?"

"If you want to stay for dinner. He worked all night and with that detective sitting across the street, he won't want to come out of hiding until dark."

"In two weeks, then. I'll plan to come down for the disposition hearing and see him afterward."

"You want to see what he's doing before you go?" Sherwood checks on Jamie, who seems completely absorbed in his task of sticking wood scraps to the board, then shows Brodie the basement workroom; the low benches and pieces of guitar and the artificial legs, one of them nearing completion now with carved panels of hardwood fitted to the framework, a shoe and a sock on the foot and a system of web straps put aside, ready to be attached to fittings in the thigh. "I think he means it this time, Doc. He's going to get out on his own."

"Nice work." Brodie picks up the finished limb, tests the joints and runs his hand over the sanded wood. "You may be right," he says, "but don't count on it."

Eight o'clock Tuesday morning Sherwood calls Doris Ransler. "You have one hour to clean up that mess. The court gave me temporary custody of Jamie yesterday and I suspect the reason I'm the first to let you know is that someone wants to give your place a quick look-over. A friend of mine will bring Jamie in half an hour. She'll stay with him until Pat Chapman and I pick him up again at nine." Something falls with a crash in the background. He can hear her breathing and he poises his finger above the cradle button. "You have about an hour to clean up. Got that?"

"You son-of . . ."

The finger mashes down. *Got you, lady.*

At nine Pat Chapman parks behind Erica's car and she and Sherwood make their way across the unkempt yard to the front door. Doris surprises him. She is dressed in jeans and a crisp white shirt; isn't saggy or greasy and looks almost pleasant. The living room is shabby, but clean. Jamie perches nervously on the sofa, the goat coat heaped around him, his hair slicked back and parted on the wrong side as if to point out the black-and-blue mark from his crash into the doorframe. His, "Hi, Sher," is not as spontaneous as Sherwood would like.

"What happened to your head, Jamie?" Pat asks.

"I fell."

She looks at Doris.

"He came back from a visit and that's all he'd tell me." Doris grimaces at Sherwood, smiles. "You know kids."

"Bumped into a doorframe," Sherwood says. He wonders where she hid all the filth. "You ready to go, small friend?"

Jamie hops off the sofa and drags the coat to Sherwood, who picks him up and slips into the sleeves with a practiced motion.

"Ready, Sher."

"Let's go, then."

"What about his things?" Pat asks.

Slipped up, O'Neal. Is she suspicious of me? Doris?

"Oh your suitcase, Jamie." Doris clumps up the stairs and comes back with a small overnight case. "I didn't bring any more of his things than I needed and Jamie has taken most of those back on his visits." She puts the suitcase down a foot from Sherwood, pulls a red bandanna out of her hip pocket and coughs into it.

Got to watch out for her. Just because she lives in filth some of the time doesn't means she's stupid. "Thank you," he says. He picks up the bag and brushes by Pat, beats her out of the house and into the car by a more than reasonable interval.

"You don't like her, do you, Sherwood?"

"No. Not much."

"Why?"

"An uneasy feeling is all. Can I be a little eccentric about people without getting written up as antisocial?" Doris Ransler is out of it now. Isn't she? What more could she do?

"I just wondered. I don't like her either, but I couldn't tell you exactly why. I do like you, though, and I feel good about your situation. I'll try to get down early next week for a visit, but I do have a heavy caseload. Several things go to court soon. If I can't get down, I'll call. If you have any trouble, any at all, I want you to promise to call me. I think you'll do fine, but if any problems come up, let's not let them get serious, okay?" She drops Sherwood and Jamie in front of Marion's, leaves copies of the custody papers.

"I'll call," Sherwood says.

He files the papers in a tin box with his birth certificate and his discharge, Jamie's birth certificate and various documents that deal with house and insurance. "We're on our way now, little dude," he says. "All we have to do is get along for two more weeks, then show the judge we still like each other."

Jamie seems a little dazed, a little unsure of himself. "That was the bad place," he says.

"Yep. It was, but you're done with it. You won't have to go back there. Ever."

"Sher?" He scuffs a foot on the kitchen floor and gives the act all his attention.

"What, Jamie?"

"Will Mommy come back? Did she go away forever?"

Finally. Quick, how to answer? He sits down and leans elbows on the table. "She didn't go away. She died."

"Died?"

"Yes."

"But where did she go?"

"She didn't go anywhere. She died and her friends cried and they took her to a cemetery and buried her in the ground so her body could spread out in the earth and be taken up again by the grass and trees and flowers." Bothered by what he knows is a lie, Sherwood considers his sister for the first time: her body encased in a thick plastic casket and pumped full of chemicals to keep it more or less intact. Uncorrupted. Incorruptible. The very material of her removed permanently from the cycle of life. The thought leaves a hollow panic in his stomach.

"Did you take her, Sher?"

"No. I was away in South Dakota. I didn't know she had died."

"You were sick in the hospital."

"Not then."

"But Sher, you got well. Why didn't Mommy?"

"Sometimes people don't. There are a lot of reasons why, but none of them would make sense to you. They don't make all that much sense to me."

"Are you going to die too, Sher?"

"Someday."

"When?"

"I wish I knew, but I don't. Most people manage to get very old and die because their bodies wear out. That's the best way, I think." You're as good as lying to him, O'Neal. But what else to do?

"Was Mommy old?"

"No, but at least she didn't know she was going to die until she did. That's the second-best way. It's hard on you and me and her friends like Erica and Josie, but it wasn't very hard on her. The worst part of dying is worrying about it. Are you old enough to understand that? It's like if I tell you I'm going to spank you after breakfast, you can't eat, can't enjoy your pancakes and that's a lot worse than if I just spanked you and got it over with so we could enjoy our breakfast."

Jamie's serious face twists into a short laugh. "That's silly, Sher. You don't spank."

"No. I haven't had reason to, but I said it to help you understand. It's the worrying about the spanking or the dying that's hard. Actually dying doesn't take too long and as soon as it's over with, it doesn't matter anymore."

"Then you go down in the ground?"

Sherwood nods.

"Where?"

"You mean where is your mother?"

"Yes. Where?"

"In the cemetery, I imagine."

"Can we go?"

No, man. You don't want to see that she's buried in a hole, and your uncle Sherwood sure as hell doesn't want to see it. "Sometime," he says.

"Now."

"You want to go see, don't you?" No way out. Go look at the grass and know she's under it: the little girl you used to fight with over the wishbone?

"Let's go now, Sher."

Sherwood pulls Jamie into his lap and rests his chin on top of the soft, dark hair.

"Too tight, Sher."

"Okay. Just let's sit a minute and let me get myself together." He takes several long breaths, shakes his head. "If you'll get the Gerry pack in case it's a long way, I'll try to find out where the cemetery is."

Jamie climbs off his lap and trots into the other room. Sherwood finds the phone book, flips through, stares at the pages with eyes that don't seem to want to focus and finally comes up with an address for "Community Cemetery."

Warm coat for Jamie, Sherwood slips into the goat coat and shoulders the pack. "It is a long way, so you might as well ride. Settle back and enjoy it."

The cemetery is about a mile and a half from Marion's. Hiking at a fast clip, trying not to notice the lively profusion of crocus and tulips and budding trees that brighten the winter lawns, Sherwood casts around for some distraction that might postpone the visit for a few hours or even days. "We could stop at a toy store," he says.

"After, Sher. I want to see Mommy in the ground."

Tall stonework posts with a wrought-iron arch between them mark the entrance to the cemetery, a loop of paved road makes a circuit around most of the graves. Beyond the loop a few occupied plots give way to lawn that flows down a shallow depression of old slough and then up a hill obviously built with a bulldozer. Site of future graves; dug entirely in landfill. A chapel that looks more like an apartment-complex recreation center sits at the end of a winding walk on the right flank of the hill.

"A park," Jamie says. "I want down, Sher."

Sherwood shrugs off the pack, lifts Jamie out and turns him loose to cross the pavement, cut through the area of newer graves and disappear into the shallow valley. More slowly, Sherwood picks his way between small headstones and little metal markers pushed into the ground on thin spikes. Jamie appears halfway up the hill and stops to examine the head of a sprinkler that sticks out of the ground. Maybe a run over fake hills will be enough for him. Sherwood scans the markers ahead of him, misses Marion's name, but catches it as he passes the foot of the grave.

MARION O'NEAL HOWARD

BORN OCT 1 1947   DIED DEC 18 1974

He stops and looks at the little plaque. The emotional drain, the burden of expected memories that had kept him away, seems suddenly silly. There is only grass and a metal plate. No sadness, no revelations, no face visible just beneath the surface of the soil. Only a piece of ground. Squatting on his heels, he examines the plot: no mound to mark the exact place, no indentation. Should have brought flowers. Even the sod strips they must have rolled over the dirt have grown together to make this part of the lawn indistinguishable from any other.

Nothing. No response.

A soft swish of feet in the grass alerts him that Jamie has come back. Sherwood points to the grave. "There it is."

Jamie leans against his knee, slides down to sit on the ground. "How can we see her?"

"We can't, small friend."

"Then how can it look like she's here?"

"That little metal thing has her name on it. Funny, even though this is where her body is buried, she's more at your house than she is here."

"She likes parks."

"Couldn't be better, then, could it?"

Jamie shakes his head.

No tears? Maybe he doesn't really understand. "If you want to cry, go ahead," Sherwood says.

"Do you feel like wanting to cry, Sher?"

Exactly—like wanting to cry, but not like crying. "No."

"I shouldn't cry when I don't hurt. Now a toy store?"

"That's the best idea I've heard today." Sherwood finds a 7-Eleven store on the way back, buys a couple of chocolate bars and a little plastic car, then stops to let Jamie play in both small parks they have to pass to get to Marion's. They don't reach the house until almost four.

"Is tonight a Josie night, Sher?"

"Josie and Erica both. Why don't you get that truck out of the dining room and stick it in your toy box with that new car. I'll put supper in to cook and make the bed. Fix this place to look like we're expecting company." He gives Jamie a piece of cheese to hold him until mealtime, then puts a small roast and potatoes in the oven. While Sherwood is making the bed, a mailman passes the living-room window, turns at the walk and approaches the house. The flap of the mail slot squeaks and a letter drops into the front hall.

"Mail," Jamie says. He scoops it up and brings it on the run.

The address is handwritten to "Woody O'Neal," rather than to Marion or Sherwood or Occupant, and the return address is Golden Goose Motel No. 3, Reno. Special gambling vacation offer to recently bereaved veterans? He tears open the envelope and reads, "Dear Art, I know you don't think we can work out, but I wouldn't be me if I didn't try one more time to convince you that I know . . ." Whoops. Three pages. Karen. Don't think *we* can work out? Sherwood takes the letter to the back hall, raps on the attic hatch with the broom handle and listens while Art crosses the ladder, hooks his rope and slides down to tap back. "Mail call." He pushes up the cover, wedges the envelope into the broom straws and passes it up. "Sorry I opened it."

"It's okay. Maybe later tonight you can mail one for me?" Art hauls up a length of rope that has dropped through the hatch, then lets the cover fall into place.

"I hope you can work it out, man," Sherwood says quietly. He checks on Jamie, who is playing with the new car in the living room, gets a bundle of broccoli out of the fridge and trims it over the sink. After several minutes he hears the ladder creak again and Art bangs on the hatch. He has managed to pry up the cover by the time Sherwood gets into the hall, and he sits on the edge of the frame to peer down, chin in his hands and eyes worried. "Art?"

"Did you read it, Woody?"

"Only as far as your name."

"She says she's coming here. Get a job, set herself up."

"That's great." Sherwood rubs his neck, already stiff from looking up. "Isn't it?"

"I don't know. Not as great as you sound like you hope. Isn't there some way you can start asking about those people? Soon? Woody, I may want to be able to get out of here in a hurry."

"I already said . . ."

"Don't put me off. I mean it."

"We can talk about it tonight if you want."

"Yeah"—Art nods—"tonight. Good," and lets the hatch fall with a bang.

Sherwood puts on water for the broccoli, checks the potatoes. The momentary anticipation of the letter addressed to him has pulled up unexpected memories: summer nights roaring up backcountry gravel roads to the little towns with their drive-ins and maybe a school dance. Don't want any of that back, do you, O'Neal; but you could miss it if you let yourself. Shaking his head, he opens the oven and pokes the roast. ". . . don't think we can work out, but I wouldn't be me . . ."? That bit of line suggests a side to Art you haven't seen. Once he has had time to think about it, he realizes he wouldn't have expected Art to turn down a woman.

"Hey, Jamie," he calls into the living room. "Find me a car and we'll play until Josie gets here."

When she does arrive, Josie is acting a little surly. First she won't play cars, then she perches on the bed and won't crawl under the coat until Jamie is almost in tears. Erica also seems upset in a yes-she-likes-rare-roast-and-no-she-doesn't-care-for-firm-baked-potatoes-and-yes-Doris's-house-was-like-a-pigsty-piled-behind-all-those-closed-doors sort of way. Sherwood puts on the food and then, before he calls them to eat, makes up a plate for Art and leaves it in the oven.

"Isn't your friend putting in formal appearances yet?" Erica asks.

Is it our "army" here that's bothering you, or is it something else, he wonders. He checks out the window. The Lincoln is gone. "Maybe tonight if that detective doesn't come back. We'll see after the kids are asleep."

She nods and with the nod manages to imply that she hadn't intended to stay that long.

Presumptuous in spite of yourself, O'Neal. "You don't have to stay if you don't want to."

"That's okay, Sherwood. I'm just tired. Haven't had a minute to stop and take stock of myself since Friday. Maybe a cup of coffee in front of your fire is what I need."

After supper Sherwood makes a fire, and the four of them roast the last of the marshmallows. At seven-thirty Erica opts for the dishes. Sherwood reads to Jamie and Josie, tucks them in, takes them water until they quiet down. Though they seem to be more keyed up than usual, Erica isn't finished with the dishes when he finally wanders into the kitchen. He pours her a cup of coffee. "You're bushed. Drink this and I'll wrap up." She moves from the sink to a chair and sits heavily. "Not as young as you used to be? Too much social life and all?"

"It isn't that," she says, then lets out a soft, ironic laugh. "Not all that, anyway."

"Sorry."

"It's all right." She laughs at herself again. "Have you ever thought you were in love, Sherwood?"

How long since you thought about it at all, O'Neal? "I suppose. Once in college, maybe. Maybe once right after I went in the Army, but that was a long time ago."

"Do you think you've outgrown it now?"

"In my particular case." He nods.

"Funny. That's what I thought. He's . . ." She lifts her hand off her knee, drops it palm up on the table and lets it flop over. "The really important thing is that Josie gets on his nerves and she doesn't like him at all. He says he just can't relate to children."

"That wouldn't be an essential thing, would it? For being in love?"

"It's damned important if you're a single mother trying to raise a daughter. I don't want Josie to grow up in a house with someone who doesn't love her, or at least like her. You must have noticed the way she's been tonight."

"Yes. I wondered. But why do you have to live with him? I can take Josie any evening. The two kids are easier than Jamie alone."

"That's fine as long as it lasts, but . . ."

"Maybe he'll change."

"Maybe."

Sherwood pours himself a cup of coffee, then wipes the last of the crumbs off the counter onto a clean plate and puts it beside the sink.

"What did you do that for?"

"The crumbs? Jamie puts them on the lawn in the morning. We watch the birds."

"Makes sense." Erica laughs and shrugs. "I never thought of that. Bird feeders, maybe, but not just crumbs on the grass."

"I have a whole flock of juncos back at the cabin."

In the attic the ladder creaks. Sherwood hears the hatch cover scrape against the frame, and the rope drops into the hall. "Let me take Art his supper."

"I still don't get to meet him?"

"Maybe." He looks out the window. No car parked on the side street. "Art?"

"Yeah?"

"You want to come and eat supper in front of the fire? Meet Erica?"

"What about the detective?"

"Not in his usual place. Let me double check." He leaves his cup on the counter and saunters through the house, hoping he looks like a man about to grab a breath of air after supper. The sky is clear, but the stars look sparse. Be like a dust storm up there from outside the cabin. The Lincoln is gone, but to make sure, he walks up and down the street, checking all the parked cars. Either the man has given up or gone off after a hotter lead. Finally Sherwood crosses the yard and re-enters the house through the back door. "Art?"

"You scared hell out of me, Woody. Didn't know who that could be coming in the back." Art comes hand over hand down the rope.

"It's clear. Maybe he got a look at that letter and is on his way to Reno. I can fix you a place in the corner under the windows so he can't see you if he drives by later."

"Is Erica out there?"

Sherwood nods. "I'll get your platform. Erica, turn off the kitchen light and take my coffee in, would you?" Without waiting for her answer he ducks into the basement, drags the platform upstairs and slides it under the swing so Art can drop onto it. In the dark kitchen he sets up Art with plate and silverware.

The combination of streetlamp and firelight puts the corner in shadow and, once there, Art is barely visible even from the chair Sherwood pulls into the middle of the room. Art's response to his introduction to Erica is a grunt and the scrape of fork against plate. Erica drops onto the bed, says, "Pleased to meet you," and leans against the wall, watching Art, as if she expects him to start something. After a tense silence, she sits up.

"You realize, Sherwood, if you're going to take care of Josie for me, I'm going to have to reciprocate."

"You already have. While I went to court. And this morning."

"That's over now."

"I have another court date in two weeks."

"But besides that, you have to be careful, Sherwood. Constant company of four-year-olds can drive you buggy. If you don't keep something going on an adult level, you'll turn into an overgrown child yourself."

"I'm doing okay."

"Think of it this way. You can't help Jamie prepare to cope with an adult world if you've lost touch with it yourself."

"Naw." Sherwood shrugs. "Well, maybe. Am I screwing up that badly?"

"You aren't screwing up, Sherwood. You're amazing." A chuckle from Art's corner puts a more urgent note in her voice. "I never met a man who could do so well with children. That first afternoon when he was just sitting there and all you'd do was look at him, I thought you were going to be terrible for him. I almost grabbed him and left." She rubs one eye with the back of her hand. "Except that he didn't want anything to do with me.

"What I'm trying to tell you is that you need to take time for yourself. Whether you know it yet or not. It's fine to get into being four years old again. Great fun, for a while. But no one can do it all the time and stay sane."

"I don't pretend to be sane."

"Nonsense. Scared, maybe, but you're sane."

Art grunts. "You tell him, girl."

Pulling her feet under her, Erica stares at the corner, then looks back to Sherwood. "Friday night there are a couple of good movies on campus. *The Maltese Falcon* and *King of Hearts*. Take your pick.

"I'll feed the kids. You can go over and have supper at the coffeehouse. That will give you an hour to find a party or whatever before the seven-o'clock showing. If nothing else comes up, you can catch one movie at seven and the other at nine."

"You got another cup of this coffee, Woody?"

"Right." Hard on you, isn't this, old friend? What wouldn't you give to go out to a movie? Sherwood takes Art's empty plate into the kitchen, returns with the coffee pot. He fills Art's cup, then Erica's, puts the pot on the hearth, and waits for an end to their uneasy silence.

"Just like it used to be at home." Art's laugh is short and bitter. "Hide in a corner and stretch my toes to the fire."

"Ease up, man."

"Erica understands, don't you, Erica? How else would she know about keeping sanity and why would she be wedging herself in here between fugitive cripples?"

"For crying out loud, Art."

"Come on, Erica. Let's have your story."

Unmoved, she watches the shadow. "It's drab. Not so dramatic as a war and none of the wounds show."

"With a disclaimer like that, you can't stop."

Fencers. Circling. Wanting to fight.

Art pushes himself into the firelight and waves a stump. "I wear mine. Show yours."

"Enough of this, man. Let her be."

"No," she says. She takes a swallow of coffee and smiles a faint apology to Sherwood. "I married a man who was too young for marriage. He was only eighteen, but already financially independent. That impressed me since I was twenty-three and just getting away from home. A long and pleasant childhood.

"He was a mechanic for a man who drove stock cars and he made us a good living. I had time to myself. During the day I took courses at the local college and then at night we'd go to the speedway and honky-tonking. It was fine. I lived in two worlds and thought I moved through both rather well."

Art laughs. "School and hot rods," he says.

"Pretty much, but then I got pregnant with Josie. I guess I expected him to lose interest in me while I was carrying her. After she was born I waited. Nothing happened. I'd stay home and read and take care of the baby while he went to the speedway and the bars. Three months of that and I got a little crazy. He hadn't hardly kissed me in a year. And he wouldn't talk to me. I'd ask him if he loved me and he'd say, what-the-hell-you-ask-that-for-I-married-you-didn't-I?

"By the time she was six months old I was so depressed I wanted to kill myself. God, was I lonely. I finally went to a women's counseling center on campus to get someone to tell me what was wrong with me. And in one afternoon, two very patient women managed to show me it wasn't all my fault.

"After my third session I picked a fight with him and got him mad enough to tell me he couldn't stand to touch me. I had produced a child inside my body and that horrified him. At the same time it made me some kind of goddess or something. I was a

mother. You know? A man just doesn't make it with a mother."
She laughs.

"I don't see how you lost anything, then," Art says.

"You wouldn't if I told you either."

"Self-pity is all you have. No wounds."

"And you recognize that readily enough, don't you?" No malice
in her voice.

"Bullshit."

"Would you rather call it something else? Bitterness?"

"Lady . . ."

"You don't fool me. I've been there, but I had Josie to think
about so I couldn't wallow in it."

Art leans into the light, face thrust forward and fist cocked in
front of him. "Damn it anyway." He jerks up his pushsticks, sending the coffee cup to bounce across the floor, and catapults himself out of the room. Sherwood hears the blanket rip, then the
platform crashes down the basement stairs.

"Bullshit is right," Erica says. She lets out a long breath and her
shoulders sag. "I didn't need that."

"I'm sorry."

"He's really swimming in it."

"Art's okay. He's had a tough time and right now there are people looking for him and all he wants is to be left alone. I'll show
you what he's working on sometime. He'll make it. He has the
will and the guts."

"I need some sleep." She shakes her head and stands up.
"Could I leave Josie here tomorrow night?"

"Sure," he says.

After she has wrapped Josie in a blanket and carried her, still
sleeping, up the street, Sherwood gets the envelope of hundred-
dollar bills he has kept hidden under his mattress, counts out two
thousand. From the top of the stairs he can hear Art plunking on
one of the finished guitars and he climbs down to stand in the
doorway and watch him play: left hand already good at the
chords, but right hand clumsy with thumb and fingers that tangle
as he tries to pick out a syncopated rhythm and melody line.

"She's bitchy," Art says without looking up. "Guts. How come
you're not getting someone else to watch the kids and seeing her?"

How come you're talking about fake ID and traveling light, and still working so hard on something that's going to be a lot of baggage? Sherwood shrugs.

"Can't answer that one, can you, Woody?"

"The answer's the same as ever."

"The same as ever." He taps the guitar. "Isn't everything always the same as ever?" and reaches up to take the sheaf of bills Sherwood holds out to him. "Karen thinks she's still in love with me."

"Is that as bad as you're making it sound?"

"Why would a nice-looking woman like her want to be saddled with a two-stump carcass like me? It doesn't make sense, Woody."

"It must make sense to her."

"Naw. She's just got some cockeyed theory left over from when we were in college. We lived together. And she was taking psych courses and somehow she got me convinced that what was wrong with me was that my parents hadn't given me love, that they'd bought me off with presents. Things instead of love.

"Problem is, Woody, I still don't think she was far from wrong. I probably would have married her if I could have gotten into grad school, but I went to Nam instead." He shrugs. "You know how that was. *Things changed.* I started sending her letters back and after a while she didn't send any more."

"So what's wrong with now? Just your legs?"

"No, man. It's as much her. Standing there with my father, coming like a dog when he called her, living right there in the house in the room next to mine; and all the time she couldn't see what he was doing. The same damned thing as ever. Another present. Come-on-home-boy-see-this-nice-nurse-I-bought-you. He got me her." Art strums the guitar strings with his right hand, but damps with his left so only a dull, thunking sound comes out. "You really don't need that money?"

Something wrong here, Art. Whatever changed was more important than you're saying. I can hear that. What did change? He shakes his head. "Marion had things set up so the estate is all but settled, but thanks."

"I can kick in for food."

"If you want, but with the insurance to cover the house and anything else that's part of what belongs to Jamie, I think we can all eat on my disability. There's something else you can do, though."

"Okay."

"Suppose I tell the judge I got into your things and that I'm making these guitars?"

"What?"

"Think about it a minute. What am I going to tell the cops about this if they come around again?"

"Tell 'em you're renting the space."

"They know those crates were yours. It'd be easier to convince them I was doing this. I'd just have to hide your legs."

"That's crazy . . ."

"If I'm going to get Jamie, I'm supposed to show that eventually I'll be able to support him without taking the disability."

"No way. You earned that money. The hard way."

"I know that and you do, but the judge just sees another bum. If I take credit for the guitars, you're covered and I can look like I'm becoming a productive citizen. By the time I would really have to stop taking the army check, I should have Jamie fixed up somewhere and it won't matter what the judge thinks. I'll help you work. Keep my hand in long enough so I can talk a good game. Make them think I know what I'm doing."

"Sure," Art says, but he shakes his head.

It's our only choice. "Not if it makes you feel that bad."

"No. It's reasonable, Woody. Damn it. Just, you're going to have to make your own guitars because I don't want to have to count on you helping make mine. You understand that?" He taps the bench. "Another thing: Did you take some scraps out of here?"

"Erica did yesterday. She and Jamie glued them onto a piece of board. Jamie calls it his boat, wants to take it in the tub, but it'll fall apart if he gets it wet."

"Uh." Art hunches his shoulders, stares at the bench, then puts down the guitar and reaches out to pick up a thin strip of mahogany and turn it over in the light. "Polyurethane," he grumbles. "Know what I really wish, Woody? When you go to that movie, steal the film and the projector and bring them back for me, would you?"

"I could pick us up an old TV."

"Yeah. That'd be better than talking to myself all night, for sure. Now, either start cutting yourself a workboard on the other bench or get out of here so I can concentrate on some work."

Taking care of both children, one trip with Jamie in the Gerry pack to pick up a used television set bought through the classified section of the local paper, two phone calls to Donald Holmes to set up guitar-making as a possible profession, one surprise visit and one regular visit by Pat Chapman to check the condition of the house and Sherwood's progress with Jamie, trip after trip to the store, three loads of wash, one workboard set up in the basement and a guitar front cut and glued and braced and presto: Sherwood's week is gone. He is not prepared for Erica, who brings Josie and a small overnight bag to the door at five forty-five Friday afternoon; not at all prepared for her cheery, "Come on, Jamie, you're coming with us to Sambo's and then we'll have popcorn and stories so Sherwood can get out of here and shake the cobwebs out of his brain." He expects Jamie to balk, but Jamie doesn't. Instead, he gives Sherwood the goat coat and takes off down the street between Erica and Josie.

No ceremony required, no hesitation, just: Here's the coat, see you in the morning, Sher. At a loss, he paces through the house, picks up the coat and a black plastic rain hat he finds in the hall closet and finally ends standing at the head of the stairs. Art isn't down from the attic yet and even if he were, he wouldn't have any sympathy for Sherwood's timidity, so Sherwood sets out; feeling awkward and flappy in the coat and pinched in Marion's hat, scuffing his feet on the sidewalk and then the grass as he crosses the park.

At the corner he stops. He has directions to the coffeehouse, but he doesn't know where the movie is supposed to be. Stopping by Sambo's to ask is out of the question. Jamie would probably be too intent on his pancake supper to notice or say anything, but Sherwood doesn't trust himself. Too much chance of wanting to join them, saying, "Okay, let's forget about this free-time business."

It occurs to him that he could throw off caution and start trying to make contact for Art's ID, and for the first time since he has come back he looks at the commune house. Where there were heavy drapes the year before, thin curtains now hang from clean windows. He can see books on shelves and stretched canvas. Large rolled sheets of paper and tubes of oil paint clutter tables in the front rooms. Either the group has changed, or has changed focus. *You're not keeping up, O'Neal.*

At length he gathers his resolve and takes the street past the old commune to the edge of campus: playing field and wide bike-path lined with small, skeletal silk trees—one hung with a small red flag that reads VIVA TANYA—and signs advertising *The Maltese Falcon* at 194 Chemistry. The location means nothing to him. He guesses that someone in the coffeehouse will know where it is, but the coffeehouse, when he finds it, is too crowded. He isn't in any shape to elbow his way through the lines so, hoping for popcorn at the movie, he sets off west among classroom and office buildings. Later he turns north into an area of coed dorms, then angles west again and south across playing fields and vacant lots bounded by roads laid out to anticipate campus expansion. Near seven o'clock he circles back to the center of campus, and half by luck comes across a small crowd that he follows to the lobby of a large classroom building. A girl in a red sweater asks if he is a student. He tells her no, and pays two dollars to get in.

The students look young. All around him he catches words and phrases about Dashiell Hammett and Lillian Hellman, about Jay Lifton and Kurt Vonnegut, Jr., and Joseph Campbell. For some, apparently, the movie is assigned work. Everyone sounds friendly, but Sherwood feels uneasy. Students as he knew them were anti-war and he half expects someone to notice his age and ask him, "Where were you during Vietnam?" Eyes and smiles seem attracted to the coat and once inside the auditorium Sherwood finds his way to the left-front row where he will have to crane his neck to see, but won't notice people staring at him.

He is hungry, half disgusted with his own discomfort and the fear that has made him pass up food and a decent seat and, to make matters worse, the movie depresses him: first with its image of Archer shot in the chest and then with Sherwood's own slow recognition that the Humphrey Bogart projected on the screen is already dead. Dead men and the shadows of dead men are too close to home. There is no hope in the plot or in the final credits or on the blank screen that follows. Blindly, he rises, jostles his way to the exit and finally becomes one of the fragments that break from the edge of the main crowd as it flows down the street like blood in an artery. "Supper, then," he says to himself. Pacing the dark sidewalk he moves with the crowd and eventually reaches the quad. Through a screen of trees, the windows of the coffee-house appear bright with interior light.

A small group of students is gathered around one table, engrossed in a chess game between two older, bearded men in jeans and jean jackets. One of the younger men gets up to take Sherwood's money for coffee, apple and tunafish bagel, and returns to the game without comment. Sherwood carries his meal outside to a large, glassed-in porch that is darker than the main room. He drops into a chair, kicks feet up on the table and stares out at the quad. The movie has left him with a pain in his chest and he scratches his scar idly. Soggy bagel, but the coffee isn't bad and the apple, when he gets to it, is crisp. One more cup of coffee and the walk back to Marion's should be enough to make a night out. Enough to satisfy Erica. Sherwood crunches on the apple. A noisy group of people comes onto the porch, takes a table halfway across the room from him and then an unexpected voice near his ear asks, "Who are you?" Sounds like she thinks she deserves an answer. He can hear her move as she takes a chair beside him, but he continues to watch the quad.

"Just another electric shadow," he says.

"I bought you a cup of coffee, but you haven't answered the question."

"Ah but I have. Take Archer in that movie they're showing across campus, chest blown open on a hillside, and then take Bogart animated beyond the grave, mix well and with a little imagination you have Sherwood O'Neal. War casualty far from the front, the idiot. Blown away by an explosive device of unknown origin, but he's still on his feet thanks to a miracle of modern medicine that is not now and never was intended to be permanent." So go away, would you? Please?

She leans forward to push the coffee cup near his hand and he catches a glimpse of red neck scarf, dark hair shot through with blond streaks. "I saw you at the movie," she says.

"Fellow fugitive from Sambo's."

Her laugh sounds genuinely amused, but the end of it is forced.

Not easy for her to bring this offering, O'Neal. "I'm sorry about
the message, but you looked lonely that morning. A lot like I felt.
I thought it might help to know you weren't the only one."

"Yes. It did help. Thank you."

"It was a mistake."

"Why?"

"I'm essentially dead." He takes his feet off the table and turns
to look at her sitting, legs toward him, tan raincoat belted at her
waist, red scarf poking over the collar. In her, he recognizes a certain weight, a seriousness he missed in the overheard snatches of
conversation at the movie. She is tall and slender, and her face is
surprisingly round. The streaks in her hair don't run all the way
up—as if she has put them in and is now growing them out. The
length of her hair, the shape of her face, both remind him of
Tsuko, and in the dim light he can't be sure she isn't part oriental.

"You don't have long to live?"

He shakes his head, surprised that her voice makes the question
sound serious without a load of phony grief.

"How long?"

"I don't know. Not long, though."

"You remind me of someone. Does that bother you?"

He shakes his head again.

"I don't usually like the coffeehouse. Do you want to go somewhere else?"

No. Time to get back to Marion's.

"A ride in the rain, maybe? I love driving in the rain and there
was a big cloud moving this way when I came in."

"Okay." Something to tell Erica or Art when you get back,
O'Neal. Dead man takes life in hand and rocks out. Ha.

Her car is a Jaguar, old and rounded at the ends, and painted a
color that he can't make out in the dark corner of the parking lot.
Inside the passenger compartment she shakes out her hair as if letting it down. "Hang on." The engine runs silently, but she backs
out of the space with a whine of tires against the damp pavement.
"This is my vice," she says. Her driving reminds him of riding a
good horse, surging against the bit from stop light to stop light
along the deserted street. The first drops of rain come down at an
angle after the last signal and then increase to a downpour that

charges straight into the headlights on the freeway. He has no idea where they are. A junction turns them west toward San Francisco at eighty or ninety miles an hour, jockeying around scattered cars that seem to putt along behind beams of headlight. Sherwood is aware of his tenuous life inside the long steel body that hurtles down the asphalt. Off through the fence, he thinks, rolling, tumbling, sliding, both of us dragging feet in wet grass. Trying to stop.

"How far do you want to go?" she asks.

"I'm just riding."

"Should we stop for coffee?"

"It doesn't matter."

"A hot buttered rum?"

"Fine."

"My place is best for that." She maneuvers through a complex interchange in Vacaville as if she were familiar with the route and heads back toward Dawville at a more relaxed speed. "I'd like to hear what happened. With the unknown device."

"I don't know what happened. Isn't that funny? It essentially ended my life and I don't remember what it was. Sometimes I flip out and have a dream about things that went before, but the dream always stops short of the end."

"Tell me."

Drops of water push up the windshield to catch the lights of oncoming cars, sparkle like silver discs. She wants to hear about it. Why? What would she do if you flipped out, O'Neal? "The dreams always start in a bar, a place I used to go to watch a friend of mine dance. I'd go see her four or five nights a week. She is always dancing and there are decorations, little round pieces of mirror hung on a red ribbon and they sparkle all behind her head. . . ."

He goes over it carefully, following the course of the dream but adding details from the life he remembers, the men adrift in another culture with no way home until their time is served, all of them depressed and crazy, hating it and at the same time loving the time as the greatest adventure of their lives; the crowded markets and the small *mama-san* stores in the villages, tiny gardens carved out on every foot of usable land, the use of plastic to manufacture everything imaginable, pottery shards mixed with old rubber zoris and bamboo chopsticks and Styrofoam packing on the beaches, the drinking, Kenny and his Vietnam stories, Bolo Point, boots smashing wet grass, and then . . . nothing. He doesn't flip out, exactly, but he loses himself in the story, succumbs to a certain savage delight in telling it that surprises him. By the time he finishes, the car is parked in a place surrounded by a complex of two- and three-story condominiums. "I got carried away," he says. "Sorry."

Beside him the woman rests her head on the steering wheel. "No. Come in."

Her apartment is directly ahead of the Jag: two stories with kitchen, dining room, half bath and spacious living room downstairs and, he assumes, several bedrooms up the circular stairway in one corner of the living room. She hangs her raincoat on a rack and reaches for the goat coat.

"I'd best stand it in a corner. It's too heavy to hang."

"Make yourself comfortable. I'll fix drinks."

She moves around a corner into the kitchen and Sherwood crosses thick carpet to a massive leather couch. Magazines: a *Scientific American, California Quarterly*, and several law journals arranged neatly on the coffee table, all carry address stickers with the name E. T. Stringham. The time is ten o'clock by the brass hands built into the rock above the fireplace. Should be back with Jamie.

Barefoot and carrying a tray just big enough for two glasses, she comes toward the couch. "Sherwood." Her voice plays with the sound of his name as if with some new word in another language.

"E. T. Stringham?"

"Tara."

In the light he can see that she is not oriental, but her round face and high cheekbones still remind him of Tsuko.

"Something to drive out the chill." She hands him the drink, sits close and touches her glass to his.

Sherwood's hand trembles a little. He leans back and stretches his arm across the sofa back. The tremor in his hand and a tired buzz in his head both give him an odd sense of time gone haywire. As if the accident had never happened. Perspective slipping, like falling.

"Are you all right?"

"I'm not sure." He feels her take the drink from his hand, feels her back press against his outstretched arm, then her hair brushes his face.

"Poor Sherwood." Tears gloss her brown eyes. "Don't try to move." Her face comes down to his and his thoughts and fears scatter. The clock hands above the fireplace move in their circles. Going nowhere. Her lips move in circles around his face. "So sad," she whispers. "Fragments of metal in the heart. Such a romantic place. So sad to be lost there." She lifts one of the glasses between them, "lost," drinks and then puts it to his mouth. The liquid has cooled a little. Fumes seem to snatch breath from his nose.

This is crazy, O'Neal. Making out here like some kid. He takes a long drink of the rum before her face falls close again.

He loses all track of time. They are on the floor, still dressed but with the buttons of his shirt and her blouse undone, when she pulls away from him. "Look," she says. She sits up and stares across the room with large, serious eyes; points toward the dining room.

Sherwood makes out an object on the sideboard: a solid wood base with slender rod fixed upright in one end. At the top of the rod another member reaches out, parallel with the base and from the member a black metal cube hangs down several inches on two wires. He doesn't understand at first, then he notices the second cube, a magnet that strains upward toward the top magnet but is held half an inch away from it by wires attached to the base. The tension in that space between the magnets creates a knot in Sherwood's stomach. He understands the small machine, its constant state of suspension, too well—and he is torn between wanting to cut the bottom strings so the lower cube can rise and wanting to cut the top to let both fall.

"People are like that," she says. "They try to come together, but their pasts keep them apart. They almost touch. Not quite. Not ever. In time the magnets will lose their strength and the one underneath will fall."

He shudders as she stands. What is this? She's broken down your resistance and now she's going to split?

"May I call you?" she asks.

Avoiding your eyes, your anger. The glasses are empty, though he can hardly remember having drunk the rum. The fireplace clock reads after one. "I answer to Marion Howard's number. In the book."

"Please lock the door. I'm sorry." Without a backward look she walks to the circular stairway and climbs out of sight.

A door closes directly over his head. Except that he is in the room with the fireplace and the clock hands without numbers he wouldn't believe it happened. He reaches for one of the glasses and notices his hand: its flesh, the joints of bone. You forgot your death, O'Neal. Surprised now at his anger, he shakes his head and laughs. What a tease. "Good night," he says.

Unsteady on his feet, he swings the heavy fur coat over his shoulder and plumps Marion's rainhat on his head, sets the lock on the front door and pulls it to as he steps outside. He has no idea where he is. No stars to guide by. North of Marion's, he thinks, with Tara's door opening toward the south. He stalks through the condominium maze, through the muddy perimeter of units under construction to a four-lane street.

Across the street and a brimful ditch on the other side, he can see a park like the cemetery, wide grassy field with hills thrown up by earth-moving machinery. Wade the damned ditch and catch cold. Let the infection kill you if it can.

Moving from streetlight to streetlight he finally finds a footbridge over the ditch and he plods across the park: a valley oak that has survived the bulldozers, playground equipment like skeletons of twisted pipe, finally a pair of buildings and a street, an intersection. B and Fourteenth. His sense of direction hasn't failed. He has nine blocks to go.

Inside Marion's living room he turns off the porchlight and stands to watch Erica's face framed by the pillow and blankets and a nest of blond hair. Odors of wood smoke and of her sleeping body catch at him.

"Sherwood?" she mumbles.

"Here at last."

"You want me to go into Marion's bed?"

"No." He moves past her, not sure what his feet are doing. Jamie and Josie sleep entwined. Sherwood leans over them and places a drunken kiss on each warm cheek, watches them snuggle closer together. "Brought the coat back," he whispers. He stands it beside the bed, flops a sleeve near Jamie's hand and wanders into the hall.

He wants to crawl into his narrow bed with Erica, but at the same time he knows he couldn't just sleep tonight. She can do without that complication, O'Neal. Can you face Marion's bed? Get over the fear that her death is contagious? You're already dead.

"What are you doing, Sherwood?"

"Fighting my ghosts."

"Are you drunk?"

"I don't know." He hears her throw back the covers. Her feet smack softly on the floor and she appears, wrapped in a quilted robe, and leans against the doorway.

"Can I help?"

His head tips forward and he shakes it slowly. "It's all on me."

She stands a minute, then turns back to bed. Sherwood grips the knob of Marion's door, twists and enters her room; lets his clothes drop to the floor and rolls between her crisp, waiting sheets.

"Good night, Sherwood," Erica calls.

"Good night," he whispers.

8

During the week before the second hearing Jamie finally throws off the general moodiness that has persisted since the visit to the cemetery. Monday at breakfast he asks where birds come from, turns off after a short explanation about mother birds hatching eggs, but perks up again when Sherwood begins to talk about migration, about how the ducks and the geese and many of the smaller birds move down the valley going south in the fall and pass again going back north in spring. They make a trip to the library and study a book full of bird pictures and colored arrows on maps that show migration routes.

Two or three days later Jamie's breakfast question is, "Do cars grow up into bulldozers?" which he clearly understands is absurd, but wants Sherwood to make up an answer complete with illustrations of freeway construction. Precarious, but he bounces back with even a fledgling sense of humor intact. Bumps and scrapes seem to heal in a matter of days, but as much as Sherwood is amazed by Jamie's resilience, the child also worries him. He still tires too easily and his falls increase in number as he gains confidence in himself. Sherwood can't imagine that so many accidents could be considered normal. Twice he tries to talk about falling down, but Jamie becomes unresponsive in a way that is too like his condition in Doris Ransler's shitty room.

On that Thursday Sherwood tries to get advice about the falls from Pat Chapman, but gives up because his worries sound like

disapproval of Jamie. The interview is a little rocky. At least the
house is clean and Jamie is affectionate and obviously happy. Pat
leaves just as Erica drops Josie at the door, and for that Sherwood
scores points. In less than two weeks as legal guardian he has arranged reciprocal baby-sitting in his neighborhood. He is set up,
established as responsible and capable in the eyes of CPS. He is in
the best position he can be for the disposition hearing.

The day of the hearing Sherwood finds both lawyers and Pat
Chapman already in their places behind the oak tables. He
marches into the courtroom with the coat thrown back on his
shoulders so Jamie can ride astraddle of his neck. The bailiff nods
and smiles. Pat waves Sherwood to her table. "It would be proper
for Jamie to sit with us," she says.

"Okay." He swings the child off his shoulders and sits him on
the edge of the table. "You heard the lady, little dude. I'll prop
you up on the coat and you can keep an eye on me at my table.
This is it. If we behave ourselves, the judge will most likely let you
come back with me and that's all there is to that. Okay?"

"Got that, Sher."

Packing the coat into the captain's chair, Sherwood puts Jamie
on top of it and folds the flap over his legs. Trying to be brave,
but it's hard. "See where that other man is sitting, Jamie? I'll be
right there."

Pat offers pencil and paper. "Would you like to draw, Jamie?"

"This shouldn't last too long, small friend."

"I'm going to draw you and me, Sher. At the park."

"Fine." Sherwood takes Donald Holmes pictures of the guitars
Art has made and they go over the proposed career schedule.

Doc Brodie slips out of the judge's chambers, nods to Sherwood
and takes a seat in the front row of benches beyond the railing.
Across the floor, Jamie is absorbed, drawing sometimes directed
and sometimes random lines on the paper.

"Amazing how much he looks like Marion," Holmes says.
"How is he?"

"Seems to be okay."

"No . . . ?" The lawyer hesitates. "Trauma? About his
mother?"

"He won't talk about it. I don't know whether I should worry about that or not."

Sherwood doesn't notice the judge until the bailiff announces "Juvenile Court of Valley County, state of . . ." Rising with the others, he glances at Jamie, who stares with wide eyes at the black-robed figure. Before Sherwood can prevent it with word or gesture, Jamie is off the chair, under the table and on his way across the floor, dragging the coat behind. Judge Gavin ignores the commotion, but then Jamie runs flat against the end of Sherwood's table. Whoa, boy. No points for this. Without hesitation, Sherwood steps around the table and scoops up child and coat.

For one long minute Jamie's eyes look dead. His body is neither limp nor rigid, but he doesn't move. "Hey, little guy." No response. Like he's back in the foster home and we're not rid of Doris Ransler yet, not now and maybe not ever. "Jamie, man. Say something," he whispers. A welt shows on the child's cheek and finally he cries. Relieved, Sherwood carries him away from the tables, past Brodie, between the chairs and pewlike benches to the back of the room. "Get it out as fast as you can. We need to finish this business. Take a look at the trees from here. We can see right into the tops of them. Bunch of cars, a fire station across the street." Jamie's sobs fill his ears. There is silence behind him. Sherwood half expects the bailiff to tap him on the shoulder. Five days for disorder in the courtroom. Oh, brother.

Finally, Jamie stifles a last whimper. "That man scares me. I want to stay with you, Sher."

"Okay. Let's go back. I don't think anyone will mind." Sherwood shuffles to his place, not daring to look at anyone, then he sits down and keeps Jamie on his lap.

The gavel raps once lightly. "This court is now in session. Mr. O'Neal, if that was staged, it was not at all necessary."

"Staged?" Sherwood croaks, then adds a hasty "Your Honor."

Judge Gavin clears his throat. "May we proceed, gentlemen? Mrs. Chapman? I would hope that since we're in basic agreement, we can do this quickly. I don't want you to think, Mr. O'Neal, that the court is rushing your nephew through these proceedings without giving serious attention to his interests. However, no one is contesting your request for custody, and Dr. Brodie maintains that there is no question about your being able to handle the responsibility. Mrs. Chapman is particularly impressed with your ability to care for this child." He clears his throat again, consults one of his three-by-five cards. "I mean, Jamie."

Jamie perks up at the sound of his name, but when nothing happens he settles back into Sherwood's lap.

"The last thing I want to resolve is this matter of support."

Already on his feet, Donald Holmes opens the envelope of pictures. "Your Honor, Mr. O'Neal has realized that he does have a skill that he might turn to earning a living. For some years he has been making guitars as a hobby. I have with me pictures of three of his guitars, valued between three hundred and seven hundred dollars each.

"We propose he continue working at home. He will be self-employed and will supplement his disability income for a year. This would seem reasonable since his primary responsibility will be to care for Jamie. After the first year, if he cannot support himself, he would like to apprentice himself to a guitar maker or guitar repairman, perhaps making use of the apprenticeship program available under the GI Bill."

The judge dips his head. "That does seem reasonable. Mrs. Chapman, you will include in your reports a record of Mr. O'Neal's progress." He glances at the clock, then back at Sherwood. "If there is nothing more, the court grants Sherwood Patrick O'Neal custody of James Patrick Howard, his nephew, under the supervision of Child Protective Services. We will require weekly inspection of the home for a period of two months, periodic inspection to be continued for one year, frequency after the initial period to be determined by the caseworker. This hearing is adjourned." Judge Gavin pushes away from the bench and stumps out of the courtroom.

Jarvis and Pat Chapman and Doc Brodie gather around to shake hands with Holmes and Sherwood. In the jumble of conversation Jamie squirms to the floor and pushes an armload of coat up to Sherwood. "Come on, Sher. Let's go to the park."

"Yes, sir, my friend, let's just do that." He half hears Pat say something about contracts and court orders and getting things all together to bring down to him in a couple of days. He says his thanks and she is gone and Jarvis is gone. Donald Holmes packs a few papers in his briefcase. "Thanks," Sherwood says.

"Keep in touch. I'd like to know how you get along and if you need any help, call me. Okay?"

"Thank you." Maybe an adoption when it comes up, but that's for later. He shakes hands, watches the lawyer leave and then meets Brodie near the door.

"You play a good game, Sherwood. Art has you making guitars?"

"Sure," he says, shaking his head to warn Brodie away from any comments about living dead men. "Let's go."

Down the hall and the stairs, out the front door and down the steps; Jamie wants to stop and play in the little courtyard in the center of the grounds, but Sherwood promises him a park in Dawville instead. In the car Sherwood sits with Jamie on his lap and watches the town unfold past the window. Brodie pilots his big Oldsmobile through streets and onto the highway, then slumps in his seat to drive and tug at his sideburns. "I want to talk to Art this time," he says.

"Stay for supper."

"Can't."

"We can try to wake him up."

"I'll want to see him alone, Sherwood."

"Fine." Matter, Doc? You don't sound good. "Jamie and I are going to a park. We'll be out of your hair."

Fingers tap the wheel, grip to pass, tap, grip, tap, reach to brush mustache or earlobe. "I want to talk to you too."

"Okay."

"After I see Art."

"Sure, Doc. I'll point out the park on the way by. You can come there when you're through at the house."

They take B Street and turn past the school. No detective again, and that's almost a week this time. Sherwood nods to himself. "Art will make it."

"I'm a little worried about both of you, Sherwood, but Art isn't the one I stuck my professional and personal neck out for."

So *that's it*, Doc. Sherwood lets the statement pass, gets out of the car with Jamie, opens the house and goes into the back hall to rap on the attic hatch with the broom handle. To his surprise, the ladder creaks immediately. Art pulls up the cover and skins down the rope.

"You get the kid, Woody?"

"Yeah. Brodie's here and wants to talk to you."

"Well, hell." Art lowers himself onto the swing seat and rubs the corner of his eye. "Congratulations."

"Thanks. You want to see Brodie, or should I send him on his way?"

"Sure I'll see Brodie. Send him down to the shop." Art pumps the swing into the stairwell to grab the rope he and Sherwood have hung there. He slides down without a backward look.

Brodie pushes around the blanket, Jamie right behind him.

"Downstairs, Doc." Sherwood takes Jamie's hand, locks the front door behind them.

The sky is clear, the air warm. Jamie hangs on Sherwood's hand, runs ahead and falls on the grass to roll as if he had planned the tumble, and comes back half proud that he didn't cry and a little sheepish in case Sherwood noticed. The park is deserted. Jamie grabs one of the swing chains and dangles, kicks his feet. "I want to climb like Art," he says.

"Good thing to learn. Build strong arms. You have to start by trying to pull yourself up. Don't climb, just grab hold above your head and try to pull your face up to your hands." Jamie flails his legs and strains and manages to lift himself an inch or two. "Keep trying. Even if you don't pull up, every time you try makes you stronger."

"Swing, Sher."

"See if you can get into the seat by yourself." He watches the child struggle onto the swing, then Sherwood pushes and watches again as the little body hurtles out and back, legs moving in time, a little out of phase, but almost pumping. "Good, man, keep it up. You're almost there. On your way."

Half an hour of swinging, climbing on the jungle gym, hanging on the bars and trying to slide down the pole leaves Sherwood a little anxious about what is happening between Art and Brodie. "You interested in going back to the house?" he asks, but Jamie wants to move from the jungle gym to the slide.

Eventually, Brodie parks his car near the play pit and comes to sit beside Sherwood on the raised lip of concrete around one of the trees.

"What's the verdict, Doc?"

"Verdict," Brodie says. Elbows propped on his knees, chin on his hands, he watches Jamie try to climb the slide the wrong way. "The analogy doesn't fit, Sherwood. I don't track down ailments like a police detective: Find out all the facts and then reach some kind of verdict. It seems that way, sometimes, but it isn't. More than I like to admit, I'm not even like a doctor. Would you believe that a lot of the time when I do come across some symptom of what can clearly be called a mental illness, I'm rarely sure whether I should treat the symptom or simply leave it alone.

"Sometimes a certain amount of plain craziness is healthy, damn it. When you start talking about more subtle aspects of mind, the best course gets harder and harder to determine. As far as I can see, Art is fine, but you know that. Better than I do. You see him every day. He seems one hell of a lot healthier mentally and he feels one whole hell of a lot better about himself than he did when his parents dragged him down to Martinez in that motorized wheelchair they had him in. But be careful, Sherwood. Your situation here is in flux. Do you understand that and how much difference it makes? You've been a kind of anchor for him and now you've taken on new responsibilities. He has stored up a lot of bitterness—and not only about the war—that he hasn't faced in any way yet."

"He'll be okay once he gets on his own." Sounds like a prayer, O'Neal, an incantation.

"Could be."

"What about this woman? The nurse?"

"Karen," Brodie says. "I'm in contact with her. Talked to her a number of times. She cares about him. A lot. I don't know how Art feels about her. He treated her badly and he's ashamed of himself. That I do know. In some ways Karen might be considered a war-related casualty. Psychologically. I may write a paper about it eventually." He strokes his mustache. "I wouldn't count on her to take Art off your hands, though.

"If Art could get himself in shape to really face her, as a person, not an object, I wouldn't worry about him at all, Sherwood. That sounds a bit vague. I apologize, but I'm afraid most of it is privileged information. Does it make any sense?"

"More than anything Art has said about her. Something else

I've wondered about: One of the cops who came looking for Art said he was back for a second tour when he was wounded."

"That's right."

"I thought he was angry at his family because he felt they'd pushed him into the Army and losing his legs. Vietnam wasn't a place you went back to unless you liked killing, was it?"

Brodie shakes his head back and forth, lets out a tired breath. "Even you, Sherwood. Sorry. I expect you not to have those ideas, but you weren't wounded there and you can't know more than what you've been told or what you've read. You're completely wrong.

"I'm not going to tell you Art's story. It's for him to tell you if he wants to. The thing you have to remember is that Art's problems didn't start with him losing his legs; and they didn't stop when he got out of the Army and out of the hospital, no matter how much he expected them to."

"Losing his legs didn't do him any good," Sherwood says.

"No, but you have to quit thinking that's the answer to everything." Brodie lets his attention wander back to Jamie where he climbs the jungle gym.

"The way you sounded in the car, I thought you had something urgent you wanted to say."

"Maybe I did. Going over your records and Art's probably got me a little worked up about this and that clinical aspect of what you are doing. I'm not immune to misconceptions." He shrugs. "We had a man break out and go off the roof last week. He wasn't one of mine, but now I wish I'd taken him. Share shrapnel scars, you know? It all adds up to make me worry when I probably don't need to. Just keep your wits about you, Sherwood. Be a little careful and you'll do okay."

"We'll get by."

"I'm sure you will. One other thing: Do you still plan to leave Jamie somewhere?"

"Not like that. I'll find someone who'll adopt him. Good permanent home. Take it through the court or whatever I have to do to make it right. I won't just dump him and run out."

"Have you checked the legality of it yet?"

Across the play pit Jamie struggles into a swing and begins to kick his feet. "Not yet," Sherwood says.

"You think that judge is going to let you take custody of Jamie so you can give him to someone else?"

"There's always an angle, Doc. I guess we'll do what we have to do and get away with as much as we can. Make sense?"

"Yes." Brodie's face breaks into a grin. "Keep in touch, would you? Especially if Art gets depressed or starts throwing things."

"Right, Doc." Sherwood walks him to his car, watches him drive away. "Let's go to the store, Jamie," he calls. "Now that we're legal, we ought to get something special to celebrate."

"Josie too?"

"That's right, man. Come on. We'll get things ready."

Sherwood makes supper an occasion with hot dogs baked in biscuit dough for Jamie and Josie, two bunches of fresh spinach lightly steamed and another bunch torn up with butter lettuce in the salad, baked potatoes and three steaks that he has found at a day-old price. There is no detective in evidence, but Art refuses to eat at the table. He gives Sherwood two sailboats, "the half-pint was wanting a boat, wasn't he? And one for his friend," and four military payment certificates—small green bills with an absurd caricature of a woman's face on the front. "Army phony money," Art says. "Use 'em for finger napkins. I know they're small, but grease them up good and let me light the fire with them when you're ready. I want to have a little ceremony of my own."

Josie brings a handful of flowers for the table; Erica, a bottle of Cabernet Sauvignon she says "someone" gave her. "I should have thrown a party for you. And don't give me that hangdog, shuffle-your-feet look, Sherwood. If you aren't feeling a little smug tonight, something is the matter with your head."

"I've had a lot of help from you and plenty of good luck."

"You've made some of your luck too." She pours the wine, grape juice for the kids and puts the salad on the table while Sherwood drains the spinach, takes the meat out of the broiler and makes up a plate for Art.

When he returns from the basement the others are seated and waiting.

"To Sherwood and Jamie," Erica says.

Halfway there and needing luck for the rest, Sherwood thinks.
They touch glasses over the table, then with Jamie and Josie.

Josie tastes her grape juice, makes a face and then drains the
glass. "Who was that food for, Sherwood? The man in the attic?"

"Yes, but I don't want you to tell anyone about him. Okay?"

She nods, but doesn't look like she means it.

"If the wrong people find out he's here, they might take Jamie
away and none of us wants that. Got it?"

Her second nod is more emphatic. "I thought Jamie made him
up in his imagination. Does he really have his legs cut off?"

"Yes."

"How?"

"Some grown-up nastiness that children shouldn't have to hear
about," Erica says.

Just whack at 'em with a sheet of flying metal splinters and
they're gone. Mention them in the wrong places and spirits
dampen. The air in the room gets noticeably colder. "Your
mother's right, Josie. You don't want to know how."

The celebration bumps along from there at an uneasy pace,
starting and stopping again with toasts to good lawyers and to
friendly social workers and to kindly, informal judges. Erica is
clearly not pleased with the MPC napkins. Things pick up a little
at the ice-cream dessert. Sherwood presents the boats. Jamie and
Josie are delighted, but Erica remains aloof from any approval of
Art.

Long before Sherwood expects, the stairway rope groans under
Art's weight as he climbs out of the basement, then his rolling
platform comes bumping up the stairs on the end of the another
rope.

Josie puts her boat on the table. "Is that him?" Her eyes are
large with fear and anticipation.

Sherwood puts a finger to his lips, waits for the sounds of Art
going into the attic. Instead, the casters rumble in the hall and he
emerges around the blanket. "Couldn't wait," he says. "Are you
ready to light the fire?" His own military-payment-certificate napkin is wadded on top of a fatigue shirt that still has unit insignia
and rank in place. "You got the rest of the funny money,
Woody?"

"I haven't heated the coffee yet."

"Skip it. I want to get to work anyway." He pushes himself through the kitchen, picks the rest of the bills off the edge of the table and rolls into the living room.

"When can we sail the boats, Sher?"

"Soon. Let's see what Art wants to do, then we'll fill the tub."

They straggle into the living room, Jamie hanging on Sherwood's arm, Josie as close to Erica as she can get; and they gather behind Art, who has pushed the firescreen aside and stuffed the fatigue shirt around the waiting logs and newspapers.

"To the end of it," Art says. Without looking at the others he strikes a match and lights the corner of the first bill. "The end of phony nickels and the phony bastards to nickel-and-dime me to death; sergeants and fathers and senators and shrinks and those three damned Presidents who thought we ought to get our asses shot off because they survived a war one way or another. End of dead crazy kids and 4F flag wavers and every sorry hero who was too stupid to be scared or too scared to remember how scared he was." A second bill flares from the first and Art touches it to the newspapers and the sleeve of the fatigue shirt. "And the brothers who wanted to get home and the ones who came home and then wanted to get back." He watches the flame. The third bill catches. "And rich contractors building roads we were supposed to die for and oil companies and cautious diplomats." Fire flickers on and off the shirttail to send up a column of thick smoke. "Career soldiers who found ways to stay stateside and crying fraggers and pushers and whores, bless the selfish bitches; and the chickenshits who ran for the borders and rotted in jail and captains and generals and fathers and sergeants . . ." Art drops the last bill on top of the now smoldering shirt, pushes his platform around so his face remains away from the rest of them and rolls out of the room. His dolly smashes down the stairs with the sound of splintering wood.

Sherwood feels Jamie's hand on his arm. Josie looks up at her mother, whose face is hidden in her hair, then looks at Sherwood. "Why is he angry?"

The last of the bills rolls off the shirt onto the hearth.

"Did it hurt when they cut off his legs?"

"It still hurts him, honey." Erica's voice is matter-of-fact, as if she has refused to let herself be moved by Art's confused litany.

"Would you like me to fill the tub so you and Jamie can play with your boats?"

For a moment Jamie hangs beside Sherwood, then he follows Erica and Josie into the bathroom. Absently, Sherwood picks up the unburned bill and tosses it between two of the logs. Whatever your past is, old friend, there is an end to it. There has to be an end. Cut off that damned bottom magnet and throw the thing away. He watches the bill flare up. From the bathroom comes a laugh and then the sound of running water. Downstairs something heavy hits the wall and runs a shudder up through the floor. Art? Sherwood turns away from the fire and starts for the basement; past a quick glimpse of Erica down on one knee beside the tub, her face level with two bobbing heads, Marion's untouched piano in the dining room. They can sell that if money gets tight in spite of the insurance. At the head of the stairs he hears the thump again and he climbs down in time to see Art pull himself up the doorway at the end of the hall, artificial legs strapped over his pants and spraddling awkwardly away from his body. His face is contorted with effort and rage. "Should have started weeks ago. Damned things'll work or I'll kick them to pieces." Holding with only his arms halfway up the frame, he lets out a high-pitched laugh that momentarily silences voices from the bathroom above, then he strains upward until his wooden limbs dangle. Slowly, he positions the legs. Gets them directly under him. Feet pointed straight ahead. Lets his weight onto them. "Look, Woody. No hands."

Incredible. Art stands motionless three or four seconds. A hand goes out to steady him against the frame, pulls back, flicks out again. "Let's see you do that with your heart." The hand moves out again and grips wood. Art shifts his weight, cocks one hip to raise the leg under it. With effort he swings the foot eight or ten inches in front of the other. Again he lets go, shifts his torso side to side in order to stabilize. "Now watch this." He pulls his arms close to his body, clenches his fists in front of his chest. For a moment he bobs and weaves like a clumsy fighter, then with an impatient heave he tries to pull the back leg even with the front. And falls. His shoulder slams into the wall and he twists so the same shoulder takes the shock of the floor. Air rushes out of his throat in a grunt.

Sherwood waits.

Art pushes himself up on his hands, works himself around to the doorway and sits, ready to climb the frame again.

"Guts," Sherwood says.

"Damn right." His massive arms strain against the sides of the door and he begins to force himself up.

"If you survive long enough to get tired, I'll dig up some lumber tomorrow and we can build railings. Something to steady you while you get the feel of how to move them. After you're done and walking, you can help me build a jungle gym for Jamie."

"We'll build it, but I don't need any damned railings."

Not much else in the way of helping you, then, is there? All Sherwood can do is keep an ear out for the sound of falls and check if they stop for too long. Even that might be too much. He goes upstairs one step at a time, aware of the ease with which his legs lift, bend and push through hip, knee, ankle and intricately boned foot.

Through the bathroom door, the kids appear half in and half out of the tub. Jamie's sleeve is soaked to the shoulder. Several of Josie's curls hang limp and wet against her cheek. Erica reclines across the bed in the living room, shoulders propped against the wall that trembles every time Art hits it below.

"What's he doing?"

"Learning to walk."

"I must seem callous."

How could you understand what he's been through and then had to put up with? How could I explain something I barely know myself? He lifts his shoulders and lets them drop in a tired shrug.

"Sometimes I'm even ashamed of myself, Sherwood. I don't know how to explain. I feel I'm fighting for my identity here in a funny way. Like there's a special club. No girls over five allowed. Does that make sense? I don't have to justify myself to Art. Or to you. The war wasn't all my fault." She stares out the window, then looks him in the face. "I'm sorry. It was supposed to be a celebration."

Only of the halfway mark. What about the other half, O'Neal?

Art on his own and you gone? He watches her eyes. "You said once that you almost took Jamie."

For several minutes Erica hardly seems to move. Even her breathing is so shallow that Sherwood can't detect the rise and fall of her shirt. Finally she scratches the top of one foot with the other, looks at him, looks away and then looks back again in a way that makes ritual of the gesture she has taken from Marion. "I thought you might have decided to stay."

"That isn't possible."

"Do you realize what you're getting ready to ask?"

He nods. A thirteen- or fourteen-year chunk out of your life. "What if I were to die? Instead of going back to the mountains? What if I finally got it over with?"

"No matter whether it should or not, that would make some difference."

She thinks you have a choice in this, O'Neal. Can't imagine death right here in front of her. Marion was an isolated accident. Never had friends alive in the morning and dead by the end of the afternoon, no letters delivered after the writer was gone, no watching the black B-52s take off and climb away to kill out of the sky at random without any real reason or even passion? No sense of how precarious life can be. "Maybe it's the brutality of everything. Even the equipment. The bolt on the M-14 slams back and forth with a kind of blind, metallic vengeance. And the grenades . . ." *Wrong tack.* He feels lost and out of control and for a moment he is struck by the realization like a shadow image across the back of his mind that no matter how much he tells her, it won't be real for her. Insofar as he tries to tell her *anything* that took place before his injury, it won't even be accurate or, he suddenly realizes, even real to him. The accident seems an insurmountable block between him and the rest of his past.

Erica shakes her head. "Josie, honey," she calls. "Five minutes and then we're going to have to go home."

Sherwood pinches the bridge of his nose between thumb and forefinger. "I just remembered something. About the grenade." *How could you have forgotten, O'Neal?* He watches her, still shaking her head. *She doesn't want to hear this. Have to make her understand.* "We threw grenades in basic training," he says. "Our company cadre had to supervise, and they hated doing it. Scared out of their minds. Green kids and explosives. That morning they had us throwing practice dummies, going through the motions again and again, first in pantomime and then with these hollow lead things loaded with a small charge that went bang. Then in the afternoon they had us go down in a trench and we'd move up to the bunkers three at a time, two men in concrete-shelter areas and one of the sergeants and the guy who was going to throw in the main section."

All of a sudden he can taste it again, the dryness in his throat and the nervous sweat on his upper lip. He remembers the falling leaves, red and gold and brown on the hillsides; and the sharp scents of drifting smoke through thin Missouri air. Bodies clothed in unfaded fatigues crouched over their rifles in the trench.

"When I went up, the sergeant was just a tense face and scared eyes. He held my grenade while we waited for clearance from the observation tower, said something like, 'If you screw up, O'Neal, they'll scrape us off the walls.' We were standing, looking over a shoulder-high wall and down an embankment piled against the other side. The ground was all torn up. Trees at the edge of the range were splintered and dead and some of them had been cut off by the blasts and the shrapnel so they leaned against the dead ones that were still standing.

"The grenade was odd-shaped, like two miniature flower pots jammed together with a raised seam. Its handle and pin were tinny. I couldn't believe that was all that kept the thing from going off. The body of it was heavy enough to have been solid lead. We got the order to throw: Hold it in front of the chest, grab the pin, pull grenade and pin apart, keep a grip on the handle. Don't drop it. Throw. I hadn't thrown the practice dummies very well, but that time I threw it up and out in a long arc and I could see the handle start to fall away.

"The sergeant put a hand on my shoulder, pulled me down. It seemed there should have been enough time to watch it land, but then a couple went off up the line, then mine. The power of the blast was incredible. It made the ground feel fluid. There was mud in the air, like it was hanging there. I could see smoke drift back on us, then dirt and rock and metal started to hit the ground. None of it touched me, but just as the sergeant leaned against the wall to wait for the 'all clear,' a thumb-size gob of mud

fell on the toe of his spit-shined boot. He swore, but his face had
this grin; and I realized he'd been expecting something to happen
to him all day, and it finally had and he was relieved. It wasn't
anything."

Below, Art hits the wall and sends a heavy whump to shudder
the house. Erica sits up on the bed as if pulling away from the impact.

Didn't do yourself a bit of good, O'Neal. Made her feel uncomfortable. But odd flashes from that story. There was another kind
of grenade. *Round*. Where was that? He shakes his head. "I guess
I understand how the sergeant felt. Except that I know what I'm
expecting to happen and I know it's something."

"Come on, Josie. Get dried off." Erica stands up, taps her foot.
"Do you want me to take care of Jamie this Friday?"

Sherwood nods.

"Here or at our place?"

"Here, I think. He's settled in, but I'm not sure he's ready to
spend a night somewhere else."

"Okay." She picks up her coat and Josie's from the back of a
dining-room chair. "If you could just get yourself away from it,
Sherwood." A whirl of coats, she spins into the bathroom and he
hears her, "Come on, honey. Dry off and I'll bring the boat. It's a
nice boat. We'll have to write Art a letter to say thank you."

"But Mommy, I like to go to sleep with Jamie."

"Not tonight, baby. We'll do it on Friday so Sherwood can
have some time for himself, okay?"

"No. Tonight."

"It's been a long day, Josie. We're both tired so let's not argue."
They come out together, Josie pouting but tractable.

"Is Joe coming tonight, Mommy?"

"Not until after you're in bed."

Josie looks at her mother, then at Sherwood with eyes that are
too knowing. "Why can't Sherwood be your boyfriend? Then
Jamie and I can sleep together every night."

"I don't think every night would be wise, Josie."

In spite of her matter-of-fact voice, Sherwood thinks he sees her
blush. "Good night, Josie," he says. "Good night, Erica." A
thump shudders the wall.

As soon as they are gone, Sherwood joins Jamie to push the

sailboat up and down and watch the child's eyes light up as they study the craft's straight path through the water, the rippled wake and the shadow image of the wake projected on the bottom of the tub by the bathroom light. Beautifully made toy. Tiny mahogany planks in the hull. Cabin of spruce with railings and fittings painstakingly hammered out of fret wire. A seagoing guitar, actually; mahogany back and spruce top. Bowsprit a little too thick, suggesting a neck. And something else: a harshness of design. A severity of line. Mass concentrated in the foredeck. Aggressive, O'Neal? Almost hostile if you think about it that way.

"What is that noise downstairs, Sher?"

"It's Art. You remember the legs he's been making? He's trying to learn how to walk on them."

"Does he fall down?"

"Yeah. A lot." Like you, little guy. "We may have to help him once in a while. Same as we're going to have to help you. If you keep falling down, you're going to hurt yourself."

Jamie looks away.

"I'm not getting after you. Falling is hard on your body. All I want to do is talk about it a little and maybe get you to think about what your feet are doing. Doesn't that make sense?"

Eyes on the wall, Jamie doesn't respond.

"I won't hit you and I won't put you in any shitty room just because you fall down, but we have to learn to talk about things like this."

No response.

"No?" Not yet, at any rate. "So, we'll forget about it for a while, but Jamie, there are some hard things and sooner or later we're going to have to talk about them. Understand?"

Jamie's gaze remains unfocused on the wall. After a few minutes he stirs. "Do you have to go away again?"

Oh-oh. At his age, wouldn't five months seem like forever? "I'll be here as long as you need me."

"But Erica said you would go away again and I would sleep with Josie."

"Oh that. Yes. I'll go to a movie or something on Friday. Erica will put you to bed and I'll come back after you're asleep. Same as last time. Okay?"

Jamie looks up and nods. "Take coat, Sher?"

"Sure. And you'll think about not falling down."

Though he doesn't respond, his eyes don't blank out again.

"Bedtime now. Let's get you ready for bed."

Friday night Sherwood takes a different route to campus: along the wide, windowed wing of the abandoned school across the street, through a grassy playing field and asphalt tennis court a block to the west. The sky is clear, but a sharp wind blows out of the north.

Without Sambo's for incentive, Jamie has been less willing to let him out of the house, but this time Sherwood needs the time alone and he knows it. He needs to be able to walk without a companion who has to be constantly coaxed or carried, given lengthy explanations of every odd object or unexpected event, who has to be denied or granted constant requests for candy or milk or juice.

Going to a movie doesn't appeal. The crowded coffeehouse sends Sherwood on a long walk around the duck pond behind the administration building, through an area of fallow garden plots that remind him of Okinawa's rich, well-worked earth laid out in paddies with raised, packed pathways. Beyond the gardens he comes to railroad tracks that shoot a straight line under the freeway and into the wide, machine-worked fields beyond.

"Something you're trying to understand here, O'Neal," he says. Relationships. From primitive agriculture of the family garden plot to tractors and bulldozers dragging huge plows across the land. Differences. Transformations with time and place: like the fireplace. Nothing in a straight line from this to that. Brodie's memories of the war: impure. Sherwood walks west and shortly after dark finds his way around the creek that has been dammed to create the channels and lagoons of stagnant water along the south end of the campus. "What's really bothering you is that you aren't sure how much of that grenade story might be like the accident, isn't it?" No answer to that. No response.

Moving east now, he passes the horse barns with their familiar childhood odors of fresh straw and leather and road apples scattered over the too-small paddocks that have been churned to mud by the animals' hooves. Sherwood tries to resist the memories that work their way into his thoughts around these images of animals, fields and gardens, but before he can shake free of them he feels caught by pine scent from trees along the lagoon. Yellow-brown prairie floor, fast-moving rain clouds, a ceiling of gray that hangs low over the land. Marion's last message to him, ". . . tell Jamie who his family was," carries more obligation than simply recounting lineage. There is no telling the child who his mother was without taking him to some of the places where she spent her childhood, no telling him who his grandparents were without showing him the mountains and the ranchhouses, horses, haystacks and herds of cattle. For a moment he is sorry he never met Jamie's father. That influence will have to be only genetic.

When Sherwood finally circles back to the coffeehouse, he finds it all but deserted. A few tired students with streaks of oil paint on their clothes and in their hair drink coffee in the main room. Sherwood buys a bagel and coffee and takes them onto the porch. He expects to feel depressed, but doesn't. Three oriental girls come in together and send him into a brief reverie about taking Jamie to Okinawa, but that isn't a solution. North Dakota would be a more reasonable place. Sherwood has cousins there, cousins he hasn't seen since childhood who live in a town near the Montana border. Are they a real alternative to adoption? Custody is all you've managed, O'Neal. Now you have Jamie and Art both depending on you, and you have to find a way to cut them free. Erica involved in your death now. Tara too, if you aren't careful. Watch out. Simplify. Don't get more involved. He sits in the dark and watches people come and go, talk and laugh and fill the lighted inner room with cigarette smoke and finally trickle away into the dark outside. At eleven-thirty the white-aproned workers empty coffee pots, wrap food and put it away in the bank of refrigerators, drag brooms around the floor and turn unoccupied chairs onto the tables.

No Jaguar ride tonight. Sherwood has 152 days to finish his business among the living. Tired from walking and tired of sitting, he drops his empty cup into a trashcan and makes his way back to Marion's house.

PART
TWO

1

In the mornings Jamie wakes refreshed, Sherwood less so. First thing he marks off the day on his calendar: Eighty-nine left and no progress beyond custody. Jamie breaks eggs into a bowl, and Sherwood cooks them; scrambled today, but as often over-easy or sunny side up. Mid-April sun falls thick through the kitchen windows, throws bright warmth across the table. Chinese hackberry branches scratch the screen with pale new leaves.

"Is today a Josie day, Sher?"

"Nope. Just us tonight. Tomorrow Josie and Erica come for dinner."

"Sunny today."

"Uh-huh." And here comes your pitch for the park.

"Good day to swing."

"We have to work first. If I can put in four hours downstairs, it will be lunchtime. We'll have a picnic."

"Got that." He looks at Sherwood, eyes wide with disarming innocence, turns away as if to make sure the piano hasn't disappeared from the dining room overnight, then confronts Sherwood with eyes gone crafty.

Too much on a Tuesday morning. Looks exactly like Marion trying to con me into taking her to Spring Creek or like Erica determined to hold her own even when things are more than she can handle. How did he pick this up? Sherwood reaches over and ruffles Jamie's hair. "What is that look for?"

"Today can I pound nails?"

"Let's see your hand." He examines the child's left thumb and first finger: black mark almost grown out of the fingernail, and the thumbnail only half black. "I don't know. If you forget what you're doing and mash another finger, Pat is going to be mad at me."

"I won't."

"Don't tell me that. Head first off the slide yesterday? And if I hadn't been there to catch you, we'd have stitches in your lip this morning."

Jamie twists around in his chair and stares toward the living room.

"Tell you what. I'll make a deal."

No response.

"Jamie? You want to pound nails and I want you to be more careful with yourself, so how about this: You go for a week without falling and I'll take you to the hardware store and buy you a hammer of your own so you can pound all you want. Okay?"

The small head swivels back. Jamie's eyes fix on his plate. "How long is a week?"

"Start with today when Erica and Josie don't come. Tomorrow they come to dinner, then Thursday it's just you and me, then my night out, another Josie day, Sunday when we don't have to work in the basement, and Monday when Josie comes again. If you haven't fallen down after that much time, I'll buy the hammer the next morning. How about it?"

Pushing leftover egg across his plate with a fork, Jamie nods. "Okay, Sher."

"Good." Almost two months of trying and finally we've talked, agreed to do something. Breakthrough. Amazing how good it feels. Sherwood carries his dishes to the sink, afraid his near ela-tion will give him away. "Finish eating while I clean up and we'll work."

At seven-thirty they clatter into the basement where Art, hair pulled back in a ponytail and beard already full of sawdust, perches on a stool at his waist-high bench and rubs patiently at the finish of a mahogany guitar back. Jamie stops at the shelf Sherwood has made for him, picks up a two-foot square of ply-wood and the box of scraps, carries them to his corner of Sherwood's bench that is still only two feet high on its original pack-ing-crate legs.

"Ready to work, huh?" Art nods to them and holds out a plas-tic bottle for Jamie. "Here, half-pint. I filled your glue." Before Jamie is able to drop his materials and get to the bench, Art loses patience and puts the bottle near the edge of the table.

"You're in a good mood," Sherwood says.

"I should be." He puts down the guitar, leans on the bench to turn himself and walks with an exaggerated roll of hips to the far wall. Selecting one of two assembled instruments, he carries it back to his workplace. "Made it up and down my practice steps three times this morning. I moved those damned mattresses out of there."

Sherwood winces. Three steps of white pine up to a five-by-five platform. No railings and now nothing between Art and the con-crete floor of the back bedroom. "Be careful. You'll split your skull."

"Not me, Woody. I'm going to do my first solo tomorrow night. Down to the park and back. No crutches. I'll have these sticks working by Arbor Day. Go out and uproot a damned tree in their honor." He lets out a bitter laugh, picks up a scraper and be-gins to scrape the unfinished guitar. "My father. Every year since I can remember he'd have me out behind wherever we lived about the middle of April, digging a hole so he could plant another stinking tree on Arbor Day. Always a place where some other tree, sometimes last year's, had died and I'd have to dig out dried-up roots. Mother would water the things every so often. He must have always picked places with bad soil. You'd think that one of those years, one of them would have grown, but no, he'd just plant them and swear a little when they died."

Sherwood nods, vaguely guilty that his mind is elsewhere. Still have to find a place to sell these guitars. He looks past Art to his first finished guitar where it hangs to one side of the ten Art has done. Not a bad piece of work, O'Neal. Didn't get the neck on perfectly, but it's close enough for a beginner. No. 2 is better.

"So I'll rip one up this year. In honor of these stumps I've built myself."

"I suppose I'd do the same." Yesterday's letter from Karen still

unopened on the bench. Sherwood touches his shirt pocket where
he carries a note that came in the same mail:

Dear Woody O'Neal,
    I can think of no reason why you would want to talk to me,
but I would appreciate it very much if you would come to the
fountain in Young Hall courtyard between eleven and noon on
April fifteenth. I can assure you that Arthur's detectives gave up
on me long ago. Thank you,

The card is signed Alissa Karen Schumwalter. Dawville post-
mark. In spite of her hostility he is curious to meet her. This
morning.

"Something I want to talk to you about, Woody." Art concen-
trates on pulling the scraper straight down the back of the guitar.
"Don't know how else to bring it up. I need you to set up my ID.
Soon."

"You'll be able to do it yourself."

"No. I'd be too conspicuous poking around, asking questions
about who to deal with. I'll meet whoever you get when it's time
for the money to change hands, but I need you to get out there
and break the ground. Cover me, man."

"Would you watch Jamie?"

"Don't put conditions on it, Woody. I can't keep up with him
and you know it."

Jamie sits at his corner of Sherwood's bench, head lowered, a
little too intent on squeezing glue onto the plywood. Why can't
you give him just a little time, Art? Sherwood thinks. It could
mean a lot if you would just hold the glue bottle a second longer
and hand it to him. You try, but then you pull back like you're
afraid he'll bite you if you make any contact; then as soon as
you're sure he's feeling bad, you make him some toy to patch
things up. Back where you started, but no better.

"I have to be ready to get out of here," Art says.

"Is everything okay?"

"Why shouldn't it be?"

With a shrug Sherwood turns to the task of sanding the inside
face of his fourth guitar, preparing the surface so he can put on
the sides. The wood is smooth and the tangy scents of sawdust

and slightly acid glue remind him of his father's workshops. Soon Art's lacquer covers all other odors in the room. Jamie spreads a maze of glue and scraps on his plywood base, then starts a slender tower of small pieces that slide apart time and time again.

"Try bracing it," Sherwood says. "Either make it bigger at the bottom or lean some sticks against it to keep it standing until the glue dries."

He has to sand down the tail block several times before the sides finally sit flat on the guitar face, then he begins working the lining blocks to fit the curves of the sides, shaping and sanding until everything will go into place with minimum use of clamps. Jamie loses interest in building, wanders into the other bedroom, and then comes back to get Sherwood to pull the mattresses under Art's practice steps so he can jump. Across the workroom Art mutters about the quality of the lacquer.

Why doesn't Jamie ever hurt himself when he's in there jumping? Any other time he can trip over nothing. Sherwood sands and fits, falling into the rhythm of the work.

Two hours later Jamie's tower finally stands, the base broadened and the top leaned precariously against two redwood strips. Sherwood has the sides glued to his fourth guitar and is getting ready to shave the braces on the back of his third.

"Let's go to the park, Sher."

Should stick with it longer. Aw what's the use? "Okay. Let's go. Just remember, no falls."

Jamie tears out of the room, hair flying and arms churning wildly. The crash and cry Sherwood expects, don't come.

"Quitting already, huh?"

"It's enough."

"You could be good, Woody. You have the eye and the hands, but with the kid you just can't stick hard enough. Put him in school or with a baby-sitter and you'd be making a lot of fine instruments in not much time at all." Art taps knuckles on his wooden thigh, then reaches with curled fingers to comb sawdust out of his beard. "Sorry. I forget you're just putting in time down here. Do something about my ID, would you? Before your time runs out."

You don't want to get involved with this, O'Neal. Bad for Jamie. But every time you turn Art down, he resents Jamie more.

"All right," he says. As easy as that? Just say yes. Throwing up his hands, he leaves the bench and follows Jamie upstairs, through the house to the front yard.

"I didn't fall, Sher." He sits on his trike, head down on the handlebars. For a moment he looks up, then down again. A narrow line on his forehead is already turning into a thin welt.

"That's good," Sherwood says. "You look a little sad. Like you need a hug or something."

Jamie nods.

Down on his haunches, arm around the thin shoulders, Sherwood feels the heave of a repressed sob. "Bad news, huh?"

"I didn't fall."

"It's okay. We won't count this one."

"But I didn't." He takes a long breath. "I bumped."

"It's okay, then. Wasn't a fall. Does it hurt?"

"No." Jamie pulls away, wipes nose and cheek on his sleeve. Sherwood rubs the child's back, stands to watch him pedal slowly off the lawn, his tears already half dried in the crisp morning air. Together they make their way down the block, Sherwood walking on the parking strip to stay away from the wheels of the weaving trike.

"You wouldn't tire out so fast if you'd ride in a straight line," he says. The comment brings only accentuated wobbling and a few giggles. At the corner, Sherwood waits, trike over one shoulder and Jamie by the hand while cars shoot by, takes the first break of clear street in both directions and runs. The trike bounces against his back and Jamie dawdles, pulls away to look at a piece of chrome embedded in the asphalt. "Come on, man. Cooperate."

The park playground is occupied by half a dozen mothers pushing toddlers or preschoolers in the swings, watching them climb or coaxing them down the slide. Pumping the trike wildly, Jamie looks like the other children, but in spite of the mothers' smiles, Sherwood reads uneasiness in their eyes. Poor child. Another mark on his head. What can his life be like if he comes every day with this awkward man—not wearing that ratty coat today, I see— whose cheeks always look dirty with whiskers even if he has shaved, which you haven't this morning, have you, O'Neal? He shudders, finds a place to sit in the sun at the edge of the play pit.

Jamie makes a circuit of the area, comes back to slide his trike to a stop near the swings; hops off and falls as his feet hit the ground. Sherwood looks away, looks back. Jamie rolls in the tanbark.

"What are you doing?"

"Swimming in water." He gets up and climbs into an empty swing seat. "Push, Sher."

"Okay, but you pump too. Get started on your own. Throw your legs out, back. . . ."

The mother whose three-year-old tries to pump in the next swing looks at Jamie. "How old is he?" she asks.

"Four."

"Cute. What's his name?"

"Jamie."

"I've seen you quite a bit. He's lucky to have a father who has time to take him to the park."

Tone pleasant, backhanded question. Probing like a needle. "I'm his uncle."

She nods and lets out a sigh that sounds like relief. "Here on vacation?"

"No."

"His parents are on vacation," she says as if that settles it.

You don't want to know, lady, so why are you asking? He shakes his head, "His father left them when he was a baby," gives Jamie a hard push and times his voice so the swing is at its most distant point, "and his mother is dead."

"Shame," the woman says. Cluck goes her tongue. "Poor thing." A silence, then she pulls her son out of the swing and carries him across the pit to huddle with three other mothers who already roost like birds on the walk around the edge.

"Let's go, Jamie. I want to check something for Art, then I'm supposed to meet a lady, and we'll have our picnic."

"Was that a mean lady?"

"No."

Jamie slides off the swing seat, holds up his hand for Sherwood to take. "You carry the trike, okay?" They leave the park side by side, Sherwood looking straight ahead with the trike over one shoulder, Jamie hanging by his hand and looking back. "Everyone is watching, Sher."

"We're an odd pair. People don't know what to make of us and

I'm not much help to them." He pulls Jamie across the street and hesitates in front of the commune house. Could go to campus now and stop on the way back. Could skip it the way you really want, O'Neal, but sooner or later Art has to get on his own and if this is what it takes . . . Finally he walks up and knocks at a thick door that opens at once. A tall man with puffed brown beard stares first at Jamie, then at Sherwood through large, stoned eyes. "Y'all come at a bad time," he says.

"Is there someone here who can tell me about the people who lived here a year ago?"

"I haven't been here a year ago. Far out. Man. What are you saying?"

"Is there someone else I could talk to?"

The question takes a long time to sink in. The man looks around the empty hall behind him and laughs. "Man? You want to know somebody before here?"

"That's close. If you could find someone else in the house and tell them, I imagine they'd get the idea."

"Hang tough a minute." Turning as if his head were fixed rigidly to his shoulders, he yells into the house. "Hey Red, there's a guy and a dwarf and I can't handle it."

"What do they want?" The voice is a woman's and it cuts a clear note in contrast to the man's befuddled slur.

"Somebody here before."

"Not that brush salesman again, is it?"

"Don't think so, Red."

"Bring him back, then."

Jamie's grip tightens as Sherwood puts the trike on the porch. "It's okay, man."

Sweeping his hand along his side for Sherwood to follow, the man starts down the hall. He stops at the third door and stands with his arm pointing inside. The room is large, the windows covered with butcher paper. A round-faced blond woman reclines in a nude pose on the table. The Sambo's waitress. Eight or ten people work at easels and sketch pads. The air is heavy with odors of cigarettes and turpentine. After a moment a tall woman turns away from an oil portrait of the blonde and clips toward the door. She wears a paint-smeared smock, and her reddish-brown hair is pulled into a bun that gives her a severe expression.

"Mean people, Sher. They look at that bare lady."

"This isn't the park, little dude. They aren't really staring. That lady is helping them by letting them paint pictures of her. In a while, before she gets very cold, she'll put on her clothes and paint her own picture of the person who gets up there next."

The woman fingers her bun and stops in front of them. "I'm sorry. I should have known he wouldn't be a dwarf. We can talk outside." She steps into the hall, holds the door for them and pushes it closed behind. "Are you a painter?"

"No."

"What can I do for you?"

"We're looking for whoever lived here a year ago."

Lines around her eyes and mouth become harsh, as if to match the pull of her hair, but all she says is, "They were crazy."

"A friend of mine wants to get in touch with them."

She shakes her head.

"You don't know where they are? This friend wants help finding some ID. I knew about this bunch from helping someone get away from them. This was the only place I could think to start asking. You can't give me a name? A phone number? I won't say where I got it."

"Sorry." She shrugs, starts to turn away, then turns back. "Look, whoever you are. You don't want to get mixed up in that kind of thing. A nice-looking guy and a cute kid? Those people were kooks. They wanted to wreck things. They completely wrecked this house before they left it. The co-op, Dawville Artists and Craftsmen, picked it up cheap because the building was next to worthless. There were tunnels under the floor, holes hacked through the walls, sandbags under the windows till the floor joists cracked. You're standing here as if you thought you could just walk in somewhere and talk to these nuts the way you're talking to me, but I'm telling you, no way. You should have seen it. Give you the creeps. I know it did me."

No help here at all. This ID business has been Art's main hope. What happens if you can't pull it off for him, O'Neal? Trouble, for sure.

"Okay?" Her eyes soften as if to acknowledge his dismay, and then follow the length of his arm to the hand that rests on Jamie's arm. She lets out a laugh that makes her sound pleased with her-self. "You really aren't an artist? Wood sculpture, maybe?"

Looking down, Sherwood sees sawdust and shavings embedded in a smear of glue on his sleeve, flecks of varnish still on his finger-nails. "I make guitars."

"Really?"

"Yeah. Really." Turned friendly too fast. Watch out.

"Is anything the matter?" she asks.

"No."

"You look a little like George when he's stoned and I run through something faster than his brain wants to go. What I'm getting at is that we're opening a co-op sales gallery next month and if you're interested in maybe selling guitars through it, I'd be glad to set up a time to come and see what you're doing." She smiles. "Quality control. You understand, I hope. We don't want to keep anyone out, but we want good work."

"Sure." Sherwood nods. "Okay."

"Still too fast for you?"

"A little, but I get the idea."

"How about Sunday? Will that do? Evening is best for us. Let me get your name and address." She disappears into the studio, comes out again with a clipboard. There are four names and addresses already on the top sheet and she watches while Sher-wood adds his with the red pencil. "That's close to here," she says.

"Across the park and up a block."

"Good." She shakes his hand. "Don't be a stranger, then. We're having a party Friday. Come. Bring a friend. Plenty of places for the kid to crash if you can't find a sitter."

"Thanks."

"And about those people you're looking for." Her mouth turns down at the corners. "Don't. Whatever trouble you're in, there has to be a better way."

He nods. "Could I leave Jamie's trike on your porch for a while?"

"Sure. I won't let anyone weld it into a sculpture." An older man with short hair comes down some stairs at the end of the hall and disappears into a studio that looks smaller than the room full of painters. "Bonnie's only going to hold that pose another few minutes. I have to get back to work. I'll see you Friday at the party, I hope." She opens the door, steps back into the room and waves as the door closes. "I'm Celia, by the way."

Jamie wags his hand back and forth and looks up at Sherwood.

"Feel a little like we've been run over by a friendly whirlwind, do you?" He catches sight of a clock in the last studio on their way out. "Almost eleven. Let's go to campus. I have to meet a lady and after I do, we'll get bagels and juice to eat on the quad."

"Got that."

With Jamie perched on his shoulders Sherwood is off to campus where girls fly to class on bicycles and shirtless boys throw Frisbees or baseballs on every open stretch of grass. "How do things look from up there, small friend?"

"Can we get one of those things to throw?"

"I imagine we can, but we we'll have to wait until we're in a toy store."

A coed at the information desk in the Student Union directs Sherwood to Young Hall, a three-story box with east and west ends open as walkways under the floor above. He carries Jamie into the courtyard, lifts him off his shoulders onto a wooden bench near the fountain. There is no breeze there and heat hangs heavy over the concrete. Rows of plum trees dangle leaves and branches thick with tiny knots of fruit. Water trickles from the fountain pipes. Jamie climbs off the bench and goes to float a leaf on the pond. "Bagel, Sher?"

"Soon. Let's give this lady a few minutes."

Two kids stroll by, arms around each other, then Karen appears under the east end of the building. Even at a distance he recognizes her: small and thin with the fringe of black hair that seems to tumble down her neck. Instead of the nurse's uniform she wears a white shirt open at the throat and a pair of snug jeans, but she walks with a professional assurance that sets her apart from the students. She stops just beyond comfortable range for talking. "Woody O'Neal?"

"Most people call me Sherwood. This is my nephew, Jamie, wet to the elbow. Jamie," he calls, "this is Karen."

Jamie looks up from the water, then back. Sherwood shuffles his feet and sits down, watches the woman who now seems more the coed with her head cocked to one side and her hip to the other.

"I didn't expect you to come," she says.

"That's what your note said."

Her gaze is steady, a little hostile. "Is Art still staying with you?"

Should have talked to Art about this. She doesn't even know if he's still here? What gives? "Hasn't he been answering your letters?"

"You admit you know I've been writing to him?"

The anger in her voice attracts Jamie's attention. Sherwood waves to him and winks. "Yes. I've been getting the letters and passing them on to him, so if you're having problems communicating, you'll have to blame it on something else. I'd appreciate it if you'd be civil. Jamie is easy to upset and if you upset him, this conversation is finished."

"You're sure he gets the letters?"

"Yes."

"Does he read them?"

"I assume he does. I've mailed replies for him. The last one was a couple of weeks ago."

"Three weeks."

"Okay. Three." Images of Karen taking Art's chair in the airport, of Doris Ransler's filthy house and her nurse's cap hung on Marion's rocker. Too easy to dislike this woman. "Did you have something to talk about or did you just want to stand here and convince yourself I'm stealing Art's mail?"

"Is he with you or not?"

Leaning back, Sherwood stretches his legs in front of the bench. "Art can take care of himself. I'm not holding him against his will and I'm not isolating him from anyone he wants to see, and if you're his friend, we aren't enemies."

"You're wrong," she says. "Not about being friends. I'm his friend, but you're wrong about not isolating him. You are isolating him, and it isn't good for him. Believe me."

"He was better off with his parents, maybe? Stuck up on the third floor so he couldn't get out. Or did they put in an elevator he wasn't telling me about?"

"It wasn't that way. Don't you see? He has to come to terms with them and he can't do it by hiding."

"I doubt he was doing much better as a virtual prisoner."

"He didn't think it was so bad for a while."

Sherwood stares at her, wondering if she meant him to hear the wounded intimacy in her voice. Almost immediately her eyes widen and she blushes. "Look," he says. "I don't know anything about your relationship with Art, but getting mixed up in whatever his family wants from him isn't helping you. He doesn't want anything to do with them."

"You're sure of that?"

"Yes."

"Then why didn't he just leave? He could have. Any time. Why take five thousand dollars of his father's money with him? The truth is he took the money because he was afraid that this time they'd let him go and he had to have something to make sure they couldn't."

Interesting idea. The lady's not lacking in subtlety, O'Neal, watch out. "If that's all, I think Jamie and I are ready to get some lunch."

"Wait." Her body goes rigid and her fists tighten. "I want to see him."

"That's not my decision."

"It damn well is. If you don't let him know I'm here and want to see him, you're as good as making the decision for him."

For a moment she reminds him of Doris saying, ". . . if you impose a different authority. . . ." "Lady," he says, "Art makes his own decisions and from what he's told me, you blew it when you went to work for his father."

"What?" Her eyes glisten with anger.

"Bought and paid for. Something his father got him to keep him home and quiet."

Karen's anger goes out like a light and is replaced by grief so naked that Sherwood is ashamed of himself. He glances at Jamie, still playing in the fountain, to make sure the child hasn't overheard.

She shakes her head, eyes large and damp and avoiding his. "I didn't know any other way to find him. All those years I thought he'd been killed; then I saw one of the classified ads his father put in the paper."

Classified ad? No wonder they were always catching up.

"And it's funny." A strained laugh slips out with the words. "I recognized the phone number. It was his father's office phone and

Art never could remember it so he kept it written on a slip of paper taped above the phone in the kitchen. I called and found out he was alive." She has to stop and turn away. "My timing was rotten," she says. "I was vulnerable. My mother thinks I've become obsessed. Am I embarrassing you?"

"No."

Her eyes flick up to his face and study him with interest for the first time. "I doubt you can imagine how it feels to love someone and think he's dead and then find him again. So changed. But the same too; still that same . . ." Balling her fist, she shakes it as if trying to squeeze out a word. "He still has that way of understanding people. And he doesn't bullshit." She lets her eyes drift beyond Sherwood, stares at something in the distance.

We're not talking about the same Art. No doubt about that, Sherwood thinks; but before he can say anything she squares her shoulders and takes a deep breath. "At first, I thought he'd let me think he was dead because of his legs. As if losing them had erased everything that went before. Kevin helped me work out how wrong I was there."

Kevin? "You mean Brodie?"

Karen nods. "Art really thinks that? Something his father bought for him?"

"I'm sorry," Sherwood says.

"It's not anything you did. Please tell him I want to see him . . . my phone number isn't in the book yet, but he could call information for it."

"All right. I'll tell him." To his surprise she offers her hand, then she turns on her heel and walks back down the courtyard. She doesn't look as confident as she did when she arrived, but something of her professional manner remains in her gait. Sorry, Sherwood thinks. He's a fool to let you go. "Okay, Jamie," he says, "let's get some lunch." He loads the child onto his shoulders. "Art isn't going to be happy about my progress with his ID. Even if it probably isn't a reasonable alternative."

"What is ID, Sher?"

"Pieces of paper that say who you are."

"Do I have ID?"

"Yes, but you don't have to carry it with you. I do, though, and so does Art."

"But Art needs one."

"He needs new ones. He doesn't want to be who he is anymore, which is tough to start with and maybe impossible when it comes to getting the right papers." He can feel Jamie become too still on his shoulders.

"Art doesn't want to be Art?"

"That's right."

"But . . ." The child fidgets. "What will his mommy say?"

"Hey, small friend? He's grown up. It's not serious when you're old enough to fight a war." *Better avoid this.* "You ready for that picnic? Bagels and juice?"

A woman passing by gives Jamie a strange look. Sherwood cranes his neck, tips Jamie off his shoulders to catch a glimpse of drawn mouth and distant gaze. At first he doesn't seem to hear, then his eyes focus and he pulls himself upright. "Bagels and juice," he says.

"On our way, then," Sherwood says. He heads toward the center of campus, thinking: stupid, O'Neal. He'll have to talk about Marion sooner or later and it would be better to let him get it done before you leave. Afraid of it, though, aren't you?

The coffeehouse is jammed with noon crowd. Sherwood manages to get one large paper cup of juice and two bagels. He hands the bagels to Jamie to hold while he pays and flees the chaos through the enclosed porch and across the more heavily used half of the quad to the sidelines of a touch football game. "Looks like a good place," he says. "We can eat and watch the game."

"What is it, Sher?"

"You don't know football?" He holds the cup to Jamie, who drinks a little and spills a little more down his shirt. Three months and still you don't have sense enough to grab napkins. At least there aren't any park mothers to disapprove. An entirely more grubby, earthy-looking bunch of kids running around the quad. He unwraps a bagel, hands half to Jamie.

Apparently absorbed in the action of the ball game, the child tastes, then leans against Sherwood's leg and chews. "I like this, Sher."

"I do too."

"Footabeel."

"What? You mean football?"

Jamie laughs. "A footabeel. Everybody runs and fights." He waves one arm and laughs, says it again and again as if the sound of the word pleases him.

"Where do you get this footabeel?"

"Footabeel." With a shrug and a smug look Jamie turns back to the field. "More bagelabeel, Sher."

"A real nut, my friend. Or is that nutabeel?" He unwraps the second bagel and gives Jamie half. A chime rings twelve-thirty from the top of the Student Union. Scents of the tall pine and fir trees along the walkway mix with the odor of crushed grass in the still and warming air. People drift across the quad, skirt the playing area. Sherwood is aware of four or five people who have found places to sit some distance away, but someone settles too close and Sherwood's neck and shoulders go tense. What are you afraid of? Knife in the ribs to cheat a ruined heart of its death? He laughs at himself, shakes his head and leans back on one arm to sneak a look.

E. Tara Stringham.

She has been watching him and she drops her head to hide behind a magazine. After a moment she looks up. Sherwood motions for her to come over. "Are you sure?" she asks. She is so close he expects her to close the distance between them by scooting on hands and knees. Instead she gets up, takes two short steps and sinks down again with her legs curled under her.

Jamie twists around, looks at her and turns back to the game.

"Hey, Jamie. This is Tara," he says and, when the child doesn't respond, "aren't you going to say hi?"

No response.

"Sorry. He's lost in the football game."

"Footabeel."

"Right, man. Footabeel. You were going to call."

"You could have called. I'm in the book."

"The address looked wrong."

"I kept the same number."

He nods, shrugs. Jamie's elbow pokes into his thigh as the child shifts position to follow the action upfield. Sherwood lets out a long, controlled breath.

"I'd like to see you again, Sherwood."

"Same here, but there isn't a lot of point in it."

She stares at Jamie and then at her hands folded in her lap. "We could make it good, though. Do crazy things, things we've always wanted to do but didn't feel like we dared. . . . I know I should have called. I did say I would. When can we talk?"

"Friday night? There's a party."

"Oooh." Her voice sounds distressed and is loud enough to pull Jamie's attention from the game. "I can't. Not then. Saturday?"

"You could come over. I take care of Jamie and his friend."

"No. That isn't right."

"Sher, I want my trike." Jamie pulls on Sherwood's arm. "I want my trike."

"Hang on a minute, man. A week from Friday?"

Tara nods.

"Want trike, want trike, Sher."

Baby talk? "Are you getting sick?" The forehead does feel a little warm under his hand and Jamie's cheeks look flushed.

"Pick me up?" Tara asks.

"No car. Meet me in the park. That little one on B Street between Fourth and Fifth."

"Trike," Jamie yells.

"Easy, man. We'll get your trike in a minute." He stands up with Tara, feeling like he is moving away from Jamie, who kicks and begins to scream.

"Trike. Trike, trike-trike."

"A week from Friday," she says. She turns away and leaves with long steps that seem timed to Jamie's shrieks.

"What's gotten into you, Jamie?" Drawing stares again. Unsympathetic eyes. What-have-you-done-to-that-poor-child? stares. Pitying glances of "Tough to be stuck with a rotten kid, isn't it?" He loads Jamie still screaming over his shoulder and angry, embarrassed he strides off the quad.

Trike duly retrieved, Jamie quieted and put down for a nap, Sherwood settles at last onto the basement floor beside his low bench and begins to shave the rough-cut braces on the back of his third guitar into the tapered, elegant shapes that will provide strength without deadening the sound. Art stalks up and down the room with his hip-twisting gait.

"So that's the end of it? Some woman tells you she doesn't know where they went and that's all?"

"I don't know. No flood of better ideas comes to mind. She said the way they left the house looked nasty. Too much like the military. Same mentality, Art, just pointed in a different direction."

"You with a short sheet upstairs, talking about the same mentality?"

"It's not the same, man."

Art swings himself around on his wooden legs, and his angry eyes meet Sherwood's. "Same or not, I have to do something. Soon."

"Do you have to change your identity?"

"What else am I going to do? Another three months, you'll be gone and here I'll be. Vulnerable. Damn, I hate that."

"What about Karen?"

"What about her?"

"I saw her today."

"You saw her? Where?"

"On campus. She thinks I haven't been giving you her letters."

"And you stopped and talked to her?"

Blew it, O'Neal. No idea he'd be this upset. "I didn't tell her where you are. Not that she didn't want to know. She wants to see you."

"Oh man." Art shakes his head. "What am I going to do about her? It'd be easier if I could just disappear."

"You could see her and tell her to get lost."

"No," he snaps. "Keep out of it, Woody. If you can't do the things I want, don't do anything. Don't see her again. Nothing."

"Ease up, Art. Jamie gave me a hard time this morning and I don't need more from you." He pushes the chisel, slips and takes a deep gouge out of the brace across the lower bout.

Art stumps out of the room and down the hall, turns and comes back, his hard-soled shoes whacking against the floor. "You're not my goddamned father," he says.

The statement surprises Sherwood. He stares at the marred brace. "No. I'm not. I'm not making you stay here either."

"You going to throw me out?"

"No, man. And if you want to come back to the cabin when I go, that's okay too. Just ease up, huh?"

Throwing his body to turn his legs, Art leans against the door-frame. "I can't go back to the cabin. Can't hide all my life. I'm not another tree and I'm going to survive, but to do it, I'm going to have to travel light. It's just me, man. Alone." He clatters down the hall, then his shoes thump against the mock stairs in the back room.

Sherwood looks around the shop at the tools and benches, instruction manuals, cans of lacquer and varnish and shellac, glue, forms and workboards, the hot pipe for bending sides, finished guitars hanging on the wall. You keep talking about it, but how are you going to travel light, old friend?

Art falls with an angry grunt. Sherwood listens until he hears the wooden legs scrape the concrete; Art's muttered curse. Upstairs, Jamie is quiet in his room, cried out and sleeping after the tantrum that Sherwood doesn't understand. Putting the chisel to the marred brace on the guitar back, he works carefully, trying to erase the damage he has done.

2

The Wednesday chicken that Erica delivered on her way to work is in the oven and will be ready by six. Side dishes of rice and broccoli simmer on the stove. Sherwood sets the table for four and joins Jamie in the front yard to watch the shrubbery-covered little house wedged between duplexes in the next block.

"They came home, Sher."

"Then they'll be along in a minute. Sit down and we'll wait." Dropping onto the parking-strip grass, he pulls Jamie down beside him. "You realize you haven't fallen all day. Only five more to go."

"I *want* a hammer."

"Good." The door of Erica's house opens and Erica comes out hand and hand with Josie. Sherwood waits to let Jamie see them first.

"Can we buy it tomorrow?"

"No. If we get it now, you'll be miserable because it'll be there but you won't be able to use it." He expects some argument, but Jamie says, "Got that," and watches down the street. He seems to Sherwood to take too long to notice Erica and Josie. Going to need glasses like his grandmother?

Finally Jamie jumps up and points. "Josie, Josie." By this time Sherwood can see that Erica is balancing a long cardboard tube— from a roll of rug or canvas—on her shoulder.

Within a few feet of the curb, Josie shakes loose from her

mother and runs to give Jamie a hug. "See what Mommy got for me and Jamie, Sherwood?"

"Joe bought new carpet," Erica says. "Josie wanted the tube, but we don't have any place to put it. Can you find room?"

"Room we have." Both children latch onto Sherwood's legs. He takes one end of the tube and drags it and them toward the house. Erica slips inside and disappears into the kitchen ahead of him. "Here, kids." He dumps the tube on the living-room bed. "Maul that instead of me, okay?" Another long day, he thinks.

"No Art tonight?" Erica calls.

"He's working."

"Sulking?"

Josie still has a hand on his ankle, and Jamie clings to the other leg. A sleeve of the goat coat sticks out from under the bed. Sherwood grabs it and holds it out as if to make a tent. Sulking? It's only Wednesday and already you're needing your Friday night? "Crawl into the coat, would you, kids?" Sulking? The coat draws Jamie immediately and Josie follows. Sherwood lets the fur drop over them and then ambles into the kitchen feeling foolish and a little fed up. "Last night he sulked. Tonight, he's working."

"Oh." Erica is near the stove, a potholder in each hand.

"Lady, it's not like I'm married to him. He does what he pleases and I don't ask questions. We don't seem to need each other much anymore. You, I do need for my Friday nights. Okay?"

For a moment her back goes rigid, then her eyes flash and her mouth forms a tired smile. "I had a rough day too."

"Yesterday was worse for me, but today hasn't been worth a lot in its own right. Truth is, Art's in great spirits. He's going solo to the park tonight. Nervous, maybe, but he's not sulking."

She shakes her head, not interested in Art, but wanting to talk. "Crazy as it sounds," she says, "I almost do feel married to you."

His jaw goes slack. "I'm sorry."

"Shit, Sherwood." The obscenity surprises even Erica. She raises the potholders in front of her face, drops them again and chokes off a laugh. "Damn it anyway." Her knees give and she lets herself slide down the cupboard until she sits with her back against it, laughing quietly and wiping her eyes with the knuckles of her thumbs. "What's Josie doing?"

"Helping Jamie try to figure out how to put one of them at each end of that cardboard pipe without either if them getting out from under the coat. If they don't figure out it's too long, they may be busy all night."

Her laughter flares, but this time it's under control. "You know she doesn't like Joe and the other way around."

"She makes a point to tell me. Every chance she gets."

"Sometimes I think I've lost all the sense I gained the last three years." She raises one hand in an almost helpless gesture. "I'm sorry to put this on you."

"Go ahead."

"The funniest thing is that I feel like I'm cheating on him when I come here. I even feel like I'm cheating on him when I leave Josie with you. You have to trust someone a lot to leave your child with him. I wouldn't leave her with Joe. Not for longer than five minutes. And where do I come when I need someone to talk to?" Pursing her lips, she laughs. "Same as ever. Marion had such a good head. Had your number too, Sherwood. And you're like her. A lot like her." Erica breaks off, stares at the oven door then looks back at him. "You remember you asked me about what was between Marion and Don Holmes?"

"Yes."

"They were lovers; and don't look so surprised. Yes, he was married then and had children. He only got down to see her every other week or so and then he'd stay three or four hours and have to leave again. A couple of times she took trips with him."

Well, O'Neal, it makes sense, doesn't it? Poor Marion. Husband run out on her, parents dead, brother half dead and half crazy. How could she help but do something a little rebellious? Out of kilter with her upbringing.

"Sherwood, I can see it on your face that you don't understand."

"That weekend she was in Fresno? Job hunting? I took care of Jamie?"

"She'd just met him."

No wonder she felt so bad. "It doesn't matter," he says. "She was my sister and nothing can change that, so don't worry that anything you tell me could change the way I feel about her."

Erica looks surprised. "She told me the same thing about you once. I suppose that's how I feel." She studies his face, ducks her head to brush hair behind her ears with both hands, then lets her eyes fix on his chin. "I don't know how to put this, Sherwood. In all the time we were friends, Marion had three boyfriends. All married. You know?" She looks at him. "No. How could you? She was an attractive woman. Never hurting for offers. I think she picked married men on purpose. It wasn't some half-conscious, self-destructive thing.

"A couple of times she almost laid it on the line for me. We'd be drinking wine after the kids were in bed, and she'd be talking about her parents and about you, and about Jamie and what she wanted for him. When she'd get to her men friends, she'd balk. Like she couldn't quite bring herself to tell me. But from all she said, particularly the last year, I got the idea that she'd decided Jamie was the main focus of her life. Everything else had to fall into line behind that, including anything she wanted for herself."

She twists a strand of hair around her finger, shakes her head. "You realize you've filled her place in my life almost as well as she did?"

Shifting uneasily, Sherwood is relieved that she is looking at the floor and not at him.

"I mean, we sat for each other, and would have shared a house except it was handy to have two so we could take the kids. Between us we even managed a wardrobe that neither of us could have afforded. It got so we didn't know who's clothes belonged where.

"But that isn't what I'm trying to say. This is hard. I've been thinking about how single-minded she was, and how you're the same way. With Jamie. And this other business." She glances up, whispers, "This being dead," and shakes her head again. "I've started to realize again how much of my own life is devoted to Josie and how I've had such lousy luck with men."

Touched by her hesitation, O'Neal, and bothered, too. Something here you don't want to think about. He tries to divert her by asking if some of the clothes in Marion's closet are hers, but she cuts him off before he can get three words out.

"Every time I've gotten involved, it's been with someone who didn't like kids, Sherwood. I'm afraid I'm doing the same thing Marion was, but she knew what she was doing. I'm afraid I've been doing it to myself. Unconsciously."

"No," he says, "I doubt it. Marion was always like that. Even when she was little she'd make crazy decisions and stick by them, make them work out for her more often than not. Dad used to say she reminded him of his older sister, like it was genetic. You couldn't have picked it up from her."

"It's not that I could have picked it up. I'm just wondering." She looks away and then back and finally looks up at him. "About myself. Marion always said you should look at things at least twice."

"Yeah." Sherwood wipes one eye. "Did you mean to say some of those clothes in there are yours?"

"Some of them." She nods, finally ready to let him change the subject.

"Why didn't you take them?"

"Guilt. I couldn't when I cleaned the house. I kept thinking it was all a mistake and that she'd be back. After you came I didn't want you to think I was a ghoul."

"Take them. Tonight. I've been freezing with the windows open trying to keep the smell of them out of the room. I was going to have someone come and take them away. I didn't think they'd fit. . . ." Idiot, O'Neal.

"It's my earth-mother image, Sherwood." Her eyes sparkle at his embarrassment and she laughs. "Don't feel bad. I know I come on a little larger than life."

"You might as well have the things in the dresser too."

"No place to put them."

"Take the dresser."

"No."

"If you argue about it now, we're going to burn the rice," he says. "Want to get the kids washed? I'll put the food on."

In better spirits she gets up, hands Sherwood the potholders, and herds Jamie and Josie to the bathroom and back. She doesn't seem particularly hungry and neither, Sherwood discovers, is he. The children divide their time between the table, and the coat and tube in the living room, and finally come to sit in the kitchen doorway, where Josie tells Jamie about the bad boys at her school who sneak toy guns in and then shoot the girls in the playhouse.

"You can footabeel them," Jamie says.

"I never heard of that."

"Chase and fight."

The idea appeals to Josie, but Erica breaks in, "If the boys aren't supposed to have guns, you should tell a teacher, honey."

"The boys are bigger."

"You mean you're afraid they might hurt you?"

Josie turns her face away. "Oh Mommy."

"Maybe Jamie could go to school with you one day," Sherwood says. "You could both try his footabeel."

"That isn't any solution, Sherwood. Josie, if you want, I could talk to one of your teachers."

"No."

"That's what teachers are there for."

"But they *aren't* always there," Josie says.

"Limited usefulness of authority figures," Sherwood says. "Maybe it's better they're catching on so young."

"It isn't the same as the Army at all, Sherwood."

Josie pokes Jamie, and the two of them inch away, dragging the coat with them into the living room.

"So we hope." He scrapes chicken bones, bits of rice and broccoli from his plate onto Jamie's and carries both to the sink.

"It isn't. Maybe you should put Jamie back in nursery school. Get involved and find out."

Won't be here that long. "I'm sorry. I should have kept my mouth shut."

"Don't take it that hard. Josie knows your view of things isn't the same as mine. She can do things here she can't get away with at home and, lately, I think that's been good for her. With Joe around so much, she needs to feel a little independent."

"That reminds me. Jamie did something yesterday. Threw a fit. Kicking and screaming. I've never seen him like that before."

"What were you doing?"

"We were watching a touch football game, then someone came over and was talking to me."

Erica cocks her head, stacks odd pieces of silverware on her plate. "If you were really involved in the conversation, he was probably just jealous. That's one of the things Josie does about Joe." She laughs. "You look so surprised. It's almost a relief to know you don't think of everything."

Jealous. Better let it drop.

They clean up the kitchen, then move into the bedroom to pull things out of the closet and spread the contents of drawers on the bed. Sherwood finds boxes in the garage, and he and Erica fill them with belts and sashes, cutoffs and T-shirts, blouses, body shirts and overalls. Things she doesn't want go into sacks for the Goodwill. Jewelry, more of it than Sherwood expected; they arrange on top of the dresser.

"Most of it is junk," Erica says. "The wedding set and the pearls and the diamond necklace are worth quite a bit."

"You might as well take it all."

"Not a chance, Sherwood. You can't afford to give that away. I know you've figured out by now that money is tight."

"I'll never sell it."

"Save it for Jamie, then." She turns away, opens the top drawer of the nightstand. "I can't. . . ." With a quick intake of breath she falls silent, reaches into the drawer, "I'd forgotten she had this," and pulls out a .22 pistol that she holds between thumb and forefinger as if afraid a more sure grip will fire it.

Sherwood takes the gun and pops out the cylinder. A little paranoia must have run in the family. He knocks the bullets out and they fall to rattle together on the bed.

"God. If the kids had gotten hold of that . . ." Erica's face is pale.

The weapon doesn't bother Sherwood. He wouldn't have given it a second thought without Erica to point out its potential for disaster. Whistling through his teeth, he pokes bullets back into the chambers.

"You're not going to leave it loaded?"

"They won't get it here." He puts it on the empty top shelf in the closet. "I know a place where they won't be able to find it."

"Take it to the police. Just give it to them and get it out of everyone's reach."

"I'll have Art stash it in the attic."

"That makes about as much sense as giving it to Jamie," she snaps, then she waves a hand in front of her face. "I just don't like guns."

Hard shoes clack in the hall, move through the kitchen and dining room. "Art's on his way," Sherwood says. "I want to see him off."

In the front hall Art stands, looking out the door. His hair is slicked back, beard combed, and he wears a pair of new-looking jeans. The shoes on his feet are military and spit-shined, his fatigue shirt is freshly ironed. He taps the floor with a rosewood cane that he grips like a sword in his right hand.

"Good luck," Sherwood says.

Arts grunts.

"Are you going to the park now?" Jamie asks.

"That's right, squirt."

"Can we come too?"

"Not this trip. Some things are best done alone." He grins at Sherwood. "Decided I better take the cane." With a heave of his shoulders he stumps out.

Sherwood waits for the sound of a fall, but it doesn't come. After a discreet interval he slips into the hall, opens the door a crack and watches Art make his way down the walk, hips churning and cane raised over his head in a gesture of triumph. Go, man. All the way. He hears steps behind him and turns to see Erica with a load of dresses over her arm. "I'll take these home and bring the car back," she says.

Josie and Jamie have the cardboard tube propped against a chair and are trying to slide down it. Jamie loses interest a few minutes after Erica leaves, and he wanders without apparent purpose into his room. Sherwood gets a fresh cup of coffee, stops on the way back to watch Josie straddle the tube and bend over to look through it.

"Sher?" Jamie's voice comes into the room sounding small and far away.

"Hello, Sherwood." Josie heaves the tube onto a chair and watches him through it.

"Just a minute, Josie." Head cocked, he hears Jamie again, talking almost to himself.

"Where did Mommy go?"

Legs heavy as if in protest of what he knows is coming, Sherwood makes his way into Marion's room, where Jamie looks from the piles of clothes in boxes to the heaped bed and the now half-empty closet. He seems to be concentrating. His eyes move and stare, glaze over with blank indifference, then flicker back to life. A muscle in his cheek quivers. "Sher?"

Sherwood squats beside him and rubs the small back gently. "She doesn't need these things now, small friend."

"Down in the ground," Jamie says.

"We could go see again, take some flowers to make it look pretty."

First Jamie nods, then shakes his head. A tear rolls off his lower eyelid and spreads across his cheek. "No flowers." He wipes the tear with the back of his hand. "Not for *her*."

"It wasn't her fault, little guy."

For a moment he clenches his fists and screws up his face, a caricature of fury three and a half feet tall. "She went down in the ground and she won't come"—his voice breaks—"back." The angry look falls apart. Jamie sobs, throws himself out of Sherwood's reach into a box of blouses and burrows down. His cries are muffled in the dead room.

Nothing else to do. Dig down into her things and the smell of her and let it out. Sherwood moves to the box and tries to put his hand on Jamie's back. Jamie squirms deeper into the clothes. "When you're ready." Back to that first day? Or will the crying help? "I'm here, Jamie."

The sobs ease for a moment, almost stop; then Jamie rears out of the box to gulp air and look around the torn-up room. He lets go a wailing cry and dives in again. The volume of his scream is hardly bearable. His body rocks back and forth against the cardboard walls.

Reaching down again, Sherwood touches one shoulder. No response. He feels Josie's hand on his arm. She doesn't try to talk, just stands as if she sympathizes and isn't bothered by the cries that rise in a series of sharp, gasping barks. Sweet little girl. Bright. Bet she could handle this by herself better than you can, O'Neal. He nods to Josie and she slides her hand down his arm, kneels to pat Jamie's head. "Josie is here, Jamie. I'm here." What else to do but be here? Can't vent his grief for him. Can't even find your own grief, can you, O'Neal? Damn it, Marion, you weren't supposed to die. You were the youngest, the strongest; going to do things your own way no matter what.

He massages the rigid shoulder. Josie rubs damp black hair and finally Jamie's sobs taper off to long, heaving breaths. "Come up, Jamie. Come on." Her tugs at the shoulder and Jamie crawls out of the box into Sherwood's arms. "That should help, man. Everyone has to cry when someone he loves dies." Standing on legs cramped from kneeling, he carries Jamie into the living room.

Josie trails behind, sits on the bed with her arm around Jamie's shoulder. "Did you cry too?"

"I cried when I found out she had died," he lies. Amplifiers and drums. Woman with a magazine. Snow and ice and Art's detective on the street. *Didn't feel a thing. All tucked away and dead.*

"Mommy cried, but I didn't."

Your eyes are wet now, though. He puts an arm around her. "Are you feeling better, Jamie?"

Jamie nods.

"We are going to let Erica have your mother's things, aren't we?"

Eyes on Sherwood, he holds his head deliberately still.

"Someone should use them and we can't. I'd look silly in dresses and they're too big for Josie. They're too big for you and, anyway, you'd look as silly as I would."

A faint smile plays at the corners of Jamie's mouth and he gives a slight nod.

"You could help me carry some of the things outside, then. So we can put them in Erica's car." With Jamie and Josie close behind him he goes to pile blouses back into the box and carry it to the curb. The lights of Erica's station wagon are on. While he watches, the car rolls down the street and makes a wide U-turn.

Erica parks, then comes around to drop the back and prop up the rear window with a piece of broom handle. "Sorry I took so long."

"It's okay."

She watches the children turn back toward the house. "May I ask a personal question?"

"I suppose."

"This person you were talking to when Jamie had that tantrum was a woman, wasn't she?"

"Yeah."

"If she gets through to you, Sherwood"—her breath catches and she coughs—"you should grab hold. Forget what you think you owe Art. Or anyone. For as long as you can leave Jamie with me, forget all of us and live as much life as you can." She whirls away, takes the lawn in long strides, and bounds up the front steps.

By the time Sherwood gets to the living room, she is on her way out with a box. Jamie and Josie have moved under the coat. Sher-

wood lifts the collar to peek in at them. Jamie looks subdued, but
okay. "You two could help if you wanted. Carry light things."
Three boxes later they abandon the coat and follow Erica outside,
where they pick up things Sherwood has dropped from an over-
load, then chase up and down the lawn, Josie calling, "Footabeel,"
and Jamie running behind. He is game, but the wildness of running outside on a spring night doesn't quite take hold of him.

At last Erica lifts Josie into the front seat and closes the door.
"Say good night to Jamie, honey. We'll see him Friday."

"You want us to come help unload?"

"No thanks, Sherwood, but thank you. For listening. I'll see
you Friday."

Sherwood picks Jamie up, brushes leaves and dead grass out of
his hair. His face is flushed and he is still breathing hard from running. Grass stains mark the knees of his pants and the toes of his
shoes.

"Let's go to the park, Sher."

"Not tonight, man." He looks down the street, hoping to catch
sight of Art, but sees only sporadic traffic on Fifth. "You look like
you've had enough for a day. How about a warm bath and then
maybe a cup of hot chocolate before bed? Sound good?"

Jamie shakes his head, but doesn't offer any resistance.

"I know. It's hard to quit."

"Do people die in sleep, Sher?"

"Old people sometimes. Children don't. They're more likely to
get hurt because they're too tired to see straight. Not look where
they're going and smash into something. Know what I mean?"

Jamie nods. He lets himself be undressed, watches Sherwood
squirt bubble bath into the tub.

"Hop on the scale. I want to see how much you weigh. Hmm.
Twenty-nine pounds. Not bad." Still twenty-nine pounds? Why
doesn't he grow? "Not bad at all." Sherwood laughs to himself
and lifts Jamie into the tub. Leave it, O'Neal. When he's ready
to grow, he'll grow, just like he cried when he was ready to cry.

"I want my boat."

"Okay." He gets the sailboat and a couple of plastic farm animals from the shower stall. The boat sinks to half mast in the
bubbles. "You play a few minutes, I'll mix the chocolate."

"With marshmallows?"

"If we have any left. Keep singing or something so I can hear
you're okay in here."

"Sailboat, sail boat." Jamie laughs and pushes bubbles over the
side of the tub.

"And try not to soak the floor."

One ear tuned to Jamie and the slosh of water, he mixes cocoa
and milk in a pan. Still no sign of Art along the half block of walk
he can see from the window, and Sherwood decides that if Art
isn't back by the time Jamie's asleep, a quick trip to the park will
be in order. "It's getting quiet in there. You okay, Jamie?"

"There's a slide, Sher. Come see."

"Be careful." Leaving the pan on the stove, he fast-walks to
the bathroom in time to see Jamie perch on the sloping back of
the tub.

"See, Sher." He pushes off, slides into the water with a splash
that shoots spray to the ceiling.

"No more, man. Too dangerous."

"Aw." Twisting like a fish, Jamie stands as if to climb the back
of the tub again.

"I mean it. Sit down." He sees Jamie step and slip, grabs
for an arm. Soapy flesh squirts through his grip. Lights flash on
the surface of heaving bubbles.

Jamie's chin hits the edge of the tub. His head snaps back.
Frightened eyes go dull. He half bounces, half slides into the bubbles that splash red against the wall. The slippery body thrashes in
a canyon of harsh porcelain. Sherwood gropes. Don't flip out,
O'Neal. He doesn't know if five seconds or ten minutes have
passed by the time he puts the child, pale and gasping, on the
floor. Face, neck and chest are smeared with blood. Punctured
heart on the sailboat mast? Torn jugular? Smashed lung? Sherwood's own heart seems to be missing beats. *Not yet. I'm not
ready yet.* He wipes Jamie's chest and neck, then around his
mouth. All the blood comes from a small, ragged tear under the
point of the chin. Band-Aids won't stop the flow; towels seem to
soak it up as if sucking the pale body dry. Finally he wrings out a
cold washcloth and folds it over the chin. "Put your hand here,
Jamie. Hold this."

He positions the hand. Jamie is too quiet, too pale. In shock.
"Now don't move. I'll get something warm on you, then we're

going to the doctor." He paws through drawers for pajama bottoms, a plaid cotton robe, warm blanket. Trying not to move Jamie any more than necessary, Sherwood slips clothes on the limp body. "Keep hold of that cloth, man." Feeling a little shocky himself, he stops in the living room long enough to slip into the coat, then he is outside.

"Where are we going, Sher?"

"Erica's first." Already across the intersection, he realizes he didn't know where he was going until he had to say it. Her car is pulled nose to tail with Joe's Porsche at the curb.

"Can Josie see my cut?"

"Man, we just need the car."

Already he is more calm, but he can feel his heart smash against his ribs and hear blood whistle as it rushes past his left ear. He pounds on her door. Erica opens it.

"He split his chin," Sherwood says. "Let me use your car?"

"I'll drive."

"It's all over. I just want to see if he needs stitches. Okay? Where's the hospital?"

"I can take you," Joe says.

"It's okay. Erica? I'll get it back as soon as I can."

She picks her purse off the chair, drops a large bunch of keys into Sherwood's waiting hand. "Eighth west to Oak, turn right to the county road. Take a left and go all the way across the highway. It's in the first mile after you're out of town."

Waving a hand, Sherwood is on his way; stuffing Jamie and the blanket onto the front seat, climbing across. He finds the right key and drives, fast at first, then more slowly. "How's the chin, Jamie?"

"It doesn't hurt."

"Keep the cloth on. No sense letting it bleed any more." The child looks pale in the dashlight. How much blood has he lost; a pint, a quart? He's too calm.

"Why are we going to the hospital? I'm not sick. Will I die?"

"Not a chance. Don't worry about dying. You've just lost some blood and I want to make sure you didn't lose too much or that you didn't hurt your neck or back, and the doctor will probably want to sew the cut closed so you don't have a scar."

"Like on your chest, Sher?"

"Right."   ✺

"Will it hurt to sew?"

"Maybe a little, but not as much as it did when you cut it."

"Like pin pokes?"

As fast as Sherwood can answer questions, Jamie asks another in a monotone that gives equal weight to "Will the nurse be mad at me because I went pee in the tub?" and "Did my sailboat get broke?" "I'm cold," he says, finally.

"Scoot over here, then." He opens a flap of the coat and pulls the child inside. Off to the right he can see the silhouette of Tara's condominium building. The units that were under construction are completed now and he can't pick out her apartment. The left turn off Oak takes them away to the west past a shopping center he hadn't even known was there, then to a stoplight at the highway where a sign guides him toward the hospital straight ahead. Beyond the intersection he follows the center line through open plots of plowed land. There are no clouds and whatever light that comes from surrounding cities is lost in black, star-scattered space. "I'll have to take you to South Dakota sometime, Jamie. They have five times as many stars out there."

The hospital is small, a flat-roofed building at the edge of a parking lot in the middle of nowhere. Sherwood has half expected an older, more humane-looking place. This island of asphalt in a rich sea of tilled land gives him the shivers. His fear of it is so strong that he has to sit several minutes after he parks in order to make his hands stop shaking. "Okay, little dude. Let's see if we can get you patched up."

"Is this the hospital?"

"This is it."

Inside, the threatening atmosphere he has anticipated evaporates. Several patients in green pajamas and robes watch television in the lobby, and a young woman in white works on record folders behind the glass reception window. A siren wails in the distance.

"What's the problem?" the nurse asks.

"He cut his chin. He's lost a lot of blood and he'll probably need stitches."

Tired as she looks, she manages a reassuring smile. "It's never as bad as you think. Take him through that door behind you and go all the way to Emergency. Through the double doors at the end of the corridor."

"Where are we going, Sher?"

"To find the doctor. Hang on." They push into the back corridor, follow it through the second doors and down yet another hall toward a metal desk with a two-way radio mounted on the wall behind it. As they approach, the back doors slam open and white-coated ambulance attendants wheel in a woman on a stretcher. The radio spits static. The woman moans. Her eyes are glazed and her fluttering hand is chalk white where it moves against the sheet. Wet grass clippings glisten on one exposed red shoe.

A dumpy, dark-haired nurse pokes her head out the door of an equipment-filled room and barks, "In here with her." The voice is harsh and familiar. Doris Ransler looks from the gurney to the goat coat and then at Sherwood. "That'll make the night. Hysterical suicides and now Tarzan to the rescue. Pop him for pissing on the floor?"

Sherwood ignores her, skirts the stretcher as it passes and stands in front of the unoccupied desk. Jamie's eyes are large and his body is stiff. "Don't worry, little dude. If she gets close enough to touch you, I'll pull her toes off and feed 'em to her one at a time."

For a second Jamie looks shocked, then his mouth forms a smile. "That's silly, Sher."

"Yeah, but I won't let her near you anyway."

"Got that," Jamie says.

Over the commotion in the treatment room, Sherwood hears Doris. "Got another waiting, Mary. You better take it."

A gray-haired woman comes out as Doris's voice cuts off. She moves heavily on white, rubber-soled shoes, picks up a clipboard with a pencil dangling from a string, and hands it to Sherwood. "Fill out the first part and sign at the 'x'es. What's the problem?"

"He split his chin."

"How?"

"Cracked it on the back of the bathtub."

"Cute little guy. Let's have a look." She reaches for the wash-cloth, but Jamie whimpers and pulls away. "What's the matter here?"

"Come on, Jamie. This lady knows how to take care of cuts and she wants to look at your chin. Lean back and let her see."

"Don't touch it," Jamie says.

"Will you need to touch it?"

She shakes her head.

"Okay, man. She only wants to look." He carries Jamie to a chair, sits down and tips him back. The child winces as he peels away the washcloth. Pale skin, pink flesh and paper-white gristle lie exposed in a ragged second mouth pulled open by the angle of Jamie's head. Sherwood feels queasy and sees dancing spots.

"It's clean, at least," the nurse says. "Fill out the form. Soon as we're done up the hall, I'll send the doctor. He'll want to take some stitches."

"How many?" Jamie asks.

For the first time the nurse smiles. "About three, I should say. He'll give you something to deaden it. You won't feel anything."

"He looks awfully pale," Sherwood says.

"Mild shock. You're doing the right thing. Keep him warm. The doctor shouldn't be long." She goes back down the hall to the treatment room.

Through the open door Sherwood can see Doris and the heaving form of the woman with the red shoes. The woman moans incoherently, tries to speak, but Doris grips her by the chin, pulls back her head and feeds plastic tubing into her mouth. "Swallow this." Gagging, the woman rolls away as if to throw up over the side of the bed.

"How many did you take?"

A groaned "No" comes out a guttural "Naawgh."

"If you hadn't taken them, you wouldn't be here and I wouldn't have to do this, so let's get it done."

Low voice like a record playing too slowly, "Oye Mwant-thoo Die-gh."

"What are they doing to that lady, Sher?"

Now the other nurse, Mary, leans over the bed, obscures Sherwood's view. "Too rough. She's fading. Hold her head and I'll put it down. Easy, honey. Wake up, now. Here goes. Swallow." Protests cut off in a gurgle.

"Why are they hurting her?"

"She ate something that was bad for her. They're trying to put that tube down her throat so they can pump the bad stuff out."

"But she said she wanted to die. I heard her."

"She may think so now, but when she feels better, she'll be glad they didn't let her die."

"Because she's sick? That's why she wants to die?"

"Close enough."

"Why didn't someone put a tube down Mommy's throat when she wanted to die?"

"It wasn't like that. Your mother was in a car and it crashed and she was killed. She didn't want to die."

Grotesque sounds erupt through or around the plastic tube. Sherwood begins to feel queasy again and he tries to divert Jamie's attention. Finally one of the nurses pushes the door closed.

"But you said Mommy didn't care."

"I said it doesn't matter to her now that she's dead. Now she doesn't care. That doesn't mean she didn't want to live. Believe me, she did want to live. Had every reason to."

Looking pale and tired, Jamie nods. "If you get sick in the hospital again, you should want to die, Sher. Then someone can save you and you can stay with me."

Sherwood pulls him closer inside the coat. "Okay. I'll do my best. Now, sit up so I can fill out this form." He writes his name and Jamie's; Marion's address and phone; relationship—uncle; father—address unknown; mother—deceased. He leaves "Occupation" blank, signs three times on the lines marked with an "x."

"Did you almost die when you were in the hospital?"

"Almost."

"You got well."

Still have to talk about that. He nods. "You warm enough?"

Jamie shivers, but says he is. Too pale. What's keeping that doctor? According to the small clock on the desk, they have been waiting fifteen minutes. With the treatment room closed and sounds through the door all but inaudible, Jamie's questions drift away from death and hospitals to curiosity about the radio that occasionally crackles with police and ambulance callls. Finally the nurse, Mary, comes out and takes the clipboard from Sherwood.

She looks tired and maybe inclined to be impatient, but her face softens as she reads. "What a shame. Will you be responsible for payment?"

"Yes. How much will it be?"

"Ninety dollars for emergency room. About thirty for doctor and supplies."

Bad bite, but damned if I'll let on how hard it'll be, lady. Can't have Doris find out we aren't living like kings. Double damn. Thought we were through with her. "I'll pay it," he says.

"The doctor will be with you in a minute. I'm sorry about the wait."

Her minute stretches to ten, but finally a bearded young man in white coat, stethoscope around his neck, sandals with socks, comes out of the emergency room. "One split chin," he says. He approaches Jamie and with a sure hand peels off the washcloth.

"Don't touch," Jamie says.

"Not this time. I want to see what we'll have to do. What's your name?"

"Jamie."

"Okay, Jamie. That looks clean. How did you do it?"

"I . . ." Jamie's eyes widen and fill with tears. He glances up at Sherwood. Looks away. The light goes out of his eyes as if someone has flipped a switch.

"What's the matter, man? You fell in the tub." Doctor and nurse staring, shocked. "Quit fooling around and tell them what happened."

"I fell in the bathtub and hurt my chin," Jamie says without expression.

The doctor clears his throat. "If you'll bring him across the hall, we'll put in some stitches," he says to Sherwood, then to Jamie, "I'm not going to touch it yet, but I'll have to give you a shot. It won't be much worse than a mosquito bite and it will stop the hurting. When I sew you up, you won't feel it at all."

Withdrawing. Eyes already faded, now going blank. Sherwood puts Jamie on the examination table. "What's the matter, Jamie?"

"You may wait outside, Mr. O'Neal."

"Will you be okay, little dude?"

Jamie nods to Sherwood, then the nurse all but pushes him out of the room and closes the door behind him.

For the first few minutes he sits, then he paces up and down the hallway. The odors of the hospital bring back flashes of nights in dark rooms. Soft footsteps in the lighted halls and the drugged realization of his own powerlessness. Paralyzing fear. He tries to shake off the memories, afraid that if he lets them come, they will be worse than flipping out.

Eventually the nurse named Mary lets herself out of the small room. "You say he fell in the tub?" She reminds him of Pat Chapman, the way she poises her pen over a clipboard.

"He fell in the tub and he bled like crazy. I don't know why he was like that with the doctor. We were doing fine until then. He does that sometimes, comes up against something he doesn't want to talk or even think about and he goes blank. He does it . . ." The emergency-room door opens a crack and he can sense Doris Ransler listening from the other side. "Probably because he's just beginning to understand that his mother is dead. He can't quite face that and I imagine there are some other things he can't face either." The crack opens a little wider and he catches a glimpse of Doris's eye, watching. "You think I hit him, don't you?"

Mary, the nurse, flushes, but he can't stare her down. "I don't know," she says. "You and the child both say you didn't, but his behavior isn't normal."

"I wish I could explain it to you."

The treatment-room door eases open and the young doctor carries Jamie, Band-Aid on his chin and a Tootsie Pop in his mouth, into the hall. "He's a brave little guy. Not a whimper out of him."

"Good, small friend," Sherwood says. "How do I pay? Will you send a bill?"

"At the end of the month," the nurse says.

"What about changing the Band-Aid? Should I do something to prevent infection?"

Jamie wiggles down from the doctor's arms and walks on shaky legs to Sherwood, lets himself be gathered into the coat and blanket.

"You could change it tomorrow. Change it if it gets wet. After a day or so, he doesn't really need it. You should be aware of the possibility of infection, exercise due caution, but it's rarely a problem with facial wounds. There are a lot of blood vessels in the face and they keep the tissue cleaned out.

"It's a common injury, on the chin like that. Interestingly enough, the cut comes from inside. The chin bone cuts out rather than something cutting in. You will need to make an appointment with his regular doctor to have the stitches out in about a week."

"We don't have a doctor. This is the first time we've needed one."

"Bring him back, then. Next Wednesday. About six o'clock."

"Here?" Sherwood shakes his head.

"Yeah. That ninety-buck entry fee is a little steep. Call it a package deal. He's a good little guy and I'd like to see him again."

"Thanks," Sherwood says. "That will help a lot."

During the ride back, Jamie snuggles inside the coat and hardly says a word. The light is on behind the basement window shade, and the front door is closed. The house smells like caramelized sugar and scorched milk, but the stove burner is off and the pan of burned chocolate sits half full of water in the sink. Art made it back, and a good thing too. Sherwood takes Jamie into his room, tugs off the robe and slippers and helps him into a pajama top.

His color looks better, but he still acts subdued. His eyes are big, no longer dead. "I fell down, Sher."

"You're telling me. You ought to be more . . . oh cripes."

"Now I can't have the hammer."

Freaked out and I didn't have sense to remember the blasted hammer. Ought to call, talk to the nurse at least. No. Too phony. Jamie can tell them on Wednesday. "Didn't want to remind me."

The bottom lip protrudes and begins to tremble. "But how can I have a hammer?"

"It's okay, man. I don't even think we have to start over. It was partly my fault. I was afraid you'd fall and my grabbing for you might have made you fall, so it's almost as if I accidentally pushed you. You're going to have to tell the doctor why you clammed up the way you did. He and the nurse thought I hit you."

"That's silly." Jamie cocks his head, laughs, then becomes serious as he studies Sherwood's face. "Got that," he says.

"We know I don't even spank you, but other people don't know that." Beautiful, little guy. No idea how strange we can look to the rest of the world.

"Okay, Sher." He lets himself be put to bed, lets Sherwood drop the covers over him and lets his eyes go closed.

Small and mortal. That was too close. Sherwood touches the soft hair. Already he can hear Art's heavy tread up the stairs, but he waits a minute to let Art get settled in the kitchen. A chair scrapes the floor.

"Woody?"

"Right here."

Art sits at the table, chair turned so his feet can splay in front of him. "What happened? It's not like you to try to burn the house down."

"Jamie fell down. Split his chin . . ."

"It's a good thing I got back." He leans back and scratches his beard. "You know what I did, man? All the way to Sambo's with all those pasty-looking bug-eyed guys and gorgeous chicks. I had a cup of coffee. God, was it good." He laughs. "Someone looked at the cane and asked if I'd had a skiing accident."

"Great." You sound almost manic. Better than you have since the cabin. "Hang on a minute. I have something I want you to stash." Sherwood slips into Marion's room and takes the pistol off the closet shelf. Like giving it to Jamie? Back in the kitchen, he hands it to Art.

"Damn, Woody. Where'd you get this?"

"With Marion's things. Stash it in the attic where the kids can't get hold of it, would you?"

"Sure, man. We should have had it at the cabin." Spinning the cylinder, he sights at the kitchen light. "No. Maybe it's better to have it now."

"Careful. It's loaded."

"I may be crippled, but I'm not blind. I feel so good I could go out and shoot up a few stop signs."

"Just don't blast through the wall. You might hit Jamie."

Art lets out a high-pitched howl. "You're getting so damned domestic. I don't see why you want to go back to the cabin. You could lock yourself away right here and be just as happy."

"I've thought about that."

"You could get a good woman in that Erica, too. Sexy chick. If she had it half as much for me the way she does for you, I'd have her in the sack so fast my stumps'd smoke. She called, by the way. Wanted to know how the half-pint was."

"He's fine."

"Don't tell me. I'd go down to her place and tell her, if I were you."

"Her boyfriend's there."

"She'd dump him in a minute. You listen to old Art. If you're sticking around, grab her."

"I didn't say I could stay, only that I'd thought about it."

"You think too much." Art swings the pistol from the light fixture to the doorframe above Sherwood's head. The phone rings and he takes aim at it. "There she is. Hand me the phone and I'll say you're on your way."

Too aware of Art waving the pistol behind him, Sherwood pulls the phone out from under a corner of the living-room bed and picks up the receiver.

"Sherwood?" a woman's voice asks. "This is Tara."

"Hello."

"You didn't get another date for that party, did you?"

"No."

"Are you still game? I got out of what I had to do."

"Sure."

"Aren't you alone?"

"No."

"I'm jealous. Is she pretty?"

"He's the ugliest thing on stumps."

In the kitchen, Art scoffs, breaks the cylinder out of the pistol, knocks shells onto the table and aims the empty gun at Sherwood's head.

"He's dangerous too. You want to meet me in the park?"

"Okay. Seven-thirty? If you can't talk, I'm going to run. See you Friday."

"Seven-thirty." He lets the receiver back onto the cradle.

"That wasn't Erica," Art says.

"No."

"How could you do that, Woody? A straight shot at a woman like Erica and you get some phony chick on the line?"

"Stash the gun in the attic, would you, Art?"

"Yeah, yeah. Those people are coming to look at guitars on Sunday?"

"Right. Sunday." Sherwood leaves him sitting there, gun empty and pointed at the phone. Digging the keys out of his pocket, he climbs into Erica's station wagon, tickles it with the starter until the engine turns over, and makes a wide U-turn up the street. The silver Porsche is still parked out front. Sherwood leaves her car the way he found it, nose to tail with Joe's car, and drops her keys through the mail slot into the darkened house.

3

Friday evening is cool with a light south wind and mottled overcast that has threatened rain all afternoon. Odors of fireplace
smoke mix with the scents of stocks and roses and a few lilacs.
Sprinklers hiss in the far corner of the park. Free of the house and
the kids and Art, Sherwood sits in the swing and kicks himself
high, head back and goat coat flapping, into the lower branches of
a tulip tree. In the late twilight he can just reach back to scattered
sensations of childhood; the desire to swim triggered by the sight
or smell of any body of water, legs that used to itch with the urge
to run. Can't watch Jamie without remembering what it was like,
can you? He sticks out his legs and lets the swing coast. "Back to
the real world, O'Neal," he says. Someone else is in the park and
coming toward the swing.

"Back to the real world? That's no greeting." Tara sits in the
next swing and steadies it with one foot on the ground. Long dark
skirt, shiny-toed boots and a coat of some rich-looking fur that
she wears tight around her throat; she is dressed for a fancier party
than the one Sherwood expects at the co-op. His own boots are
scuffed. Jamie has managed to leave an indelible spot near the
knee of his new corduroy pants and his chamois cloth shirt is
shiny at the elbows. "Sorry I'm late," she says.

"You're not. Want to swing awhile?"

"I'm not dressed for it."

He twists his swing to face her and is surprised at how pretty she is: eyes that turn up at the corners, giving her that slightly oriental look, and a wide, serious mouth. Something about her, O'Neal. What is it? "You're dressed for a party, aren't you?" Pulling himself out of the swing, he offers his arm.

"My car is over there."

"Won't need it. We're just going across the street. Some artist types I met. They said come and bring a friend."

"Is it that place on the corner?"

"You know it?"

She hesitates, shakes her head. "I pass there on my way to work. It looks romantic. And on days I walk, there's that paint smell."

"They all seem to work hard at it."

"I'm sure they do, but it looks exciting to me. Know what I mean?"

Nodding, he slips an arm around the soft fur of her coat and starts across the play pit. The sprinklers have gone off, but the grass soaks their boots as they pass under the sycamores. Tara pushes close to him. Her arm finds its way around his waist. "This feels right," she whispers.

In the downstairs hall of the commune, the air is already thick with cigarette smoke mixed with odors of marijuana and beer. Sherwood finds a room full of coathangers strung on clothesline rope, stands his coat in a corner and takes Tara's.

"Wait." She reaches into her pocket and comes out with a fifth of rum. "I thought in case it was a bring-your-own."

"Sounds right." He leads her down the hall, past circulating drinkers in the smaller studios, to the main room where the easels have been taken down and stacked beside rolls of canvas and boxes of precut stretcher bars along one wall. Tables on either side of the sink serve as bar for chips and crackers and cut-up vegetables, bowls of dip, a keg of beer put down in a washtub of ice, and a small assortment of liquor bottles. Near the door the man with the puffy beard grabs Sherwood's arm. The man is stoned again, or still, and he stares a long time before he speaks.

"Where's your dwarf, man?"

"Home in bed. He's a four-year-old dwarf."

"Man. Maybe he'll get bigger, then."

"You're George, right?"

"Far out." He waves a lighted candle in front of Sherwood's face, lets go of Sherwood's arm and Sherwood notices a thick, green stick of twisted paper in George's other hand.

"Is that a cherry bomb?" he asks.

"Far, far out. You got good eyes, man. In a guitar maker's head, right?" He shakes the candle as if trying to remember. "Sherwood," he says, then turns to several people who pass a joint back and forth along the wall. "Sherwood here lives in Robin Hood Forest."

One of the smokers frowns, the others smile and a blonde, Bonnie the Sambo's waitress, breaks into desperate giggles.

"Hey, Bonnie's on her way," George says. "You want me to launch you, Bonnie?" He lets go of Sherwood's arm, brings the cherry-bomb fuse near the candle flame and starts toward her.

The frowner stops him. Bonnie slips out the door and Sherwood catches up with Tara at the bar.

"I don't care for that kind of thing," she says.

"Would you rather not stay?"

She shakes her head, but he can see she isn't sure.

"We can hang around the windows. First sign of trouble and we're gone." He glances one palm off the other.

"Okay."

The hard-liquor supply is not sufficient to last the evening. Sherwood mixes rum with Coke, then stashes the bottle under the table in an empty potato-chip sack. "You want to look at paintings or find the crowds and music?"

"Paintings," she says. "I still feel a little prim for dancing."

Drinks in hand, they wander through the downstairs studios. Tara seems distant. This could turn into a downer, he thinks. "If you see anyone you know, introduce me. The freak with the firecracker is the only familiar face I've seen and he wasn't someone I'd want to get close to."

"I know." Her voice is flat, but her eyes devour paintings one after another. She seems to prefer figure studies and landscapes, and she ignores the abstracts until, in the last studio, they confront a huge painting. Blue and green, red, white and black rectangles and triangles and a number of oddly organic-looking curved lines. "Ugly," she says. "Flat and closed. I think it's depressing."

Sherwood agrees, looks around the room for something else and is surprised to discover that the painting is the only one in the room. He looks at it again: done on two canvases, each six feet by eight feet with a gap between them that appears to swallow parts of the geometrical figures. There is an engaging complexity about the thing, a use of the space between the two canvases as an element in the painting and then, with a rush that is almost physical, he sees the flat surface appear to collapse into itself and form cubes, empty boxes, pyramids, thick triangular wedges and long, curving walkways that remind him vaguely of Marion's street as he saw it that first morning in the rain. "Amazing," he says.

"What?"

"It's three-dimensional."

"No."

"The perspective is too complex, I think. Too many vanishing points, and that makes the overall pattern two-dimensional, but if you get back a little and concentrate on that empty space between, the back falls out of the whole picture."

"How? I still can't see."

He looks at her, her brow knit in concentration, and when he looks again, the painting has become a slightly garish flat surface. "Neither do I now. No. There it is." He feels excitement as the pattern shifts, the elements seem to move as if the act of seeing has created the third dimension. "Like a huge optical illusion."

"I don't believe you," she says.

"You probably just need a fresh drink. Or maybe I don't." He laughs, turns to leave. Bonnie is just coming in the door and she smiles at him.

"Far out," she says. "After that second morning I didn't think you'd get together. A shame, but no one ever does in Sambo's. That's my job. This is my home. You're Sherwood. And . . . ?"

"Tara."

"Do you like my painting?"

"You did this?" Sherwood asks.

"It probably isn't finished yet."

"Not finished?"

She shakes her head. "Everybody thinks it looks too much like a sick patchwork quilt. Everybody except George and Celia and,

well, maybe one or two others. I thought I'd put in some arrows
or turtles to show where the spaces are supposed to be."

Tara nods agreement. "That would be a shame," Sherwood
says.

"You see it?"

"It slipped up on me. It's amazing."

"A lucky accident," she says, but then her face opens into a
broad grin. "You really see it? Far out. Wait'll I tell George."
The grin fades. "No. George is being a pain in the ass tonight."

"Someone should take that firecracker away from him before he
blows his hand off."

"Yeah, but who's going to do it? I'm glad you like the painting
and that you two finally met. Bring those kids in again and I'll
slip you some free pancakes." Clearly happier than when she came
in, Bonnie darts out of the room. Sherwood and Tara follow, work
their way back to the bar, where he makes fresh drinks. The Coke
is running low. Someone else has found the rum, taken a couple
of shots and returned the bottle to the potato-chip bag. The party
is thinning out in the lower part of the house, but loud music
comes from upstairs.

"Now the music," Tara says. She leads Sherwood away from the
table, but their way is blocked, first by Bonnie and then by
George. He still has the candle and the cherry bomb and with
them he backs Bonnie toward a corner.

"Come on," he says. "It'll be far out."

Sherwood gives Tara's hand a squeeze, slips up behind George
and blows out the candle. "Robin Hood Forest strikes again, man."

"Hey, really far out." George stares at the smoking wick. "How
come nobody thought of that before?"

"Maybe they want to hear it go bang."

Bonnie edges along the wall, grabs a cup of beer and runs for
the door.

"She got away, didn't she? Again?"

"I don't think she wants to be launched, George." Sherwood
looks around for Tara, but she is gone. He threads his way
through fragments of a crowd that seems to be arriving, and
checks the hall. She isn't there. Her coat is still in the front studio. From there a systematic search takes him to the stairway and
the second floor.

Upstairs is living quarters: two kitchens, a maze of halls and rooms furnished with mattresses propped on bricks and boards, desks and dressers with dust-free patterns that show the shapes of articles now hidden away. The flow of traffic carries him the length of the house to a large room that shakes under the blast of a stereo. Dancers pack the floor and around the edges people rest on pillows or the sills of open windows overlooking the park. He finds Tara near the record changer, sitting on a thin cushion with her head tipped forward and moving in time with the music. Dropping onto the floor beside her, he touches her arm.

"I was afraid he'd light it," she says. "Loud noises frighten me."

"We're in the wrong part of the house then, let's find a quiet place."

Hand in hand they go back down the maze of halls and rooms. The number of people seems to have increased since Sherwood came upstairs. Bonnie brushes past them. Sherwood catches sight of Celia, deep in conversation with several other women. In a long stretch of hall near one of the kitchens they meet a couple coming out a narrow door. "What's through there?" Sherwood asks.

The girl giggles. "Closet," she says.

"That's what we're looking for." He holds the door for Tara.

"A closet? I don't believe it."

"Private and quiet."

"I'll need another drink. Mine's disappeared."

"Save my place."

Handing her his cup, he passes through the kitchen, down the stairs and into the lower hallway, which is now congested with people all wearing coats. Tara's bottle of rum is no longer under the table. The potato-chip sack is tracked into the debris on the floor. Sherwood finds the bottle on the table, still a third full. He tips two cups upside down over the neck and carries it upstairs to knock at the closet door.

"If your name is Sherwood, you can come in." She sits on the floor, back slumped against one wall and feet braced against the base of the wall opposite. In the light from the hall he can see she has finished the drink he left.

He pulls the door shut. "I rescued our bottle," he says and slides down the wall across from her to sit with his leg against hers. There is hardly any light with the door shut. Her hand finds his and she takes the bottle, pours, hesitates, then gives it back.

"What now, Sherwood?"

What indeed? "We could swap life stories. It's your turn. I told you mine last time." He expects her to laugh, but she doesn't.

"This isn't working," she says. "I have to be honest. I couldn't stay with you that night we met." He can feel her moving, as if casting around for the right thing to say. "I'm attracted to you, but part of it is the story you told me in the car. Your accident and being dead."

There it is. That seriousness. Another walking wounded, O'Neal. You can hear it if you listen. He feels his scar start to itch and he lifts the bottle, takes a drink. "What happened?"

"I don't usually tell people, but even that first day in Sambo's . . . You look a little like Bill."

"Vietnam?" he asks, and when he feels her nod, "Who was he? Brother? Husband?"

"I met him the month before he went over there. We were going to be married in Japan when he got R&R."

"Killed?"

"Missing in action, they called it. Not dead, not alive. Just gone and it all happened so fast I never even met his family."

"When was this?"

"Spring of 1969. Were you . . . ?"

"No. In the spring of '69 I had a little less than a year to go." Art was already back in the States. Legless.

"Where's that bottle you saved?"

Guiding his hand up her leg, Sherwood finds her hand, takes the cup, fills it and gives it back. Her weight shifts in the dark and he can hear her take two long swallows.

"I just thought," she says. She takes another quick drink. "When you told me about being dead and not knowing how it happened, I thought you might understand."

"Yeah. No end to it."

"No end," she repeats. "But it's worse than that. Not just something that doesn't have an end; it keeps coming back, getting in the way of my life."

He nods and gives her leg a squeeze. Don't want to think about that too much, do you, O'Neal?

"About a year ago I met someone and we started to get serious, but then I'd have these nightmares about Bill coming back. Angry. Something terrible was going to happen, but I didn't know what." She cuts off.

"And?"

"No end to it. I quit seeing the man and the nightmares stopped."

"You quit seeing him?"

"What else could I do?"

"Told someone, seen a psychiatrist. A guy I know, Brodie, specializes in that kind of thing."

She drains her cup, finds his hand and gives it to him. "It seemed so silly. Fill that, would you?"

"It's not silly."

"Like a neurotic teen-ager or something."

"You haven't told anyone else this, have you? Parents? Brothers or sisters?"

"No."

"You weren't married to him. Didn't know his family and they didn't know about you. No one to talk to. No support group. Completely outside and alone and thinking it was silly?" At least Art and I have had each other. "That's rough, Tara."

She leans across the closet to him. Her mouth finds his eye, his mouth. He can feel the tears on her cheeks. Her hair tickles his nose, and her lips taste of rum. "Thank you," she whispers.

Feet scuffle past, create irregular rhythms on the hallway floor. Stoned, drunk bodies thump against the wall. The hall light goes on and then off again. Several times the closet door opens, but they ignore apologies and each time the door closes again. A firecracker, either George's cherry bomb in a distant part of the house or something smaller nearby, explodes. The noise jars Sherwood enough for him to wonder what he's doing at his age, necking in a closet at some artists' party; but he takes another drink and memory of the explosion fades. The volume of the music rises through a raucous, jangling series of songs that then give way to a more sedate orchestral piece that flows and builds and finally ebbs away to quiet.

"It sounds like the party's about over."

"What about us?" Tara leans back and starts to straighten her hair.

"Do you think it's good for you to see me?" he asks. The question stops her. He can feel her leg tighten against his. "I mean, won't it be worse for you if we get involved and then I die?"

No response.

"No," he says, "maybe it won't." It's just the opposite. You remind her of this guy Bill. You were in the Army; were wounded. If you could take his place and die on schedule, you might end it for her. Get rid of her nightmares. Cheap therapy. He laughs, and only then realizes that her measured breathing probably means she has thought the same thing—at least half consciously. Be careful of her. She doesn't have the cushion of your practiced irony. She thinks she's alive. "How about next Friday night?"

"I have to go out of town next weekend."

"Two weeks then?" Her unseen nod becomes a gentle motion of her leg, and her hand squeezes his knee before she goes back to working on her hair. "So, let's see if there's any party left," he says.

Bottle in one hand, Tara holding the other, Sherwood emerges into the startlingly silent hall. The kitchen is deserted and only one couple sits on the stairs. "What time is it?"

"Almost two. Did you know you were carrying an empty bottle?"

Celia and two other women who look like co-op residents have put down folding chairs near the demolished food table in the main studio. Their conversation appears intense, but Celia looks up as Sherwood drops the bottle into the trash. "I thought you'd gone."

"Just on our way. Thanks for the party."

"I didn't get a chance to talk to you. Did we arrange to meet?"

"Sunday evening. About eight?"

"Fine. I'll bring . . ."

A manic, high-pitched giggle cuts her off. It sounds so much like Art that for a moment Sherwood expects to see him come churning through the door. Instead, George backs into the room, hands raised in surrender. Bonnie follows. Her shoulders are hunched together and her arms, extended like a television cop about to shoot an advancing criminal. Dark wine drips from her hair and soaks her shirt, and in her hands she carries George's lighted candle stub and the cherry bomb. "You shit," she hisses. Blank and stoned, her eyes are hardly mobile in their sockets.

"But you're such a far-out chick, I thought you oughta get into space." George's giggle drops by half steps to a belly laugh. He stops in the center of the room.

"Bonnie. Watch out." Celia is on her feet. She stares as if fascinated by George's hand as it reaches out and taps Bonnie's wrist, knocks the cherry-bomb fuse into the flame. In an instant George is around her and out the door, leaving her to stare vacantly at the sputtering green stick.

Time drags as if the air were jelly. Celia is rooted, chair tipping slowly beside her. Tara's arms move up to protect her eyes. One of the women pushes toward a window and another reaches slow motion for a paper cup of beer. *Déjà vu* squeezes like a vise around Sherwood's chest. He feels grass under his feet, pain in his lungs; tastes the thick, sweet blood in his throat. He is falling and reaching out. Falling. Then he has the cherry bomb in his hand, sees the fire spit down the green twist of paper toward the red ball, sees Bonnie's empty gaze, the shocked, frozen faces of the others, knows it is too late and everything is finally finished, knows that the shock of having his hand blown to pieces will kill him. Reaches up. Reaches and plucks the fuse like the stem off a cherry and lets it fall sparking to the floor.

The firecracker is an angry red eye in his palm. It catches the light, blurs from red to gold to silver and then to flat-black blank.

"What time is it?" he asks. "Art?"

CLUB TEXAS cuts a vertical slash of blue neon down the front of the building. The light dances and shimmers in the hot night air that hangs thick with odors of the benjo ditches, cheap perfume, food cooking in sesame oil and soy sauce. Lonely plunking notes of a samisen drift out the open window of an apartment above the bar. Sherwood steps into the recessed doorway and pushes inside. Tsuko, Kenny and Lisa, the bargirl, are all there ahead of him, and with them are two others: Lieutenant Lang, the company commander, and an MP sergeant Sherwood knows he ought to recognize, but doesn't. Something menacing about the officer and NCO. "Not yet. I'm not ready yet," but even as he protests the unfamiliar current of the dream pulls him deeper.

"You drink one drink, Sherwood." Tsuko meets him, takes his arm. "I dance soon." Kenny moves over to make room at the table, whispers that he is going to kill Lang, who sits two booths away. Off to the left the MP sergeant pours beer from a bottle.

Sherwood studies his image in one of the mirror discs. He looks older and has lost weight. His hair hangs over his shirt collar, thin on top now, with gray showing in the sideburns. "I've changed."

Tsuko is changing too. She is herself, but she is also Tara as she mounts the stage, kicks off zoris and waits. The man Sherwood thought was Lang is Art's father and he stands up, drops a hundred-dollar bill beside his half-filled glass and leaves without even a passing nod. Brodie comes in, sits across the room and waves.

"What time is it?"

Kenny slides out of the booth with Lisa and they walk away, she with a nurse's cap and he, hips churning, a cane raised above his head. Tara grows taller, fuller in chest and hips, steps into the spotlight. Her hair is the color of straw. Erica. The band plays and she begins to dance, eyes casting back and forth until she finds Sherwood. He expects her to smile, but instead her hand moves to her mouth.

"Not yet."

He is running across grass. No fatigues. Jeans and an old wool shirt. The goat coat flaps around his legs. Art is straight ahead, distraught. There is a grenade in the air, its handle falling away. Pockmarked earth banked against the bunker a little way off. "Stay back, Woody. Get back."

Human silhouettes stare down at him from the muddy, bullet-torn embankment. Wind off the East China Sea cools his cheek, carries the salty, decaying odors of low tide. A wide circle of long-needled pines surrounds him, scraps of red rag fluttering from their branches. Jamie appears among the trees, running on short little legs and stopping every few steps to pull up the loops of coat sleeve that hang around his shoulders. "Get back, Jamie. Art. Run." Art can't run. He sits on the edge of some kind of crater, beating the earth with fists and stumps. Sherwood runs faster.

Behind him, metal strikes metal. He knows the sound is a rifle.

He should be able to stop the bullet, reach out and catch it. Fear fills him, paralyzes him. Art flops on the ground. The grenade is nowhere in sight. Sherwood's terror grows like an exploding red flower that overpowers him as it blossoms. Then, nothing.

He wakes, expecting the hospital but finding himself instead on the field, where he plods toward the place Art should have fallen. Fires burn in the scorched grass. The wind smells of fish. A little way off an Okinawan woman and two children cook a catch of turban shells over one of the fires. Hungry, Sherwood approaches, but the children hide from him in tall grass. The woman comes to intercept him. Her eyes are troubled. "You need a doctor," she says. She holds up a small, round mirror.

The coat has fallen back on his shoulders. His shirt is peeled open and with it, the skin and muscles of his chest are parted along the line of his scar. Breastbone, white like gristle, is exposed and between the ribs he can see a spongy gob of lung. There is a long welt on his heart where the metal is lodged. It looks like a small sailboat mast completely covered with tissue. "It didn't break loose."

He is making the children uncomfortable so the woman walks with him, changing as she moves up the cliffs to the promontory three hundred or four hundred feet above the barnacle-covered ledge. Beyond the ledge the waves heave smooth swells toward the land and in these swells Sherwood can see a square of red cloth, half submerged, rising and falling in the glass-green sea. "I could jump here and miss the ledge," he says.

Erica leans close, gives him a friendly hug. "We could go to Moon Beach tomorrow."

Tomorrow.

Watching the cloth bob and slowly begin to sink, Sherwood wonders what has gone wrong. It isn't supposed to be this way, this lingering half life. He leans over the edge of the rock and stares down.

A quick ripple of fear courses through him like a shiver.

"Sherwood. Sherwood."

"Time? How long was I gone? Art? I'm coming out."

"God, his heart feels like it's going to blow itself up."

He turns his head away from bright ceiling lights and opens his eyes. The potato-chip sack is trampled flat on the floor several inches from his nose.

"Lie still. The ambulance is on its way."

"Ambulance?" He fights off the hands that try to hold him down. "No ambulance. I just flipped out. Did someone call an ambulance?"

"I think I hear it," Celia says.

Scrambling up, Sherwood grabs Tara's hand. "We have to get out of here. Tell 'em you don't know who I am." He half drags her down the hall and into the studio for their coats. "Get it on. Come on."

"I don't *believe* this."

"Move." He can imagine the headlines: EX-MENTAL PA-TIENT FLIPS OUT AT ARTIST DRUG BASH. COUNTY MOVES TO REVOKE CUSTODY. Tara is in her coat and he pushes her ahead of him into the hall, where the red ambulance lights throw eerie flashes across the paintings on the walls.

"Too late, Sherwood."

"Give 'em a nice smile on their way by." Arm around her, he opens the door and steps onto the porch. The attendants already have their stretcher out. They wheel it to the house, lift it up the steps. This is the way I'll end, this infernal narrow bed with handles and wheels. Sherwood holds the door open for them. "Up the stairs at the end of the hall," he says.

"Thanks, buddy."

Hand in Tara's hand, he strolls to the corner. Police cars come from both directions on B Street, lights blazing and sirens on full blast. "Gawk a little." He spins her around, puts his arm over her shoulder. The sirens cut off in unison and the cars stop, one behind the ambulance on Fourth, the other on B. Doors slam shut behind running men. "Hey, what's going on?" he calls. All four cops ignore him. "Come on, Tara."

They run across the street, across the soft thick grass of the park, and finally come to rest against the side of her Jaguar. "What happened?" Her cheeks are flushed from running and she gasps for breath.

"I flipped out."

"I thought you were dead." One hand presses at the middle of her chest and she stares down at the street, color draining from her face and eyes widening. "My God."

"Are you okay?" Scared. But it's more than that. What's the matter?

"No. I have to get out of here. Sherwood, I'm sorry. Terribly sorry."

"I'll call you tomorrow."

"Not tomorrow. Sunday." She opens the car door and gets in, moving carefully. The keys jingle in her trembling hand as she starts the car.

For half an hour after she has gone Sherwood sits on one of the swings and stares across the park at the sycamores all lined up row by row. The ambulance leaves the co-op, then both the cop cars leave. Finally he gets up and walks back down the block to Marion's. Erica is asleep on the living-room bed, light still on, and the book she was reading askew in a fold of covers. He turns off the light and climbs downstairs to the workroom.

Art looks up from the new leg he has been building since Thursday morning. "What happened to you, Woody?" He winks. "Good party?"

"I flipped out."

"Bad?" Pulling a hinged panel off the back of the calf, Art shaves the edge with a rasp. "You don't look like it's left you shaky."

"It was different. All changed. There was an MP sergeant who was never there before. There was a grenade too. And a rifle."

"Sounds like a fragging. It'd add up."

What's the matter, man? You sound tired. Discouraged. "I don't know if those were real or not. Almost everything was changed. Like a dream. Tsuko kept turning into Erica or Tara."

"Tara, huh?"

"And Brodie and your father were both there. Then instead of ending in the hospital, I was out on the rifle range with Jamie and you. . . ."

"No." Art slaps the rasp against the table. "You keep me out of that kind of thing. Flipout, dream, I don't care what you call it. I'm not some crazy kid who's going to get killed doing something stupid. You hear me?"

Blew it. Sherwood shakes his head. Didn't mean that at all, Art. He starts to say so, but Art cuts him off.

"I'm sorry, Woody." He stares at the rasp and the panel in his hands. "Watched the damned news tonight. Cambodia's gone. Nam won't last another month. What a fucking waste."

"Yeah. But it's not like we just figured it out."

"No. You're right," Art says. "At least, it sounds like you're making some progress. Shook something loose so it's not like a stuck record anymore. Even if you never remember what happened, it'll probably help to be thinking about it."

Help what? "Different, anyway."

"Brodie'd be glad." He tries the panel again, then searches the bench until he finds a scrap of paper that he hands to Sherwood. "See if you can buy me one of these tomorrow, would you? It's a latch. For a small door. That's actual size; and I can't use anything bigger. If there isn't anything exactly like that, bring me an assortment of the closest you can find."

"Right." Sherwood stuffs the sketch into his shirt pocket and stands there, not really seeing Art, wondering if Brodie was right— if he *should* try to remember what happened.

4

Saturday is lost to a fuzzy-headed hangover. Sherwood manages to clean house and make one trip to the hardware store for an assortment of the latches Art wanted; but Sherwood's efficiency is low. Where he has needed to do three loads of wash he only does one, and that one he forgets in the machine overnight.

After breakfast next morning the grass in the backyard is long and bent over with dew. Sherwood shuffles up and down the lawn, pins clothes that smell slightly of mildew to the line and watches Jamie where he runs a rusted dump truck along the narrow sidewalk. Shirts and pants so small. Almost insubstantial. It's not warm enough out here; I should have put a coat on him. "Aren't you cold, little guy?"

Jamie looks up from a pile of sand he has dumped out of the truck. "Come on, Sher. Play trucks."

"For a minute, but we fooled around all yesterday. I want to work this morning."

"Is today a Josie day?"

"No. Tell you what. Fifteen minutes with the trucks, then we go to work." Sherwood finds a plastic VW bus in the garage, fills it with sand and runs it down the walk to where Jamie sits with his back to the sun. "Where do you want this sand?"

"How do you make roads?"

"Roads? Hmm. We could cut some roads out of the lawn. They'd be rough, like building roads through a jungle."

"Got that, Sher. Then put sand?"

"Sure. Why not?" It couldn't look any rattier back here. "I'll clip. You bring the sand, okay?" He takes out his pocket knife and goes to work on the lawn, slicing through Bermuda grass, something that looks like crested rye grass in miniature, clover, a little dicondra; cuts a wide, twisting path around broad sprays of crabgrass. A tiny version of the world down here; smells like a hay field. "Have you ever looked for a four-leaf clover, Jamie?"

Jamie dumps sand next to the sidewalk and spreads it onto the grass without apparent regard for the clipped road.

"We could set up a whole city if you wanted."

"That's silly, Sher. What would be the houses?"

"You could build them in the shop. How about it? I would like to get some work done."

Head tilted, Jamie looks at the sand he has spread and at the five or six feet of path Sherwood has cleared. "Okay," he says and he is off across the backyard, up the steps.

"Don't fall." Sherwood follows, tensed for the crash and cry of a missed step, but it doesn't come. Halfway down the basement stairs he hears Art's gruff, "Hello, half-pint," and the clatter of Jamie rummaging through the scrap box.

"What time is this woman coming to look at my guitars?" Art asks. He stands the almost finished new right leg on the table and checks the catch of the door in the back of the calf.

"About eight."

"How long do you think it will take, Woody? An hour?"

"Probably."

"Okay, look. I don't want to meet her. Not yet, so after she leaves you can turn off the porchlight or something. I'm going out and I'll want to know when it's safe to come back."

"Sure."

"One other thing. You told the court you're in the guitar business and that's fine, but I want credit for my own work when she comes to check us out tonight."

"I'd planned on that. Unless I miss my guess, she's been around —she'll be able to see the difference."

"Good. Maybe I'll want to meet her."

"How do you build houses, Sher?"

Nodding to Art, Sherwood draws a square on the plywood

Jamie has picked. "Four walls here. Straight up from these lines, then a roof."

During the first hour of work, Jamie doesn't ask that the television be turned on and he takes fewer breaks than usual to play on Art's practice steps. Jamie manages to put together a reasonable house. There are no windows and the door is a gap in one corner, but he knows what he wants down to the gabled roof that frustrates him until Sherwood cuts two triangles to support the sloping sides. By about ten o'clock Jamie has half obliterated the basic shape with glued-on chips of wood that he calls chimneys and windows and shingles.

"Looking fine," Sherwood says.

Jamie nods, pleased with himself. "I hear knocking."

"At your door? You already have people living in there?"

From the other bench, Art waves for both of them to be quiet. "I think he means it, Woody. Upstairs."

Sherwood crosses to the high, narrow window, pulls the shade back an inch and finds himself looking almost up the leg of a woman's pantsuit. "Pat Chapman," he says. "Jamie, go up and answer the door. Quick. And remember, this is just like one of her regular visits. Don't say anything about Art."

"But Sher . . ." Jamie hesitates, starts toward the stairs, turns back.

"Keep a sharp ear, Art. If I stomp on the floor, get under the bathroom, and take that extra leg."

"Damn it, Woody. How'd you get us into this?"

"Just do it." Sherwood turns on his heel, picks up Jamie, who hasn't gotten past the door. Hope they haven't found out it was me at the party. By the time he reaches the door, she has ceased to knock and is just standing, a dark look on her face. "Sorry," he says. "We were in the shop and didn't hear you."

"Good morning," she says, sounding more businesslike than usual. She strides into the house, stations herself in front of the green chair and pulls out her clipboard. "I understand you had a little trouble last week."

"Trouble?" Someone *did* tell her I flipped out at the party.

"Three stitches. Or wouldn't you call that trouble?"

"Oh, that." Bad words and worse inflection. Makes her want to ask what else happened. "Show her your chin, little dude. He scared the bejesus out of both of us."

"Come here, Jamie." She sits down, catches his jaw between thumb and forefinger, and tips his head back. "How did this happen?"

"I fell down."

"Where?"

Jamie pulls back from her and puts his hands on his hips. "On my chin."

"I can see that. What hit your chin?"

"The bathtub. I fell down on my chin in the bathtub."

She looks relieved, but not convinced. "Why didn't you tell that to the doctor?"

"Sher wouldn't buy me a hammer."

"He wouldn't buy you a hammer," she repeats.

Jamie nods.

"He wouldn't buy you a hammer?"

"If I don't fall down for a whole week, he will buy me one."

"I see." She watches Jamie several seconds, then turns to Sherwood.

"He's been falling a lot. Not paying attention to where he's going or what he's doing, tripping over things. He also wants to learn to drive nails so I said I'd get him a hammer if he could go a week without falling down."

"And?"

"The deal was only a day old when he cut his chin. Neither of us thought about it until the doctor asked Jamie what happened, then he remembered. He didn't want to say because that would have reminded me he fell and he'd have to start over again for the hammer."

Pat slips a fresh tablet into the clipboard and writes on the top sheet. "You sound as if you think that's a perfectly logical explanation, but the doctor said Jamie was withdrawn. Extremely withdrawn, not just reluctant to remind you of something."

"He was in shock."

"Dr. Goldsmith can tell the difference between shock and emotional withdrawal, I'm sure."

"Okay. Sometimes he withdraws. There seem to be certain things he doesn't want to face and he just doesn't."

"How long has this been going on?"

"Since the day I picked him up. He's been doing it less, but I have to watch out for discipline he might consider arbitrary."

Jamie has wandered into the dining room and pulled the coat off the chair. "What is arbitrary, Sher?"

"Something done without good reason." That must look good, lady, a natural response to a reasonable question. "Like if I came over and spanked you right now, that would be arbitrary."

Slowly, Jamie cracks a smile. "That's silly, Sher." He looks at Sherwood and then at Pat. "Sher doesn't ever spank." The response is spontaneous, but not as impressive as when he did it the first time.

"Why haven't I heard about this before? It isn't in any of my reports."

Sherwood shrugs, notices that the gesture causes immediate tightening of the skin around her eyes. Her eyes take on a wary light he hasn't noticed since their first meeting. "It hasn't been a problem."

"I'd call it a problem."

"I've gotten around it, sometimes through it. If it had been getting harder to handle instead of easier, I would have said something, but it was just something he did when he first came."

Her pen scratches the paper. Jamie drags the coat over to the bed and crawls into Sherwood's lap.

"You aren't telling me everything."

"Everything I know."

She shakes her head. "If this child was withdrawn, something had to happen to cause it. Whatever it was either happened here or at the foster home."

"Wasn't he somewhere before the foster home?"

"The shelter home, but he wasn't there long and there are reports on his condition. As a matter of fact, I remember him from the shelter home."

"You wouldn't consider it normal that he was having trouble handling the fact that his mother died?"

"I could consider a lot of things normal if I could just figure out what it is you're trying so hard not to tell me."

Come on, lady, you're not clairvoyant. Ease up.

"I recall that you were reluctant to talk about the foster home the first time I mentioned it. Do you want to tell me now?"

"There's nothing to tell."

"Sherwood."

"Are you out to get Doris Ransler, or something?"

Dropping the clipboard, Pat throws up her hands, flops against the back of the chair. "What is going on here? This conversation isn't even going in circles. I'm batting my head against a wall." She pats her hair as if to make sure it's in place, then picks up the clipboard again. "I want to start over. This time, Sherwood, look at the situation from a purely logical point of view. There is no record of Jamie being withdrawn in the shelter home. Very attached to the coat, yes; withdrawn, no. Unfortunately, he was not under our direct supervision in the foster home. We had an abnormally large caseload, and it seems no inspection was made during the month and a half he was there. From the twenty-second of December until the fourth of February.

"He has now been with you two and a half months and he is exhibiting emotional withdrawal."

"He's not. . . ."

"Don't talk, Sherwood. Just listen. Three things are possible. Either there is something physically wrong with him, or something happened to him at the Ransler home, or something has happened to him here."

"Am I sick, Sher?"

"No. You're healthier than I am." And Pat's sharper than I thought. How am I going to get out of this?

"It may become necessary to have a doctor verify that, but I suspect you're right. That leaves two possibilities."

"Are you accusing me of something?"

"We aren't communicating at all. I get a strong feeling that you haven't heard anything I've said."

"Yes, I have. Nothing has happened here to make Jamie withdrawn. He's been withdrawing. I've been dealing with it. Frankly, it hasn't seemed anything to be alarmed about. I've done a certain amount of withdrawing myself and I think I understand a lot of what he's had to go through. Does that make sense?"

"More than the rest of what you've said. Or haven't said."

"If something happened to him beyond . . . Marion's death, I don't know what or when."

Jamie stiffens against Sherwood. "Mommy went in the ground," he says. "Sher took me to see."

Pat's expression is more sympathetic as she breaks off writing. "How does that make you feel, Jamie?"

"Sad." He looks at her, suddenly angry. "She went in the ground in a big park and she likes parks."

Jamie sounding brave, Pat having trouble controlling her face. Maybe we haven't blown the deal yet. Sherwood shakes his head. "I'm sorry," he says. "It didn't occur to me to say anything. I thought it was normal. Dying is always hard to take. I thought I could handle things and I still think I can."

Pat watches his face, finally softens. "Okay. I apologize. I have been grilling you. Maybe I'm wrong, but I still have a feeling there's something you don't want to tell me."

"No."

"I will start making one or more unscheduled visits a week for a while. That wound on his chin makes it necessary. I don't know. He isn't withdrawn now."

"Come as often as you like. If you come in the morning, knock on that basement window by the front steps. We're usually working in the shop and we can't hear the bell."

She sighs, checks off a couple of boxes on a form under the tablet and drops her pen into her purse.

"We don't have anything to hide." Except Art. Oh brother.

"I hope not. You and Jamie have been an easy case. Almost too good to believe, I'm afraid. Last week I was considering cutting my visits to one every other week. We had best let that wait. I'm not against you, understand, but I am concerned." She gets up, crosses the room and stops in the front hall. "You're sure there isn't something you want to tell me?"

"No. See you later this week."

Nodding as if half ashamed to admit she will make a surprise visit, Pat Chapman opens the front door. "Good-bye."

"Good-bye," Sherwood says. He watches until she gets into her car and drives off, then lets out a long sigh. "That blows work for today." Hands too shaky to build guitars. "Let's go tell Art she's gone. Then we'll do whatever you want."

Day of roads and houses in the backyard, day of slides and swings, cream-cheese bagels and orange juice on the Sunday-quiet quad, footabeel with a Frisbee among the sycamores in the park, leisurely supper, story and bed for Jamie. At a quarter till eight that evening Sherwood sees Art out the door, bound for the park with a red-and-white bandanna puffed out of his fatigue-shirt pocket like a boutonnière. Ten minutes later Celia and George ring the bell. Seeing George puts Sherwood off, but he offers them both coffee.

"That would be nice," Celia says.

George shakes his head. "Nothing extra in the body tonight. I want to apologize for Friday. And thank you, too. She could have been hurt, man."

"It's okay."

"Are you all right?" Celia clutches her purse briefly, then puts it on the dining-room table. "We thought you were having a heart attack."

"It was far out, man. Very far out."

"Yeah." Sherwood laughs. Far out it was. "Did you get rid of the cops without getting busted? I didn't dare get caught. Flipping out like that might give me custody problems I can't afford to have."

"The little boy?"

"My nephew." Sherwood nods to George. "The dwarf."

"We told the cops we'd never seen the guy before. Just a party crasher. They groused around awhile and left. They're pretty loose, only bust people who flaunt it." She gives Sherwood a sly smile, takes the coffee he brings her and casually inspects the sparsely furnished living and dining rooms. "George is our best guitar player. His ear is as good as his eye."

"Even stoned, man." George wanders into the kitchen.

"Straight back and down the stairs," Sherwood says. "The workshop is first door at the bottom. Guitars on the north wall."

George ambles out of sight. "You could use a painting or two on these walls," Celia says.

"I couldn't afford even a small one."

"We do a lot of trading."

"Can't afford that either right now. The truth is, a friend of mine made most of the guitars we have. He's the craftsman. I'm a novice."

A muffled plunk of fingerpicking drifts up the stairwell.

"Could I see?"

By the time they reach the basement, George has arranged the guitars against the far wall, six of Art's and Sherwood's first guitar on the right, four of Art's in the middle, and Sherwood's second finished guitar all alone on the left. Odd he put my second one last, Sherwood thinks. The neck is on right and it even sounds better. He wonders about the order while Celia walks the line of instruments, stopping to tap out one from the first group, two from the second and the one of Sherwood's on the end. With a nod, she crosses the room and studies the ones she has chosen as George turns each to give her a view of all sides.

The silent communication between this calm, strong woman and spaced-out man surprises Sherwood. They seem to understand each other; she his original grouping of the guitars and he, her choices. Finally, George leans the last guitar against the wall. "They sound from good to very fine," he says, "but it's freaky. These"—one hand flicks toward the center group—"have the best tone."

"Interesting."

"They're harder to play, action a little high, and they're as clunky to handle as they look. The elegant one is much easier. You can see how it is with the finish." He holds up two fingers. "Two people working here."

"Your friend makes these boats too, I take it," Celia says.

"Yes."

"It comes out more here where he's not working with preset restraints. The guitar body takes its shape from forms, doesn't it?"

"Took him three months to figure out the first one." Back in Martinez, that place with the green walls and cockroaches. "He took the basic shape from a Martin Dreadnought, then pushed a little here and there, I think." All that work, Art. So maybe the boats are harsh. You make the necks thick because you have big hands, damn it.

"The one on the end, and that one, in the last group are yours," Celia says. The statement doesn't require a response. "We'll take the one of yours and three of his. I'd bet you play guitar and your friend doesn't."

"You'd lose. I've never tried. He plays a little."

"Oh? What's he like?"

"Like anyone."

"With big hands." George laughs. "You're living with a dwarf and a gorilla."

"I'll never have the patience to rub a finish the way he does."

"Yeah. That *is* far out. I'd like to have one of those around just to stare into sometimes."

Celia puts her half-empty cup on Art's bench. "How long has he been doing this?"

"About three years."

"You?"

"I've been helping off and on the whole time."

"But you've worked with wood before?"

"Nothing this intricate. My father was a ranch foreman and in winter he did a lot of carpentry and some cabinet making. I built things when I was a kid."

"It makes a difference, man. This other dude is like he's making clubs instead of guitars. No. They sound good. Musical clubs."

"He made both the legs he walks on, so he might feel like he needs a club to go with them."

"Bummer." George clicks his tongue. "It doesn't make his guitars any nicer to look at."

"Having legs doesn't make mine sound better, either."

"Time will, man."

"Do you want these for your gallery or not?"

"We aren't trying to cut him down, man."

"Then stop. He works hard and he deserves all the breaks he can get. Both his legs were blown off in Vietnam."

"It doesn't make . . ." George cuts off the rest at a shake of Celia's head.

Capitalize now, O'Neal. "How about trying a couple of the boats too?"

"They would be expensive as toys."

"Isn't anyone interested in well-crafted things?"

"Form is part of craft, man."

"A little tact doesn't hurt either," Sherwood snaps.

"Far out."

"We'll try one of the boats. All right? If it sells, we can bring up another one or two."

"Aw man, it'll sell, don't worry," George says. "People around here can't tell good from bad as long as there's that much spit and polish involved. Call your heavy-handed lines symbolic and even the ones who can tell the difference are likely to bite. It's a college town."

"We plan to take things on consignment, Sherwood; 30 percent commission. I'll call you as soon as we're ready to take them. You should be thinking about how much you want to charge." Celia picks up the cup. "Don't be a stranger at the studio. We have access to the Art Department woodshop. If you do any sketching, we have life drawing Tuesday and Thursday about nine."

"That isn't exactly my line."

"We also have quite a few sculptors who either live there or come around. They can probably put you onto supply sources. It's a cooperative. All of us find it easier if we pool skills and knowledge."

"Makes sense."

"And bring your friend. We'd like to meet him. And the child."

"Jamie."

"Jamie," she says.

George holds out his hand. "No hard feelings?"

Sherwood shakes without comment.

"We'll get along better in time, man. I'm about to start a new series of paintings. Off the chemicals. I'll get more coherent for a while. No more cherry bombs."

"Okay." He follows them upstairs, flipping off lights as he goes; sees them out the door.

From Marion's porch the park looks deserted. Sherwood sits on the step and watches Celia and George until they pass out of sight around the play pit, then reaches up and turns off the porchlight. The house is dark. No light to guide you home, Art. A bat makes its fluttering shadow around the streetlamp as it scoops gnats and mosquitoes out of the air. Jamie moans in his room, says something in his sleep and quiets again. Sherwood feels restless. He wants to slip down the street to check the park and make sure Art is all right, but he is acutely aware of Jamie. Crawl out of bed, come looking for me and fall down the stairs. There could be a fire. How could I have left him alone a year ago?

Ten minutes Sherwood watches from the porch, wondering about Marion and her lawyer and about why Art seems so intent on driving Karen away, thinking about that amazing silent communication between Celia and George. Joe's car is parked in front of Erica's. "Why does that bother me?" he asks. Finally, he goes into the house and dials Tara's number. One ring runs to five and then to ten. He hangs up, stands by the phone intending to try again in a few minutes, but Jamie cries out and something heavy hits the floor of his room.

"Jamie?"

Fingers scrabble like some small animal trying to gain traction, then Jamie calls, "Sher," and comes padding into the living room. "I fell out of my bed," he says.

"You want me to tuck you back in?"

"No." He comes to lean against Sherwood's leg and Sherwood picks him up. "I was afraid."

"Of what?"

"I don't know." For a moment he rests one hand on Sherwood's shoulder. "Why is it dark?"

"I was just sitting here thinking and didn't want to waste money on lights."

"Art isn't working in the basement?"

"No. He went to the park. In fact, I was starting to worry about him."

Jamie sits unnaturally still in his arms. Sherwood can just see his eyes, wide open and fixed as if looking in instead of out.

"You wouldn't be trying to figure out how to get me to take you to the park this late at night, would you?"

No response for a moment, then Jamie nods.

"Well, you're in luck. If you'll go try to dress yourself, I'll leave Art a note, then come help."

Without hesitation, Jamie wiggles down and trots into his room to flip on the light and make rustling noises around the dresser. Sherwood finds paper and pencil, scribbles, "Art, turn on light," and tacks it to the front door; then he goes in to find Jamie, wearing pants and pajama tops, trying to pull on one sock. "Not bad, man." He puts on the other sock and then the shoe, and by that time Jamie has the first sock on well enough that Sherwood only needs to straighten it before he slips on the shoe. "You realize, three months ago, you could barely get into a pair of underpants by yourself?" Grinning, Jamie pulls off his pajama top. Sherwood helps him on with a sweatshirt and then a jacket. "Just let me get the coat and we're ready."

Out of the house and down the street, Jamie sticks close to Sherwood's leg, leery of the dark places between houses. "Is it midnight?" he asks. "Sometimes Josie gets to stay up until midnight."

"It's almost ten. That's only two hours from midnight."

"Can I stay up till then?"

"I doubt it, but we'll see."

Fifth Street is deserted. Mercury-vapor lamps create bright areas in the upper branches of the trees and cast rippling shadows across the ground. The thumping strains of "Bad Moon Rising" drive through open windows of a car pulled to the curb at the far end of the park. Jamie runs out into the play pit, goes down the slide once, then comes back to where Sherwood sits in a swing, and climbs into the next one. He kicks, trying to get started, until Sherwood gets up and gives him a push.

"I like the trees," Jamie says.

No sign of Art. There are four, maybe five people in the car with the loud radio. Their cigarettes glow in the dark, and once a volley of beer cans clatters across the pavement. Sherwood climbs through his swing and kicks it to move almost in time with Jamie's. "It just smells good tonight."

Jamie takes a deep breath, exaggerating the gesture solemnly, and nods. His eyelids are starting to droop a little, but he looks good. Better than I ever thought he could look when I found him, Sherwood thinks. A sparkle in those eyes, even when they're tired. The swings slow almost to a stop. Jamie sits thoughtfully, his head nods. He jerks it up again and looks at Sherwood. "I want to swing in your lap," he says.

"Sure. Come on."

Slipping off the swing seat, he lets Sherwood gather him up again, and pulls the flaps of coattail over his legs.

"You ready to go back to bed?"

"No."

"Not sleepy?"

"No, Sher." He settles against Sherwood with his head tipped back.

Eyes wide to the sky, but not for long. I wish Art would show, small friend. You need your sleep. The wide eyes fall closed. Sherwood hears a muffled cough and turns to see Art standing on the grass about ten yards across the play pit and a narrow walk. His legs are spread a little and he leans back in three-point stance against the cane rammed against his hip.

"Didn't hear me, did you?"

"No. Man, that was good."

Art pushes off with the cane and crosses the walk, shoes now smacking against the concrete. "Grass is getting easier. Can't move quiet on cement worth a damn, though."

"Have to get you a pair of sneakers. Those army dress shoes weren't made to be quiet in."

"Yeah," Art says. "Sneakers. Fast ones too." He stops beside a raised lip of concrete protecting a willow that has died back to trunk and one precarious branch. "Fast ones," he repeats and lowers himself onto the wall.

Sherwood twists the swing around and shifts Jamie to a more comfortable position. "What happened? You don't sound good."

Shaking his head, Art stares at them. For a moment he looks oddly wistful, then he shakes his head again. "I may be in a bind, Woody. Went to Sambo's and there was a guy in there who was at my parents' house a couple of times while they had me. I don't know if he's a detective, but he works for my father."

"Did he recognize you?"

"I don't know. I've grown the beard since then, and I'm on legs now. He didn't pay any attention while I was sitting. Just another hippie. But when I walked out, he still didn't look." He taps the cane on his knee. "Maybe I'm paranoid, but everybody looks at me, man. I walk funny. People look."

Just what we don't need.

"Any ideas, Woody?"

"We have to assume he recognized you," Sherwood says. Jamie shifts in his arms. "I can't run with you this time. Best I can think of is hole up and don't talk to strangers."

"Damn." He hits the wall with his cane. "If only the ID thing had worked out."

"Sher?" Arms and legs tense, Jamie squirms around to look at Art. "No bad place," he whimpers.

"No. No bad place. It's okay. Remember when we talked about that, the judge still hadn't said you could stay with me. Now he has and nothing can change that. Hear me?" The legs relax a little, but the arms still feel tight and Jamie's right hand grabs a handful of Sherwood's shirt sleeve. "I have legal custody. You're not going back to any bad place. Got that?"

"What are you talking about, Woody?" Art's mouth is twisted and his eyes seem shiny.

"Some stupid story I told Jamie so he wouldn't mention you by accident and get us caught. It worked, but I shouldn't have done it."

Jamie finally relaxes and turns around on Sherwood's lap. "Got it, Sher," he says.

"How about you tell me back at the place." He pushes up from the wall and puts out the cane to catch his balance. "I feel exposed as hell out here."

"Right." Sherwood lets the swing unwind, lifts Jamie onto his shoulders and crosses the tanbark. Art is already on his way, hard-soled shoes making angry whocking sounds with each step.

"Will they put Art in a bad place?" Jamie asks.

"Not if we can help it."

"You can't help it," Art says over his shoulder. "You have your own problems, damn it."

Holding Jamie's legs, Sherwood runs to catch up. "I'm in this with you, man. We are."

"No, Woody. This time I have to solve my own problems my own way." He stops abruptly, braking with the cane. "Now either go on ahead or slow down, either one. Just get the hell away from me for a while. I gotta do some thinking."

Bad news, old friend. What is this anger all of a sudden? He stops, takes a backward step. "I'll watch your back trail for a few minutes."

"Yeah, Woody. If that's how you want to think of it." Art moves out again, grinding his way up the sidewalk, off the curb and across Fifth Street. Every few steps he catches himself with the cane.

Sherwood swings around and peers through the park. "You see anyone who might be following Art?" he asks. He feels the shake of Jamie's head as slight pressure of the arms that hold around his neck for balance. "I don't either, but that doesn't mean he isn't there." No. That's not right. Get him thinking that way and he's paranoid before he's five.

Jamie doesn't respond.

"You okay?"

"Sleepy, Sher."

"I bet. Give Art a few minutes and I'll take you back to bed."

"Got that," Jamie says. He leans forward and puts his cheek on Sherwood's head. By the time they get to the house, Jamie is sound asleep. He rouses a little but doesn't open his eyes when Sherwood rolls him under the covers.

"A little night air's good for you," he says. "Puts color in your cheeks." He goes into the living room, takes the phone to the green chair and sits down in the dark.

There is no sound from the basement, but soon the ladder creaks in the attic. The hatch opens and then Art's feet hit the floor. "Woody?"

"Out here."

Art comes slowly, as quietly as he can, and lets himself sink onto the bed. "Was there anyone following?"

"Not that we could see."

Nodding, Art leans back so his head goes out of the light from the corner streetlamp. After a minute he rolls up his pantleg, taps the side of his wooden calf and the door in the back drops open. Blued gunmetal gleams in the streetlight. Art checks the cylinder, slips the pistol into its wooden holster again and snaps the door shut.

"What's that for?"

"I thought I might need it." Art shrugs.

"Why don't you just leave it in the attic so the kids can't get it and let it go?"

"You don't understand, do you? I've about run out of options, Woody."

And I'm not helping much, am I, old friend? "You're still welcome to go back to the cabin with me."

A derisive laugh stabs the dark. "I used to think you were smarter than that."

"Smarter than what?"

"You can't go back. Ever. Everybody knows that. You even hear it on the radio."

"It isn't like that," Sherwood says, but Art sits forward into the light, shaking his head and waving a hand for Sherwood to be quiet.

"Let me tell you about trying to go back." He stares across the room. "I was in Vietnam for a second tour when I got hit. I never wanted you to know that. You'd been so completely screwed by the Army, I didn't think you'd understand. The first time, I was in Saigon. Had a clerk job that didn't amount to anything and I had a woman. Chinese. Tall." He knocks on his thigh and laughs to himself. "But I was taller. Then.

"The night I met her I was stinko drunk. My CO had just gotten me a deal on three sapphire rings a friend of his had smuggled in from Laos and I was feeling salty. Bayonet in my boot and a couple of the rings in my pocket. Incredible rings, man. This one had eight sapphires set up on eight gold stems, like a flower of jewels. So this Chinese chick's name was Mei Hua. That meant beautiful flower. And I was just drunk enough to give her the ring. No strings attached, you know? I get like that sometimes. Just want to give someone something.

"Next morning I woke up at her place. My uniform had been pressed. The bayonet was right where I could reach it and everything from my pockets, money, keys, wallet, the other ring; it was all there in a lacquerware tray. It was unreal, man. She fed me breakfast and sent me on my way.

"That night I showed up at the bar sober with a box of candy, went back to her place after closing and she had a six-pack of American beer waiting for me. It went like that for a couple of weeks. I'd take her something and she'd have something waiting for me at her apartment. After a month we got her a bigger apartment near the base.

"I met her family. Great people. They weren't rich, but they got by and after a while I'd help them out here and there. I loved

them as much as I loved her. Couldn't go over there without
them trying to give me everything in the house."

And this is why you started sending back Karen's letters, Sherwood thinks.

"What's that look for, Woody?"

"Nothing."

"I know what you're thinking. Like Karen always said about my
parents—buying affection. But this was different. It was so simple.
Natural.

"We planned to get married, but she didn't want to leave her
family to come to the States. Right after Christmas '67, I had to
rotate home. Promised her I'd be back. Came stateside and
reupped for another tour, but you see how it is, Woody. I
couldn't go back even then. The Army hung me up until mid-
February and I got back to Saigon after Tet.

"They'd all been home, man. Celebrating the New Year. Fucking mortar round right in the middle of the table. I found one of
her brothers in the hospital at Tan Son Nhut. He said she'd been
right there. Dead for sure."

Art raps fingers on the right side of his calf. "I stayed drunk for
a month. Tore up a couple of bars, the barracks, the day room a
couple of times. Got Article 15s. It was easy to get into a combat
unit. Nobody wanted to be a grunt. I didn't either after a couple
of days, but I thought I'd make it." He shakes his head. "Three
months I lasted. Almost three. Eighty-seven days."

There is nothing Sherwood can say, so he waits, watching the
shadow that is Art's face and uncomfortably aware that he is fully
visible in the streetlight.

"I really loved her," Art says. "I don't think I knew what love
meant before. Giving like that because I wanted to. At home it
was always 'give something to get something.' Always what was
expected. Some awful sense of shame lurking in the background.
'Go Army and I'll buy you a Mustang,'" he mimics, reminding
Sherwood of Arthur, Sr., pointing with his hand full of money.
"You can't disgrace us like your uncle George's boy did." With a
sneer, Art waves both hands in front of him to dispel the appari-
tion of his father. "Uncle George's boy went to Canada, which is
why my parents came out here. Uncle George was stuck with his
job in Omaha—and anyway, he didn't think it was such a disgrace.

My father, though, *my father* was so ashamed of his brother's failure to raise a patriotic American son, that he had to leave town. He was ashamed of his nephew who left his country, ashamed of his brother who wouldn't send his own son to prison, and now he's ashamed of me, the legless wonder who couldn't fight through a war intact.

"You wanted to know what it was like when they had me down there? Shame and guilt, man. And control: All of us always trying to get control of the others. It's the way they live, the way they are. And I can't stay out of it because it's in me too." He flops his hands aimlessly against the bed. "Worse this time because they had Karen there. My folks think I quit writing to her because I didn't want her to know I'd lost my legs. I never told them about Mei Hua."

The house is silent for almost a minute, then Art shakes his head. "I don't know what Karen thinks happened, but she's sharp. Quick memory for facts, dates, numbers. She didn't let on while I was there, but she has to have figured out that those letters started coming back almost a year before I got my"—he hesitates, hits the inside of his knee with the edge of his hand— "ticket home.

"I don't know why she's hanging around. I was shitty to her down there, Woody. Guilty about the letters and angry that she got mixed up with my parents; angry about my legs. But once or twice when I was by myself, I got to thinking about when we lived together. Almost ten years ago. When I moved into her place. It was a big decision then. And we were just kids. Seems silly now, but damn it, it was something."

Sherwood takes a long breath, lets it out slowly. "How can I help, man?"

"You can't. You have to help Jamie."

"After that."

"There isn't any 'after that,' Woody. Even if I had time to wait, there won't be any *after*." He shifts his weight in preparation for standing and his face moves into the light.

Tears in his eyes. "Hey Art . . ."

"Don't you see anything? You and that damned kid love each other. Really love each other."

For a stunned second Sherwood watches Art heave himself off

the bed, stand and sway back and forth. "That doesn't mean I have to forget about everyone else."

"I'll listen to that kind of bullshit when you've thought about it enough to know what it does mean."

"Now, wait a minute. . . ." Before Sherwood can stop him, Art stumps across the living room. "Are you going to be okay?"

His "yeah" comes without expression as he turns out of sight in the kitchen.

Sherwood listens until Art is downstairs in the workroom, then gets up to look in on Jamie, who sleeps with his head thrown back, his face relaxed and the three stitches visible on his chin. There has been too much in the evening to make sleep a reasonable possibility, but Jamie will be up between six-thirty and seven no matter what else happens, so Sherwood goes to bed. Sounds of Art's rasping and scraping come up from the basement and, after half an hour of staring at the ceiling, the familiar pattern of noise puts Sherwood to sleep.

5

Though he has worked all night, Art skips breakfast and stays on in the shop. Jamie eats little and complains that he doesn't feel well. "You're just missing sleep after our trip to the park last night," Sherwood says; then he breaks a plate and a glass doing dishes. Missing a little sleep, myself. "Maybe we'll both take naps this morning."

By the time Sherwood is ready to work, Art has come upstairs, grabbed a couple of apples and retreated into the attic. For Sherwood the morning is short. He manages to get the binding bent for his third guitar, but the assembled instrument isn't dry enough to cut the channel. Jamie tries to build, becomes frustrated over nothing, and finally turns on the television. Halfway through "Electric Company" he falls asleep. Sherwood carries him up to bed. If he naps until noon, I can get started on guitar No. 4, Sherwood thinks; then while he's heating the coffee, Pat Chapman knocks at the front door. She is more cautious this time and not at all cordial. "I have had a rather disturbing communication," she says. "Disturbing as much because it was anonymous as because of its content. An unknown informant has charged that you have someone living in the house besides Jamie. He also claims that this man is in hiding."

Art's father. Or someone working for him. That guy spotted Art in Sambo's for sure. Sherwood shakes his head. "A friend of mine, an old friend from the VA Hospital, is using the basement shop with me. He doesn't live here."

"Where does he live?"

"I don't know."

"You don't know," she says.

"He *is* hiding. His father wants him home. As a matter of fact, his father has sent detectives after him before, so we both felt it would be better if I didn't know where he lived. He had his legs blown off in Vietnam so if his father gets him home, it's not much trouble to keep him there." No points for the war this time.

Pat's eyes are hard with suspicion. "I'll have to look into this," she says. "The man's name is Arthur Johnson?"

"I think he spells it with a 't.' Johnston. But I've never seen it written, come to think of it." A little lie for you, Art. To slow her down, but she doesn't look convinced. Not at all.

Tapping one foot, she takes her clipboard out of its plastic case. "I want you to show me the house, Sherwood."

"You don't believe he's not living here."

"Just show me the house," she says. Her inspection is thorough, down to counting the number of brushes, combs and toothbrushes in the bathrooms. The practice stairs in the back bedroom cause a raised eyebrow, but beyond that and the workshop, Art has not left any evidence of his presence in the house. Custody of Jamie, Pat informs Sherwood, is not in question. Yet. However, the combination of anonymous call and last week's injury calls for extreme caution on her part. He should, in essence, watch his step —and to punctuate that message her parting wishes that he have good luck and a nice day are perfunctory.

Flipout time. Pressure building. If I can't get settled down, I'm going to have a good one. Have to warn Art. Sherwood knocks on the wall, but gets no response. Catch him tonight, he thinks.

Later in the afternoon Erica calls to say that she has been offered a cabin on the coast and, since she has been needing to spend time alone with Josie anyway, she's going to take a vacation and get away for a week. They will leave Wednesday night or Thursday morning. "So if you want your night out this week, you better take it tonight, Sherwood. Josie would like to have Jamie come stay at our place. We have a surprise for him, and Josie wants you to bring that rug tube." Her voice sounds bad: tired, angry, and some other mix of emotions Sherwood can't identify. "I'll feed them dinner, but late. Bring him about seven-thirty. Okay?"

"Okay," he says.

When he and Jamie arrive that evening Josie is wearing the surprise, a yellow pullover shirt with bird wings sewn from the middle of the back to the cuffs. "We made Jamie's too," she says. "Put it on him and we can play mommy sparrow and little lost baby bird." A cardboard box of blankets in her bedroom is the nest. The tube is supposed to rest on the edge of the box and extend into the living room.

"It's a lookerscope, Sher, so she can find me." Sherwood helps him into the shirt and the children are off, tweeting and bouncing on the broken-backed couch.

"Mommy's in the kitchen," Josie says.

"I suppose I should say hello, shouldn't I?"

At the back of the living room a waist-high bookcase marks off a six-foot-square nook with a desk and chair pushed up under the swamp cooler in the window. The desktop is well-aged mahogany, a clear slab of it with straight, closely spaced grain and a fine patina of scratches. Opposite the desk, an open door gives him a glimpse of Erica's room: mattress on plywood and bricks, an old oak dresser with a mirror mounted on it, another bookshelf loaded with paperbacks, a piece of carpet cut to rug size.

Erica appears around an L-shaped jog at the back of the kitchen. "Small and shabby, but it's home." She moves into the kitchen, checks something in the oven and stirs a pan of soup on the stove. "Are you going out?"

"No." Have to get back and warn Art about that anonymous caller. But what about you, Erica? You look like you've lost every friend you ever had and on top of that you're tired enough to fall asleep where you stand. "I could take the kids to Marion's," he says.

She turns away from the stove, holding a ladle that drips chicken soup on the floor. "Running on automatic pilot, okay? I can't handle any change of schedule tonight. You're welcome to stay for supper, all the same."

"You're sure I can't take them?"

"They're both keyed up to be here for a change."

"You don't look like you need the hassle."

"Sherwood."

"It wouldn't be any trouble for me to take them. . . ."

"For crying out loud."

"Sorry." He backs into the living room and sinks onto the couch while Josie and Jamie chirp at each other through the cardboard tube.

Erica follows him out a few minutes later and slumps into a straight-back chair. "I'm sorry," she says. "It doesn't have anything to do with you, but unless you can let things alone, I'd rather you didn't stay."

It? You're looking so down, all bent over in that hard chair the way you were that first night. "You want to talk?"

"No. Yes." She shrugs, thinks a minute and finally shakes her head.

"All right."

Oblivious to the uneasiness above them, Jamie and Josie sit on the floor, one at each end of the tube, which they lift first to their mouths, then to their ears. Slowly they shift it across the restricted space until Josie is sitting on Sherwood's feet, and Jamie is beside Erica's chair. "Let Mommy play," Josie says.

Jamie gives up his end to Erica and scoots across the rug to the door of Josie's room.

"Hi, Mommy."

"Hi, honey. What are you doing down there?"

"What do you think? Talking to you. Are you still sad?"

"Not now."

Josie looks up at Sherwood. "Do you know Mommy was sad almost all week?"

"It occurred to me I've seen her happier," he says. Then, when she wrinkles her nose as if to say his answer is not definitive enough, "She seemed a little sad when I came in."

"See. Sherwood thinks you're sad," she says into the tube.

"He doesn't know everything either, honey."

They look natural, mother and daughter at play, talking to each other through a cardboard tube. All the time we've had it at Marion's, I haven't talked to Jamie through it. Must be losing my sense of fun. He feels Josie's hand tug on his pants leg and then she is pushing the tube up to him. "Thanks," he says. He takes the end, looks down the slightly curved brown tunnel at Erica's mouth and the tip of her nose. For a moment the fact of focusing on only part of her face makes him feel like a voyeur. The gentle shape of her lips surprises him as they twitch and part.

"We've been set up, Sherwood."

No doubt about it. Josie is beside Jamie in the doorway. Putting the tube to his mouth, Sherwood looks over the length of it. "Who made the rule grown-ups can't play, too?"

"It's natural law. If we sit here and talk through this silly thing, the biscuits will burn."

"Right." He lets his end onto the floor and watches Erica prop hers on the chair. She looks more relaxed; no happier, but the edge has gone off her anger.

Supper is simple: chicken soup, biscuits, and green beans with a small bowl of strawberries as a special treat for dessert. Both children bolt their food and fly back to the living room to be birds. Erica drinks the last of the soup. Sherwood polishes off the biscuits and the beans, watching her. She wants to talk, but can't. Something wrong. I better see if I can help. Art's careful. He can hold out another couple of hours without getting caught. "You look tired," he says.

She nods. "I think I'll put the kids to bed."

Maybe she doesn't want to talk. He does the dishes, amazed at how few she has used to cook and serve. Always extra plates, cups, bowls, spoons in Marion's kitchen. A snatch of song comes from Josie's room—a scratchy phonograph record: "Sunny days chasing the clouds away/ Friendly people there, that's where we meet/ And you only have to guess how to get to Sesame Street." The lyrics drag up tag-end memories of those mystical childhood places he once thought he'd reach but forgot about instead.

The record player shuts off. Wiping his eyes, Sherwood leans against the counter and listens to the rhythm of Erica's voice as she reads through three or four stories he can't quite hear. At length she tells them good night and promises to send him in with glasses of water. He fills two enamel cups, ready to take them in as she comes out the bedroom door.

Kiss for Josie, give her the cup. It used to be improper for men to kiss male children. Wonder if it still is? He laughs, half to and half at himself, kisses Jamie on the cheek and holds the cup for him to drink. "Good night, small friends."

"Night, Sher. Night, Josie."

Josie's "good night" is muffled by blankets pulled over her face.

Sherwood finds Erica in the living room, sprawled on the couch and staring at the blank television screen. "You look a little down yourself, Sherwood."

"It's nothing." You've had enough of my troubles. "That blasted song the kids were listening to."

" 'Sesame Street'? It got to Marion too. Gets me. The kids buy it so completely. That they could actually be there with those other kids. What can we do? Let them have their childhood and hope it's enough to last. . . ."

"Did yours last?"

"Oh, damn, Sherwood. This isn't a time to ask me that. I'd have to say no."

"Mine wasn't long enough either."

"Joe and I are quits," she says.

There *it* is. "I'm sorry," and mildly pleased and, all of a sudden, feeling more than a little guilty about it.

"It had to happen. That thing between him and Josie has been like Jamie's tantrum over your woman-on-the-quad, but at slow boil for almost three months." She brushes her hair out of her eyes. "I could have handled it if I'd had sense enough to call things off, but he did it. Left for Portland last Tuesday. A short vacation, he said. Quit his job. All that fixing up his house with the new carpets was so he could get more when he sold it and, dummy that I am, I thought he was making a cozier place for us to lie in front of a fire. And he couldn't even tell me to my face. Sent a postcard."

I am sorry, he thinks. "This is going to sound like an echo, but if you want to get drunk, I'll stay with the kids."

She laughs. "I was planning that for tomorrow night. Bought myself a gallon of cheap wine and thought I'd just get it out after Josie went to sleep. An evening of cop shows and sloppy self-indulgence."

"That sounds reasonable."

"It sounds stupid to me, but it was all I could think to do."

"I'd probably do the same."

"Would you? I thought you'd dried up all that." She drops her head to hide her face. "Sorry. I warn you I might get a little bitchy, but you're welcome to get into that gallon of wine with me."

"I'd be honored."

"You really would, wouldn't you? You have a very expressive face, Sherwood. Wine, then. Drown my sorrows and you can listen to them gurgle all the way down."

Shortly, they are set up: Sherwood in the recliner that doesn't recline, and Erica at the near end of the couch, bottle of wine and two plastic glasses on the end table between them. She fills both glasses, drains hers and refills it. "And don't tell me to slow down. I intend to become unladylike as quickly as possible."

"I didn't say anything."

"It's your face. Does a lot of talking for you."

"You have to admit it's interesting that even the drug generation still drinks for its sorrows."

Erica's shrug looks a little exaggerated. "Aren't we all our fathers' creatures?"

"We must be." Fathers' creatures?

Spare, angular, hard-working man. Those years he used to wait up for me past midnight with the *Stockman's Journal* or one of his travel magazines and a drink on the arm of the chair.

He was fifty the year we took that walk on the meadow, Dad saying, "You should know about my affairs, Sherwood. In case anything happens."

"Nothing is going to happen." Words a charm, sounding thin out there. Crisp autumn air and all that space.

And his answer, "Not at your age. Nothing can happen." He worried about his heart. It fluttered sometimes, and sometimes it was hard for him to catch his breath.

"The thing that gets me worst," Erica says, "is that I'm not going to have many more like Joe. I'm thirty years old, Sherwood. What am I going to do when I can't attract a man anymore? Body sags. Crow's feet around the eyes."

"That isn't everything."

"I didn't say it was, but it's part. I'd almost forgotten what it was to be head over heels for someone and now that it's gone, I hurt when I think I might not feel it again."

"You have nice lines in your face."

"Yeah. I'll make a cute grandmother, won't I. I knew a guy in high school, back when boys were shy of tall girls, who said that about me. I'd make a good grandmother." She slaps the table, "I'm not ready for that bullshit," and pours herself another glass of wine. "Sometimes I don't think I'm ready to be a mother. How does that grab you? You're not drinking enough, Sherwood. If you're going to watch me get crocked, get crocked yourself. It's only fair."

"Why not?" The room seems warm and he can feel his heart working against his ribs, pushing blood up past his ears. A long gulp of wine tastes harsh going down, settles like a shifting weight in his stomach, but after a few minutes he ceases to hear his heart. Is that why Dad drank? Shut off that ceaseless, essential pounding. A worry to hear and a terror if ever you think it's stopped?

"That's better," Erica says.

"Like Darvon in the Army. The pains don't stop, but you quit caring about them."

She nods.

"So what now, Erica?"

"Nothing. Nothing changes. Monday morning I'll drop Josie at school and go to work. I won't mind having things simple for a while. Damn it all." She takes a gulp of wine. "I will too mind. That cold-blooded bastard, coming over here every night to this crummy little place and all the time he was getting his house spotless to put it on the market."

Sherwood shrugs.

"Don't give me that innocent act. You damn well understand how he could do it. Men. There's Art in your basement and he's kissed off the entire human race, you included. And you've kissed it all off, including yourself."

"I didn't have much choice."

"At least Joe wasn't pathological about it. The only one he kissed off was me. How long have you tucked yourself away planning to be dead before morning? Five years? You think in all that time nobody cared? Marion used to cry about it, Sherwood. And you outlived her. You could outlive me. I could finish this gallon of wine, stumble out into the street and get run down by a truck, and you'd still be here and I wouldn't. What then?"

The thought of Erica hit by a truck sends a pain running down the length of his scar, and for a second he remembers himself tearing down a mountain road on a motorcycle. Twenty-three and immortal and I didn't feel alive unless I was tempting Fate. "I know," he says.

"So?"

"As you say. Nothing changes. What I know doesn't change the way I feel about things. You really think this has anything to do with drowning *your* sorrows?"

Sinking against the sofa back, she lifts an eyebrow in question, "It might," then drags the wine jug into her lap and pours her glass full.

"You'll do okay."

"Sure I will. This time and the next and the next." She glances at him out of the corner of her eye, stares away toward Josie's half-open bedroom door, then turns back.

The gesture catches him by surprise, reminds him of Marion as a child, Jamie wanting to pound nails, and Erica herself in front of Marion's fireplace. It's the initial glance that gives the game away, he thinks. Like testing the water, then pulling back for a breath. How could I grow up with Marion and not understand that she always must have been afraid I'd reject her?

"I tried to tell you before, Sherwood, but now I've thought it out. Part of my problem has been that the men I've found haven't been very good for me. They haven't liked children."

He shakes his head.

"Don't do that. I'm not just thinking out loud this time. Before I met Joe, there was one man who liked Josie. The three of us spent time together, but he paid so much attention to her and she liked it so much that I started feeling they didn't need me at all. I wasn't very clear about what was going on, not then. I thought I was jealous of Josie and that seemed neurotic so I dropped him. Now I think it was the other way around. I'm afraid of risking my relationship with Josie. Always, before, I've looked for men who didn't threaten that."

He can't help thinking of Bonnie's painting that could be a flat-surface or three-dimensional landscape, depending on how he looked at it, and for the first time he understands that Marion might have taken his effort to spare her pain as a judgment against her. Too late, now, to tell her I'm sorry.

"What are you thinking, Sherwood?"

"Isn't important."

"It's making you unhappy, whatever it is."

"I suppose."

"Are my quirks that shocking?"

"What? That you won't sacrifice your relationship with Josie for a social life? It isn't shocking. Makes perfect sense. That's you, Erica. What amazes me is that no matter what you're doing, you can't ever be sure you won't think differently about it later. Not just you, everyone. Human beings. We get things figured out, then turn one small mental corner. The light changes. Focus changes. Bingo. Everything looks different even though nothing has changed at all."

"That doesn't make sense," she says.

"Won't make any difference. You've already figured out where your responsibility lies."

Erica sips wine, puts down the cup and scratches her ear. "Where my responsibility lies," she says. "You aren't trying to set me up again, are you? To take Jamie so you can go back to South Dakota? You could go back there for a while, then take off somewhere else with this other woman."

"I never would." We aren't understanding each other at all. I've been brooding and not listening. He drains his cup.

"Well, if you wouldn't, I'm a step ahead of you. How do you like that, Sherwood? In spite of everything, I have thought about dumping Josie on you and running off with Joe. Tell me about working out my responsibilities." She laughs, shakes her head. "Come to think of it, you're just like Marion. You're the one who has his responsibilities all worked out. I only think you'd run off because I've thought about doing it"—eyes tired and sad, she looks at him—"a couple of times. Am I making sense?"

"Yes." He watches her tip the bottle again, then he takes it from her and fills his glass.

"Why do you have to leave, Sherwood? What am I going to do with you gone too? I didn't think I could stand it when Marion died and now Joe's turned rat on me and in a couple of months you'll go and I'll have to start all over. You could . . ." She tips her head back, looks straight up. "It would be a lot easier, damn it, on me, if you'd just . . ."

"Die." He nods. That was the original idea.

She stares at him, wide-eyed, shocked. "Oh Sherwood I didn't mean that."

"It's okay."

Her hands fly to her face and she jumps up. Her glass skitters across the floor, leaves a wet trail of wine on the rug. "I have to get some air." She stumbles to the door and pushes outside. Sherwood hears the sharp, uneven beat of her shoes against the walk.

Not feeling drunk enough to stand the chilly night, he grabs the goat coat and sets out after her. Running across lawns damp from watering, he rounds the end of the block, expecting to see her, seeing only empty, shadowed sidewalk and splashes of light from the full moon. She isn't along the back of the block either, but he knows she wouldn't go far from the kids. Across the street a line of shrubs and pine trees screen a playing field. There. He sprints the pavement and comes up behind her where she walks huddled into herself at the edge of a football field.

"You weren't supposed to follow." She shivers and keeps her face away. "You really weren't. Someone has to watch the kids. Doesn't that make perfect sense?" With a shrug and a laugh she starts back toward the house. "Does anything make sense? Happiness is so simple. All you have to do is be happy, but hardly anyone manages. Always something in the way, somewhere to go to get whatever it is.

"I can't even get my jollies helping other people, Sherwood. After this thing with Joe, Josie's barely under control. Try to comfort Jamie and he screams at me and runs."

"What? When?"

"All the time. Since the first day he came back. I've been half afraid to touch him. That morning at Doris Ransler's was awful; and I don't think I could take care of him on Fridays if I didn't have Josie to help me. And you, Sherwood." She stops, turns to face him. "Is the reason I can't reach you because I don't kid around and play games?"

"You're going to get cold." He tries to wrap half the coat around her, but she spins away.

"Don't change the subject, damn it. You're probably the only friend I have. Except Josie. And maybe Jamie, sometimes. I want to know how you see me?"

"You're going to freeze. If you won't get into this coat with me, take it."

"Damn it, Sherwood O'Neal. Give me a straight answer."

"You're a woman I like and admire and I wish I had the time to find out how much I do like you. Does that help?"

She sniffles, gives a grudging nod.

"Come on. Let's go back." He slips the coat off his shoulders and drapes it over hers.

"Sure. It feels wrong, leaving the kids, doesn't it? I'm sorry. It just gets to be too much sometimes. Alone with all the roles: working woman, mother, cook, cleaning woman, professional drudge. I even have to arrange baby-sitting in order to be someone's lover. Probably I'll be happier now that I won't have to juggle him against Josie, and you, for a while." Erica holds out a flap of the coat to invite him inside.

"He must be incredibly stupid."

Her body relaxes against the arm he holds around her waist. "He didn't know how to behave with children. A lot of men don't. Maybe his father didn't have much to do with him. I don't know. Sometimes I think Josie—and Jamie, too—are lucky not to be around men who are uneasy about them. Then sometimes I'm afraid that they won't be able to get along with men at all because they won't have known any as children. You've been good for them, Sherwood."

He coughs, shuffles, listens to the wail of a police siren across town.

"I'm sorry for what I said. It wouldn't be easier if you died."

"You didn't say that."

"But that's what I was thinking."

"It's okay. I wish it myself, most of the time."

"Most."

"Yeah. Most."

"Like tonight?"

"I'm a dead man. Night is my time. I grow warts and hair on my teeth and howl. . . . But I whimper a lot in the morning."

"Vampire?"

"More like the haunted rabbit. Afraid I'd leave clumsy gashes instead of those elegant little fang marks."

Moonlight through lower branches of the pines casts spiked shadows on the packed earth. Erica slips out of the coat, knocking it off his shoulders, and backs away. "All right, rabbit. Catch me if you can." For a moment headlights of a car on the side street make her eyes glow like the eyes of an animal along the highway, then she sprints away.

Middle of South Dakota. Dusk. Flashes of broad lawn. Rich odors of moist dirt and crushed grass. Marion at age ten and the two girls from down the road toss manes of long hair near a field of half-grown oats and call, "We're horses. Catch us, Sherwood." For a moment he imagines himself as he was then, toy pistol on his hip and lariat of clothesline rope in one hand. Having to pick up the goat coat slows him, then he is after her, arms pumping, heart pounding dangerously, fresh blood spreading exuberant warmth through his thighs and calves. She has fifty yards on him at the start. By the time she rounds the lower end of the block he has cut it to forty and he gains steadily until he is on her heels in front of the house. She takes the steps in one leap, tears at the door; but he bangs it closed and goes for her neck. Laughing, she pulls her head down to fend him off. Instead of her neck, he finds her mouth.

Faint scent of perfume. Her breath smells like warm wine, and her lips taste salty. "Are you sure about this?" she whispers.

"No."

"It doesn't have to mean anything except for now."

Lying, Erica. To both of us. "It will, though," he says. "To me. But I can't see that what it means will change anything."

"You think too much, you with your little orphan and his shaggy coat. Come on."

In the beginning he tries to think of her in one dimension, tries to concentrate on the flesh she uncovers as she lets her blouse drop to the bedroom floor, the curve of her back, the heat of her body. His hands can't get enough of her; her skin soft and loose over muscle and bone. Not like the tight, younger bodies he remembers. Better. *I haven't done this for five years, and the last time was with a prostitute.* Emotion boils inside him like laughter. Bubbles of elation. Confusion. Erica: tossing under him; and at the same time the frightened woman who came with her child to Marion's that rainy night, hurt by husband and lovers, concerned about Jamie but feeling rejected by him, determined to drown a broken romance in a gallon of wine. In the end he can find no way to separate the startling, animal force of their lovemaking from who she is, and as they rock together his elation peaks, crosses some line of sensibility and becomes sorrow. He knows her better than he has known any human being in his life and if she feels anything of what he is feeling, he has just done the worst thing he could do to her.

They lie quietly afterward, first together and listening to their hearts slowing out of phase, then apart with Sherwood on his back and Erica curled away from him. At about one o'clock he gets up and makes a pot of tea, takes it back to share with her. "We probably shouldn't do this again," she says.

Sherwood nods. You too, then? More than I can handle. I wish I could wake up alone at the cabin with this all decided.

"What *are* you going to do about Jamie?"

"I don't know. If nothing else, there are some distant cousins in North Dakota. I'll give myself until June to find something here, then I'll take him back and see what's to be done."

"That's pretty unfeeling."

I must appear that way to you. "The alternative is worse. I could stay here and die. He'd go back to CPS and Doris or someone like her." He sighs. "Maybe not. They can't all be that bad, but if I could get him in with a family of second cousins, they'd care. Maybe I could even stay near there as long as he had someone to fall back on when I died."

"We could"—she raises up on one elbow, tries to get him to look at her, but finally he feels her shake her head—"get into the rest of the wine," she says. "That might put us to sleep."

"What time is it?"

"About one-thirty."

"Damn." Forgot about Art. He bounces to a sitting position.

Beside him Erica stiffens, as if his alarm is contagious. "What? Are you all right?"

"Our caseworker was grilling me today. Someone called her and told her Art was living in the house. I was going to go back and warn him." Getting up, Sherwood pulls on his pants and pads barefoot through the house to the front porch. Marion's is all dark: No light in the workroom, not even the porchlight is on. Maybe he split for the night. For a moment he realizes how lonely it must get in the tiny attic cubicle, but he blocks the thought immediately.

Back in the bedroom, Erica is curled up with the covers over her head. "Turn off the light," she says, her muffled voice sounding angry even through blankets.

He hits the switch, goes over to lie on his back and stare at the ceiling. Erica is so quiet beside him that he thinks she has fallen asleep, but then her arm moves over his chest. She kicks at the covers until she has him pulled inside, pants and all. Her breasts press against his side. "Good night, Sherwood."

"Good night." Not tonight. No sleep. I'm sorry, Erica. He forces his eyes closed.

The next thing he knows, the room is charged with daylight. He can hear the kids whispering outside the bedroom door, and a few minutes later Erica's alarm goes off. She rolls over and punches the button, then sits up and looks at him. "Oh," she says, then, "Good morning."

"I hope you feel better than you sound."

"Better than I felt last night, at least." She looks away to the door where the children have fallen silent, looks back. "Two workdays left. . . . There's room for two more at that cabin."

Can't do it. Can I? "Let me think about it." He shakes his head. Have to make sure Art's okay. "How about you and Josie come down for supper tonight, and we'll decide?" He gets up, pulls on his shirt and goes out to shoo Jamie and Josie away from the door. "If you kids get dressed right now, I'll make you pancakes for breakfast."

"French toast," Josie says.

"Right. That's what I said, wasn't it? French toast. Now hurry."

He feeds the children first and cleans up, then he and Erica eat. With clean clothes and fresh makeup she has completely erased any suggestion that she might be hung over; Sherwood finds it hard to believe he has spent the night with her. Too soon they are all out the door. Erica loads Josie into the car. "Supper tonight," she says to Sherwood.

And I have to decide whether we all go to that cabin on the coast together.

Jamie watches the car until it turns the corner, then runs down the walk after Sherwood to grab his hand. At the corner he stops to sniff some poppies. "Sher?" he asks. "Are you going to be Josie's daddy?"

"Josie already has a father somewhere."

"But I mean and they come live with us. Josie said you would."

He shakes his head. "Even if they did live with us, which is not something Erica and I are planning, it wouldn't make me Josie's father. Any more than living with you makes me your father. I'm just an uncle." He feels the tension in the child's hand as they cross the street and lawn to the front porch. There is a box on the top step, addressed to him, though there's no stamp on it. "You'd like them to come live with us, wouldn't you?"

"Yes."

Scooping up the box in one arm, he digs out his key and unlocks the door. I've let things slide too long. Waited for Art to solve his problem of where to go and for Jamie's problem to solve itself, and now they've both caught up with me. The only thing right is that Jamie is normal and happy again. "It isn't easy," he says. "I don't suppose it makes sense to you, but there are problems about living together that children can't understand. People get older and they grow a certain way, and they can't change. Aw that doesn't make sense either. Maybe if we sit down and I have another cup of coffee, I can figure out a way to explain it."

"Okay," Jamie says. He follows Sherwood through the house, watching the box, but not asking about it; climbs into his high chair. There is a closeness between them that reminds Sherwood of Sunday night in the park. He sits down and slices paper off the package with his pocket knife.

"Will you go away again, Sher?"

"Not this week, I don't think, but I need my Friday nights."

"No. Far away and me in the bad place?"

"Not a chance, man." The response is automatic. He shakes his head. "No more bad place. I already told you," he says, hoping the half lie will carry enough truth. "Let's see what's in here." He slits the taped-down flaps, opens them.

Under a layer of wadded newspapers he finds base, upright, top member, strings and magnets. Tara's magnet sculpture. What's this for? He stands it on the table in front of Jamie.

"What is it, Sher?"

"Just a thing to look at." There is a folded piece of paper in the bottom of the box. He opens it, then lifts the lower magnet to give Jamie something to think about while he reads:

I'm sorry. I'm afraid this will hurt you, but I can't see you again. I didn't know who to turn to Friday so I called the man I told you about. This sounds so callous. Please understand. The nightmare is gone. I think I just needed to tell someone who could understand. Thank you, Sherwood, for listening.

"Neat, Sher." The magnet hovers. Jamie pokes it hard and it falls, hits the table with a bang that makes him jerk away in fright. "It's not broken. Just put it up." Sherwood raises the magnet again. What do you know? Something came out right. Tara's nightmare gone. Maybe I died her lover's death for her. Now if I could just straighten out the rest of them—and me. He gets up, puts a pot of coffee water on the stove and starts toward the basement. "I'll be right back, Jamie. I have to see if Art's downstairs."

From the hall he can see Art in the workroom. He has cleaned off his bench, put all his tools in order and hung his guitars on the north wall; now he sits up on his tall stool with rags and oil and a cleaning kit Sherwood has never seen before. Apparently he has just put the pistol back together and he loads it slowly. Then he pulls up his pantleg, twirls the gun twice on his finger, taps his calf with the barrel and slips the gun into the holster door as it drops open. "Where you been, Woody?"

The question catches Sherwood off guard. He doesn't want Art to know. "Pat Chapman was here yesterday about you. Someone called her and told her you were staying here, so probably that guy in Sambo's did recognize you. She searched the house. Knows you're working here, but doesn't know where you're living. I'm not sure what we ought to do."

Art shrugs and taps his calf. The door drops open and he draws the gun, closes the door with the barrel. "I'll think of something." He winks and laughs softly to himself.

Bad news. Sherwood goes back up the stairs without another word, stops halfway up and sits on one of the steps so that neither Art nor Jamie can see him. He wishes he could flip out at will. Get it over with. There's another one coming. He can feel it and he knows that unless he can find some way to ease the pressure, this one will be bad.

Forgetting the coffee, he makes hurried preparations for the evening meal: cut-up meat and vegetables oriental style for spring rolls, oyster-sauce beef and stir-fry asparagus and snow peas. It isn't quite enough to be elegant, but he can round it out with a couple of packages of ramen. By nine-thirty he has rolled the last spring roll and put everything away in covered dishes in the refrigerator. "Let's forget work today," he says to Jamie. They catch a bus for Sacramento to visit the petting zoo, have lunch on the K Street Mall and then blow the afternoon; first in a little park full of winos and old men playing chess, then on the Capitol grounds. Hiding out from Art, Sherwood thinks. From Art? I hope he cools it with that gun tonight. Have to get things straight with Erica. A couple of days at the ocean to think, then just come back and do what I have to. And if we're going, I should let Pat know so she doesn't get worried and come after us with cops. Maybe it's finally time to tell her the whole story.

A little after five-thirty the bus drops them in the Fifth Street park. The sun is already behind the trees, and the air is beginning to cool. As they start up the block toward Marion's they see Erica and Josie sitting on the steps. Josie comes flying down the walk to meet them, shouts her hello to Sherwood and grabs Jamie's hand. "We're going to play," she calls over her shoulder. "You can talk to Mommy."

The two of them race up the parking strip. Sherwood follows at an easier pace. Erica waits on the step. Her hello sounds tired and as soon as he opens the door, she goes into the kitchen, where she sits down at the table. With motions that seem to require all her concentration she takes a crumpled business envelope out of her purse.

"We have to talk, Sherwood."

Something wrong. "Okay. Do you want a cup of coffee while I start supper?"

"No thank you."

"What's the matter?" The only thing he can think of is that Pat Chapman has talked to her and that he's in trouble.

"Are we going anywhere?"

Going anywhere? No, wait. There's enough gone wrong already.

She watches his face, then shakes her head. "I'm sorry. I can see that we're not, but I want to hear it." Her hands smooth the envelope onto the chipped Formica tabletop. "This is from Joe. He says he's thought about things and he wants me to pack up Josie and come to Portland and we'll try for real this time."

"Are you going to do it?"

Her mouth makes a tight line, goes slack. She bites her lower lip.

"You won't go," he says. "You know you won't do it."

"How can you be so damned sure?"

"You told me yourself. You're not going to let anyone get between you and Josie."

"But it would be so much easier," she says. "How can I stay here, knowing you'll be gone as soon as you do whatever it is you're going to do with Jamie? Pressure me to take him."

"Erica, I'm not pressuring you."

"It's the way you do things, Sherwood. Fill Marion's place and Jamie's father's place and Josie's father's place. Make me think I should be able to do it. I know I should have taken him when I knew she'd been killed. Sometimes I think if you'd just stay, I'd have time to figure out from you how you manage it, but that's just a dream because the only reason you can do it is that you don't care. You're not human. You're so selfish with this 'already dead' nonsense that this is all just some minor annoyance you have to get through before you can leave Jamie and crawl off into your mountains to die." Her voice chokes off.

Following her horrified gaze, Sherwood sees the children framed
in the doorway, both of them reared back as if they have just
come out of the coat still heaped around their knees, Josie looking
concerned; Jamie's face gone blank with terror. Sherwood can almost smell Doris Ransler's shitty room. "Jamie."

The eyes are coals of resentment.

"We better talk about this, small friend." Sherwood reaches for
him, but Jamie wails and lurches out of reach. Things happening
too fast. Jamie tearing through the dining room, taking the
corner into the back hall. Safety of his room already in sight. Feet
slipping, body beginning to tilt, going down. Woodwork around
the doorframe, sharp and nasty. Down.

Before Sherwood can move, Jamie is sliding along the living-
room wall. His body makes a screeching sound against the floor;
feet hit the leg of the bed with a force that snaps his head down,
and his forehead crunches against the molding. Erica cries out.
Sherwood can feel rather than hear the "Oh no" that resonates in
his own throat. The distance from the kitchen to the hall door
seems too great and the time too short. Already thick blood
spreads across the floor, sinks between the boards.

Only half conscious, Jamie is still stiff and his resistance seems
to make the blood flow faster. Sherwood jerks out his shirttail and
wipes at the wound, trying to see how deep it is and at the same
time trying not to wipe hard enough to dislodge any bone fragments the doctors might need to repair damage to the skull.
"Relax, man. Relax. I'm not going anywhere. Try to relax and let
it slow down so I can see how badly you're hurt." The glaze over
Jamie's eyes is part shock, part withdrawal from an impossible
world. "Don't go away, little guy. This is Sherwood. Sher? Remember?"

He is half aware of Josie beside him. Erica presses a towel into
his hand and he drops the drenched end of his shirt. The cut is
above the eye. There is no apparent eye damage, no pieces of
bone after all, but the bleeding won't stop. Sherwood finally
winds the towel around Jamie's head. "Let me have your keys. I
have to get him to the hospital."

"I'll drive."

"No."

"My God, Sherwood. I'm sorry. Don't shut me out."

"Let's move, then." Jamie's body goes limp as he lifts him up and he is out the door ahead of Erica. Her feet and Josie's clatter behind him on the sidewalk.

Once inside the station wagon they are all silent, lost in the engine noise, the groans of the frame in protest against each stop and start and turn. Erica drives too fast, eyes ahead and knuckles like pale knobs at the top of the wheel. Josie is quiet, Jamie withdrawn. Headlights on the darkening streets dance in front of Sherwood's eyes and he wonders if he is going to flip out.

This time he is glad the hospital is so far from town. Cart my guilt away from the lights and the people. No difference to Jamie whether I leave or die. Either way he's alone again. Fail anyway I turn. Can't help. His head buzzes and reflections of light he can't see wink off the glass of the rear-view mirror. His legs feel heavy. Let it come. This time I'm ready.

The images that hit him are not like flipping out—more like a memory or a hallucination that starts as shapes and shadows and then grows, sharpens. Dim light from outside, probably a street-lamp, slants up through venetian blinds and throws a pattern of bars across the ceiling. Odors of alcohol and rubber. Door ajar, the hall outside deathly quiet. His own body swathed in gauze. Pain running from throat to abdomen. Tubes trembling down from suspended bottles. A wind? Who is trembling? Finger on the call button. Buzzer sounding in the distance. No one has said anything, but he is aware that his parents have been killed in their car. Soft squeak of crepe soles approaching the door, turning away. Throat too dry to cry out. Body drugged and heavy. Finger numb on the buzzer. Don't leave. Don't give me up to die here alone. Kenny is dead and he knows that in some way it is his fault. His parents' death is his fault too. *I was supposed to be the one who died.* He lets out a cry and the hallucinations stop.

Jamie is in his arms. Sherwood loosens his grip on the child's leg and stares across the fields. Something tickles his cheek. Reaching up to scratch, he finds his face and scalp are soaked with sweat. His hand shakes as he wipes his eyes. He doesn't realize the car has stopped, doesn't even see the hospital until Erica says, "We're here." With foot and elbow he pushes open the door.

"Can I help, Sherwood?"

Without a backward glance he is out, kicking the door closed and loping across the parking lot to the emergency entrance. Jamie's eyes are blank. His lips are pale and even his hair looks as if something essential has retreated to leave only a vaguely corporeal ghost.

This time the hallway is deserted, no suicides, broken bones or high fevers; nothing to take the focus of attention away from Jamie. Doris Ransler creases the page of a magazine as she looks up from the duty desk. "You again," she says.

"He fell."

"I bet he did. Third door on your right. Put him on the large table. I'll get a blanket. He looks like he's in shock."

Mute, Sherwood shuffles down the hall.

"Gonna be fifteen minutes before I can get a doctor here."

"Try for ten." He puts Jamie on the wheeled bed. In the reflector of the light above he catches a glimpse of himself, hair disheveled, blood on his arms and the front of his shirt and blood still dripping down his pants leg from the soaked shirttail. "I'm not looking all that respectable," he mutters. "Jamie? You have to listen to me. Erica was angry. At me, not you. She was saying I'd die or leave you because she knew it would hurt me to hear her say it. Can you understand that?" How could you? All that nonsense has to be learned.

"I'm not going to leave you. Okay? Hear that? I'm not leaving."

Jamie doesn't respond.

Too much all at once. Sherwood stares up at his image in the reflector. I'm not going anywhere, am I? Art had it pegged. There's no leaving now. "I'll stay. Got that?"

The dark eyes remain blank. Doris comes in with a clipboard, hands it to Sherwood. She gets a blanket from the cupboard and moves to put it over Jamie. Sherwood takes it away from her and covers him. "Let me have a look," she says.

"Don't touch him. If you want to do something, hurry that doctor."

Her eyebrows go up and she looks smug. "You're familiar with our form. Fill out Part One and sign on the lines marked 'x.'"

"Right. Now you get out of here."

Familiar with the form. Our names, Marion's address. Write "apprentice guitar maker" in the space for OCCUPATION that I left blank before. Father, split; mother, dead; relationship, guardian. He signs Part One, skips down the page to the section on financial responsibility, but stops midway at a small, heavily bordered box with the heading AUTHORITIES NOTIFIED. Of four tiny boxes and a blank line for 'other' Doris has checked two: POLICE and CHILD PROTECTIVE SERVICES.

Uh-oh. He signs the two remaining lines automatically, drops the clipboard on the metal cabinet, then stands over the bed. "Jamie. Snap out of this. That lady with the shitty room is going to drag us through it, man. If you can't believe I'm going to stay, if you can't bring yourself around enough to tell these people what happened, they're going to lock me up and take you away. Doris is going to say I hit you and they'll believe it unless you can tell them otherwise."

Eyes still blank, Jamie turns his face away.

Sirens and flashing lights, sure as hell. No ambulance, just handcuffs and doors without handles on the inside. *Child beater.* Leaving Jamie for a moment, he steps out to look up and down the hall. Erica and Josie haven't come in. Doris ignores him. If there were another nurse, he could go outside and alert Erica, but there is no one else in sight and he doesn't want Doris to make Jamie any worse.

Grab Jamie and run? Get to Erica's and spend the night, call Pat in the morning. Stall a confrontation until all the witnesses are lined up and ready. Jamie in better shape. Ex-mental patient brutalizes child. Bad news. He slips back into the treatment room and grips Jamie's shoulder. "Come on, little dude. Let me see your head. We're going to have to split." Gently he peels back the towel.

Jamie's eyebrows twitch. The cut is about an inch long and it gapes open so that the movement of the brows produces a ripple in pale, exposed muscle. Can't run out, that cut needs stitches. He pulls up a stool and sits down to rest his elbows on the bed beside the child's arm. "This is it. I'm not leaving, got that? I'm staying with you. You have to believe me." He hears a rustle, then footsteps in the hall and turns to see Doris whispering to the doctor, the same young, bearded doctor who did the stitches in Jamie's chin. The doctor appears annoyed. Finally he and Doris separate and come toward the treatment room, she a step behind.

"I don't want her in here, Doc."

"You see, Doctor? What did I tell you? We're going to need help."

The doctor waves her back into the hall. "If I need help, I'll call you." He closes the door in her face. "What happened?"

"He fell down and hit his head on the doorframe. He was running, turning a corner and he slipped." Sherwood slides one hand along the other. "His feet hit a bed and his head snapped down." He takes a breath. Give him the whole story?

"You better finish whatever you were going to say." The doctor's eyes look concerned or angry, or both. "Nurse Ransler says you're a mental patient. Also that you once threatened to kill her and that she was afraid to stop you from taking this child illegally."

Now the whole story. "That's close, Doc." He takes a long breath. "I said I'd kill her. I was tempted, but I wouldn't have killed her even if I'd had her ugly neck in my hands. I'm an ex-mental patient, not a mental patient; and I was never *that* kind of crazy.

"I was in an accident five years ago. A military accident. Shrapnel in the chest. They said they got all the junk out of my heart. They'd tell me that, then I'd hear them talking when they thought I was asleep, and they weren't ever sure they got it all. I've had psychiatric help because I can't function. For the last five years I've been expecting to die any minute. That's the kind of crazy. Make sense?"

Nodding, Dr. Goldsmith pulls back the towel and pokes at the cut. Jamie doesn't move. "Keep talking," he says. "I'll get started." He checks the stitches on Jamie's chin, then spreads a green sheet of paper on his chest. "Sterile surface here. Don't touch anything on it."

"A friend of mine who lost his legs in Vietnam and I got out of the hospital together," Sherwood says. "We lived a couple of years in Martinez, where we were seeing a psychiatrist who had worked with us both in San Jose and then transferred. About a year ago we decided to get out of California, went to South Dakota and got a cabin in the mountains. That's where I was when I found out that my sister, Jamie's mother, had died.

"Jamie was in a foster home about a month before I heard. I came out to see about him. He was a mess. The house was filthy

and he wasn't getting any care at all. I took him out of there and
we did all right together. He accepted me after a while and, I'm
afraid, trusted me. I had planned to find him a better home, a permanent home, and then go back to the cabin.

"It's crazy. I was going to go back because I was afraid I'd die
and mess him up."

The doctor grunts, but nothing more.

"Tonight he overheard a conversation about my planning to
leave. He was running from me when he fell. The way you see
him is the way he was when I took him from the foster home.
Like a frightened animal, almost a vegetable."

"That's hard to believe. I know something about the foster-
home program here and it's very good."

Sherwood shrugs. "They made a mistake."

"Why didn't you report it? Didn't the social worker go with
you to pick him up from the home?"

"I didn't report her because I did tell her I'd kill her and her
daughter heard me, and with my record I was afraid she'd blow
my chance to help Jamie."

"Doris," he says as if he hadn't understood before. "Doris?"
Shaking his head, he changes direction abruptly. "What color was
the woodwork?"

"What?"

"The doorframe? The woodwork he hit his head on?"

"Mud brown."

"You're going to have to prove everything you've told me. Even
if it's true, you ought to be prosecuted. There's a new law about
having to report child abuse." He pokes at the cut. "Nurse
Ransler has already notified the police and CPS."

"I know."

"You know?"

"It was marked on the form I had to sign."

The doctor holds up a swab to the light and looks at the dirt on
it. "At least you got the color of the paint right. Get on the other
side of the table and hold his hands while I sew him up."

"I don't think he'll give you any trouble."

"Just do it," the doctor says. He sounds angry and tired, and a
little like he'd rather not be involved.

Moving to the other side of the bed, Sherwood takes Jamie's

hands loosely in his. "Cold hands, man. Have you paid attention to what's going on? I'm staying. We're going to have to talk about the possibility of my dying, but we'll know it's coming and fix things so you won't have to end up in some shitty room. Okay?"

Still glazed and half distant, Jamie's eyes turn toward Sherwood. He nods.

"Hold still."

"Don't move a minute, Jamie. The doctor has to sew you up."

Jamie's hands twitch, grip the thumb of Sherwood's left hand and the little finger of his right. The doctor slips a long needle under the lips of the wound and injects local anesthetic. Jamie doesn't flinch. Sherwood closes his eyes.

"If you're going to get faint on me, I'll have to call Nurse Ransler."

"No. I'll manage."

With sure hands, Dr. Goldsmith prods the discolored skin around the wound. "Can you feel this? How about this?" Jamie nods, then finally shakes his head.

The sewing takes only a minute. Four stitches, four knots. The doctor steps away. "I'll have to ask you to wait, unless the police are here already."

"We'll wait. This time we're going to do it right."

They don't have to wait. Pat Chapman and a plainclothesman are standing outside the door. The man shows Sherwood his badge. Doris is nowhere in sight. A woman Sherwood hasn't seen before sits at the desk. "Am I under arrest?" he asks.

"No. Not at this time."

Pat looks tired and annoyed. "What happened, Sherwood?"

"He fell again."

"I want to believe you." She shakes her head. "Were you alone? The two of you?"

"Erica was there. Erica Riggs and her daughter."

"How do I get in touch with her?"

"She brought us. Last I saw her was in the parking lot."

"What kind of car?" the cop asks.

"A Ford station wagon. Beat up. Old."

"I don't think it was there when we drove in, but I'll double-check." He strides back down the corridor and outside.

"If she isn't there," Pat says, "I'll have to take Jamie with me. I can't leave him with you unless I'm sure." Jamie moves in Sherwood's arms to look at her and she puts a hand on his shoulder. "How did you hurt your head, Jamie?"

"I fell down." His voice is soft, almost a whisper, and the words are pronounced without inflection.

"What's the matter with him? Is he in shock, Doctor?"

Dr. Goldsmith motions her down the hall. They retreat out of Sherwood's hearing, Pat listening with head tipped forward and the doctor talking in low tones. The plainclothesman comes back inside. "She's not there now," he says.

And you doubt she ever was. Sherwood shifts Jamie to hold him against his hip. Things aren't looking all that good.

"You say she brought you out? How did she expect you to get back?"

"I don't suppose she thought about it. She was angry. And something she said caused the accident." Acts like he'd be happier to find out I'm lying.

"What's her address?"

"I'm not sure. It's on C Street between Sixth and Seventh. West side of the street between two duplexes."

"That little house?"

"Right. Her name is Erica Riggs. She's in the phone book."

"Don't try to leave." The man walks to the duty desk, pages through the phone book, then dials.

Pat and the doctor split up and Pat comes back shaking her head. "Was your friend there?"

"No. He's trying to call her now."

"I can't believe what I just heard. You're saying now that you had Jamie two weeks before we went to pick him up?"   .

"That's right. He was asleep in the other room the first day you came."

"And you claim he was this withdrawn when you took him?"

"Worse. He wouldn't talk, walk, even look at me. The only thing he would do was cry if I separated him from the coat."

"I even asked you about Doris Ransler. The first day. And you wouldn't tell me. Didn't you trust me? Did you think I was stupid? That no one would understand your reaction to something like that?" She takes a deep breath. "It makes sense. That feeling you weren't telling me everything."

"No one answers the number for Erica Riggs," the cop says.

"Maybe she isn't home yet." No idea what time it is or how long we've been here. Maybe she went out for a drink?

"Well, I'm not going to wait around here until someone locates this woman. I can't leave Jamie with you."

Just like that. Something awesome in that power—the ability just to take him from me. "Where will he go?"

"To the shelter home. There will have to be another hearing, a detention hearing. Thursday or Friday at the latest. Doris has reported possible abuse against you. She'll have to file a written report in the morning. You should have reported her." She cuts off, too angry to continue.

Sherwood turns Jamie away from Pat. "Do you understand all this? You're going to have to go with Pat tonight. If she'll write down where you'll be, I'll come visit you tomorrow. Do you want me to bring the coat?"

Jamie shakes his head.

"Keep it so I'll have to get you back, huh?" A nod. "Okay. You go with Pat. I'll get Erica to tell her what happened and come let you know how we're doing as soon as I can get there in the morning." He tightens his grip and Jamie finally lifts his arms to hug Sherwood around the neck. "Just don't worry, man."

Pat takes a card out of her purse and scribbles an address on it. "If you're going to take him, let's not drag it out."

She nods and reaches for Jamie, who clings to Sherwood for a moment, then turns passive. The nurse at the duty desk looks up and away again as if she has been caught spying. "Is Doris Ransler off now?" Sherwood asks her.

"No. She went on break. If you want to wait, she'll be back in a few minutes."

"Thanks. No." He follows Pat and Jamie and the plainclothes cop outside. "If you want to see what it's really like at Doris's, one of you ought to sit on her front step and check the house as soon as she gets home from work."

"I'll see it in the morning," Pat says.

"She'll probably have it together by morning. She's beaten your inspections before and she knows that now I'll tell you what I've seen."

"I see." She studies Sherwood. "You *really* took this child two weeks before the court gave you custody?"

"Go there tonight and I'm betting you'll see why. If my chances for keeping Jamie are riding on what you find, I'll go wherever you're taking him and drag you to her place as soon as he's settled."

"John?" she asks the cop. Her mouth makes a tight line across her face and her fingers tremble as she straps Jamie into the shoulder harness and seatbelt of her car.

"I'll go," the cop says. "I have to check in and I'll want to see your house too, Mr. O'Neal. Will you be there after eight?"

Sherwood nods; stands on the sidewalk and watches them both get into cars and drive away. Across the fields the lights of town sparkle and beckon. Must be a criminal. Neither of them thought to offer me a ride. Should go in and call a cab, but Doris is there, and the curious nurse and Dr. Goldsmith who doesn't want to be involved and is, and who probably resents the living hell out of me.

The short way in across the fields, but Sherwood crosses the parking lot and starts down the shoulder of the road, back hunched and hands in his pockets. The sun is down behind the Coast Range and the sky is going dark. Chilly. Feeling a little cramped in the forehead. Cold coming on if I don't watch out. Chug a bunch of vitamin C, hot bath and bed. If I make it back to Marion's. Just plain scared to take the short way. No one goes there. Alone. It isn't the being dead that makes dying so hard, it's the loneliness of lying down and listening to the organs shut off one by one, never to go again. Fall into a plowed furrow out there and stare up at the stars alone until my eyes go gray.

Lost in thought he walks, dwelling on the terror. Impact of metal against flesh. Am I awake? Am I flipping out? How do I stop this?

Marion alone in her car. Fingers touching lightly on the wheel, lifting the cigarette to her mouth. Thinking of home, thinking about Jamie or the next time she'll see Donald Holmes. Daydreaming at the wheel? How do these things happen? Metal screaming, heating up, bending out of shape. Odors of flaked paint, fluid spewed on the hot engine block, insulation burned off shorted wires. View of the spinning world fragmented through the

smashed windshield. Purse and papers scattered on the floorboard.
Mom and Dad went the same way. Together in the car. Machine
swerving. The end of hope. One last terror before peace.

He hears himself sob, feels the tears begin as he sinks into the
weeds beside the road to stare up at the evening star that dances
like a fluid spark. All dead. I couldn't help any of them. Blood
pounds in his ears. Going to flip out. He squeezes his eyes shut.
Have to stop it. Count heartbeats. "One, two . . ." Blood flowing
back to its source. My heart. Inner walls scarred and scabbed,
sprouting bits of dirt and metal. Threads, buttons from Kenny's
uniform. Pieces of keys. Tatters of letters from home. His fingers
trace down his shirt, following the operation scar from the top of
his breastbone to its end near his navel. Points of light float across
his closed eyelids. Can't flip out. He tries to remember Kenny's
face, but instead sees Jamie, fighting back tears while Pat straps
him into her seatbelt. "Couldn't help," he says, then his grief ob-
literates all sensation.

When he regains control and is able to get himself up again the
sky is completely dark and filled with stars. No cars pass him on
the highway. His eyes adjust until he can count the fenceposts as
he passes them, can see the rank grass left from winter and the
mustard plants growing to cover the ground with new green leaves
and yellow flowers. Eventually he enters town, where the lights
seem oppressive on the pavement. At least I didn't flip out.
Fought it off this time. Down the boulevard, past apartments
with tall fences to shut out the noise and fumes of traffic, past the
high-school football field to the park, with its man-made hills.
Dirt hauled in from who knows where, thrown up by earth-moving machinery. Break up the flatness. Maybe anything is better
than nothing at all.

Across the street he can see the condominiums. That way to
Tara's stone fireplace and clock hands without numbers on the
stones; but he moves south across the spongy grass of the park to
the narrow streets and full-grown trees of the central part of town.

Marion's house is lighted as if for a party. The interior is plainly
visible from the street; the chair and single bed in the living room,
piano and table and a couple of straight-back chairs in the dining
room, the chipped blue table and Jamie's high chair and dishes
stacked in the drainer beside the kitchen sink. The front door is

wide open. Oblivious to all that has happened, Art saws something in the basement. Sherwood walks softly into the kitchen,
opens the refrigerator door. He is hungry, but there isn't anything
to eat; only the stacked, covered dishes of chopped and wilting
vegetables, pieces of raw meat that remind him of the pale muscle
inside Jamie's forehead. Finally Sherwood closes the door, slips
out of the house and walks down the block to Erica's.

Her car isn't parked in front, but a light is on in the bedroom.
Sherwood knocks. No response. He knocks again, then pounds,
but his beating on the door brings no sound from inside. "It was
my fault, not yours," he calls. "I was all wrong."

Nothing.

A side window in the far duplex slides open. He can see two
faces in shadow behind the screen and an angry voice growls,
"Would you shut up."

"Sure," he says. He wanders back to Marion's, feeling aimless,
tired and used up. The time is eight-thirty and he wonders if the
cop has already come and gone away again. In the kitchen cupboard Sherwood finds half a bottle of vitamin C. He takes a handful, wanders toward the basement stairs; but before he gets
through the back hall, he hears a car door slam outside.

"Art?" he calls.

"Yeah. Gotta talk to you, Woody."

"We're going to have a cop here for a while. Lie low."

Hoping that Art's silence means he understands, Sherwood goes
back through the house to meet the plainclothesman from the
hospital at the front door. The man introduces himself by name
this time, but Sherwood doesn't pay any attention. There are one
or two more questions—eleven by Sherwood's count—all of which
seem pointless. At least Pat hasn't thought to mention the anonymous phone call. Art remains quiet in the basement and the cop
doesn't ask about him. Last, he takes scrapings from the woodwork and blood-stained floor.

"Pat got somebody out of bed," he says as he leaves. "The detention hearing will be Thursday morning at ten o'clock."

"Thanks." Before the cop is off the steps, Sherwood dials
Erica's number and lets it ring and ring.

He is still listening to the hollow clacking inside the receiver when Art clomps up the stairs and grinds past the kitchen doorway with a wool blanket thrown over one arm.

"Erica isn't home, Woody."

"How do you know?" Dragging phone cord, Sherwood goes into the kitchen.

"Hang up and give me a hand." Art passes one corner of the blanket across the table and moves to drape his end over the curtain rod. "You were right about who called your damned social worker. My father was poking around here this afternoon. Big, heavy-set guy with him. I hid out, but they'll be back."

"I'm sorry, Art." No time for this now. "You know where Erica is?"

Art fusses with the blanket until it hangs straight to cover the window, then leans against the counter. "She called. Sometime after eight." Rubbing his chin, he watches Sherwood.

"Don't fool with me, man. They took Jamie and I can't get him back without her. Where is she?"

"Headed north. She called from someplace up there, Willows or Williams. I told her she ought to come back, that you weren't going anywhere even if you weren't smart enough to see it. Said if she did come back and I was wrong about you, I'd take her; but she just swore and hung up."

Going to Portland? "She didn't sound like she'd come back?" Did you blow it for me, Art?

"Not as mad as she was. It's just us again, Woody. Us and my father. You ready to run back to the cabin?"

"I can't leave Jamie. You're right about that."

"Yeah." Art lets out a dry, mirthless laugh. "It's my curse. Being right. I'm going to call Brodie, then. You got the kid to watch out for and I can't handle fighting my father about going home."

"Brodie?"

"Let him put me in the hospital. It's the only way. Call Brodie and find myself a bar." He tilts his head. "You want to get drunk?"

Drunk? No, man, but I can't let you do it alone. Too near a flipout to be alone myself.

"We could get blown away, Woody. Just like old times."

"Smoking pot on the hospital roof?"

"I mean the real old days. The old army days. Condemned men; every drunk might be our last, you know? Like in Saigon. And that place you used to go . . ."

"Koza."

"That's it. Koza. Mourn our dead and wind up in the gutter."

"A good grovel, we called it," Sherwood says. Need something and I feel too bad to stand being alone.

Pushing himself away from the counter, Art picks up the phone and stumps into the living room. "That sister of yours keep any booze in the house?"

"Probably." Sherwood goes into the back hall and digs through cupboard shelves until he finds half a fifth of scotch. Better to start drinking now. If I don't, I'm going to think; and anything I'd think about, I don't want to. He slops liquor into two glasses and carries one in to Art, who breaks off talking and covers the mouthpiece of the phone against his hip.

"My cane's in the shop. Would you get it?"

Something wrong here. I can feel it. Taking a swallow of scotch, Sherwood climbs down to the workroom. The cane is on Art's workbench, next to the gun-cleaning kit. Get him drunk, drag him home and then maybe call Brodie myself and find out what's going on. . . .

By the time he gets back upstairs and makes a pass through the bathroom and Marion's room to wash up and grab a clean shirt, Art is on the front porch, leaning against the doorframe. "Come on. Let's get on with it." His empty glass is on the floor beside the phone.

Sherwood gulps down the last of his own drink, puts his glass beside Art's. The receiver is off the cradle, held up by a doubled piece of cord caught between the two. Using the tip of the cane, he jerks the cord free. Something flakey. He pokes the phone one more time to make sure the receiver is down tight, then he takes the cane out to Art. "Are you going to be able to make it all the way to town?"

"Damn right. One drink in me, I can walk anywhere for another one. Move out." In spite of his claim, the eight blocks to town tire Art. The first two bars they try serve only beer. The third is too well lighted to suit either of them. They end up in an old house divided into basement beer bar and a restaurant with adjoining hard-liquor bar on the main floor. Art doesn't like this place either, but the waitress who brings them their first drinks says that the one bar they haven't tried is mostly suit-and-tie crowd.

"This is it, then. A little quiet, isn't it?"

"Tuesdays are always slow." The woman takes Art's ten-dollar bill and makes change. "The rush doesn't start until after ten."

"Well, just keep our drinks coming, rush or no rush. We'll treat you right." Art slides his cane under the chair, downs half his first scotch and looks around at the hanging light fixtures, framed pictures of turn-of-the-century Dawville, the wall of open brickwork between the bar and the front dining room of the restaurant. "It isn't much, but it's better than getting blotto in some hooch."

A sign behind the bar says MAXIMUM SEATING CAPACITY 56, but the only other people are two waitresses, the bartender, three loud college kids and a small group back in the dark. What are we doing out in the middle of the room? Do you feel as exposed as I do?

"What do you think, Woody? It's just the two of us again."

"Erica didn't say anything about coming back?"

Art shakes his head and his eyes go distant.

"What's the matter?"

With an abrupt shrug, he finishes his drink and waves to the waitress who brings two more.

Art folds a five-dollar bill over his middle finger and passes it to her, waves away the change.

"Take it easy with your money, man. We want to go the distance." Better this than going back to the house. "Last until midnight and see what happens to Dawville when the days change."

"Not a problem, GI. I got a hundred bucks to blow. Then if we can't find a slope taxi driver, we'll crawl home."

Too loud, Art. One of the men at the dark table sends a nasty look their way and Sherwood, eyes now accustomed to the dim light, notices that the woman beside him is oriental. "Hey, easy. There's a guy behind you with a Japanese wife or girlfriend."

"Hot shit," Art says, but he swings around, waves and calls, "Waitress, give those people a drink on me."

"No thanks," the man says. His low, menacing voice carries across the room.

Art turns back, mutters, "Mother. Always a sorehead. I ever tell you about the night we got drunk and went to get laid in the *ville* across the river and ended up blowing away half a dozen VC coming down the other bank for the same . . . ?" He is off and running: Eight dead here, three laid, half a dozen joints smoked, six more dead. . . . Drinks appear on the table like incoming shells to punctuate his stories. Sherwood sips scotch and edges his half-full glasses into a growing jam at his elbow. Most of the empties are carried away on the waitress's tray, but one ends up on the floor, where it rolls between his shifting feet. At first he worries that the man with the Japanese woman will overhear something else he doesn't like, but the bar begins to fill at about ten o'clock, and by ten-thirty it is crammed shoulder to shoulder with drunk college kids. The extra chairs disappear from around the table. In a large group that seems to move back and forth behind him, Sherwood hears propositions encouraged and brushed off in voices that bubble with high spirits. Through the din and chatter he can occasionally make out music from the jukebox, and in one lull he catches Joan Baez singing half a verse of "The Night They Drove Old Dixie Down."

He can no longer follow the whole sense of what Art is saying, but Sherwood still hears enough to know that the funny stories are all done, that the drift toward the tragic and the pathetic has begun. The contrast between the boisterous activity around them and the drawn look on Art's face bothers him. Bodies lurch back and forth, some in time with the beat from the jukebox, some half out of control. What are all these kids doing here? Sherwood has had enough scotch to know he has been drinking, but he doesn't feel drunk. The taste is familiar in his throat and it drags up memories. Two years in the Army and two to go. Education already wasted. No civilian skills. No place waiting on the outside. He had finally realized the only sensible thing to do was to re-up. Take his bonus and stick it out to retirement. Combat duty a vague risk. Drank then and plenty and with good reason; wanting to blot out the possibility that every stupid, strutting E-6 or new warrant officer might be a sign of the life to come for Sherwood O'Neal.

Across the table Art straightens himself in his chair, smooths the shirt over his chest and leans forward. "You been looking at these kids, Woody?"

"Yeah. I don't understand it."

"I can see us wanting to get ripped. We've seen plenty, man. Things we want to forget, but most of these punks are just barely shaving. None of 'em ever saw a man gut shot. . . ." Art shudders, closes his eyes and then opens them again.

The thought of someone gut shot reminds Sherwood of the Custer post office and the clerk's friend; and it sends fingers of pain radiating from his solar plexus. He reaches inside his shirt and scratches his scar. "We don't belong here, Art."

"They sure as hell don't. That's a fact. Three good men with me and I'd throw all their asses out."

"Let's go."

"Rather drink with a bar full of VC. At least they'd know what kind of shit came down."

Sherwood tries to push his chair back, but finds feet and legs in the way. "Excuse me," he mumbles. Three kids in jeans and sweat shirts press into the backs of more kids to make room for him to get the chair out of his way, but before he can move, an oriental woman slips through the space on her way toward one of the doors. Art catches sight of her, says something in a language

Sherwood supposes is Vietnamese. The woman doesn't notice, tries to brush past. Art catches her arm and drags her onto the tabletop. "I makie talkie you, you lissen-up, honey, hear?"

She twists half away, her face a mask of anger and fright.

"This isn't some *ville*, Art. Let her go."

"Aw. She doesn't mind, Woody." He pulls her onto his lap.

Her anger flashes surprise at landing on solid wooden thighs, and Sherwood has to fight back a laugh. "He's a bitter old jungle fighter," he says. "Keep cool and we'll straighten him out, get him on the road home."

She nods. Bright and aware of what's going on. Maybe she had a brother over there and understands. Some vein of sympathy, and anyway, she's a little blitzed herself and inclined to be generous. Sherwood reaches for Art's shoulder. "Let her go, man. There are forty wise-ass kids in here and I can see at least ten guys who wouldn't need more than a fast thumbs-up from anywhere to clean the floor with each other and us in the bargain."

The woman's eyes and Art's give warning at the same time. Sherwood feels a hand bite into his shoulder and hears a deep, drunken voice ask, "What the hell is going on?" Before he can answer, another hand latches on and he is thrown up and back, carrying the chair with him into a wall of bodies that collapses under his weight.

In the stunned silence, he has time to hear Joan Baez slide through the line about tearing up tracks, then a roar erupts to rip away the music. The lights above shift and dazzle; he fights for control. Two people begin to struggle underneath him. Three pick themselves up to one side. A foot kicks past his face and Sherwood grabs it and twists, scrambles to his feet, takes a fist on his forearm to protect his throat and breaks free of the jostling mob. Across bobbing heads he can see women run for the exits. In addition to the scuffle he has escaped, a fight with five or six antagonists has started along the bar and two men go at each other in relative isolation near the front windows.

The Japanese woman is nowhere to be seen. Her date shakes Art by his shoulders, but while Sherwood watches, Art swarms onto the man's neck and head, and gets a firm grip on one of the hanging light fixtures. Dangling, one arm waving free, he punches twice. His fist rebounds from his assailant's temple and the man staggers back, regains his feet, sights a blow at Art's groin. Too late. The wooden legs come up together and catch him, one on the shoulder, the other on the chin, and the man sinks backward into the crowd. Two glasses sail across the room and shatter against the brickwork wall. "Come on, you sons-of-bitches," Art roars.

Sherwood maneuvers under him, pushes tables and chairs out of the way, motions frantically toward his shoulders. "You fight. I'm the footwork."

Eyes wild with anger, Art clubs someone behind the ear with one thrashing leg, then nods and drops onto the back of Sherwood's neck, dress shoes pointed forward like caps on twin battering rams. A fuzz-faced kid careens toward them, a beer bottle raised over his head. Sherwood spins away from him, looking for a door.

"Get that little bastard," Art yells.

At the end of the brickwork wall—a passage. Sherwood runs for it, ducks into the dining room. Art yanks at his hair. "Back, back. Into the shit." Startled diners, already retreating from the shattered glass that sprays through gaps in the wall, stare as the two gallop through the room knocking over tables and scattering empty chairs. Sherwood has misjudged the door; he blunders through a maze of place settings, empty bowls that reek of salad dressing, plates covered with half-eaten steak and coagulated grease. Waiters like bullfighters wave white towels, try to catch the falling glassware.

Three women, refugees from the bar, streak by, fling open a glass door and Sherwood follows them onto the porch that is gradually filling with fighters. Sirens cry in the distance, coming fast to cut him off from Marion's. Hampered by Art's attempts to turn him, Sherwood bounds down the steps and dashes across the street. His feet puff up dust from the bulldozed parking strip, then crunch on the rock fill of the railroad embankment. There is a screen of trees to his right and he makes for its cover, out of breath now and grunting from the impact of his heels against the ground. Art's weight beats down on his shoulders. Red lights flash in the leaves. Back at the bar, three cop cars stop at angles in the street. The exultant roar of fighting shoots up an octave to cries of "Cops!" and "Raid!"

"Damn it, Woody." Art's voice is a moan. "I can't fit."

"Naw. A bunch of drunk kids is nothing." Placing his feet on the ties, Sherwood trudges down the tracks, across the street overpass, past a wide, tree-covered lot that looks like an abandoned orchard. Heart beating like a hammer. He breathes deeply, smelling the leaves. At the next bridge over Pewter Creek he cuts away from the tracks and through a settlement of student housing —block-shaped units stacked three and four high among old trees and worn lawns and chipped playground equipment.

"Let me down," Art says. "I gotta be sick."

"Hold on, man." At the far edge of the next parking lot, Sherwood finds a grocery cart, probably loaned by the white-haired woman in the downtown market, and he dumps Art into it. "Now get sick, GI."

"That's it."

"What's it?"

"GI. Like a goddamned disease. You get it and you can't get over it. The only part finished is the fighting. The rest is just the same."

"It's all over."

"That from you—" Art coughs, leans forward and spews scotch through the bottom of the cart.

Sherwood turns away, fighting to keep his own stomach under control, and walks across a narrow street and onto a bridge over the creek. He can still hear shouts from the bar, now about six blocks away. Another siren wails. Behind him Art retches. "You going to live, man?"

No response from Art.

This is no way to be. We have to stop it. He looks back at the man doubled forward in the wire basket. The streetlight behind Art throws his face into shadow and illuminates the trunks of a stand of young pine trees at the edge of the pavement. Art sits back, fumbles with his leg. His hand comes up with the pistol and he raises it until the barrel pushes into the junction of his jaw and neck.

"What the hell, Art?" Sherwood shuffles off the bridge.

"Your way's too slow. If I can't be alive, I'll be dead." Art shakes his head in a series of side-to-side wags that pivot on the muzzle of the pistol. "You better stop where you are," he says.

"You can make it."

"Can't. Once I got in, I never wanted to be on the outside. Brodie tried to get me to see that and I couldn't. The Army was easy. It was home. Family. Uncomplicated. It gave me the best year of my life. Then in the field there were guys who had lost girls or buddies. Had a good platoon. Sergeant who took care of us like he was a father. Not trying to run our lives for some damned reason of his own, but watching out for us. We were all in it together." He shrugs. "Sure I counted days. That was part of it. But I didn't want out, and look at us now. Just a little Army here. Ex-soldiers against the world, but now that's gotta end too. I have to get out, and I can't, Woody."

Karen was right. "I have kept you . . . isolated. I'm sorry." He steps forward, but as he does, Art dips his head, lowers the pistol and then raises it again to point at Sherwood's chest.

"I'm not going to shoot myself by accident. I'll do it when I'm ready. I'd as soon shoot you by accident, though. If you rush me. Wouldn't matter. You're dead anyway. Right?"

Stitches of pain along his ribs, Sherwood is surprised by the strength of his fear. He can feel his heart begin to labor. The parking lot looks unnaturally bright.

"Isn't that right?"

I have too much to do. "Art?"

"You're already dead so it doesn't matter if I shoot you. Wouldn't even be murder."

Sherwood can see the blunt bullets in the cylinder and knows that if the light were stronger, he would be able to see the one lining up behind the barrel. The hammer edges back, cylinder inches around. Art's neck is a column of straining tendons. His left hand comes up to cradle the butt of the gun. Everything seems suspended by the springs and levers that hold back the action of the pistol. Who will take Jamie? Hammer clicks past half cock, moving faster.

"Check it out, Woody. Are you really dead?"

Dropping his legs out from under him, Sherwood sprawls backward. The pavement stuns him, but he rolls and comes up on one knee in time to see the twisted anger of Art's face change to a look of horror and then, rage. Lips curl to bare his teeth. Art swings the pistol away as if searching for a target, fixes instantly on the pine trees, and fires. Chips of wood spray like sparks, fall like fragments of mirror that glitter in the streetlight. He fires again.

"Art? What time is it?"

The little .22 makes popping noises. The slugs whack against the bark. Two more throw up pieces of tree, but the others disappear without visible traces. "I'm not another goddamned tree."

"What time is it? I'm flipping. . . ."

No Club Texas. No Tsuko dancing. No Kenny, miserable beside Lisa the bargirl; reliving the terrors of his war and threatening to kill Lieutenant Lang, the company commander. It is morning and red flags fly along the perimeter of the rifle range.

A platoon of MPs patrols the road. Sherwood moves up the line of shuffling men toward the truck where Kenny, who has extra duty again, pulls rifles from the racks and hands them out. Maybe Kenny has decided to let the lieutenant's harassment slide off him. He looks calm, but as Sherwood reaches for his weapon he can see that the young face is too calm. "Hang in there, Kenny," he says.

"Can't, Woody."

Lieutenant Lang snaps off a string of commands that Sherwood doesn't catch. Kenny cocks his head in exaggerated attentiveness, then straightens, lifts Sherwood's rifle shoulder high and drops it over the side of the truck. "No more, sir." His pack slides off one thin shoulder and falls, and Kenny's hand comes up holding an olive-drab ball as if for a game of catch. It looks innocent, but the protruding firing mechanism and handle make it unmistakably lethal. "I'm going to kill you, sir."

A breeze slides into a clump of graceful, long-needled pines and hangs there. The waves that roll onto the beach several hundred yards away seem suspended. Sherwood's chest aches and he realizes he is holding his breath. The lieutenant's eyes widen, fix on Kenny's hand as it pulls the pin from the grenade. None of the others have noticed yet. Only Kenny, the lieutenant and Sherwood stand frozen with the waves and the trees. Kenny throws the pin and it lands with a metallic ping.

The lieutenant pivots with a grace that is part military precision and part dance. His dash for the firing line breaks the tableau. Sherwood can hear shouts as men scatter from the line behind

him. In a motion that looks unnaturally quick, Kenny leaps off
the truck and gives chase; maybe ten or fifteen yards behind.
Three MPs and the range NCO start up from an ammo can they
are trying to open. "What the hell?" One of the MPs draws a pistol, but Kenny menaces him with the grenade and he and his
companions scramble for cover behind the observation tower.
MPs begin to converge from the road, homing on the commotion
at the tower. Sherwood sheds his field pack and jacket and begins
to run, but he is too late. The MPs cut Kenny off from the lieutenant, who dives behind one of the human silhouettes and disappears. Kenny is caught between the first target embankment and
the firing line.

For several minutes the situation is chaotic. The MPs' boots
beat a thick dust out of the grass. Sherwood can taste the dust as
he runs, seeing what he has to do, but moving too slowly. Kenny
races in ever-tightening circles, arms flailing and voice breaking
into incoherent shrieks that rise above the shouts of the MPs. The
lieutenant appears at the end of the target row and lopes toward
the firing line. Kenny sees him, tries to follow, but is cut off.

Out of breath, Sherwood arrives at the observation tower as the
lieutenant begins to call, "Give yourself up, soldier."

"Come and get me, you chicken shit, sir." Kenny backs off.
Above his head, his hand makes a knot of white knuckles around
the grenade.

"Sergeant," the lieutenant barks.

The MP staff sergeant salutes. "Sir?"

"Shoot that man before he hurts someone."

"Kill him, sir?"

"No, damn it. Just stop him. Shoot him in the leg."

Grabbing a rifle that leans against the tower, the sergeant fits a
clip of target ammunition into place.

"I'm his friend," Sherwood says. "Let me talk to him."

"Shoot him, Sergeant."

"Are you crazy?"

The sergeant drops to one knee. Without thinking Sherwood
kicks the man in the shoulder and sends him sprawling. "Get rid
of it, Kenny," he yells. "They're going to shoot you." He runs.
Targets to his right, grass spongy under his feet. Kenny is just
ahead. Not more than thirty yards. "Don't shoot." If I can get the

grenade. Flip it over the embankment. Kenny will end up in a psych ward until he can be discharged. Twenty yards now. Sherwood hears the bolt slam shut. *If I can't make it . . . I'm not ready.* The rifle pops.

Kenny falls as if someone has jerked the legs out from under him. The grenade hangs in the air. Plenty of time. The handle falls away in a slight arc, then the olive ball drops straight down. Kenny lets out a grunt as it bounces off his back into the grass.

Sherwood is still ten yards away. His feet brace to stop, slip out from under him. Terror now. Odor of bruised grass stems. There should be three seconds or so, but he hasn't counted. *I'm not ready.* He spreads his arms and beats the air in an effort to claw himself away from the blast that comes as a quick red flower and a wave of overpowering force.

For moments afterward his parents seem to be there, but he can't touch them or even talk to them. My fault. The sharp scents of road tar tickle his nostrils. He tries to roll over and his hand strikes hard asphalt. Sharp points of light stand in front of his eyes. "Kenny," he says and the weak sound of his own voice brings him around. The points of light are stars. "Flipped out."

"Broke my watch," a voice says.

"Art?"

Silence for a moment, faint noises from the distant bar fight, then Art mumbles something incoherent. He is close, scooting backward on hands and buttocks. The grocery cart lies on its side in the parking lot. "What the hell happened? It wasn't the same."

Seeing Art on the ground confuses Sherwood, and it takes him almost a minute to sort out the image of Art, sitting on the edge of a crater, from what has just happened. "You okay?" he asks. Kenny and the grenade. That was real.

"Damn. I don't know."

The reek of gunpowder remains in the air. "Kenny tried to frag the lieutenant," Sherwood says.

"Shit."

"He had the pin out of the grenade. I was trying to get there, but they shot him anyway. In the leg."

"And he dropped it." Art shakes his head back and forth. "And you couldn't save him." His wooden legs make a hollow sound against the pavement as he tries to turn farther.

Sherwood sits up. He is cold and trembling so hard he can't hold still. "I tried."

"Just like in your dream, Woody. And then he was me." At first he looks like he's going to cry, then he starts to laugh, coughing out tight bursts of words. "All this time. Hanging on you. Scared. Jealous of the kid. Feeling guilty for it. And you were as stuck as I was. Using me. To stop up your own guilt." Pulling himself all the way around, he takes a deep breath. "Are you okay? I didn't hit you or anything?"

"No. Only the tree."

"Check. The tree." Art picks up the pistol by the barrel.

"You're right. I was trying to help Kenny, should have been able to save him. Then my parents were killed; by the time I was conscious and not full of drugs, they were dead. Somehow their dying got mixed up with not being able to do anything for Kenny." Brodie tried to tell me that. Makes perfect sense. Why didn't I see it then? "I'm sorry, Art."

"No," Art snaps, "don't tell me you're sorry. We have to quit that. Break the patterns. Right now."

"Break the patterns," Sherwood says. He shudders.

"We can do it, Woody. We have to."

Going to have to change something if I'm to stay with Jamie; and I don't see how I can leave him. "We can try."

"We can do it." Moving carefully, Art puts the pistol aside. "Could you get that cart? We have to go back to the house and I'm not going to be able to walk."

Sherwood's legs are rubbery, but he doesn't feel drunk. By the time he has stood the cart on its wheels and run it across the lot, Art has his right leg off. "What are you doing?"

"Just give me a hand." Art pulls himself up on the basket. He is shaking as hard as Sherwood is and he lets Sherwood help him in; then he arranges himself with his left leg doubled to his chin. Loose leg and pistol across his stump rattle together as the cart starts to roll. "Lots to do," he says half to himself. On the bridge he takes the gun by the barrel and flips it over the railing. "Hold it a minute." He heaves the leg after the weapon.

"Not if you're going to jump . . ."

"No more bullshit. I mean it."

Below them, ripples spread up the channel of Pewter Creek.

After a moment the leg floats out of the shadow of the bridge, its holster door open and light glinting off the toe of the shiny military dress shoe.

"Let's go," Art says. He slumps back against the basket. "Didn't get out to tear up a tree on Arbor Day. I guess shooting one to death'll do for now." The wheels click over cracks in the sidewalk. "You're not saying much, Woody?"

"I think I've made it, Art. I think remembering is going to make a difference." How can that be?

"Right."

"Life is going to be harder if I'm not dead."

Down the first cross street, red lights still flash in front of the bar. "A lot of things will be harder," Art says. "You know? I never thought you were as dead as you said you were, Woody. You'd flip out and you'd toss and mumble and none of it made any sense until you'd get where you'd say, 'I'm not ready.' That part was always clear. Even in the hospital when you were out of your head more than you were in." He watches the dark apartment buildings that they rattle past. "Remember how bad it was? Guys giving up and just taking any drugs they could get?"

"Yeah."

"But not you, man. Even when you said you were finished. Dead and given up on yourself for good, but you did it in a way that let you keep going. Until you could find out . . ." Art beats a clumsy tattoo on his stump, falls silent, takes a breath as if to speak and then shakes his head. Finally he nods. "It sure felt good to waste that tree—"

Maybe we have found an end to it. "Yeah. I know."

"I have to get out of that attic. Put my mattress in the back bedroom. Tonight. And don't let me forget to call Brodie and tell him things are all right."

"Sure."

"I mean as soon as we get back. When I called him before I was pretty low and I left him a message on his recorder thing that I was going to get drunk with you and then blow myself away."

"You what?"

From the park they can see two people waiting on Marion's

front step. "Probably my father," Art says, but by the time they have made it halfway up the block, Sherwood recognizes Brodie. He is talking to a woman. Dark tight curls down the back of her neck.

"I see her, Woody."

Brodie comes off the porch to meet them, nervous hand playing around his sideburns. "I was out until almost eleven. I'm sorry. I didn't . . ." He checks himself and peers more closely at their tired faces, at Art's missing leg. "I thought it might help to bring her, Art. If it's awkward . . ."

"Relax, Doc."

"Right. What happened?"

"You'd have loved it," Art says. "You and Freud, man. I was going to kill myself, then I was going to shoot Woody, and then I tried to waste a pine tree. Geez, I must have been drunk. I kept expecting the thing to fall. And Woody flipped out and remembered what happened to him."

Looking from one to the other and back again, the doctor finally laughs. Both hands come up and he straightens his mustache.

"It's all right, Doc." Sherwood pushes the cart across the lawn. "Everything's finished. We got it straightened out. . . ."

"Don't tell me you have everything figured out. Then I'll worry."

"This is Woody, Doc. Remember?" Pulling his leg up, forcing the knee straight, Art grins. "He always did like to have things all set and decided. What he's trying to tell you in his own way is that we got a start tonight. I know I cleared a lot of Army out of the air. Found some other things I have to quit running from." He twists around in the basket, almost as if to avoid Karen, then turns and looks at her. "Help me out of here, would you?"

The three of them pull him free of the cart and carry him into the house. "In the bathroom," Art says. "Woody, if you'd get me a change of clothes and my old right leg from the attic? My toothbrush is by the bed. And bring the backpack hanging beside the ladder. Have to tend to that, first thing."

They split up in the hall: Brodie toward the kitchen, Art and Karen into the bathroom and Sherwood to the attic. Through the half-open door he can hear Art saying, "Okay, I don't care if you are a nurse, I can take a bath by myself. Just talk. And what we have to get straight is about those letters. . . . Damn, that was a long time ago. What *are* you doing *here?*"

Sherwood climbs Jamie's swing to the hatch, then through it on Art's rope. There is a flashlight balanced on one of the rafters and with its beam he picks his way across to the trapdoor. He can see the cop's footprints in the dust, some of them wiped away by Art's handprints and larger impressions where he must have sat on the stringers at times to think and watch the gloom of the web-crossed attic.

The cubicle is orderly, bed made with hospital corners. A few of Marion's magazines are piled on the shelf and on top of the magazines, several self-help psychology books that Sherwood hasn't seen before. Built him another institution here. Private cell with craft shop. No reacculturation desired, none possible. Didn't help at all. I wonder if I can do any better for Jamie? A shudder runs across Sherwood's shoulders. Wonder if they'll let me have him back so I can try?

Art's old leg is heavier than Sherwood had thought it would be. Substantial. Something to stand on, but not made for walking softly. Stuffing clothes and toothbrush and, finally, the leg into the backpack on top of the money Art brought from San Francisco, Sherwood hauls the bundle through the attic and into the hall. He leaves the things there and climbs down the stairs to the back bedroom, where he digs an old pair of tennis shoes out of the closet.

At the bottom of the stairs he stops, feels the excitement of the fight and flipping out finally drain away, and he stands with a shoe dangling from each hand, trying to collect what is left of his strength. Running on reserves since I left the hospital. Seems like days ago. Not much sleep last night. But if I can lift one foot . . . He plods up to the hall, collects the pack and the leg and carries them to the bathroom. As he pushes them through the half-open door he can hear Karen: "I thought you were dead. And you, of all people, should know I haven't lived like a saint. Remember? I'm older, but this is still me. What I'm trying to say is, we had a good year, Art. I don't want to try to go back. It's just that we're here. . . ." She jumps nervously when Sherwood pokes the leg into the room. Embarrassed. Not at all sure how she should act toward me. He winks and flashes what he hopes is a smile.

Now to consult the doctor. Then maybe sleep. In the kitchen Brodie has set up the coffee filter and put water on to boil. "I'm the guy who is supposed to tell someone else to heat water," he says. "It's that way in all the movies."

"Right, Doc." Sherwood slumps into a chair and leans back with his head against the counter, feet stretched under the table.

"Are you okay?"

"No. It's all screwed up."

"I thought Art said you remembered."

"Yeah. The kid in the dream was after the CO with a live grenade and they shot his legs out from under him. He dropped the damned thing and it went off."

"Son-of-a-bitch."

"A lot of things you tried to tell me make sense now, Doc. Things I ignored."

"Your folks?"

"Right. Their death got jumbled in with Kenny's along with quite a bit of guilt and maybe some other things I haven't even tried to sort through yet."

"Great, Sherwood. Amazing." Brodie stands with his hands on his hips, too excited even to tug at a sideburn. "Have you considered that the other doctors might be right, too? They got it out. All the shrapnel. You're not going to die."

"Too much all at once, Doc. That's going to be harder to handle."

"Good. It should be." Brodie nods. "We should plan to get together a couple of times. I can help now in ways I couldn't before. Remembering isn't any miracle cure. You still have to learn to live with the memory."

"Sure." Makes sense. He nods. "But my biggest problem right now is that CPS took Jamie because he fell down and split his head. They think I've been beating him."

"You haven't been." One hand comes up to stroke mustache. "Have you?"

"Are you kidding? He was . . ." Sherwood lets his eyes go closed. "It's a long story. Worst is that one of their foster mothers was a real bitch and she messed him up, and even if I do prove I

didn't hit him, I'm not sure they won't cover up their own care-
lessness. It's a government agency. Just like the Army and the
Nixon White House. There's a law on the books that will let
them get me for not reporting her."

"You still have the same caseworker? Mrs. Chapman?"

Sherwood nods. "There's another hearing Thursday morning.
What day is it, Doc?"

"It's been Wednesday for a couple of hours now."

Feels like longer. At least a week. Need to sleep. Damn. Jamie
off somewhere in a dorm room or cell or something. The thought
becomes a muted image, almost a dream; but before he can fall
asleep, the dream is interrupted by a distant thump and Brodie
asking, "Did you hear that?" Sherwood opens his eyes. At first he
is confused by the blanket Art hung over the window, then he
gathers his wits enough to pull it aside and look out.

A car has parked behind Brodie's at the curb. The thump that
woke Sherwood was the door slamming; he can see a tall figure
striding across the lawn. Oh brother. That's all we need right now.
"It's Art's father." Arthur, Sr., stops short of the steps and waits
while another car pulls up on the other side of the street. A heavy-
set man gets out and comes toward the house. "Looks like he
brought reinforcements. Stay out of sight. I'll try to get rid of
them."

Sherwood makes his way through the back hall and Jamie's
room and stops at the bathroom door. "Your father's here, Art.
Keep quiet."

"Just a minute, Woody." Art has his legs strapped on and is
working his pants over them while Karen ties one of the tennis
shoes. "Tell him I'll talk to him."

"You sure?"

"Better now than later. I'm keyed up enough." He laughs.
"And about half drunk."

A long time coming, Art. A long time. The knock comes and
Sherwood answers the door.

Arthur, Sr., carries a cane, but he makes no pretense of leaning
on it. A weapon. No doubt about that. Wonder what he thought
he'd find? The man with him isn't wearing yellow boots this time,
or the tweed overcoat; but perched on his head is the same narrow-brimmed hat with the little red feather stuck in the band.

"Come in," Sherwood says. "You like a cup of coffee?"

"I know my son is here." The voice is resonant, commanding. "I demand you let me see him." Arthur, Sr., pushes blindly past Sherwood and walks into the living room. "Where is he?" In front of the fireplace he swings around.

The detective stations himself so that he is looking straight through the central hall and into the bathroom, where Karen is helping Art steady himself on his legs. The man shoots Sherwood a questioning look, but before either of them can say anything, Brodie appears in the kitchen doorway.

Art's father brandishes his cane. "What the hell is going on here?"

Nervous. He expects violence. Maybe hopes for it. Finally realizing that the detective's position near the doorway is a tactical deployment—securing an avenue of retreat—Sherwood backs into the dining room to leave the way clear. The move doesn't help. Arthur, Sr., simply advances a step. "I'm not going to be put off this time."

"No one is going to put you off, Dad." Art stumps out of the hall, leaning slightly on Karen and carrying his pack over one shoulder. "I'm sorry we had to work things out this way."

Looking from Art, who stands several inches taller than Karen on his wooden legs, to Sherwood, to Brodie and back to Art again, Arthur, Sr.'s, face twitches from anger to surprise. His gaze finally fixes on Karen. "Young lady," he says, "I don't know what you think you're doing, but as long as you're here, there's a wheelchair in the back seat of my car."

"I don't work for you anymore, Mr. Johnson."

"Just get the chair."

Karen shakes her head. "I'm with Art now. Where I should have been to begin with."

"No one is getting any wheelchair, Dad. As you can see, I'm walking. My own feet."

"You can walk to the car, then."

Art lets the pack slide down his arm, holds it out. "Here's your money. Take it with you. My life is here and I'm not going to leave it."

"Don't make me use force."

"Force won't do any good. I'm staying."

Tapping the cane on the floor and then raising it again, Arthur, Sr., nods to the detective, and tries again. "You can't," he says, but the deep note of command in his voice has slipped a step and a half up the scale.

"It's time you understood," Art says. "I could never make you listen down there, and these goddamned stumps . . ." He slaps his thigh. "You don't have any claim on me or my comings and goings. I'm a grown man. I can vote, drink. Fight wars. All that bullshit. I'm thirty-one years old."

"But you're . . ." Arthur, Sr., stops. The cane tip sinks to the floor and rests there.

"I'm what, Dad?"

Pulling himself up with an audible breath, Art's father rests one hand on the other and finally leans on the cane. "You're a cripple."

For almost a minute no one says a word. Sherwood can hear the hackberry branches scrape the screen, and once he hears Brodie shift his feet. The detective breaks the silence with a cough. He starts to say something, but Art cuts him off.

"I'm not a cripple, Dad. I've been thinking like one. Running and hiding as if I were one, but I'm done with that and I'm done with your treating me like a damned kid because we both think I'm a cripple. And if we're going to see each other and if I'm going to see Mom, we're going to have to find another way."

"That's enough."

"No it's not enough. I've seen something here with Woody and his nephew. A way they are." Eyes searching, as if for the right words, he looks at Sherwood; looks away and then looks back to his father. "I was jealous of it. You should see them sometime. Like last Sunday—they were down in the park, just sitting in a swing." He takes a long breath.

"You have to understand that Sherwood has always made a big deal about staying away from the people he cared for, particularly Jamie. He was sure he was going to die any minute and he didn't want his death to hurt them. That made sense to me. Then I saw them together on Sunday night. There was no question they really cared about each other. Sherwood couldn't leave the half-pint. He was putting him*self* on about staying away from people. I could see they loved each other in a way I've never been able to love anyone."

Anger showing again around mouth and eyes, Arthur, Sr., shakes his head.

"People are a lot like trees," Art says. "You can't just plant them and then expect them to grow because *you* stuck them in the ground. They need more than that."

Beside him, Karen turns her face away and wipes her cheek with one knuckle.

Art gives her shoulder a squeeze, steps forward to hold out the backpack again. "I'm sorry. Take the money," he says softly. "But if you wouldn't mind, I'd like to borrow your cane. I lost mine tonight and I can't walk very well yet without it."

No response. Brodie's breathing sounds ragged and even the detective is having trouble looking tough.

"I could bring it to you. Maybe next weekend? We could meet somewhere in the city and talk?"

Standoff, Sherwood thinks, but then Arthur, Sr.'s, head tips down. His eyes fill. He gives a tired nod and holds out the cane, reaches for the pack with his other hand. They are careful not to touch, but there is an intimacy in the awkwardness of the exchange. Incredible effort. For both of them.

The detective moves aside to let Arthur, Sr., pass, then follows him out of the house. Doors slam. Motors start. Headlights come on and the two cars depart in opposite directions.

"I'll be damned," Brodie says. His face breaks into a grin that looks like it's part pain.

Art sinks onto the living-room bed. "I thought he'd yell and stomp around. Even hit me." He lifts the cane, looks at it. "I didn't think it would hurt him like that." Tears come to his eyes and he wipes at them with the palm of his hand. "I'll have to go down there. Maybe it won't be so bad now."

"I'll come if you think I can help," Karen says.

"Maybe." Art looks at Sherwood and then at Brodie. "But we have a lot to talk about. Give me a hand." He pulls himself up on her arm and churns into the kitchen to snag the scotch bottle off the counter. "You have a place somewhere?" he asks her. She nods. "Woody looks dead on his feet. We shouldn't keep him up."

"If you go down to see your father," Brodie says, "stop and say hello on your way back. Would you?"

"Official visit?"

"Half and half."

"Buy me a drink?"

"I'll do it."

"You're on then, Doc." He hands the bottle to Karen and clomps out with her, wooden feet still noisy in Sherwood's old tennis shoes.

Dr. Brodie watches through the dining-room window until Art and Karen have crossed the lawn and disappeared around the corner of the house. "You two have done more for each other than I could have done for either of you." He moves back into the kitchen, picks up his coffee cup.

"Thanks, Doc." Helped each other, used each other. Maybe it's the same thing. But I still have Erica gone off to Oregon and Jamie locked up in that shelter place. Child abuse, not reporting child abuse and lying to a judge.

"You don't look like you believe it."

"I do. Just seeing Art stand up to his father like that . . ."

"You're worried about Jamie," Brodie says, and when Sherwood nods, "Do you want to tell me about it?"

"Not tonight, Doc. I blew it from the start, but right now I haven't had enough sleep to think straight. And this time I have to think things out right. Do you have to get back tonight?"

"Yes. Appointments starting at nine o'clock, but you know I'll help."

"I'll call you tomorrow. I have to see Jamie and find out what I should do for this hearing. Marion's lawyer said to call him if I needed legal help."

"Okay." Taking a hurried gulp of coffee, Brodie puts the cup on the dining-room table.

"You want a full cup for the road?"

"No. Well, sure. I'll get the cup back to you Thursday. If I can't make it to the hearing for some reason, let's plan to spend the morning together on Saturday. After that, we can set up whatever schedule feels right."

"Fine." Sherwood follows him into the kitchen, then back through the rooms and outside. At the curb Brodie balances the

cup on the roof of his car, shakes hands, opens the door and carefully fits the cup into a tray between the bucket seats. He climbs
in, closes the door, rolls down the window as if reluctant to leave.
"You guys have made my week," he says. Finally, he starts the engine and slips the car into gear.

"Thanks, Doc." Sherwood waves and plods back into the house.
Too tired. Ought to be flipping out. He shakes his head, trying to
wake himself up.

"I'm finished with flipping out," he says aloud. Finished with
being dead. No short sheets. No end in sight. Forty minutes or
forty years.

He stumbles into Marion's room and falls onto the bed. Sleep
comes with two thoughts: one repeating, *have to get Jamie, have
to get Jamie;* and the other coursing through him like electrical
shock—*I'm alive.*

Sherwood wakes with his tongue dry and foul-tasting in his mouth. Bad night. No rest. Time to get up and fix breakfast before Jamie . . . He opens his eyes. Marion's house is quiet. No Jamie. Rolling over, he tries to shake the sleep out of his head. He has things to do: find the place they've taken Jamie, see Donald Holmes, see Pat Chapman, call Brodie. "Have to get in touch with Erica," he mutters. He dresses and shaves. Today he will have to look as respectable as he can. Haircut wouldn't hurt, but there isn't time. The goat coat is stuffed under the dining-room table; he drags it out, leaves with it slung over his shoulder.

Covering the half block to Erica's at a trot, he clatters onto the porch and knocks at the door. No answer. Her car isn't there and the light in the back bedroom is still on. He moves around the house, peers into windows. Made a mess of this too. Unsure what to do next, he makes his way to the curb and stares at the empty space where the station wagon is supposed to be. A tall woman jogs by, trailing a large dog on a leash. "What time is it?" he calls.

"A little after seven," she yells back.

Could phone the highway patrol. See if they'd stop her and send her back. Should have thought of that last night. Too much going on; all too important. Not wanting to go back to Marion's empty kitchen, he walks to Sambo's, only to discover he can't face breakfast there either. Pancakes alone seem a kind of betrayal; Jamie enjoys them so much. Little devils take over your life. Several blocks past Sambo's he catches the seven-thirty bus. He finally has a couple of bags of peanuts from a machine in the Woodgrove bus depot and calls that breakfast. From the depot he walks to the center of town, wastes half an hour trying to find someone to give him directions to the shelter home and then, when he does get directions, he has to walk across town to a new, rather small house in a residential neighborhood. He has expected an institution, but only the expensive play equipment that sticks above the side fence and a small plaque on the door indicate the building's official function.

A young, plump woman answers his knock. She gives him a once-over with a double take for the coat. "You must be Sher," she says, and when he nods, "Jamie's been talking about you ever since he got up. You may see him, of course, but you'll have to have one of the staff with you." Her voice is pleasant, but official in its lack of any inflection that might betray a feeling.

"Okay." He steps inside.

As the woman closes the door, a girl about five years old charges into the hall from one of the far rooms. She is bruised on the forehead and both cheeks. The battered face is bright with expectation, but it falls almost before she sees Sherwood. "I thought you were my daddy."

"Not yet, honey." The woman pats her shoulder. "Are you still playing in the quiet room?"

"Yes."

"I'll bring him there as soon as he comes."

The girl nods, hangs her head and wanders back down the hall.

"What happened to her?"

Probing his face with her eyes, the woman shakes her head, then in the same flat voice, she says, "Her mother spanked her for not cleaning her room. So the little girl told us. The teacher who alerted us yesterday said she had been coming to school with bruises for about a month. Nothing this bad until now. Sad. She's been so eager to see her father, but we notified him last night and he hasn't come yet."

"You think someone really did that to her? On purpose?"

"I'm afraid there's little doubt."

"Why?"

The woman shrugs, studies Sherwood. "Any number of reasons.

Alcohol, drugs, money problems, trouble over an affair. Simple tension of living too close. For all we know at this point, the mother may be taking the blame to protect the father. Maybe he did it and that's why he hasn't come. Am I shocking you?"

"As a matter of fact . . ." He nods.

"If you'd said that last night, I would have called you a liar."

Jamie's here and that alone puts me in a class with whoever hit that little girl. They aren't going to let me have him back. Grab this smug woman by the neck and throw her out of the way. Take Jamie and run? He shakes his head. "I didn't hit him. He fell down."

Finally the monotony of her voice breaks with a note of sympathy. "Look, Mr. . . . ?"

"Sherwood," he says.

"This morning he's a whole different child, Mr. Sherwood. You saw how Joanie was. Anxious. Disappointed so fast it looked like she expected to be disappointed. No sense of security. No will to be happy, if that makes any sense to you. As far as we know, the father is good to her, but still she's terrified he won't come.

"Today, Jamie isn't at all like that. When he got up he told me you were coming and that I'd know you because you'd have a big shaggy coat. He's been playing ever since. He knows you'll come. He trusts you."

"Will that help me get him back?"

"I can't say, not knowing the case."

Child abuse, not reporting child abuse, lying about my intentions. Abducting a child from a foster home, if they want to push that. Not a good case. "Where is he?"

"This way." She leads him from the hall, through a living room in which a pair of eight-year-olds sit over a board game with an older woman who seems to be watching, yet letting them alone as much as she can. One of the children has his arm in a cast.

"This isn't your average good scene."

The woman shakes her head.

Can't imagine what it would take for me to hit Jamie hard enough to bruise his face. Maybe over the long run? Not enough money. Frustration about not making enough guitars? "Do most of these kids have just one parent?"

"Only Jamie right now," she says.

Through a sliding glass door at the end of the living room, he sees Jamie and a girl about the same size sitting together on a platform made of planks bolted to peeled logs. As the door opens, Jamie stands up, waves and yells, "Lookit how high I can jump, Sher." Without hesitation he barrels off the platform.

Frozen with horror, Sherwood watches the little body plummet five feet to hit upright with a force that carries Jamie's shoulders between his spread knees. He stands straight and smiles. "Georgia taught me."

"Scared the bejesus out of me, small friend." He crosses the trampled grass and sand that separates them.

"Come on, Georgia. Jump and show Sher."

On the platform the girl gets up and retreats a few steps. She wears a Band-Aid over one eye to match Jamie's fresh Band-Aid and her eye is bloodshot.

"Show him how you showed me."

She shakes her head and sits down again.

"She doesn't want to jump right now," Sherwood says.

"But she showed me how."

"I think she's afraid of me. She doesn't know me." It looks like she has reason to be afraid. He wants to lift her off the platform and hug her until she isn't afraid. Instead he ruffles Jamie's hair and takes his hand. "Let's sit down and talk a minute."

"Can I come home?"

"Not yet. I brought the coat, in case you wanted it."

Jamie shakes his head. "Did you bring my sleeve loops?"

"Didn't think of it. I was in a hurry to come see you and I forgot."

"Okay. I get a little scared here, Sher."

"These people seem nice enough. I'll bring your sleeve loops to the hearing tomorrow. How about that?" He turns his head away and wipes his cheeks with the coat sleeve. Harder to be here than I imagined.

"Can't I come home at all?"

"I think so, but we're going to have to go to court again. Remember the courtroom? The time you were supposed to sit with Pat and you bumped your head coming to sit with me?"

"I remember, but I was home then."

"This time we're stuck. The people here are trying to do the

best thing for you. They'll have to keep you here for your own
protection until they're sure I didn't hit you."

"I can tell them you didn't."

"You may have to do that, but not here. In court."

They sit on small chairs just outside the sliding doors. Jamie
nods his head, rubs the back of one hand on his pantleg.

"I should have thought to bring you clean clothes."

"Can the court say I can't come home, Sher?"

"Yes. They can say that."

"Why?"

"You've seen the other children here. Someone who should
have known better has hurt them and the court is trying to fix
things so it won't happen again." How to tell him our case isn't
that simple? That I've made mistakes that are less obvious? "If
we're lucky, all we'll have to do tomorrow is tell the truth and the
judge will let you come home. But if that doesn't work, we'll go to
court again, and if he doesn't let you come home that time, we'll
go again until he does."

Jamie's eyes are large. He nods slightly, but he can't hide his
fear.

Sherwood looks up at the woman who still watches through the
half-open door. "Is Pat Chapman here?" he asks.

"I'll have someone check." She says something to the woman in
the living room, but doesn't leave the doorway.

"Are you scared, Sher?"

"Yeah. A little."

Jamie gets off his chair, climbs into Sherwood's lap and burrows
his way inside the coat. Still has the stitches in his chin. We were
supposed to get those out tonight.

The woman in the doorway turns back from the living room.
"Pat isn't here," she says.

"Do you know if she went to Doris Ransler's last night?"

"I'm sorry. I don't."

"You do recognize the name?"

She shakes her head. "Sorry."

"Is Pat a mean lady, Sher?"

"No. But she's not happy with me right now. Hop down a second." He picks Jamie and the coat off his lap, fishes out his knife.
"I'm going to have to go soon. We'll need a lawyer and I'd better

make sure we have one. Now, there's plenty of coat here to make
a new pair of sleeve loops." Working carefully, he slices a band of
the fur from each sleeve, slips them onto Jamie's arms. The
plump woman looks on from the doorway. "If you could find a
piece of string and tie them together in the back, they won't fall
over his arms," he tells her.

"Neat, Sher."

"Why don't you walk me to the door. I have to get busy."

On the front porch, he holds Jamie several minutes, finally pries
him loose and puts him down with a kiss on the forehead. "I'll see
you tomorrow."

"Got that, Sher. Bye." Brave, but fighting tears.

Apparently sensitive about long good-byes, the woman takes
Jamie's hand and leads him back inside. Sherwood stares at the
closed door, then turns away. He is worried, but at the same time
he is amused to notice that the coat, which he wears in spite of
the warm day, finally fits him in the sleeves.

The morning has passed by the time he walks back downtown
to Donald Holmes's office. The lawyer isn't in, but a secretary assures Sherwood that he is aware of what has happened, has already talked to "people" at CPS and plans to represent Sherwood
at the hearing.

"Shouldn't I talk to him?"

"He is out of town this afternoon," she says. "He said he'd call
you this evening if it were necessary. The hearing is tomorrow
morning at ten. Do you know where?"

"Yes." But I don't feel right about it. No preparation. I ought
to be doing something and it isn't encouraging that there's nothing
I can do. Preoccupied, he catches a Valley Transit bus and slumps
into the seat to brood; to listen to the rumble of the diesel engine
and to feel the steady thump of his heart. Final irony if it gave
out now. Organ with a malevolent sense of humor, waiting for
hope to appear before shutting down the body. Being dead had its
advantages. Took some edge off the fear.

The bus drops him at the park and he shuffles through the
freshly cut grass, ignoring the children in the play pit and their
mothers in the sun. Shaggy coat and no kid. Wonder if we made

the local paper yet? Across Fifth and up the street toward
Marion's, he walks with his head down; feeling the heat of the
day, enjoying it and recalling the heat of his first fire at Marion's,
the lingering odor of Erica's perfume. Portland? He looks up and
at first thinks he's imagining her station wagon—dented and pit-
ted and listing toward the left front wheel—parked in front of the
little house. Mind playing tricks. Heart taking off again, but not
from fear this time. Moving blood, spreading warmth. Street ap-
pearing as it did that January morning: small, oddly shaped fields
of lawn like oriental garden plots. Meadows for tiny elf horses.
But the car is real.

Running down the block his feet hit the concrete, jar muscle
and bone, and the sensation surprises him. He stops short of her
porch to catch his breath, then climbs up to knock softly. No one
is in sight inside the house. His second knock is louder and finally
a third brings Erica around the corner at the back of the kitchen.

"It's open. You don't have to knock." She waits for him, looking tired around the eyes and mouth. Her hair is a tangle around
her face. "I didn't see anyone at Marion's so we thought we'd let
you sleep. Art said something about drowning his sorrows." Wiping her eyes, she laughs. "And I could use a bit of sleep, myself.
Josie didn't even want to eat. Just collapsed. Where's Jamie?"

"In the shelter home in Woodgrove. Pat Chapman took him."

"Oh no, Sherwood."

"She thought I hit him. Now that you're here, *that* isn't any
worry."

"That isn't all?"

"No. I had to tell Pat the whole story: Doris and what I'd
planned to do. Apparently there's a law about reporting child
abuse. They've got me there. And obviously I lied about what I
was going to do after I got custody. Lied to Pat and to the judge
too. I don't know what they'll do about it." He turns away, looks
at the half-eaten sandwich and full glass of milk on the kitchen
table. "You were having lunch. Go ahead."

"It doesn't matter."

"I'm staying. Art and I figured out some things last night. I
told you about my flipping out. . . ."

"Marion talked about it. You never told me much, but I'll
listen."

He waves his hand, as if to clear away the dream like so many cobwebs. "Sometime. The thing is that I remembered what happened and I'm through thinking I'm dead." A chill runs up his back.

"Josie cheered for five minutes after I turned the car around," Erica says.

Ah Erica. You look as awkward and nervous as I feel. How am I going to tell you?

"It feels so strange to be here, Sherwood. I really thought we'd gone for good."

"I'm staying. I'm going to get Jamie back. Doesn't matter how long it takes. But once I have him, I can't imagine the two of us without you and Josie."

She rests one hand on the back of a kitchen chair, straightens it in front of the table. "There are so many problems. . . ."

"Let's see if we can work them out." His arms feel too long and he crosses them in front of him, uncrosses them. What's the matter? We've even made love. He reaches for her, and after a slight hesitation she moves against him.

"I want to, Sherwood. In almost four years I don't think I've had a lover I really liked. And I do like you, and we're good together. And Josie loves you." She breaks off, face against his shoulder, then pulls away to look at him. "Maybe that's why I'm not sure. It might get permanent."

"Would that be so bad?"

Slowly, she raises a hand to touch his cheek, then kisses him. The kiss drags on, becomes passionate, but it is interrupted by the slap of feet on the living-room floor. "Mommy," Josie says, "what *are* you and Sherwood talking about?"

Keeping one arm around Sherwood's shoulder, Erica breaks free. "I thought you were asleep," she says.

"I woke up. Hi, Sherwood."

Grin on her face, smug grin. She must have been watching a while. Through the tiredest eyes I've ever seen. He winks at her. "Are you sure you're not sleepwalking?"

Josie shakes her head. "Where's Jamie?"

"He's gone right now. Back to the shelter home, but with luck we'll have him here soon."

"How soon?"

"Tomorrow." With a lot of luck. He can feel Erica's arm tighten around his back.

"Josie," she says, "you hop back in bed. I know you're sleepy and as soon as I finish talking to Sherwood, I'm going to take a nap myself."

"Aw Mommy."

"Now."

Pouting, Josie turns and drags feet back to her room.

"We'll try." Erica leans against him and lets her head droop to his shoulder.

"You look as tired as she does."

"I caught about three hours in the car last night. Somewhere around Mount Shasta." She kisses his ear.

"Would you call Pat Chapman? When you wake up."

"That I'll do right now." She goes in to sit at her study-nook desk and pull the phone book out from under a clutter of pens and pencils. "How's she listed?"

Sherwood gives her the number and watches her dial. Erica asks for Mrs. Chapman, introduces herself, and after that the conversation contains no information. She says "yes" half a dozen times, then "no," then "yes"; shoots Sherwood a bewildered look and shrugs.

"Will you want that in writing?" she asks, finally. "I see. Can you tell me . . . ? I see. Thank you." With a tired shake of her head, she hangs up.

"What happened?"

"It sounds like you're off the hook for child abuse. She, or someone went to Doris's? Does that sound right?"

"Yes."

"They have her kids in custody, but Pat wanted to know if I knew where Doris was."

"Good. If they went there, they know what was wrong with Jamie."

"But she didn't give me a chance to ask about the other things. She said you should be sure to be there."

"I will."

"Not alone, Sherwood."

Not alone. He nods. "Thank you. Marion's lawyer, Holmes, is

going to be there too. And Brodie if I need him. I guess we'll see what we're up against and then fight if we have to."

She leans her head on one hand. "Is there anything else I can do? Right now?"

"No." Don't want to leave you, but I have to let you sleep. You look so beat. "Come down to Marion's when you wake up. You want me to take Josie now?"

"She should stay here. She was so excited about coming back that she didn't even sleep when I did."

"Okay." He kisses her once more, then forces himself to let her alone and go back down the block to Marion's.

Art isn't there, but dishes in the sink show that he has been, for both breakfast and lunch. Sherwood cleans up the kitchen, pulls down the blankets from the window and from the hall doorway, then wanders through the house. In the basement he discovers that Art has brought his things down from the attic and set up his mattress in the back bedroom; and he catches himself wondering how they will distribute the rooms when Erica and Josie move in a month or so from now. Amazing to think that far ahead just to begin something. He is tempted to start making lists of things he'll have to do, but goes upstairs and tears down his short sheet instead.

At about five o'clock, Art comes in looking rested and jaunty; even moving more quietly, as if becoming used to the tennis shoes. "I see her car's back. Why isn't she here?" he asks.

"Drove all night. She's sleeping."

"Good. You have sense enough to invite her to move in?"

"More or less. Not right away, but I think that's how it will turn out."

"I'll have a little time, then."

"You don't have to move out if they move in."

"We'll see." Art sits on one of the kitchen chairs, pulls one leg up so the knee is bent and stretches the other in front of him. "There's more to Karen than I remembered. In a lot of ways, she's had it rougher than I have."

That's saying something, coming from you. "I liked her. The one time I met her."

"I don't know, Woody. Whatever attracted us back then . . . centuries ago." He shifts his weight to get comfortable on the chair. "I should have known, building myself the legs after all that time being content without them. Kept telling myself it was because of the half-pint; but most of it was that couple of weeks with her. Whatever we had is still there. But it makes things harder too. I'm feeling like a kid again. Like my life was all bottled up before and now it's open, and I don't know if I want to shut off part of it so fast."

"Yeah. I can imagine."

He combs fingers through his beard. "What happened with the half-pint?"

"Looks better. With Erica here, I think I can get him back. Erica, and the fact that Jamie's in good shape in spite of everything."

"He's changed a lot," Art says. "Since I first saw him."

"Kids are resilient. But it's still with him: the way he was when I found him. Not walking or talking. He'd hardly look at me. And when he thought I was going to desert him, man, he was right back there. Like he had a wall all built and he just put it up. It'll be hard for him to get completely over it."

"For us too. It's one thing to know what's the matter with you. Makes a big difference, but we still have to learn to live with our wounds."

"That's the same thing Brodie said."

Doubling his fist, Art taps the table. "If Jamie can do it, we can. Have to show this younger generation what guts are." He grins. "Damn. I sound just like my father. That's going to be a fight. Me against myself."

"You sound good."

"So do you. We're going somewhere, Woody. Not running anymore. I feel like I've grown up and gotten younger at the same time."

Exactly that. Grown up and younger.

"I don't think I ever expected to feel like this again." Art leans back, looks out the window and nods up the street toward Erica's house. "Here she comes. With Josie. You've done okay."

"For a dead man." They laugh. Sherwood gets up, goes to turn on heat under the coffee pot.

Erica knocks, comes straight through to the kitchen calling, "Anyone awake? I smell coffee." She stops in front of Art with her hand out; and when he shakes, leans down and kisses his cheek. "Thank you," she says.

"What's this?" As near blushing as I've ever seen Art.

"If not for Art, I'd be in Portland." She crosses to the stove to slide her arm around Sherwood. "When I called to find out how Jamie was, he told me he didn't think you'd leave. Even though you hadn't figured it out yet. It took me two hundred miles to realize I thought the same thing; but I needed to hear someone else say it."

"And of course if you weren't leaving . . ." Art winks at Erica. "You have your blind spots, Woody, but you've never been dumb."

"Thanks, Art. Again." Sherwood pours three mugs of coffee, gives one to Erica and takes Art's to the table.

"Let's not get into thanking each other, man. All mine would take at least a week."

Josie trails into the kitchen, having made a slow pass through Jamie's room. "He really isn't here," she says. "But what am I going to do if it's only grown-ups?"

"Why not get into the scrap box in the basement and build something," Art says.

"Will you help me, Sherwood?"

With a shake of his head, Art reaches down for his cane, then pushes himself to his feet. "Woody has some talking to do, but I'll tell you what," he says to Josie. "If you'll carry that cup of coffee downstairs for me, I'll help you."

The evening seems not to last any time at all. Brodie calls to say he has talked to Pat Chapman and won't be needed at the hearing, but he arranges to meet Sherwood Saturday morning. Karen stops to pick up Art and stays long enough to drink three cups of coffee. By the second cup, Sherwood is reasonably certain that she and Erica will meet again by their own arrangement. As far as he can tell, Karen and Art are comfortable together and happy to be that way.

"Their chemistry is right," is Erica's comment after they have gone off in Karen's microbus.

A south wind blows up as the sun sets. Erica predicts rain and whistles "It's Raining, It's Pouring," while she helps Sherwood cook the meal he'd planned for the night before. Later, Sherwood reads to Josie. Erica puts her to bed in Jamie's room; then she and Sherwood do dishes together.

Neither of them has much to say. The few times Sherwood tries to make talk, his own voice sounds cracked and distant in his ears; but he doesn't feel uneasy. By unspoken agreement they build a fire they don't need, sit side by side on the floor, backs against the bed, to watch the flames and listen to the Chinese hackberry tap out the flow of night air over the rooftop until they start yawning and finally go together to Marion's room to undress each other slowly, and make love, and lie together until both fall asleep.

Sherwood wakes early on Thursday. He feeds Josie breakfast and listens to her bright morning chatter, finally lets her go to the basement to watch cartoons on the television in the shop. Sunlight streams through the windows to warm his back as he drinks his second cup of coffee. All the day needs is Jamie. Erica comes in, sweet and tousled, frowns in the direction of gunshots and explosions that come up from the basement. "I should think that would upset you," she says.

He shakes his head, automatically gets up and moves to the stove to make toast and scramble an egg for her. The act surprises him with its complexity, both of motion and motivation; and he realizes that this is how it feels to do something and expect to do it again and again. With the same sense of discovery he works through the necessities of the morning: cleaning up, making beds, packing clothes for Jamie. Josie has seen several "cowboys" on horses during the ride to Oregon, and the morning TV has reinforced her desire to be one. Sherwood finds two bandannas—one for her to wear and one to take to Jamie—and she carries those and a pair of rifle-shaped sticks into the car for the drive to Woodgrove.

Erica's predicted rain has soaked the road and fields, and then blown over. The wind has dropped to an erratic breeze that ruffles the bushes and flowerbeds in front of the courthouse. Between the little courtyard in the center of the grounds and the front steps, a crew in dungarees tears up old sidewalk with railroad bars and

loads ragged chunks of concrete into a county truck. Josie wants
to watch, but Sherwood and Erica coax her inside with promises
that Jamie will be there.

They have to wait a few minutes outside the second-floor hearing room, then Pat Chapman clips up the stairs. Jamie breaks
loose from her hand, comes tearing down the hall and leaps into
Sherwood's arms, excited and out of breath. "Pat says I can come
home, Sher." Immediately, he wiggles out of the embrace to take
the bandanna and stick from Josie. "Footabeel," he says.

"Hold on. This isn't a place for any footabeel." Sherwood col-
lars both children before they can run off. No way to calm them
down, but he manages to get them in check by the time Pat
reaches the hearing room.

"He's understandably excited," she says. "I need a quick word
with both of you. There's no longer a question of child-abuse proceedings, Sherwood. But the district attorney's office is planning
to prosecute Doris Ransler, and one of the attorneys will want to
talk to you." She stops. "You are Erica Riggs?"

"Yes."

"Good. They will probably call next week. Monday or Tuesday.
Now, if you wouldn't mind taking the children outside? Things
will go faster without distractions."

With a grin and a sigh of relief that she won't have to sit in the
courtroom, Erica takes Jamie and Josie by the hands and walks
them back down the hallway.

"We can wait inside," Pat says. "I have to have the case removed from the calendar. Judge Gavin wants to say some things
to you." She unzips her plastic case and riffles through her papers.

"You aren't going to get me for not reporting Doris?"

"Whatever gave you that idea?"

"The doctor said there was a new law. . . ."

"There is, but it only applies to professional people. Doctors,
dentists, teachers, school nurses. People who are in a position to
notice abuse and who are trained to recognize it. I can see why
you were worried, though. You should have told me."

I should have done a lot of things. He nods. "What about
Doris?"

"We found her. Rather she found *me*." Shaking her head, Pat
motions Sherwood toward a chair at one of the tables.

No mistaking that tone of voice. "What happened?"

"She slit her wrists in my office last night."

Little pains dance up and down Sherwood's chest and he shudders.

"I had quite a long talk with her. Waiting for the ambulance. It turns out, as is almost always the case, that her mother treated her the way she was treating her own children. And Jamie. From some of the things she told me, she has made amazing progress. Her mother used to beat her, and as far as I can determine, Doris wasn't violent with her children."

"She's okay?"

"Under close observation. I think she really tried."

"But the DA's office is still going after her?"

"Yes."

"What will happen to her?"

"It's hard to say. Assuming she's convicted, which seems probable, she will be eligible for a diversion program. Probation Department. Legally, she's a first offender. The welfare office will get into the act since she didn't report the fact that her husband was gone. Apparently she just left her children while she was at work. It's possible she won't spend any time in jail, though why you sound reluctant to put her there is a mystery to me. Most likely she'll end up with County Mental Health, in view of last night's suicide attempt."

"Right." He closes his eyes, concentrating on the pains. Should hate her, but I don't. Wheeled into her own emergency ward, thinking she's finished her life. And then to be dragged back. Alive and terrified that she got up the nerve or the desperation to do it. Terrified at how close she came and worse; that she still has death to face some other time.

"Are you feeling well?"

"A little queasy, but I'll be okay," he says. "I just need to sit a minute." Come on, heart. Slow down. I'm not ready.

"We have a few minutes yet," Pat says. "I'll be right back."

The courtroom is the same as before, the collection of benches and mismatched chairs, high windows with venetian blinds all the way to the ceiling. The large clock above the door reads five minutes until ten. Five minutes. Then this hearing, and then we get out of here and start the business of living. He shudders. It's not

going to be easy. Help Jamie get over something he hardly remembers. The bad place. Wounds he can't even see. Break the
old patterns. "Start new ones in their place," he says. I ought to
get Art to show me a few chords on the guitar. If I'm going to
build them, I should learn how to play one.

At one minute till ten Pat comes back into the room with the
bailiff, both of them laughing at something they have heard outside. The bailiff takes his place, watches the judge's chamber door.
Pat sits beside Sherwood.

There are only the four of them in the room at the "All rise."
The gavel clicks. Words in semi-official format buzz back and
forth between Pat and Judge Gavin.

"Mr. O'Neal," the judge says finally, "this matter of abuse has
been an unfortunate misunderstanding. It is closed. However, it
would appear that you are a prime contributor to the misunderstanding, and I would like you to explain your alleged inten-
tion to return to"—he consults a three-by-five card—"South Dakota. I distinctly recall that you told this court, through your
attorney, that you intended to remain here and care for your
nephew. You also maintained that you were engaged in a craft,
guitar making, that you hoped would lead to an income or to em-
ployment. The report I have seen indicates that, in fact, you intended to select some person or couple to adopt your nephew.
This is a serious matter, as it could easily move from an innocent
attempt to provide for a child's future into the realm of adoption
rackets. Would you please stand and address this bench. And consider your words carefully. At this time I do not anticipate legal
action against you, but if it appears such action might be necessary, I will stop you and we will call your attorney."

On his feet, Sherwood looks from Pat's composed face to the
judge's half scowl. "I didn't misrepresent myself to you, Your
Honor. I couldn't have left him. What I was doing and what I
was thinking were at odds. Does that make sense? If I lied to anyone, it was to myself."

The judge coughs, consults his cards. He coughs again. "An interesting answer. The essential thing would be that you can prove
you have begun your apprenticeship. That, more than anything
else, would seem to indicate your true intentions."

"I have been making guitars, Your Honor. I'll have one for sale in a gallery soon. I'll send you an invitation to the opening, if you're interested."

Nodding, Judge Gavin taps his cards into a neat pile. "You surprise me, Mr. O'Neal. Pleasantly, be assured. I'd be pleased to have an invitation." His gavel taps the block.

Pat and the bailiff stand. The judge pushes himself up and walks out of the courtroom. Sherwood feels a hand on his shoulder, and Pat's voice comes too close to his ear. "You can go, Sherwood. No papers to sign."

"Thanks," he says. "See you next week."

"Unless you're planning to go somewhere after all this?"

"Not right away." Too much to do.

"Fine," she says. She hesitates, as if she might say more, then moves across the room to exchange comments with the bailiff and, finally, leave with him.

Absently, Sherwood makes his way around the railing that marks off spectators from participants, out through the hearing room to the hall. Thirty or forty people have gathered in the large area at the top of the stairs. They sit or stand around the walls, all with information sheets about jury duty held in front of their faces or tucked under their arms. Most of them look up as he walks by, obviously wondering if he has anything to do with their trial, and he scans their faces wondering: Will there be witnesses for the defense? Friends of the accused? Or will there be only empty places? With a shudder he climbs down to the foyer, goes out through the glass doors to the top of the steps.

The workmen raise a clatter and a cloud of dust with their bars. Over their heads, beyond the ripped-up concrete and pockmarked earth where the walk has come up, he can see the little courtyard with its benches and planters and bushes, and the wide surrounding lawn that looks still damp from the morning shower. Someone is talking to Erica, but Sherwood doesn't recognize Karen until he finally notices Art, leaning forward on his cane and talking to Jamie. Did they come just to lend support? While Sherwood watches, Jamie reaches up to shake Art's hand, then Art says something to Karen and the two of them skirt the bushes side by side and cut across the lawn toward the jurors' parking lot. Erica sits down on one of the benches, her back to Sherwood. A little way off Josie squats to look at something near the base of a birdbath. Jamie drags his stick gun toward her, drops it suddenly and holds up his hand as if he has cut it or gotten a splinter. The red bandanna hangs askew around his neck and a cowlick of fine hair flaps up and down in the light breeze.

Apparently Erica has noticed too. She beckons for Jamie to come to her. He seems reluctant, but he picks up the stick and trudges to the bench, where he extends his hand for her to see. The light makes a silhouette of her face as she takes gentle hold of his finger.

To his surprise, Sherwood finds himself turning away from them to watch a pickup drive slowly along the front of the building. Even trying to avoid the small tableau, he feels its strong attraction: Erica's blond hair next to Jamie's black, blowing fuzz, her concern and his grudging trust; and it all catches in Sherwood's throat with a force that leaves him short of breath.

At the foot of the steps the pickup stops. Two deputies get out, help a man in denim and handcuffs over the tailgate and escort him up the stairs. Sherwood nods to them all, gets a pair of cuffed hands raised slightly in greeting; but his attention is drawn back to Erica, who has just released Jamie's finger and has put her arm around his shoulder.

And here I am: looking, looking away and looking back. Was that it, Marion? Was the world sometimes too much to take all in one glance so you had to pull back a second to keep from being overwhelmed? But you stayed in it to the end. Catching his breath, he climbs down the wide staircase to skirt the construction, his step lighter now, moving faster; feet scuffling through the wet grass on his way to meet Jamie and Josie and Erica, and to take them all home.

STEPHEN J. THORPE was born in Louisville, Kentucky, and was raised in northeastern Wyoming. Before graduating with a B.A. in Philosophy from the University of Washington at Seattle, he worked as a cowboy for five summers. Then he joined the U. S. Army.

Mr. Thorpe lives in North Platte, Nebraska, with his wife and their young son. He is currently at work on a new novel.